A LIFE REDEEMED

SECRETS OF THE QUEENS · BOOK 2

OLIVIA RAE

Please Note

This is a work of fiction. Names, characters, places and incidents are either the product of the author's imagination or are used fictitiously, and any resemblance to any actual persons living or dead, business establishments, events or locales is entirely coincidental.

Published by HopeKnight Press

For information, please contact:
www.oliviaraebooks.com
www.facebook.com/oliviaraeauthor
www.twitter.com/oliviaraebooks
www.instagram.com/oliviaraebooks

ISBN: 978-1-7320457-7-4

Books by Olivia Rae

The Sword and the Cross Chronicles

SALVATION

REVELATION

REDEMPTION

RESURRECTION

ADORATION

DEVOTION

Contemporary Inspirational

JOSHUA'S PRAYER

Secrets of the Queens

A LIFE RENEWED

A LIFE REDEEMED

A LIFE RECLAIMED
Coming Soon

Contact Olivia at
Oliviarae.books@gmail.com

Want notice of upcoming books? Join my mailing list:
Oliviaraebooks.com
Facebook.com/oliviaraeauthor

Acknowledgments

Special thanks goes to Jody Allen, Scottish historical expert extraordinaire. All your historical knowledge has made this a far better book. Words cannot express my gratitude for the hours you spent educating me on all things Scottish. You are like an angel sent from heaven.

For Yutong,
Welcome to the family. You are deeply loved.

And to the glory of God

CHAPTER 1

March 1559
Outside of London

The crisp spring air entered Audrey's lungs and lifted her spirits. So fresh compared to the foul stench found in London. Even the brown earth had given up its winter chill; delicate wildflowers were starting to dot the meadows. She chuckled as birds flitted and fluttered from tree to tree and branch to branch. Now she was like them, free from the bonds of Queen Mary's court. Thankfully, the new Queen Elizabeth did not want Mary's ladies tending to her needs. God had been merciful and returned her to her family.

Her family. That wasn't exactly true. A tinge of sadness entered her heart and troubled her thoughts, chasing away her jolly mood. Her mother was here, but her father had died over a year ago. Born a merchant, he could not fathom working the land; nevertheless, that became his life since his release from debtors' prison. Now he was gone and her brother Asher, who had bought the land and built this fine cottage, was living somewhere in a distant eastern country with his wife. Though he promised to return someday, Audrey knew she would never see him again. She shook off the melancholy thought; he deserved to be happy for he had paid his dues to Queen Mary, and now he too was free of her. Audrey pulled a shawl tight around her shoulders to ward off the morning's brisk wind before she picked up the basket at her feet. She strode down the hill to where her stepfather and stepbrother had begun to plow the fields. Neither stopped to give her a look, so intent they were at their task. "'Bout time ye got here, girl," her stepfather chided. "Place the basket on yonder rock and we will eat when this row is done."

Her stepbrother Jacob gazed longingly at the basket but did not gainsay his father. At six and ten, you would think he would have grown a backbone, but no, he was as weak as the rest living at the cottage.

"What ye standin' like a limp saplin'? Do as I say and then fetch us a cool drink from the river." Her stepfather spat on the ground before putting his shoulder to the plow.

Audrey shook her head and stared at his round back as he struggled on. The man never had a pleasant word. Truly, what prompted her mother to marry such a person? Leaving the basket, Audrey picked up the empty jug her stepfather and Jacob had discarded. What freedom was this, doing the same thing over and over every morn? 'Twas not much different than attending to Queen Mary's needs.

With a heavy sigh, Audrey made her way to the river. Her brooding would serve no purpose. She had a roof over her head and food in her belly, what matter if the tasks were mundane and the company chafed? Things could be far worse. "At least I am far away from the deadly games of the court."

"Agreed. They can be bad." A crow cawed and flew away when a woman wearing a black cloak and heavily veiled stepped out of the foliage.

The hairs on Audrey's neck rose as a band of men dressed like peasants but carrying swords common with the royal guard circled around her. She straightened her spine. "What do you want? I have no coin or goods except this empty jug. If you think it is of worth, then it is yours." Her heart racing, Audrey hefted the jug above her head and threw it at the woman, who deftly stepped out of the way. The jug hit a rock, fracturing into pieces, shattering her confidence as well. The guard charged forward while Audrey dodged left, desperately seeking an escape route.

"Stop." The cloaked woman waved a dark-gloved hand in the air. "Cannot you see? You are scaring the girl."

The men halted, not taking a step closer nor retreating. Audrey's feet stalled. How fast would it take Jacob to come if she called out? But what would his presence do against these armed men?

The veiled woman moved to the edge of the circle and held out her hand. "Come walk with me. I promise no harm will befall you."

Audrey folded her arms across her chest. "Nay. I shall not. You wish me ill. There is nothing I can give you. Leave me be."

The woman huffed. "Good heavens. If I wanted you dead, you would not be drawing breath. I just wish to have a private word with you."

This woman was not a leader of a band of thieves. No indeed. Her speech was that of a lady's. Her gait and straight back bespoke of noble breeding. There had been many such women at court. Why this one would create such an elaborate disguise was a bafflement. Unfortunately, the curse of being curious was starting to get the better of Audrey. "What do we have to talk about?"

"Why, your family, of course."

The lady knew how to set a hook. "My past family or my present one?"

The woman laughed. "Come walk with me and find out. The others will stay here."

One of the men rushed forward, clutching his sword in a tight fist. "But my—"

"Stay here and say not another word." The woman then motioned to Audrey. "There is a smooth path up ahead. Let us take a stroll."

A circle of men formed around her. What choice did she really have? The woman was going to have her way. Besides, it would be easier to escape one female than a band of armed cutthroats. Audrey acquiesced with a quick nod.

Her mind racing, she walked on in silence surveying the woods around her, wondering if there were other hidden attackers. Her feet stomped on the dirt path. Could she strike the woman before she alerted her men?

"So, tell me, have you heard much from your brother recently?" The woman did not break her stride and carried on as if they had been acquaintances for some time.

Audrey's stomach toppled and rolled over. This was about Asher. Being a spy for the late Queen Mary, who else lived a life of such intrigue? To steady her jumbled thoughts, Audrey took a deep breath. "Mistress, I have not seen my brother in years, and I rarely receive word from him. I cannot help you find him for I know not where he is."

The path widened to a small opening; rays of sunlight filtered through the leafy canopy. Hardy wildflowers peeked between the lush green foliage. The woman stopped and sat down on a large boulder that graced the side of the path. "Where he is does not concern me. That is not why I have sought you out."

With slim hands, the woman raised her veil. 'Twas a face Audrey had seen only once before she left court. Her blood turned to ice. She curtsied deep and reverently. "Your Majesty."

A layer of fine sweat rested on Queen Elizabeth's pronounced cheekbones. A brightness shone in her brilliant brown eyes. She seemed so much wiser than a woman of five and twenty. "Hush. Do not use such titles here. And do stand up straight. Do you wish to alert the whole of England where I am?"

They were alone on a forest path with no one present except for a few twittering birds and a rabbit or two. "Your...um... What could you possibly want with me, if not to seek out my brother?" Audrey wiped her sweaty hands on her skirt, knowing her bold words might send her to the Tower.

"I know you were one of my sister's ladies. And I know you were one of the first to leave court after she died. So eager you were to return to your family. But what I do not know is are you as astute as your brother?"

A small creature rustled in the thickness of last year's leaves that covered the forest floor. Perspiration slithered down Audrey's back. Oh, how she wished she could as easily slip away. "I do not know what you mean."

"Come, come. We both know he was a spy who helped my sister root out Protestants. I hear he was considerably sneaky and crafty, but all that changed a few years back. He just up and left with my sister's blessing. I thought nothing of it until I came across some of Mary's scribblings. My, my, they were a busy pair—my sister and your brother."

What she spoke of was a mystery to Audrey. Uneasiness knotted her shoulders. One thing she did learn at court: If a royal fumed, best to keep silent. She dropped her gaze to her feet and clenched her jaw.

"But none of that matters now. What I want to know is do you have the same talents as he?"

"Talents? What talents do you mean?"

Queen Elizabeth rose and put her hands on her hips. "Are you dull, or are you being shrewd?"

Audrey's hands curled into fists, and she fought not to glare at her queen.

"I think you are the latter. Do not think I hold that against you. Before I became queen, there was many a time I had to hold my tongue and play the dull maid in order to keep my head upon my neck."

Audrey lifted her chin and saw a merry twinkle in the queen's eye. The royal just nodded.

"You and I are not that different. Our survival is due to our wits." The queen circled the clearing and seemed to be distracted by a wren's sweet song. But then she leveled Audrey with a sharp eye. "Are you happy here, living as a peasant?"

A wave of wariness weaved through Audrey's chest. Surely she was not being summoned back to court? "This is where my family lives."

Queen Elizabeth sniffed. "Not true."

"My mother needs me," Audrey snapped.

"Does she? She has a new husband and three new children. Must be crowded in that little cottage, especially since you are used to the comforts at court."

A cool breeze swept up Audrey's back, sending a shiver to her spine. The queen must have had her spies about to know so much. Whatever she wanted, Audrey refused to be trapped in a royal cage again. "What would a Protestant queen want with a maid of the True Faith at court?"

"Shush, girl. Keep your voice down." Queen Elizabeth's gaze darted around the forest. "Good heavens, the last thing I want is a papist around me. I have enough of those lurking about already."

The unease that had whirled around Audrey's insides receded like a wave at low tide. "Then why do you seek me out?"

The queen let out a heavy sigh and sat upon the boulder once again. She glanced upward as if contemplating how to proceed. Settling on her course, she stared at Audrey. "I told you of my sister's writings. They were most disturbing. One in particular. There is a lord, near the northern English border, who seems to be quite aggressive in his thinking. His English wife has just recently passed away, leaving him with two sons and an aging mother."

Aggressive? Disquiet began to creep up Audrey's spine once again. The intrigue and lies of court began to suffocate again. "If all of this just happened, then how could this information be in Queen Mary's writings? She has been dead for some time."

Queen Elizabeth glared. "Do not contradict me. Just listen."

Audrey rolled her tongue in her mouth and tightened her lips. She was never good at being silent before her betters. "Forgive me, Your—"

The queen cleared her throat. "This man, Gavin Armstrong of Warring, a lesser laird, has an interesting heritage. He has an English mother who clings to the Reformed Faith and a Scottish father who, when he was alive, claimed to accept of his wife's beliefs." The queen's skeptical tone relayed a different thinking. She rose and strolled around the boulder. "I came to the throne with the goal to be tolerant of those who practiced the Roman faith, but there are some who still do not view me as a legitimate queen and the head of England."

She spoke of the marriage of her mother with King Henry VIII. Some in England, mostly those of the True Faith, did not recognize Elizabeth as the real queen. They would prefer to see Mary Queen of Scots, a good Catholic, who was married to the French Dauphin, sitting on the English throne.

As was her way, Queen Elizabeth got right to the point. "I cannot trust the Scots. Some English near the border claim to be my loyal servants and others do not. The borderlands are in constant disruption. That is why I need you."

"Me?" Audrey regretted her outburst the moment the syllable left her lips. The queen's brow wrinkled. "Forgive me. I just do not understand how I would be of help."

"Do you not?"

Audrey met the queen's steady eyes.

"You served my sister. If Armstrong carries your faith and wishes to put Mary of Scots on the English throne,

8

who better would he confide in than another of the same beliefs. Who has been oppressed by the illegitimate Queen Elizabeth."

Audrey lifted her chin. "I have never thought such or been disloyal to you."

"I know. That is why I am sending you. I know you will be loyal to me, and I will reward that loyalty by protecting your mother and her brood of stepchildren."

The lashing, though heavily coated with sweetness, was well taken. Audrey could not imagine that this Laird Armstrong would tell her all his secrets. Nonetheless, she had to accept the queen's offer. "My Queen, you give me more honor than I deserve. I am neither noble nor a man, why would this Gavin Armstrong of Warring confide in me?"

Elizabeth raised a well-manicured brow. "An act of birth nor one's sex makes someone loyal. I would rather sup with an honorable digger of ditches than a prince who would sell his devotion for a bauble. It has all been arranged. You are to go to Liddesdale, in the northern marches of my realm. Those who live there honor neither my throne nor that of my cousin Mary of Scots. You will go in the guise of a companion to Laird Armstrong's mother. There you are to keep your ears and eyes open. You shall relate to me any threats to my Crown. I want to know who the man corresponds with, where he goes, whom he confides in. I want to know everything that is going on with that family."

Audrey's stomach sank. She shouldn't have complained earlier of living a mundane life for now that life seemed sublime. However, one question remained in her mind. Why this Scot and not another? Surely there was more to this story than the queen was willing to share. "And if there is nothing out of the ordinary, would you like me to talk about the weather?"

The queen narrowed her eyes and pointed a thin finger in Audrey's face. "Do not taunt me. Your very life and of those you love are in my hands."

The heat in Audrey's belly and her saucy tongue had gotten the better of her. Why could she not be cool and calm like Asher? Why did she spout off when she should not speak? No good ever came from insulting a queen. Audrey tightly folded her hands. "Forgive me. My words were vile."

A soft smile curled the queen's lips. "Your speech is forthright, and you have a strong spirit. You have just forgotten to choose your words wisely as you did at court. A few weeks at Hampton Court should cure that."

The Tower would be more preferable. But this was not about her, it involved her mother, and Jacob, and her step-sisters. Audrey tempered her words. "I am sure it will."

"You have the ability to write?" the queen questioned.

Audrey nodded her head, but briefly she thought to deny the skill. Without a doubt, the queen already knew the answer and the query was given as a test of loyalty.

"Good. It has been all arranged. Once you are in Liddesdale, you will write weekly and send your missives to a Mistress Pittman on Little Lane."

"Little Lane? I have never heard of such a place. Would not the message get lost?"

"That is not your concern. Just try to gain Gavin Armstrong's confidence. Learn and report everything he does. Even if it seems of no consequence. This might be done by keeping an eye on his son."

The last request was thrown in as an afterthought, but the queen's cryptic manner told Audrey it was not. "You want me to watch the children as well?"

"Just the oldest, the flamed-haired boy, Thomas, who likes to go fishing and has a sharp mind with numbers."

Queen Elizabeth clearly had spies watching Laird Armstrong and his family already. The hairs rose again on Audrey's neck. Then why was she needed? Once more her curiosity took root, but she was wise enough not to broach the subject. "As you wish, my lady. I will do your bidding, but if Laird Armstrong and the family are no threat to you, I want your promise that I will be returned to my mother within a year's time."

Queen Elizabeth's eyebrows shot upward as her jaw worked back and forth. Audrey could already feel the Tower chains biting into her hands and feet for her insolence. The queen opened her mouth. "If there is nothing there, why would I leave you in such a godforsaken place?"

CHAPTER 2

The cart hit every rut as it rumbled along the rough road. Audrey's backside ached from being in this wagon since Lanercost, England. Not that she could not bear the pain, but her company was not much better. Peter, a sour man of middling years, grumbled incessantly and whipped his horse more than necessary. The man stank of ale and smelled worse than a frothing donkey. As they rounded the bend in the road, he pulled the cart to a stop.

"There be the keep of Armstrong of Warrin'."

Audrey peered at the stone structure circled by a stone barmkin wall less than a rod tall. The fortified building resembled a peel tower more than it did a country home. None of this surprised her considering the lawlessness of the shared disputed lands. Claimed by both England's and Scotland's crowns, the area was under constant attack either from the English or the Scots. Few cared to occupy this land because of the constant wars and raiding. The Scottish people called this raiding *reiving*.

From what Peter had told her on their journey, the Armstrong families established their holdings on both sides of the border along the Liddel Water. The fertile valley was good for farming cattle and harvesting crops, but the constant warfare between both crowns had rendered the plentiful farms into wastelands and thus *reiving* became a necessary way of life in order to fill one's belly.

Audrey scanned the rambling hills and mountains that surrounded the valley. "'Tis a wonder anyone can find this place."

"Hey? Look at the hoof prints and droppin's on this trail, there be more bodies and horses whistlin' through here than the wind." Peter spat on the heavily rode road before looking up at the fading purple sky. "Best we get ye inside before the night falls. No tellin' what the darkness brings."

A brisk wind whipped up her back. Audrey pulled back her shoulders, trying to bolster her courage. The look of the bleak place sent spiders to her spine. What would the inhabitants be like? She wanted to beg Peter to take her back from where they had come, but instead, she lifted her chin and sat up straight with feigned courage. It was not her own welfare that she needed to think of but that of her mother and the rest of her family.

Closing her eyes, she focused on the instructions she had received from Sir Walter Pimberly, one of Queen Elizabeth's trusted spies. For a fortnight, he and his cohorts instructed and forced her to memorize almost everything about the Armstrongs, especially Lady Francis, Gavin Armstrong's mother. The questions burned within her. Where had Lady Francis been born? How long had she been married? What was her favorite spice and flower? What habits did she keep? On and on these questions swirled through Audrey's head. Sadly, to her frustration, she had not been as quick of a study as Sir Pimberly would have liked her to be. Being devious was not in her nature. The thought of pretending to be someone she was not repulsed her. She could not bring herself to use knowledge for trickery. Hence, the facts did not plant in her brain. Knowing her mother and stepsiblings would suffer, Audrey endeavored to memorize some.

Her training did not stop there, she was supposed to be alert and report who visited Warring Tower and who resided within. She had to chronicle where Laird Armstrong would go and who would come to see him. The most disturbing was the demand that she should keep a close eye on Thomas, the laird's eldest son. What interest could a boy of six be to the queen? Audrey's skin crawled with growing unease in her task of deception; yet, she had but one year to endure this deceit. Hopefully all her missives would not knot a noose around her neck.

As they approached the grey fortress, Peter gave a wave to the guard on watch at the tower's yett. A few words were exchanged before the iron-latticed yett rattled open and they proceeded into a modest courtyard. The stone rectangular tower stood near the left within the keep's courtyard walls, its narrow windows staggering up the sides of the tower. The keep's battlements on either side of the tower included the required iron basket for signal fires within the ruinous turrets, a result of years of wars and conflicts fought between the riding families and between the two crowns. A slanted stone roof protected all within these stark, sad walls.

Audrey's mouth went dry, and she had to resist the urge to make the sign of the cross over her chest. She could not move from her spot when the cart stopped in front of a stone arch that led to the ground floor of the tower.

"Here, mistress, take me hand," Peter offered, encouraging Audrey from her seat.

She hesitated, then placed her cold fingers in his grimy palm as she descended to his side. Audrey scanned the empty yard. "Is no one about except the guard?"

Peter shrugged. "May not himself, Laird Armstrong, but the old crone is within. The bat rarely leaves her cave."

"Whom do you speak of?" Audrey asked.

"Why, Lady Francis, of course." Peter spat on the ground. "She cares not for me."

Audrey thought to question him further, but this did not seem to be the place to discuss the lady of the keep.

"And the children and servants, where are they?" Audrey bit her lip and tasted brine.

A rusty chuckle creaked out of Peter's throat. "Oh, they be around." His gaze slid up the tower wall. "Probably watching you from above."

Audrey followed his gaze and thought she saw a figure slip out of view from one narrow arrow slit. "I would have thought someone would have come to greet us."

"Ah, make nothin' of it. This place ain't like the queen's place. There is much work and few to do it. Besides, to them ye are just another mouth to feed and to clean up after."

"I can look after myself." Audrey lifted her jaw. "And I do not eat much."

"That is good, mistress, because there be little to go around in this land. Come, I will take ye in."

They walked past a small stable that held maybe two or three horses. Sir Pimberly had instructed her that most Scottish Galloway ponies were left to graze in the fields and were only brought in when raiders were spotted in the area. Not far from the stable on the other side of a low wall was a block kitchen. As they got closer, Audrey could hear a servant whistle while another hummed a merry tune. She wanted to stop, but Peter wished to press on.

"This way, mistress." He pointed to an arched doorway, which led them into a bleak cellar filled with sacks, barrels, and other supplies. Toward the back of the cellar, she noticed two bulky wooden doors with small eye slots. Watching where her gaze went, Peter added, "Those be the laird's prison cells."

Her shoulders shook as she heard the squeak of mice and rats rustling through the soiled rushes. She hoped the cells were empty, for no man or beast should live such a way.

Peter's eyes took on a sinister glow. He took a lit torch from a wall sconce before he lumbered to a spiral staircase. Her throat clogged with damp dust as she followed him up the steep narrow steps until they came to another rough wooden door. Peter pulled the iron latch. Once opened, instant warmth caressed her weary bones. The hall was bright and heated from a large stone hearth. The rushes smelled fresh, though the tapestries that hung on the walls were mended and threadbare. Had she not known it to be possible, Audrey would have thought she had stepped back in time before kings and queens ruled Scotland and England.

Near the hearth sat a woman, her braided grey hair covered by a thin veil. She stroked a cat whose fur was as white as the woman's skin. She beckoned Audrey with a bent finger. "Come here, my dear, so I can have a closer look at you."

With slow measured steps, Audrey shuffled forward while Peter, without a fare-thee-well, slipped behind a wooden screen heading for what appeared to be a small scullery. An unusual thing for a peel tower. Perhaps Laird Armstrong was the cautious type and wanted another place to prepare food in case his courtyard and kitchen were breached. Whatever the case, this was her new situation. She threw back her shoulders. *Courage. You can handle an old crone.* But coming to stand before the woman, Audrey's mouth gaped and shut in a blink. The woman was neither old nor a crone. Her eyes were a light blue, her figure slim, and her braid was not grey at all but a soft blonde.

"I am Lady Francis, come sit by me. Are you parched from your journey? I shall call for a soothing drink." The cat leapt from her lap as she clapped her hands.

Relief flooded Audrey's body when she dropped into a curtsy. "My thanks, my lady."

The woman gave out a hoot. "My word, such manners. I have not seen the likes since I left London some thirty years past. There is no need for such formality here. Please sit and let me take a good look at you."

Audrey had barely settled into her chair when a serving maid appeared with a small beer in her hand.

Lady Francis raised her mug and took a long drink. She wiped her mouth; her blue eyes glinted merrily. "Though the brew is not strong, it will warm you all the way through." She then turned to the maid. "Get Mistress Hayes something to eat." The girl paused as her eyes grew wide. Lady Francis waved her off. "Oh come now, Blair. The boar is not about, and he'll never know we fed her a morsel."

With a nod, the young woman took off toward the scullery as if this boar Lady Francis spoke of was at her heels.

"You will have to forgive her. She has not been with us long." A few wrinkles hemmed Lady Francis's eyes when she smiled, but then the grin faded, and her eyes took on a look of caution. "It was kind of Pimberly to offer me a companion. It has been a while since my son's wife, Edlyn, died. Though I must say, until this past year, I have not seen nor heard a word from my cousin in close to five years." Lady Francis paused. "I suppose he did not know what to do with you, eh?"

Audrey tried to clear her throat, yet the lump remained.

"Do not fret so," Lady Francis fussed. "I am pleased that he did. I do miss Edlyn, even though she was a mouse in every respect and duller than a goose." The older woman winked, and Audrey's heartbeat slowed.

Edlyn died not long after her second son was born. Audrey took a small sip of her beer and tried to recollect the facts about the tragic death. According to Sir Pimberly, Edlyn seemed to be doing well after giving birth to her son, but then two months later, she took to her bed and then soon after died. The death was thought to be due to a woman's melancholy after giving birth. Any other questions Audrey had on the matter were quickly dismissed.

She wanted to reach across and console Lady Francis with a gentle touch, but they were so newly acquainted and such an act would seem improper. "I am sorry. I do hope I can bring a little cheer to your life."

Lady Francis leaned back in her chair and cocked her head. "I am sure you will. And I think you have more wit than Edlyn as well."

The older woman winked again, and Audrey's face warmed. When Blair came back with a meager plate of oatcakes and cheese, though not a king's feast, she was certain it would ease her noisy belly and busy her mouth.

Lady Francis took another drink, then placed her mug on the floor. "You shall have Edlyn's old room. I will have your trunk moved there forthwith."

A piece of oatcake caught sharply in Audrey's throat as she offered, "Oh, my lady, I do not think that is seemly. I can sleep with the other women in the women's solar."

Gentle laughter left Lady Francis's lips. "The other women sleep here in the hall or in their hovels in the nearby village. Nay, that will not do. Edlyn's old chamber is fitting. It is between mine and the boys' room. Children do not annoy you, do they? Thomas can be quite boisterous."

"Nay, I like children. I have two younger stepsisters who are very sweet." Audrey took one more sip of her beer before she finished her food.

"Do you?" Like an eel sliding through the water, the simple words slid out of Lady Francis's mouth. A wintry nip slipped into the older woman's eyes and then was tucked away under a cheery twinkle.

Audrey's breath hitched. She was the one that should be extracting information, not the other way around. It would be folly to let her guard down around this sharp woman. Best to start with kindness and humility. That is how she survived at court. Plus blending into the walls, which would not work in this case. Except for Lady Francis, no one else had English mannerisms.

She lowered her head and folded her hands in her lap. "'Tis one of the reasons Sir Pimberly suggested I come here. Our home was quite crowded."

"Mmm, I suppose that takes care of his problem and adds to mine."

A problem! How had she gone from being a welcomed companion to a problem? Audrey opened her mouth, but before she spoke, Lady Francis rolled her eyes and slapped her hands on her knees.

"Please do not take offense. Living here is difficult, and those of weak constitution do not last long. The fighting and *reiving* is constant. And then, of course, there is the boar."

"The boar?" Sir Pimberly had told her nothing about this boar.

Suddenly, the door to the hall burst open as four men dragged in a dead bull. A dented breastplate hit the floor with a *thunk*. Dressed in a black jack of plate and dark breeks, covered in blood, a lean muscular man led the gory parade. The leader's hair was wild like a winter snowstorm and reached straight at his shoulders. His eyes resembled chips of blue ice, and his firm jaw and cleft chin reminded Audrey of the mountains and hills that surrounded this valley. A large brown and black hound lumbered in next to him.

"We shall eat well tonight," the fierce warrior shouted.

A small band of moss-troopers, who looked incredibly young and terribly old, filled the hall. Servants appeared from the scullery and from the winding staircase. Gleeful voices rose and bounced off the walls. A cheery tune broke forth from a man's small bagpipe. Caught up in the excitement that surrounded her, Audrey began to tap her foot to the music but quickly felt the cold draft of a rigid stare. Her tap halted, and her gaze locked with the frosty glare of the man in black.

Lady Francis leaned over as the man made his way to the hearth. "Chin up, my dear. You are about to meet my son, Gavin Armstrong of Warring. Whom I affectionately call 'the boar.'"

CHAPTER 3

Gavin squared his shoulders and wrinkled his brow as he approached his mother's new companion. Anything or anyone that came out of London and was recommended by Sir Walter Pimberly brought no goodwill to Warring Tower. The lass's dark eyes grew wide, and then she looked away, but not before he saw the fear in them. Perfect. Perchance her distress would send her scurrying back from whatever dank, dreary London hole she had crawled from.

Standing close to her chair, he crossed his arms over his jack, pushing the metal strips sewn into the fabric closer to his chest. "And who be this?" he asked, laying on a thicker Scottish accent.

"This is Mistress Audrey Hayes. We have spoken of her before, Gavin." His proper English mother's strong stare would brook no mischief with their new arrival. "Do try to make her feel welcomed."

The lass rose from her seat and dropped into a deep curtsy. "I am pleased to meet you, Lord Armstrong." She gave him a wide winsome smile. Her eyes were like the night sky full of twinkling stars.

She tried to goad him by calling him lord instead of laird. Ack. She was not scared of him at all.

A twitter of laughter came out of his mother's lips. "Oh, Gavin. If you could but see your face."

Without moving a muscle, he knew his frightful glower had faded away to dumbfounded bewilderment. He quickly recovered and motioned with his blood-stained hand to the chair. "Mistress, please take your seat. We do not stand—"

"On formality. Your mother has told me as much."

Bairn, his large drooling dog, sat next to her chair. *The turncoat.* The beast's foul pant permeated the air. Mistress Audrey covered her nose with her hand, turning her gaze to the bull carcass lying in the middle of the hall.

"Where I come from, men hunt pheasants, deer, and foxes. I have never seen a hunting party return with a cow."

"A *coo,*" he boomed. "He is a bull from the same English who but five days ago stole cattle from us."

Mistress Audrey did not blink an eye. She tipped her head to the side; her long black braid bumped off her shoulder. "Now I see. It is a bull. His shoulders are unusually bulky." A tiny curve appeared on her lips as she assessed Gavin's width.

The devil take him. She teased him. Edlyn would have been swooning by now, but not this woman. Poking and prodding him as if he were truly a bull. Gavin pressed his lips into a white slash. He would have to watch this wee baggage closely.

"Quit fussing about the animal and go and clean up. And have those men take that beast out of the hall to the kitchen. I just had fresh rushes laid this morn." Lady Francis covered her nose with a cloth. "The smell is fierce."

Gavin took a tankard of beer from a servant and then downed the hearty drink. The whole room had grown merry with laughter, music, and dancing servants. Even Mistress Audrey tapped her foot and hummed along. This was not the introduction he wished to have for the lass. He wanted her shaking, shivering, shrinking at the very sight of him.

He took another swig from his drink. "I shall leave, but the bull stays. See how everyone cheers as Cook slices meat from its belly. Why ruin their joy when there is so little of it to be found. Do you not agree, Mistress Audrey?"

Her foot stalled midtap, and she tried to hide her surprise that he even cared about her opinion. "Why, my lord, I have been here less than half a day, and everyone has been kind and friendly. If they are sour, it might be the company they keep."

What was this? She jabbed him again? Did she not know that he could have her thrown out with just the wave of a hand? He examined her tiny nose and her high cheekbones. Her back straight and proud. Her hands delicately placed in her lap with her palms primly clasped. Her fair skin contrasted by her inky hair and bewitching eyes. She sat like a queen. Ah, that was it. She was not your average mistress come to console his mother. This lass had been trained in a palace. By Queen Elizabeth or another? In truth, it did not matter. He was sure she was sent here for no good.

"Then I shall leave you to more suitable company." Gavin bowed slightly.

Just as he was about to turn away, a streak of red hair and brown clothing ran behind his mother's chair— Thomas. As usual, the lad picked the most inopportune time to make his presence known. The dog leaped up and barked wildly, wagging his tail. One severe look from Gavin sent the beast to sit once again.

"Where is your nurse, lad?" Gavin snapped. "Should you not be upstairs learning your manners?"

Thomas screwed up his face. "I *dinnae* want to be upstairs with her and that cryin' *bairn*—"

"Quiet. What you want is not important," Gavin chastised, then hated himself for doing so. But the lad had to learn you did not always get what you wanted in life, especially living in the borderlands.

The lad ducked and then peeked out from behind the chair, staring with his round copper eyes.

"Stop, Gavin. You are scaring the boy." His mother reached around her chair and pulled at Thomas's sleeve. "Come here and meet our guest."

With timid steps, he shuffled to the side of the chair, turning into his grandmother, placing his head on her shoulder. "Is she nice, Gran?" the lad whispered.

A glow of warmth softened Gavin's mother's features. "Quite, and she has come from far away just to stay with us." His mother pushed the lad until he stood between her chair and that of Mistress Audrey. "Let me introduce you."

The lad looked sheepishly at Gavin and then lifted a doubtful gaze to his gran. "Will she be my new *ma*?"

Peals of laughter left Gavin's mother's throat as Mistress Audrey blushed. The dog let out a howl.

Gavin almost dropped his mug on the floor. "Nay, lad.

Dinnae be foolish. She is here to spend time with your grandmother."

Properly admonished, Thomas glanced at the woman and then twisted to his gran for assurance.

"What a fine-looking boy you are," Mistress Audrey said, giving Thomas a friendly smile.

"I am not a boy. I am six summers old. I am almost a man, and I act like one too." Thomas folded his arms across his chest and pouted.

"And so you are!" Her evaluation pivoted to Gavin. "You stand just like your father, but I wager you look like your mother."

Gavin's breath seeped soundlessly from his lips. *What a foolish presumption.* "Thomas, make your apologies and leave. Now." The hurt in the lad's eyes burned a hole in Gavin's gut. The child nodded and gave his gran a hug before clumsily bowing to Mistress Audrey. He hurried up the tower steps without a look back. The hound plodded after him.

"Truly, that was unnecessary. He is just a boy," his mother admonished.

"*Hmph*," Gavin sputtered. He was used to her scolding, but the censure in Mistress Audrey's face dried his throat and sent hot nettles to every muscle in his body. "Leave it alone, Mother."

His mother's lips thinned, and she shifted her gaze toward the dancers while Mistress Audrey watched him like a cat watches a rat.

"It seems I am disturbing everyone's good mood. I shall retire to my chamber." Gavin gave a slight bow to the ladies without spilling a drop of his beer. "Have Blair bring up a trencher when the meal is ready and have her prepare me a warm bath." With long strides, he made his way to the stairs, all the while feeling the Englishwoman's stare burrowed into his back. Let her look. She knew none of the truth, and if he had his way, she never would for she would be gone before the summer grass grew.

With keen eyes, Audrey watched Gavin Armstrong of Warring head for the spiral stairs as if he had fire on his heels, all crusty and cross. Obviously, he wanted her gone, and how she wished she could oblige him. Regrettably, that was not going to happen anytime soon. Not until Queen Elizabeth gave the order. Her Majesty might be right. Maybe he was hiding something or he was hatching a devious plan. Perhaps that was why he treated her with such disdain. Although, he was just as strict to his son Thomas. Worse. What kind of man would be cruel to a child? A boar, that is who.

Even Lady Francis called him such. But how did a man get that way? Surely he was not born with such a brutish bent. His mother seemed gentle and generous. Was his father a cold and callous man? That would certainly explain why he treated his son in such an unkind manner.

"So, what do you think of my son?" Lady Francis asked without taking her eyes off the raucous servants twirling and singing.

"He is a very interesting sort, but I do not really know him."

"What a safe answer." Lady Francis rotated toward Audrey. "Where is the pluck you showed my son? Pray tell, be honest. You will not offend me."

Even with permission, Audrey balked. What mother wants to hear ill about their child, no matter his age. "He seems a little strict with Thomas."

A look of sadness crept into Lady Francis's eyes. "It has not always been so. He used to do many things with the boy, but then Edlyn gave birth to Marcas, and all that changed. He spent more time with the babe. Then the tragedy with Edlyn..." Lady Francis shook her head. "Gavin has not been the same since... Such a pity. All of it."

Surely, Laird Armstrong loved his wife and was one of those men who loved babes too? Her heart warmed slightly at the thought. If Edlyn had not died, in time, his affections would have equally returned to Thomas.

Audrey reached over and boldly touched Lady Francis's arm. "You all have suffered much. No one ever understands why our Lord sees fit to take a mother from her children and from a man that deeply loved her."

Lady Francis pulled away. "Is that what you call it— our Lord taking someone away? I would call it something else."

Audrey worried her lip. How stupid of her. Lady Francis's pain was deep as well. "I am sorry. How cruel of me. I just meant God has a plan that we do not always know. A woman dying of female complaints is not an easy matter when she has a young family."

"Female complaints?" Lady Francis widened her eyes. "You do not know anything about Edlyn. Speak the truth. These platitudes of God and purpose mean nothing in this case."

"I-I am not trying to offend you, my lady. 'Tis that we do not always see the good in God's plan until much later."

"God's plan!" Lady Francis slammed her hands on the arms of her chair, her face curling up in a bitter twist. "Edlyn jumped from her chamber window and killed herself. Where is God in such a foolish death?"

CHAPTER 4

N ot one wink of sleep. Audrey spent much of the night staring at the narrow window, wondering how Edlyn had managed such a deadly feat. How had she squeezed her body through such a small space? Why would a woman with two wonderful children kill herself? And why didn't Sir Pimberly give her such an important fact? *Unless he didn't know how she died.*

Last eve, Audrey had been so distraught upon hearing the fateful news that once she arrived in the cold, eerie chamber, she crawled quickly into bed. With stiff hands, she pulled the musty coverlet around her as if it were a shield against Edlyn's ghost.

Now, in the early morning light, she assessed the room more closely. Dust filled the corners. A lone straight-backed chair sat next to an iron brazier. Clearly, this room had not been inhabited for some time, nor was it made welcoming for her. Under the window stood a rickety table with a basin on top. Next to the basin, she spotted a painted wood miniature of a woman. Audrey scanned the room again. This was the only personal belonging in the chamber.

Her heart quickened, and her curiosity once again

battled down her fears. Wrapping the coverlet around her body, she tentatively lowered her feet to the cool floor. With quick steps, she made her way to the table. Carefully, Audrey picked up the painting. A thin-faced woman with wavy brown hair and glassy eyes greeted her. There was no doubt the artist had worked hard to make the woman look attractive and joyful, but somehow he managed to fail. The woman's lips were slim, her cheeks sunken, and her face seemed shrouded in sadness and loneliness.

This had to be the likeness of Edlyn, but why would she have a miniature of herself? Shouldn't this small painting be in Laird Armstrong's chamber? Or was the reminder of her too great to handle? Her clothes and personal effects quickly discarded after her death to stop the grief? Possibly.

Audrey scanned the chamber again. The place was just as eerie in the daylight. Not a tapestry hung on the wall or an ornate trunk sat on the floor. Nor was there a lamp stand to illuminate the room. The bed was narrow and meant for one. This was never meant to be a lady's chamber, and yet somehow it had become one. What had caused Edlyn to wind up in such a dismal place?

And where was Laird Armstrong's chamber? Should that not be next to this one? As if the boar had heard her thoughts, a thump of footfalls on the floor above her sent a sprinkle of dust and debris from the rafters. Moans and groans and garbled speech greeted Audrey's ears. Suddenly the clip-clop of horses' hooves filled the courtyard. She raced to the window to see two broad-shouldered men sitting on their mounts, dressed in brown breeks and weathered breastplates. One held the reins of a black Galloway pony. Their scraggly appearance and long brown beards reminded Audrey of the many villains she would see lurking on the London street corners.

"Come on, Warrin'. We *dinnae* have all day. The marches *willnae* patrol themselves," one of the burly men said.

The thumping above her ceased at the slam of a door. Hurried footfalls descended the spiral stairs, and before her thoughts settled, Laird Armstrong raced to his horse with his large hound behind him. His cold gaze reached up to her chamber window, a sarcastic smirk across his lips.

Audrey knelt down below the window, straining to hear every word.

"Yer early. We should wait for the others," Laird Armstrong said.

"What for? The old man will hold us back, and I have no wish to hear wailin' of the young whelps. We *dinnae* need yer pathetic moss-troopers."

Not a word answered the bully man's plea. The next time Audrey dared a peek, clouds of dust kicked up from the horses' hooves wafted on the wind. They galloped away from Warring Tower like three demons out to do the devil's bidding.

"Well is that not a fine good morn to you," Audrey said to the miniature in her hand. She placed the picture back on the table and dropped the coverlet back onto the bed. She stretched her arms above her head, staring out at the misty grey skies. A chill shivered down her back. "Spring or not, it would be a fine day to stay in bed." But as she contemplated doing just that, she heard the stirrings of life. A rooster crowed and chickens clucked, the smell of baking bread drifted up to her nose.

Looking out the window once more, a lad with a fishing pole in hand dashed to the open gate followed by a rotund woman struggling to catch up. "Master Thomas, where ye be goin'? Yer gran will be wantin' ye to say yer mornin' prayers with her." The woman gave up her chase and stamped her foot. "Ye be just like yer *da*." Placing her hands on her round hips, the woman harrumphed and then limped back to the tower, mumbling all the way.

Audrey's plan for the day just fled through the gate. Keeping track of a six-year-old boy would not be an easy feat. Quickly she took care of her needs and dressed. With quiet steps, she made her way down to the hall. Maybe if she followed the river, she would find Thomas.

To her surprise, Lady Francis and Blair stood near the entry discussing the day's chores. After dismissing Blair, the older woman switched her regard. "Mistress Audrey, I did not expect you to be up this early after your long days of travel. Would you care to break your fast or first join me in the chapel?"

Audrey wanted to say neither, but that was not the way to gain the trust of the Lady of Warring Tower. Inwardly she sighed and plastered an eager smile on her mouth. "Oh, chapel first, my lady." Audrey's stomach rumbled in protest to her words. But God did come first, and now, more than ever, she needed to raise her prayers in help and hope.

Graciously, Lady Francis nodded. "Very well then, follow me." They made their way to a small chamber tucked under the stone spiral staircase. At the door, Lady Francis paused. "My husband built this room to house weapons, but I convinced him it would be better used as a house of prayer. There is not a kirk nearby, and with those of the Roman faith and the Reformed Faith claiming equal truths in these lands, this chapel is a much safer place."

Audrey wondered just which religious prayers, the True Faith or that of the Reformed Kirk, she would be participating in this morn. The heavy wooden door scraped the stone floor, and once opened, showed a plain room with a makeshift altar and a simple bare cross. The rest of the room was just as stark. Ah, Reformers then. A Roman chapel would be more ornate with a symbol of Christ hanging on the cross.

Lady Francis strode to the front of the chapel while Audrey followed along. Turning her head slightly, she watched as Blair, Cook, and a few others joined them. The rotund woman Audrey saw chasing Thomas appeared with a young child in her arms. When Lady Francis looked expectant, the woman just shook her head.

"Let us begin." Lady Francis faced the altar, dropped to her knees, folded her hands, and bowed her head. All within did likewise.

Like a good Christian, Audrey closed her eyes and waited, but no words were spoken by Lady Francis or anyone else in the chapel. Peeking through her long lashes, Audrey found many were quietly moving their lips and some did not move them at all, but all seemed to be deep in prayer. *Well then, I guess I shall do the same. "Dear Heavenly Father, thank you for sending your son to die for my sins. Please watch over me in this place and let me do no harm to the innocent here. Take care of my mother and my new family back in London. Guard my thoughts and lips from evil..."*

She then continued by saying the few prayers she knew from the *Book of Hours,* which Queen Mary had all her ladies recite often. When she was finished, she raised her eyes to find all staring at her. Audrey's skin heated. Had she said her petitions out loud? She hoped not for they were Roman prayers.

A peacefulness rested on Lady Francis's face as she beheld the cross above the altar. "Praise be to our Lord and Savior, Jesus Christ. May his mercy and grace support us this day. Amen."

Some made the sign of the cross over their chests while others did not. Audrey held her hands fast, not wanting to give away her true beliefs. All took their turn trailing out of the chapel, returning to the hall or to their other duties.

Lady Francis looped her arm in Audrey's, leading her to the hall. "Come, let us break our fast and then we shall take a walk."

A walk! Nay, she wanted to find Thomas. But once again Audrey had to remember her place. She had been sent here to be a companion to Lady Francis. Despite her failed plan to find Thomas, Audrey felt her spirits lift. Surely some family information could be gained from the family's matriarch. "I would love that, my lady."

They had no sooner sat down when Thomas raced into the hall, his rusty curls tousled and his cheeks pink from the morning wind. Audrey lifted her eyes upward, thanking God for his speedy answer. Just maybe she would be allowed to spend some time with the boy.

In his hands, he cradled a scrawny fish. "Look what I have caught." He proudly held out his catch to his grandmother. "Can I eat this instead of me pottage?"

Pride shone in Lady Francis's eyes as she clasped her hands together. "Why, of course you can. Give it to Cook to clean and prepare."

"Nay. I want to cook it." Thomas pulled the fish protectively to his shoulder.

Lady Francis chuckled. "All right then. Go and prepare your own meal, but do not come crying when the bones tickle your throat."

The boy skipped gleefully away and only managed to drop the fish once on his way to the scullery.

"I know what you think." Lady Francis glanced sideways at Audrey. "I am spoiling him when I should be scolding him for not being at chapel this morn."

The thought had crossed Audrey's mind, but she kept her peace, remembering she was here to be a companion, not to be an adversary. A stab of guilt pained her brain… not a companion but a spy come to learn the loyalties of those in the keep. Thus far she had learned Lady Francis was tolerant of both faiths. An action that revealed little of the family's political beliefs. But then she had only just arrived, she had at least six days before Peter would be back, expecting a missive for the queen. She should also send word to her mother for she was slightly distressed when Audrey left.

Blair plopped the pottage and oatcakes on the table. "Eat hearty. There be nothin' until this eve."

A few grumbled at the pitiful meal, but most seemed grateful and happily conversed with their fellow neighbor. One by one they finished their food and left until only Lady Francis and Audrey remained in the hall.

"Come. Let us get started." Lady Francis began to rise from her seat when Thomas appeared from the scullery, walking with measured steps, trying not to drop his bowl and oatcake.

He sat down next to his grandmother, who took her

seat once again. "Cook helped with the bones, but I prepared the fish." Dotted with black spots, the paltry fish lay limply in his wooden bowl.

"Perhaps you would like a little pottage, after all?" Lady Francis asked.

The boy picked at the fish, then nodded. Before giving the call, Blair appeared with a bowl in hand. "Thought the lad might want a little more."

"My thanks, Blair. What would this place be like without you?"

The young maid tilted her head and straightened her white cap. "It be a lot dirtier, I wager," she said as she stared at all the empty bowls on the table.

"I would have to agree." Lady Francis absentmindedly played with the hem of her sleeve before focusing her attention on a servant clearing away the mess. "I wonder, would Duncan feel the same way?"

Blair bristled and glared at the other servant. "Duncan may be swift in a footrace and may think of himself as a moss-trooper, but he's nothin' more than a son of a cottar tryin' to put on airs. I can set and clear a table faster than him or anyone else in this hall." She grumbled, scooping up bowls in her arms before stomping off to the scullery.

Lady Francis's gaze never left the maid's back. "That one does not appreciate the life she has. I am certain she would not like living in her father's cottage with her four brothers and the family's sheep again. But then we all have short memories. My cousin comes to mind."

Audrey felt the color rise up her neck. How she wanted to confess why she was really here. She bit the inside of her mouth as a lie took root. "The matter of Edlyn's death may have sprung forth a river of compassion in Sir

Pimberly. He seemed truly sad upon hearing she was gone. I am not certain he knew the true nature of her death, but even if he did not, I am sure he would be concerned."

Gad, she rambled on like a fool. Why wasn't she like her brother? Asher was always calm, even when things were at their worst. When she was growing up, Asher would shield her from the truth with his cool and casual manner.

Lady Francis drummed her fingers on the table. "Mmm, possibly. Though I always believed him to be an unfeeling man. But then I have not seen Pimberly in over ten years."

Ten years! What was the queen thinking sending her here? That was just it, she wasn't. Audrey picked at a piece of oatcake stuck to the table while her mind raced on. Finally, another lie developed. "Perchance he has changed over the years. I do believe he spoke of visiting you soon."

"Did he?" Lady Francis delicately touched her white veil. "It would be so nice seeing someone from my home." Suddenly her face softened, and she seemed to drift to a different time.

Home? According to Sir Pimberly, Warring Tower had been her home for close to thirty years. Would she not think of this place as her home?

Lady Francis directed her attention back to her grandson, watching him pack his cheeks with fish and pottage. She gently stroked his head. "I wonder what he would think of this lad?" When the boy was finished, she kissed him on the cheek. "Mistress Jonet is very displeased with you for running away this morn and missing prayers."

Thomas wrinkled his nose and stuck out his lower lip. "I *dinnae* like Mistress Jonet."

"You do not like, Mistress Jonet." Lady Francis cleared her throat. "Do try to speak like a proper English boy."

Thomas pushed his bowl of pottage away and stood, crossing his hands over his chest. "I am Scottish, and I say *dinnae,* like *Da.*"

"Like your father," Lady Francis corrected. "Now go find Mistress Jonet and I do not want to hear that you are misbehaving or I shall have to inform your father."

The boy's lips began to tremble. He unfolded his arms and dropped his chin. "Aye, Gran." Thomas shuffled away like an old man.

Lady Francis sighed. "I blame this on my son. He knows how to act and converse with both English and Scots, but he denies his son the same education. It is altogether troublesome." She splayed her hands on the table. "I know you think me rude and cruel for saying such, but the truth of what is going to happen is clear to me. These lands will never belong to the Scots. They put their stock in someday having Mary of Scots on the English throne. I tell you, Queen Elizabeth will never let that happen."

No indeed, she would not. Audrey rolled a morsel of oatcake between her fingers. "Only God knows what will happen, my lady."

"Mark my words, Queen Elizabeth will not tolerate Mary of Scots."

Audrey prudently did not answer. Obviously, Lady Francis was a supporter of the English Crown.

"If only I could find a decent nurse who had the ability

to train the boy in both customs of the Scots and English. I would do it myself, but I tire so quickly these days. We removed Mistress Jonet from the kitchen and made her nurse after…" Lady Francis frowned and then quickly brightened. "But, of course, I have you! You know English customs coming from London. Better than me, I suspect. Thomas would gain much from your instruction."

Audrey's insides tumbled. She had been sent here to observe, not to instruct. "My lady, I know nothing about teaching children."

"You are not really teaching him, just showing him how the English would act in different situations. He is young and sharp, and I am sure he will notice and mimic your mannerisms quickly. You do not have to spend all day with him, just a morning or afternoon, here and there." Lady Francis squeezed Audrey's hand. "Please."

Keep an eye on his boy. Queen Elizabeth's words bellowed in Audrey's brain. The queen would see this request as good fortune. A chance to carry out her wishes. Using a child as a pawn against the father seemed nothing less than nefarious. Had she not planned to do the same earlier this morn?

"Someday Thomas will be laird. How much better for the Armstrong family if he is able to deal with the English as easily as he does the Scots?" Lady Francis gave Audrey's hand one more squeeze. "You are my only hope."

Truly, what could the boy say or do that would betray his father's confidences? "Of course, I will do as you wish. However, do not get your hopes up. Thomas has a deep desire to please his father, and he will do anything to gain his affections."

Lady Francis released Audrey's hand and sat back in her chair. "There is the problem. The boy cannot do anything to please Gavin. Nor do I see that changing in the near future."

A twinge of sadness grew in Audrey's heart. How could a father reject his own son? "Then I shall pray that God softens his heart toward Thomas."

"You are a kind woman, Mistress Audrey Hayes." A fine mist clouded Lady Francis's gaze.

Guilt clawed at Audrey's insides. What would Lady Francis say if she knew the truth? What would Laird Armstrong say? The glacial blue eyes and granite-tight jaw floated through her mind. Just what was Laird Armstrong capable of doing?

CHAPTER 5

Gavin rode along the banks of Liddel Water, scanning the meadows and the hills around him. All seemed peaceful this day, but that did not mean they would remain so. At any moment, a *reiver* from a neighboring family, the English, or even the French might invade this quiet countryside. He swiveled to see his cousin Fraser crossing back and forth over the river with his brother, Jaxon. At present, the two Armstrong families were at peace. But tough times were known to make the best of friends into the worst of enemies. Even the buzz of an annoying fly could change the moods of the borderland families.

Their father, Hew Armstrong, was meaner than most. A lump of meadow grass turned the wrong way might send the man into a hostile berserker. Age had mellowed him somewhat, though Gavin was not allowed on any of Hew Armstrong's land. The riff came when Gavin's mother and father married. A staunch English Reformer did not sit well with Hew and his Roman beliefs.

Hence, Fraser and Jaxon snuck away to Warring Tower where rules were a little more lenient. The friendship with the brothers began years ago when they were just lads. Gavin and Jaxon had been fighting over fishing spots and soon found more could be caught if they joined forces. Fraser, always following his older brother, became a welcomed addition. Most border villages knew that when the terrible trio came riding, it was best to lock up your daughters and livestock or in the morn one might be ruined and the other gone.

Though they still rode the marches together when their families weren't feuding, they no longer caused havoc in the neighboring villages—that ended when Edlyn died.

"Ack, I am tired of ridin', and me gut is a growlin'," Fraser complained. "Let's stop in yonder village an' cool our throats."

"Are ye mad? We are on the edge of Rory Maxwell's land. The villagers will take one look at Gavin and string his English hide up on the nearest tree. Especially since he stinks like a fartin' mule, or is that yer *dug*?" Jaxon rode up beside Gavin, holding his nose. He swung his horse wide when Gavin reached out to give him a slug.

Gavin sniffed and glanced down at Bairn. The hound meandered through the fields and did smell like he had bathed in a pile of dung. "Speak for yourself. If I remember, the last time we were here, the *wummin didnae* leave me alone."

"He's right." Fraser glanced back at Jaxon. "They were holdin' their noses at ye, brother." Fraser gave out a howl, kicked the flanks of his horse, and took off toward the village.

Jaxon frowned. "The fool *hasnae* any sense. Sure as God made the earth, Fraser is goin' to get his head bashed in one of these days, an' I *dinnae* care to hear our *da* screamin' about it. I wonder what has gotten into Fraser lately. He used to be so reserved."

How true. Fraser had changed these past six months. Jaxon had always been the one to raise a ruckus, and Fraser had always held back somewhat. He even tried to talk Gavin out of playing a game of chance with Rory Maxwell, which had cost him dearly years ago. The question was what caused Fraser's change?

"Ye can wait here if ye like," Jaxon said.

On the contrary, Gavin did want to come. Now more than ever he wanted to make contact with the Maxwells. "I will go along. If we have to knock a head or two, all the grander."

"I thought ye have sworn off the fightin', havin' two wee children." Jaxon cocked his head. "Methinks ye are up to somethin'."

The mention of his sons froze Gavin's heart. 'Twas because of them he wanted to meet Rory Maxwell. "Come on or your brother will take all the best lassies."

With a swift flick of the reins, the pair took off toward the village. There they found Fraser's Galloway pony tied outside a small thatched-roof inn that served drink and food to weary travelers and hearty town folk. Inside, a few tables sat near a roaring hearth. A burly fellow served up small beer and ale to those who had the coin. His pretty daughter warmed hearts with her saucy lips and mutton stew. Gavin's pulse quickened when he noticed that at one of the tables sat Rory Maxwell and his son Ewart. Both vocal supporters of Queen Mary of Scots and the papist faith. They were robust rivals when it came to *reiving*.

According to Gavin's mother, Rory at one time had been a friend of Gavin's father, Ian Armstrong. As long as Gavin could remember, the families have always been feuding. Rory Maxwell was a rugged, repulsive man. His earthy-brown eyes resembled puddles of mud, and his long grey locks hung like a dirty mule's tail. For certain the lengthy scar that went from his brow to the middle of his cleft chin made him mean and ornery. Nevertheless, Gavin wished to speak to the man.

At another table, Fraser sat, tossing down drink as if it had sprung from an eternal well. Jaxon took a seat next to him. "Hold there, brother. We have a ride ahead of us."

Hauling out another chair, Gavin glanced over his shoulder at Maxwell and gave him and his son a nod. His friendly gesture was met with a sneer and the showing of Rory's back.

"Why ye always tryin' to make friends with him and his lot? He would rather stick ye through the gut than give ye a hug." Jaxon tapped his fingers on the table. "*Dinnae* ye like our company?"

"I like it just fine," Gavin answered, taking a drink of his own brew. "But there are advantages in getting along with the Maxwells."

Jaxon let out a puff of air. "What that be? They smell like fish, an' their *wummin* look like oxes."

"They are good staunch supporters of Queen Mary and the Roman faith."

"And so am I," Jaxon gibed. "If ye be wantin' true believers, look to yer own family."

Gavin slightly shook his head and lowered his voice. "They are close to those who wish to see her on the English throne."

Jaxon slammed his mug on the table. "Leave them be."

Gavin rubbed his chin. How he wished he could, but Maxwell was his only connection to those who might help him. "Stay here." Gavin picked up his mug and walked over to Rory Maxwell's table.

"Ye not be welcomed here, Warrin'. Best ye move along with yer cousins." Maxwell leaned over and spat on the floor. Ewart quickly moved his foot from the vile spot.

Gavin winced inwardly and then dropped his gaze to the table, to Maxwell's cup. "These men need more ale." Gavin waved to the burly innkeeper.

Rory Maxwell leaned back and rested his hand on a dagger at his hip. "I *dinnae* want to drink with ye, unless ye want another game of chance?"

The mention of that fateful day where he had almost lost Warring Tower for good curled Gavin's insides. Instead of a fist to the mouth, Gavin gave Maxwell a thin smile. "Nay. Accept the brew as a gift to better times between our families. You have a good day." Gavin sauntered back to his original seat.

Jaxon let out a low whistle. "What ye say to him? He looks like he's ready to put a dagger between yer shoulders."

Gavin took a drink before answering. "Just a few welcoming words among friends."

"May I never have friends like that." Jaxon's attention flipped to Fraser who was fast becoming well into his cups. "Come. We better be goin' before I have to explain to me *da* why Fraser is drunk and why I was fightin' with the Maxwells." Jaxon rose and grabbed Fraser by the arm.

Taking one last pull from his mug, Gavin stood and nodded toward Rory Maxwell, who returned the sociable gesture with a glare.

On the ride back to Warring Tower, the cool mist nipped at Gavin's nose and cheeks. Satisfaction rippled through his body. Maxwell didn't attempt to put a knife in his back. A good sign. A very good sign.

Not a half a day had passed and Audrey had visited every corner and cranny of Warring Tower. Truly, there was not much to see. She examined the kitchen, the hall, the pens where the sheep, cattle, and other pigs were kept when the fields were not safe. Lady Francis did not venture to the floor above their chambers. Nor did they glimpse into the older woman's room.

From the tower gate, she pointed to the hovels that dotted the countryside and housed Warring's tenants. She then escorted Audrey to the children's nursery, which was slightly larger, but just as meagerly furnished as Edlyn's room.

Mistress Jonet sat on a chair humming and rocking Marcas, who could not be older than one summer. Thomas sat straight legged in a corner breaking small sticks in half.

"Would ye like to hold the *bairn*?" Mistress Jonet held out a child with a shock of blond hair and brilliant blue eyes. There was no mistaking this was Laird Armstrong's son minus the ferocious frown.

"Very much." Audrey reached for the babe.

Snap!

She stalled. Her vision seeking out the source of the sound. Thomas held two pieces of a jagged stick in tight fists, his cheeks flushed and his breathing heavy. His gaze rigid and fixed on his brother. This is what happens when affection was given to one child and not the other.

47

Audrey made her way to Thomas's side and knelt down. "What are you trying to make?"

He leaned back, a deep glower on his face. "A pile."

"A pile of what?" Audrey asked, trying to hold her features in check.

The boy's lower lip puffed out, and he shrugged.

"If it is all right with your grandmother, we could go and find some pitch and build a tower like Warring?"

Immediately the boy's frown fled, and he scooped up the remaining sticks. He looked toward the door where his grandmother stood. "Can we, Gran?"

"Well of course. I am sure there is a bucket of something sticky down in the stables that will hold your tower together." Lady Francis touched her temple. "You go along with Mistress Audrey while I go lie down. I fear my head is pounding something terrible."

"An' what about the *bairn*?" Mistress Jonet asked, arms stretched out, holding the kicking, gurgling child.

Thomas froze and glared at Audrey. A few sticks fell from his fingers and rattled on the floor.

"I shall come by later." Audrey bent over and picked up the sticks. "Right now, we must build a tower to keep our defenses safe. Is that not correct, Master Thomas?"

A huge grin grabbed at Thomas's cheeks as he nodded and scampered out of the doorway and down the stairs. Audrey followed with light steps—a victory won. Spending time with the boy would not be such a terrible chore after all. Far better than spending time with Gavin Armstrong of Warring.

Trying to keep up, Audrey heard Thomas's laughter floating from the courtyard. When she got to the stable, shouts and cries of the stable master could be heard.

Approaching the noise, she could understand the man's complaints. A pail of feed lay on its side next to an upended bench, and a fidgeting Galloway pony banged a hoof against his stall. Clean and soiled rushes were strewn about as if a strong gale force wind had raced through the structure.

"Calm down, lad. Give me a mite an' I'll get what ye need," bellowed a grey-haired man whose back resembled a round mountain.

Audrey put a hand to her nose to mask the pungent odor. As she proceeded to the back of the stable, she marveled at the horses within. Most were Galloway ponies, but there was a beautiful grey palfrey and an old brown mare. Audrey reached out to pet the palfrey's muzzle.

"What do you think you are doing?"

The familiar roar stalled Audrey's hand. She gulped as she turned to find frost in Laird Armstrong's frozen eyes. "I-I just—"

"We're goin' to build a tower." There spotted with black pitch and bucket in hand stood Thomas with a wide grin on his face.

Laird Armstrong's blond eyebrows shot to his hairline. "And who gave you such a foolish idea?"

"I did." Audrey cleared her throat. "'Tis not foolish at all. Methinks it is a wonderful idea, and we will not be deterred." She pulled back her shoulders, and her spine stretched upward. "I have heard you are an expert on this tower. So why not put your expertise to work and help your son build this one?"

CHAPTER 6

How brash! Blood poured into his cheeks as his jaw began to stiffen. Did not the English have a handle on their women? Encouraging the lad to run off and build a tower with sticks. Nonsense. A small nugget of memory produced a time when Gavin was the same age and used to build boats, carts, and horses out of leaves, twigs, twine, and stones. Look where such playful amusements got him, in debt with a dead wife and a child that was… Gavin gritted his teeth.

He handed the reins of his mount over to the stable master, and towering over his son, he said, "Go find your nurse, lad."

The bucket of pitch slid from Thomas's hand and landed with a *thunk.* His fingers grew white around the fistful of sticks as his body began to shake. What was this? Did the lad think to defy him? Gavin smacked his gloves against his leather-clad thigh. The lad paled. He fled, holding the blasted twigs in his hand.

Unclenching his teeth, Gavin took a deep, calming breath. His attention spun to the planner of the situation. "Mistress, you will follow me."

He stomped to the steps and did not stop until he

reached the first floor. Even then he only paused briefly to make sure she trailed. Once he heard her huffing behind him, he proceeded up the stone spiral staircase to the top floor. He expected to wait for her, allowing his temper to cool, but to his surprise, she was less than a handful of steps behind him.

"My, that was altogether invigorating." Mistress Audrey dabbed a hand to her cheeks, brightened from the exertion. Her back straight as an arrow. "Now then, what do you wish to say that could not have been said down below?"

Gavin ground his teeth and pushed open a low wooden door with his shoulder. He led her to the narrow battlements that overlooked the greening valley.

"Oh my, such a lovely view. I was never allowed to admire such at..." Her mouth snapped shut, and her lips moved as if she tried to chew her words away.

"Mistress, please continue. Where were you not allowed to go?"

"I-I mean in London, we do not have such splendid views of hills and meadows. The streets are extremely dirty, and even in the near countryside, the stench of city air singes the nostrils and..." She wrung her hands to the point where Gavin believed she would twist her fingers right off.

He folded his arms over his chest and set his back against the battlement wall. "And...do go on."

She kept swallowing as if she had eaten the pitch Thomas wanted to use for his tower.

"Where Queen Elizabeth resides, are not the grounds lovely there?" he asked.

Red streaks sped up Mistress Audrey's neck and

colored her face. Her whole body began to wobble; he feared she might go over the wall. *Nay, not again.* A shadowy figure from the past wrapped his heart in horror. He reached out and grabbed her arm. "Are you all right, mistress?"

Immediately, the color in her cheeks fled, and she placed a hand to her temple. "I-I am fine."

Gavin could feel the rapid beat of her pulse when his hand slid down to her wrist. With little thought, he used his own body to shield her from the low battlement wall. Her sweet breath twisted up his neck and pulled his gaze to her lips. He cleared his throat before stepping back. "Forgive me. I should not have been so bold. But I—I thought you…"

The color in her cheeks returned to normal. Her breathing slowed, and her tempting heather scent drifted away on the wind. She brushed back her black locks and tried to feign a look of indifference, but not before he saw the heated glisten in her dark eyes. "I am fine. The walk up the steps must have winded me a little, but I am recovered now." She folded her hands to calm her shaking. "Now then. Why did you bring me up here?"

For a moment, he just marveled at how quickly she had regained her composure. She was not as weak as expected. He grunted and gestured over the land. "To see what I fight for. Though you can see far, my land only goes to the water's edge. This small piece and this tower are all that I own. Someday it will belong to my heir."

"You mean your land. Cannot your other children inherit some movable property?"

She stunned him. Why would she care what his children inherited? "Aye, but take a good look, mistress.

My lands are not plentiful. To the east lies my uncle's holding. This land was divided when their older brother died."

He paused when he noticed her frown. Aye, she too knew that wasn't how the laws went. The next eldest should inherit, but that did not happen here.

Gavin cleared his throat and continued, "To the west is Maxwell land, who would like nothing more than to take my land." He waved a hand across the open fields. "Do you not see? The Armstrong family weakens itself even when movable possessions are divided. What you see here must go to one son only. The eldest. Often, fights break out over family possessions. Did you know that my father and my uncle had another brother? The oldest brother. He had a tragic accident of questionable circumstances."

Without asking the question he saw racing across her face, she moved to the battlement wall and gazed outward. "That is a tragic story, but I have been told that the whole family would fight together when called."

I have been told. By whom? Once again, uneasiness settled on Gavin's shoulders. Mistress Audrey was a mystery that needed to be unraveled cautiously.

"Is that not true?" Again, she feigned the look of an innocent maid.

"Most of the time, but not always. A quarrel among brothers or cousins can be just as troublesome as fighting with another Scottish family or the English raiding our livestock. To this day, my uncle plots against me."

She pierced him with her fathomless gaze. "And why is that?"

He should hold his words, but the truth might frighten her enough to send her dashing back to England. "He was not happy when my father married an English lass. He cursed the day when he and my father decided to split the land. I believe he seeks to control all of it. So that some-day his youngest may inherit it."

She brushed her fingers lightly on the cold stones. "I see."

"Do you? I have two sons also. Do you think the youngest will be happy with a few heads of cattle and sheep?"

She drew in her cheeks and examined the meadows. A modest herd of cattle grazed near the river while a farmer hoed a slim slice of land. Warring Tower could ill afford to give up one animal let alone a whole herd. Audrey bit her lip, clearly unable to come up with a reasonable solution.

"Now you see my predicament."

"If Thomas inherits this land, should not he be using his days in more useful pursuit than building stick towers?"

Time stretched as Mistress Audrey contemplated his words. Surely she could see he spoke the truth—if the lad inherited. The notion unsettled him. What would his son do if he ever learned the truth?

"An heir has much to learn about running an estate, but I fail to see what education Thomas is receiving by sitting on a floor watching his nurse care for his younger brother."

By the stones beneath his feet, she wanted to gainsay him about his son's rearing. "Mistress, my son's welfare does not concern you." He expected that to be the end of it as she stepped toward the door.

"I am sorry, but that is where you are wrong." A wicked grin tugged at the corners of her mouth. "Your mother has asked me to spend time with Thomas as she fears he will not have the manners or skill to deal with his English neighbors when he comes of age. Unless you would like to take on that role? For I noticed you seem at ease with both the English and the Scots."

His jaw dropped, but not one sound came forth. Bold, brash, and bonnie. *Bonnie!* His mind was running amuck. May he be lashed with a horse whip.

"So good day to you, my lord. I have a tower to build." The wicked smile became devilish. Quickly, she curtsied and fled.

Before he could verbalize a correction, he heard her footfalls rushing down the stairs.

Gavin slammed his hands on the stone wall. What a brazen woman. Heat engulfed his temples. He took a few steps to follow her, then stopped. Barreling after her and barking like a dog would solve nothing. A stubborn lass had to be dealt with in a different way.

Laughter drifted up from the courtyard as he saw Thomas and Mistress Audrey race toward the gate with the pitch bucket in hand. She tilted her head and nodded in his direction before dashing into the meadows.

He worked his fists at his side, drawing in deep breaths. If he believed in God, then this might be a trial. But Gavin no longer believed in such myths. This was nothing more than a short inconvenience, something to be remedied… And he knew just how to do it.

Audrey swung the pitch bucket back and forth as Thomas held the timber tower gently in his hands. By all accounts, it had been a productive afternoon. Perhaps not by Queen Elizabeth's standards, but certainly by Thomas's.

Once they had bolted from the tower, Thomas led her to a nice cozy spot near the river. Pink ragged robin and meadowsweet were starting to bloom, sending up a bouquet of fragrances. The afternoon sun warmed the air and lightened their moods.

Thomas had laid all the sticks before him and then curled his lips inward to help focus on his tower. He placed four sticks to form a square. "They not be even," he cried.

"They are not even." Audrey mimicked his words with proper English speech. She picked up one of the sticks. "But that can be fixed easily." She rose to her feet and found a sharp stone and began filing the pieces of wood. "This would be easier if we had a knife."

The boy's eyes glittered. "I *ken* where to get one."

"You do?"

As quick as a vole, Thomas scurried to a large boulder by the river. Immediately, he began digging and did not stop until he produced a dull dagger. He held up the weapon like a proud warrior.

"I found it in the stables under a pile of soiled rushes. Me *da* would be mad if he knew I had it." His eyes clouded with doubt. His head whipped from side to side to see if anyone was about. Only bushes and the soft sound of the trickling stream greeted their ears.

"Have no fear, I shall not tell him."

"What about Mistress Jonet an' Gran?" Thomas itched his nose, trying to hide his fear.

"I will not tell them either." Those few simple words sealed their bond. From thence forth, Thomas chattered away as if he had not confided in anyone for a long time. He revealed his secret hiding places and all of his treasures.

The lad was an accomplished thief or a serious collector. Besides the dagger, he had long lengths of rope, a broken hoe, a flail, a woman's veil, strips of cloth, a single peasant boot, a bowl, and a mug.

"These are lovely riches. It must have taken you a long time to collect them."

The boy's cheeks pinked, and he looked around once again. "Only Hetta knew I took them."

Ah, a thief then. "And who is Hetta?"

"Me old nurse. She left after me *ma* died."

This new piece of information begged for more questions, but before Audrey opened her mouth, Thomas crawled over to a large oak and began to dig.

After a while, he pulled out a bound strip of cloth. Carefully he untied the small package. "This belonged to me *ma*." Reverently, he held up a lovely ring encased in a heavy crust of dirt. "I took it when me *da* shoved all her things into an old trunk. He *didnae* even miss it."

She wanted to examine the ring, but the boy protected it close to his chest as if fearing the jewel might magically disappear. Suddenly another find stirred Audrey's senses. "In my chamber there is a miniature—"

"That's me *ma*. I put it in there—in her chamber." Thomas focused on the ring in his hand. "Nobody ever went in there after she died. But then ye came."

Audrey wanted to hug the boy until the sun faded away. So desperate he was for love. "Would you like it back?"

He shook his head. "Nay, just leave it there...in her room." His voice cracked.

"You loved your mother very much, and I am sure she loved you too."

The boy nodded his head as his eyes glistened with unshed tears.

An ache grew in Audrey's chest. She reached out and let her fingers catch the first tear that rolled down his cheek. "You can come and look at her picture anytime. I am sure she would be happy that you have her ring and cherish it." A squeak caught Audrey's attention. A small red squirrel busily searched and dug at the ground for last season's bounty. What would this creature do if it came across some of Thomas's treasures? She flipped her attention back to the boy. "But I am not sure this is a safe place to hide such a valuable possession."

Fear settled in his blinking eyes. He pulled away from her. "I *cannae* keep it in me room. Mistress Jonet goes through me things every night."

Doubtlessly she did, looking for snakes and rodents.

"She took the silver rattle Gran gave to Marcas."

There seemed to be more than one thief at Warring Tower. "You should have told your grandmother."

Thomas shook his head. "She *widnae* believe me. Besides, Mistress Jonet would say I was lyin' and took the rattle meself."

Somehow Audrey believed there might be a kernel of truth in those words. "Have you been caught stealing things?"

For a long while Thomas sat still like the boulders and trees he hid his prizes under. Finally, he just shrugged.

"Well, I will not tell on you, but you must promise not to take any more things." She grinned. "I cannot imagine what that poor fellow is doing without his other boot."

Thomas's tears dried. "*Dinnae* worry, the man was dead."

Audrey gasped before laughter spilled from her throat. "I do hope it was not from some vile illness."

"Nay, Master Simms was plowin' yonder field when he grabbed his chest an' dropped flat. I would've taken both his boots, but I could only get one off before his son came runnin'."

Audrey clasped her hands over her mouth to cover her smile. The boy was indeed a scamp. "Then I believe 'tis safe to keep the boot since its owner does not need it."

His face lit up, and he held out the ring to her. "Would you keep this safe for me?"

Even though her fingers itched to take it, Audrey leaned away from the jewel as if it had demonic powers. If she were found with this ring, she would be tossed out without a chance to explain. What would Queen Elizabeth think of that? A chill washed down Audrey's spine. She must remember her family in England. She would not divulge Thomas's secret. The ring was the only thing he had from his mother.

Thomas's hand began to waver, and his lower lip began to quake once again. "Please."

She could not deny such trust. Surely there was a better hiding place for the ring. Audrey reached out and took the jewel, slipping it into her bodice. "I will only keep it until we can find a safer hiding place."

The boy clapped his hands and then jumped up. "I have been prayin' for a friend, an' now I have one."

Her heart squeezed and softened. Starved for affection, Thomas would claim a woman of almost twenty summers as a friend. She wanted to fold him in her arms, but she did not want to scare him. A bubble of anger started brewing deep within her. Didn't Laird Armstrong see how much his son was hurting?

Why was she surprised? The man was a cold block of ice. Lady Francis said he used to be affectionate. Bah. 'Twas nothing more than a mother seeing only good in her child and dismissing his faults. As long as she was here, Audrey vowed that Thomas would beam and laugh at least once a day, even if she had to battle the boar.

CHAPTER 7

Streaks of faded orange and red spread across the sky, pronouncing the end of the day. Gavin, hot with anger, waited at the gate as the merry pair approached. Bairn was at his side, panting loudly, eager to join the foolery.

"Look, *Da*. Look at the tower Mistress Audrey and I built." Thomas grinned as the early evening wind tousled his red curls. The dog barked and jumped in happy agreement.

The stick tower stood sturdy and straight in Thomas's hands. The gaps were filled with the right amount of pitch. Little holes were carved in for a door and windows. Thomas had done a remarkable job. He had a sharp mind and nimble fingers.

A smidgen of pride pricked at Gavin's soul before he shoved it away. Whatever skills the lad had, they did not come from being an Armstrong. Gavin grunted. "You're late. Your gran awaits you in the hall."

A familiar scene unfolded. The lad's shoulders drooped while the smile faded from his lips. His chin dropped to his chest. The tower drifted from Gavin's sight as Thomas lowered his hands. "Aye, *Da,*" he said before running away. Bairn whined and followed after him.

With his son gone, Gavin focused on the instigator before him. "Mistress Audrey," he began as practiced, "I have made arrangements for you to leave in the morning." *There, done. Now to his meal.* He gave the lady his back as he strode away.

"Nay." She ran after him and grabbed his sleeve. "I cannot leave. Not yet."

He wrestled his arm free. How dare she defy his authority. "Why not?" he snapped.

She gulped and gasped and gurgled like an old woman taking her last breath.

"Out with it, mistress. My stomach growls for a warm meal." Gavin fisted his hands on his hips and glared at her.

"I-I just got here," she whimpered.

"Aye, and now you are just leaving." He spun away and marched toward the tower, nearly running over a squawking chicken.

"Please," she cried, racing to his side. "Can you not give me a moment?"

He stopped. "Why? So you can lift your nose at how I raise my son? So you can trample my rules? So you can inflict your English ways on those who live in my tower? Nay, mistress. *Dinnae* expect us to change for you. We are Scottish and best you think on that when you make your way back to London."

She blinked several times and stood, for once, straight and silent like Thomas's tower.

"Well? Do you have anything else to say?" he barked.

A small squeak came forth. "I promise I will not question how you..." Suddenly her eyes bulged and her lips formed a perfect O. She lifted her hand to her chest where she started patting about on her breasts. Just as abruptly, the action stopped and she let out a long sigh.

Gavin let go of a breath he didn't realize he was holding. "Mistress? Is there something wrong?"

"Nay... I mean..." An odd glow entered her eyes, and with a sharp cry, she fell to the ground.

Heaven help him! The place must be cursed. He knelt down next to her and started patting her hand. What malady did she suffer from? "Mistress Audrey, Mistress Audrey, can you hear me?" She did not stir, and he was helpless. Had he caused this fright with his bluster and bellowing? Would another woman suffer because of him? He picked up Audrey and cradled her in his arms. Seeing his dilemma, a servant came to his aid. "Quick, find my mother and bring her to Mistress Audrey's chamber."

Audrey fought to keep her eyes shut and her body limp as Laird Armstrong carried her up the stairs to her room. 'Twas not an easy feat since the side of her body bumped against his hard chest. She could feel the heat rush up her limbs. Hopefully, he would think her flushed state was caused by her faint and not by her wayward thoughts of his muscled body.

Earlier, she had been ready to apologize to him, then she realized Thomas's ring was no longer tucked securely between her breasts. First, she feared it had landed in the dirt by her feet, but she happily discovered it lodged under her left breast. It was as if God had created the scare to give her a reason to stay. She feigned a faint.

But now what? She won a day's reprieve, but nothing more. Once again, her boldness had gotten her into trouble. She should have stayed at court a little longer. Somewhere she had lost the ability to keep her eyes adverted, her mouth shut, and her ears open.

A shuffle of quick feet met Audrey's ears, and a pressure on the bed told her someone sat near. Gently, a warm palm touched her forehead, followed by a click of the tongue. "Bring me a flagon of cool water and my apothecary bag," Lady Francis ordered.

An earthy scent of pine and horse flesh floated into Audrey's nostrils, and once again her memory tripped back to the hardness of his body against hers. God forgive her, but she craved to feel him once again.

"What ails her, Mother?" Laird Armstrong asked.

"I do not know, but methinks it is the screaming of the boar that frightened her."

"I was not screaming. I was correcting." His meager defense sounded laced with regret.

Audrey had to struggle to keep the corners of her mouth from turning upward.

"Go. I fear she may swoon again if she wakes to find you standing above her like a giant ogre. Go have your meal," Lady Francis reprimanded.

An odd sensation withered in Audrey's stomach on hearing the order. She so did want to see the planes of his chest once again.

"We *dinnae* need another weak English woman here," Laird Armstrong muttered as the sound of his feet made their way to the hall.

At the same time, another rushed in. The pouring of water captured Audrey's ears. "Bring me a wet cloth," Lady Francis whispered to a servant. "And close the door when you leave."

The latch clicked, and a cool rag was placed on Audrey's forehead. She stifled a gasp in order to not give away her pretense.

"Mistress Audrey, Mistress Audrey, do wake up."

The concern in the older woman's voice brought an ample supply of guilt to Audrey's being. Water trickled into her eyes, causing her lids to flutter. "I am fine, Lady Francis. Fear not," she sputtered.

Lady Francis sat back. "Thank the Lord, the boar did not frighten you away for good." Worry clouded her eyes and deepened the burden in Audrey's breasts.

"Nay, 'tis not what you think." She pushed up onto her elbows. "I did not swoon. Laird Armstrong wished to send me away, and I did not know what else to do."

"Oh child, it will take more than a faint to keep you here if my son wants you gone." Lady Francis rose and placed the cloth back in the basin.

"As I feared." Audrey slapped her hands on the bed. "'Tis all my fault. I keep provoking him, and the more I try to stop, the more I keep poking. I am so sorry. Unfortunately, I must leave you and Thomas on the morrow." She sniffed, wiping her nose, hoping her act of contrition would be passed along to Gavin.

"Now, now." Lady Francis moved to sit at the edge of the bed again. "I so would like you to stay and help Thomas...there must be a way to keep you here." She tapped a finger to her lips. "I just need to think a bit."

Time stretched, and Audrey looked on expectantly, but the lady did not voice a word.

All was hopeless. A shudder shook Audrey's body. Queen Elizabeth would have her hide and that of her family. She should have paid better attention to her brother's antics when he was around. He was cunning and a daring spy.

"I have an idea." Lady Francis pointed a finger in the air. "We just have to make you invaluable to my son. Surely you have some talent that can be useful to the boar?"

Blank. Audrey's mind was as empty as a piece of parchment without a word.

"Let me see." Lady Francis chewed on the tip of her finger. "Can you ride? Hunt? Cook delectable meals?"

With each question, Audrey's confidence waned.

"He would not care if you had skill at sewing or weaving. Nor if you had musical talents," Lady Francis mused.

Audrey sadly shook her head. "I have no skills that would change his decision."

Lady Francis rose and walked to the window. "Then I fear you will be leaving us very shortly. Too bad we are not like men and have skills in weaponry, for certain he would let you stay."

A talent from the past crept into Audrey's brain. "That's it!" She almost leapt from the bed. "My father was a merchant near the docks of London. He would trade in all sorts of things—fabrics, grains, and spices. He would store them in a large building near the wharf until buyers were found. It was a fun place to play." Audrey placed her hands on her knees. "Once as a gift, my father gave my brothers daggers."

"I did not know you had brothers," Lady Francis said, placing her back against the wall.

"My brother Asher is a spice trader and lives far away in the east. Then there was my older brother Robert."

Audrey dropped her gaze to the coverlet, not wanting to remember his awful death in Wyatt's Rebellion. "He died a number of years ago."

"Oh, I am so sorry, my dear." Lady Francis came closer to the bed.

Refusing to dwell on past hurts, Audrey turned to a brighter topic. "As children we would have great fun. They would stack up grain bags and practice tossing daggers into their centers. I begged them to let me try. Finally, they could not stand my pleading, so they did. After a while, my skill matched theirs."

"My dear, you must be a miracle sent by God." Lady Francis rushed over to the bed and kissed Audrey on the forehead. "If what you say is true and you have this skill, then you will be a gem worth keeping. This year the Truce prize is in our grasp."

"The Truce prize, what is that?"

She took Audrey's hands in hers. "Several times a year the border families, both Scottish and English, come together on a number of Truce Days. They forget about warring and *reiving* and make merry. But once a year they have a special wager with a series of events to test each other's strength. There is the *reiver* horse race, which the Armstrongs usually win, but rarely do we excel in the other events." Lady Francis sighed, her gaze wandering to the past. "We have not won since my husband was a young man. Of course, back then, there was much brawling. Things have become slightly more civilized now."

A flutter of excitement swept through Audrey. She had always enjoyed watching an archery tourney. "What else do they do?"

"They have archery, wrestling, lang spear throw, a footrace, and..." Lady Francis started to giggle. "The blade toss."

Audrey scrambled to the edge of the bed. "Truly, they have such a contest?"

"Aye." Lady Francis rose, unable to hide her delight. "And the Armstrongs have always lost that event. If you are as good as you say you are, all we have to do is figure out a way to show your talent to Gavin. Without him knowing, of course."

Bubbles of excitement spread through Audrey. "How will this be arranged if I am to leave in the morn?"

"Let me see." Lady Francis started to pace. "If I could get the servants to place a butt in the courtyard...it may work." She stopped her pace and held up her hands. "I have a plan."

"If it allows me to stay, I would be forever grateful." Audrey jumped from the bed.

Thunk!

She froze as the ring rolled across the floor.

"What is this?" Lady Francis picked up the jewel and brushed the dirt from the bright blue stone. She gasped. "Where did you find this?"

CHAPTER 8

Words clogged Audrey's throat as Lady Francis examined the ring's stone. The woman's earlier gaiety withered. Not only had Audrey's chance to stay at Warring Tower faded, but she had betrayed Thomas's trust.

"Answer me," Lady Francis snapped. "Where did you find this ring?"

"I-I found it outside." She shook her head, lying would not help her circumstance. "Thomas gave it to me."

Dunking the ring into the basin, Lady Francis carefully washed the soil from every crevice. "That boy. I should have known." She wiped the stone with a soft cloth. "This ring belonged to me. Given to me by..." Sorrow filled her face, then quickly receded. "When my husband died, I gave it to Gavin to give to the woman who would capture his heart. He gave it to Edlyn."

Stabs of sadness struck Audrey's heart. One death had caused so much pain. At every turn, she was stoking the fire. "Thomas had buried it under a tree near the river. I convinced him that was a terrible hiding place. He gave it to me for safekeeping. I am so sorry, my lady."

Unshed tears formed in Lady Francis's eyes. She

flipped the ring over and over in her hands. "On one side of the ring, a horse is engraved. Most border men are fine horsemen. The other side"—her voice quaked—"a bluebell. I was his bonnie bluebell because of my blue eyes."

Audrey wanted to reach out and take the woman in her arms, but her feet stuck to the floor, uncertain if the act would be accepted. "You loved your husband dearly, didn't you?"

Lady Francis's face filled with puzzlement. "You speak of Ian. No, not in the beginning. He was a brute with bushy eyebrows and a bark that would terrify a wolf." She sat down on the only chair in the room. "The marriage was arranged by my father and his. Ian needed the coin, and my father needed protection for his lands... later, we came to an understanding after Gavin was born."

"Well, now you have the ring back. I am certain once you tell Thomas why the jewel is important, he will be glad you have it." At least, Audrey hoped he would.

Staring at the ring, Lady Francis shook her head. "Nay, he will not. To him it was his mother's." She held out the jewel. "You take it and keep it safe for Thomas."

"I do not think that is wise. If I leave tomorrow, I will have to give him the ring, and I am sure he will put it back into the earth. Best you hold on to it, and together, you can find a good hiding place." She could see a great bond being formed between grandmother and grandson.

A hint of merriment filled the older woman's eyes. "I know of a hiding place, but what fun would there be for Thomas if I showed him? He wishes to hide things from me as well as Mistress Jonet and his father." Lady Francis rose from her seat and held out the ring. "Please take it.

Later, I will show you the hiding place. Thomas will think it is great fun."

Audrey backed away. She had caused enough hurt this day. What would happen if the boar caught her with the ring? "Lady, I—"

"Believe me. You will not be leaving, especially after Gavin learns of your skill with the dagger."

"Perhaps it is for the best."

"Nay, it is not. I have not heard Thomas laugh as he did today in a long time. You are good for him, and if he gave you this ring, he trusts you. Take the jewel, and in a few days, you will prove to my son how important you are to Warring Tower." Lady Francis placed the ring in Audrey's palm, clasping her fingers around Audrey's hand. "You will bring joy back to this family. I just know it."

Or heartache. The two words plagued her. How could she spy on such a compassionate woman?

Not sharing in Lady Francis's optimism, later that night, Audrey sat down to write to the queen. Better to let her know ahead of time and possibly soften their future meeting. But what could she say? *I have failed, Your Majesty. Instead of trying to appeal to Laird Armstrong's affections, I have harvested his rancor instead. I meddled in the rearing of his son, and he has banished me from his home.*

Those words alone would convict her and her family. How could she appease the queen's wrath? Audrey ran her fingertips over her forehead, hoping the action would bring forth the answer. None came. There was nothing she could say or do that would ease the queen's condemnation.

With a heavy sigh, Audrey decided to write to her mother instead. At least she could give warning of what was probably going to happen. Her poor mother, she had barely survived the last time she had been thrown into debtors' prison. The possibility of being in prison again would be her end. Her mother must flee. If given enough warning, perhaps she and her new family could sell the farm and leave the country like Asher had years ago. But where would they go? Her mother was not young, and her stepfather was a stubborn man. No one knew exactly where Asher lived. There would be no help from that quarter.

Dropping the quill, Audrey placed her head in her hands. *Dear Lord, I beg of you. Please protect my mother and my stepbrother and stepsisters. None of them deserve to suffer for my sins. Let the queen's wrath fall on me alone. God, I know you never want the innocent to suffer. Please, deliver them from evil and keep them safe.*

Audrey dried her eyes and swiftly wrote her letter. Once finished, she slipped it into her trunk. If Lady Francis's plan failed, the letter would be ready to send.

Trouble brewed. He should have ordered a cart to take Mistress Audrey away the day after she swooned in the courtyard. However, his mother had pleaded to give the young woman a few extra days to get her strength back. That had been his first mistake.

Three days later, the meek mistress came quietly into the hall and pleaded her case to stay.

"I am terribly sorry for what happened, and I promise, if you will let me stay, I shall never, ever question your judgment again." She stood, her hands modestly folded and her head penitently bowed. Outwardly she acted humble, but inwardly he knew the truth. She could not hold that plucky tongue forever. In no time, she would be back to influencing his mother and Thomas with foolish notions.

Gavin stood before the hearth and jabbed at the heated embers with a poker. "Mistress, we both know that is false. Your true nature will win out. I *cannae* allow such bullheadedness to be shown around my sons."

He saw that spark of spirit, which she desperately tried to hide, fill her eyes. "I can assure you, from this day forth, I will not speak a word that you would not approve. I will be a humble companion to your mother."

"And you will not interfere in Thomas's rearing?"

Her clasped hands shone white. He had his answer.

"I think not." He set the poker against the sides of the hearth and then took a firm stance in front of her. "Let us be honest. You have difficulty controlling your tongue. No doubt that is why you were sent here in the first place. Your manners at court were certainly questionable." He added the last statement to trick her, hoping to get her true purpose for being here.

"Court? I was living with my mother and my—"

"I have heard the story enough. Sir Pimberly just happened to think you would be a good companion for my mother. I do not care where you came from. You are leaving, and that is that."

Gavin expected her to rant, but she did not. She drew in her cheeks as if she could suck away the words that were begging to be released from her lips. All he needed to do was prod her a little more. He planned to do just that when his mother strolled to his side.

"A word with you, my son," she said pleasantly.

73

"Can it not wait? I am having a discussion with Mistress Audrey," he said impatiently, placing one hand on his hip.

"Are you? Looks to me like you are barking and she is mute." The twinkle in his mother's eye should have cautioned him, but it did not.

Gavin let out a long sigh. "What do you want, Mother?"

She fixed the sleeves of her gown before casting an affectionate smile. "I have a suggestion. Would it not be a good idea to place one of the butts in the courtyard to use for archery and dagger toss practice? Truce Day will be here before you know it."

"Truce Day!" Gavin shook his head and held on to a laugh. "Which might be held. Mary de Guise, the dowager queen, keeps inviting more French troops into Scotland, and the English are slipping across our borders daily. The Lords of the Congregation, whom you are so fond of, are causing all sorts of ruckus in Perth. War probably will come to us again, and I fear we will be right in the middle of it on Truce Day."

"But surely there will be some event. The tenants look forward to it. If not at its usual time, then perhaps later summer?"

Gavin squared his shoulders. She had never been interested in the feats of wager on Truce Day before, why now? The reason mattered little to him. He had other concerns to take care of, starting with the removal of Mistress Audrey.

"If setting up a butt cheers you, then by all means do so." He waved a dismissive hand.

"My thanks," his mother said, and then she gave him an unexpected hug before hurrying away.

A rush of unease poured through Gavin's body. He narrowed his eyes and rubbed his chin. But, just as quickly, the doubt fled when he looked to Mistress Audrey.

"I am sorry I will miss this Truce Day, I do so like such joviality," she cheerfully chimed.

He puffed out a spout of air. "Methinks you'd be glad if the fields were covered with English and Scottish souls." He bowed. "Good day, Mistress." He strode to the hall entry, feeling quite satisfied.

That was his second mistake.

The following morning, a cart was readied to take Mistress Audrey back to London. Once she was gone, then he would focus on more important things, such as gaining the trust of Rory Maxwell. Gavin gazed longingly at the butt standing in the courtyard. Fraser and Jaxon wildly threw blades at the cloth mark. Their skill was miserable, but their laughter was contagious. Gavin shook his head. He wished the squabbling and fighting between England and Scotland would pause long enough. They all needed to practice for the feats instead of riding the marches, then maybe they would have a chance at winning the Truce Day prize. What he wouldn't give to beat Maxwell just once. Plus, the extra coin was sorely needed at Warring Tower.

With long strides, Gavin made his way to the cart where Mistress Audrey slumped against the wheel like a woebegone maid whose betrothed ran off with a more inviting lass. He raised his vision to the bright sky as he pulled on his riding gloves. "Fine day to be traveling, mistress."

"I suppose," she said glumly, her lips in a delectable pout.

The thought gave him pause, but then he warmed to it. The lass was leaving, there was no harm in enjoying a hearty glance at her beauty. She was that. Her fine dark hair curled around her oval face while her black lashes protected her deep dark eyes. Not too tall nor too short. Even the modest plain brown gown seemed elegant on her. She was slim in the right places and wide in the hips. Someday she would birth beautiful English children far from Scotland.

The lass pulled a wayward lock from her cheek. "I am not one of your horses to be appraised," she snapped.

A smile tugged at his lips. "I agree, you are not. Even though we have had our differences, I wish you well." His horse was brought to the courtyard. "There has been much activity on the marches lately. Duncan, Clyde, and I shall accompany you until you are safely on English soil."

"Who is Clyde?"

Her answer came shuffling out from the stable leading a Galloway pony. Hunchbacked and older than any Roman ruin, Clyde had been a moss-trooper at Warring Tower since anyone could remember. Out of charity, he still rode the marches when the weather was fair and the pace was steady. Following a rumbled cart would be a perfect duty for Clyde and a green lad like Duncan.

"Heaven help us if we do meet up with any ruffians," Audrey mumbled. Then a look of mischief added to her enchanting looks. "Are you not worried an English arrow might be placed in your back?"

He chuckled. Of course, she would think of such a thing. "I fear an arrow would not be as sharp as your tongue."

Color clouded her cheeks before she looked away. Just maybe he would miss this bonnie lass.

"Mistress Audrey, Mistress Audrey," his mother called, running from the tower. "You forgot this." In her hands she held a leather sheath, which she gave to the younger woman.

"My thanks, Lady Francis. How could I have forgotten my father's dagger?" She pulled the weapon from its sheath.

Gavin stretched his neck to have a look, but the lass quickly curled her fingers around its hilt.

"My dear, you will be missed." Gavin's mother reached out and hugged the young maid.

The lass stepped back and eyed the butt. "I shall miss you too." She tapped the blade against her side. "Stand aside, sirs. I should like to take a throw," she shouted to Jaxon and Fraser.

Gavin had to squelch the hearty laugh that lingered in his throat as he watched her take a firm stance. The dagger left Audrey's delicate fingers and landed square in the middle of the cloth. Gasps filled the air. Gavin's heart kicked up a beat. Before he had a chance to examine the strike, she ran to retrieve the blade.

Duncan hooted, and Clyde coughed. Jaxon and Fraser both clapped their hands and gave her a slight bow before she returned to Gavin's side.

"A lucky strike, mistress," he said, holding out his hand. "Can I—"

"A lucky strike!" She turned and flipped the knife toward the butt again where it landed in the same spot. "I think not."

Shouts and cheers from the servants and guards ricocheted around the courtyard. Even a donkey brayed his praise. Frasier let out a long whistle while Jaxon took the blade from the butt and handed it to Mistress Audrey. She curtsied as everyone clapped.

Now more than ever Gavin wanted to inspect the dagger. But once again he was denied the chance.

To everyone's protest, she shoved the blade back into its sheath. "I am ready to leave now," she said, her cheeks pink and her dark eyes sparkling.

Gavin stood slack-jawed. Could luck have visited her twice, or did she really possess such fine skill? Perchance the blade was specially made. All he needed was one look.

"My dear"—his mother pushed him out of the way and hugged the lass again—"I did not know you were so talented. Why, your skill with the dagger is better than most men around here." Her gaze veered to Gavin.

He bristled. How dare his mother think a woman could best him. He pulled his own knife and flung it at the butt. The blade struck the cloth in the middle. In truth, it was a fortunate strike. He puffed out his chest as those in the courtyard called for Mistress Audrey to challenge him.

With a raise of her lovely lush brow, she drew her dagger from its sheath once more. A snap of her wrist sent the weapon sailing toward the butt. Her blade skidded on top of his, knocking his knife to the ground while hers stuck firm in the cloth. His jaw slacked, and he could feel the cool spring breeze on the back of his throat.

Cries erupted, and before he uttered a word, his mother, Duncan, servants, stable lads, and guards picked up Mistress Audrey and carried her back into the hall.

Clyde hacked. "Better keep the mistress." He shuffled after the joyous crowd.

Jaxon sauntered over, his hands in his belt. "Methinks

the lass should stay too." He slapped Gavin on the back and raced to join the parade.

Fraser plucked the dagger from the target, then handed it to Gavin. "Ye should send her away. She will bring nothin' but trouble." Frasier hung his head as he trod toward the hall as well.

Gavin glanced at the blade. He had seen it before. He had seen it often. The dagger belonged to his father. Mistress Audrey and his mother had played him false. As much as he wanted to take Frasier's advice, there was no getting rid of her now. All in Warring would boil his bones first.

Falling for her trap had been his third mistake.

CHAPTER 9

Within a day, everyone in the borderlands was blabbering about the maid who had the ability to outdo any man at blade tossing. No matter where Gavin went, people were either asking him about Mistress Audrey's talent or saying the best man the Armstrongs had was a *wumman*. Both comments were like a weasel gnawing at his insides. The Maxwells and the English were all quick to offer Audrey entry into any trials of feat. Hew Armstrong flatly refused until his sons persuaded him that she was the Armstrongs' best chance to win the event.

Attitudes in the tower had changed as well. You would have thought Queen Elizabeth or Dowager Mary de Guise had come to live with them. Servants bowed and fell over each other to do Mistress Audrey's bidding. Thomas followed her about and chattered continually. As the days carried on, the pair could be found picking wildflowers or at the river catching fish. Once they were spotted hoeing the ground with the tenants. Frowns curved to smiles wherever Mistress Audrey appeared.

This morn her laughter drifted up to his chamber window like an exotic potion brought from the Far East.

He looked outside to find Jaxon standing a hair's breadth away from Audrey's slim back as he whispered in her ear. Gavin's shoulders tensed. The lass didn't need Jaxon's help to throw straight. A pinch of pain squeezed Gavin's back. Bah. Jaxon adored Audrey like a besotted fool. What would Hew Armstrong say if he knew his son consorted with an English lass?

Bairn whined and scratched at the door. Probably he too wanted to find Mistress Audrey to get a few rubs behind his ears. "All right, ye beast, go. But *dinnae* get too attached to the lass, we'll be riding the marches soon." Gavin opened the door, and Bairn took off like he was chasing his mother's fat cat. Lately Gavin had warmed to the fluffy white feline since she did not seem enraptured with Mistress Audrey at all. Such a wise animal.

He made his way into the hall to find his mother working on her mending. "The world must be coming to an end if you are spending half your day lying in bed," she said, not taking her eyes off her chore.

"I *wasnae* in bed." He pulled out a chair and sat. "I was going over Warring's affairs."

"Will we survive another year?"

"If the fields remain free of blood and if our crops thrive before winter comes again. It should please you, Mother, that the Protestant reformers are calling for Mary de Guise's head."

His mother paused in her work. "You know I do not believe in such bloodshed. I want the reformers and the papists to live together in peace."

Gavin rolled his shoulders to release the kink that had plagued him all morning. "Because that is the Scottish way."

"Do not make fun of me." A deep frown settled on her face. "Your father and I put aside our religious differences to make a home for—"

"Do not lecture me. I have heard it often enough. *Da* put aside his religion for you and in doing so turned his back on his other kin." The white cat jumped up onto his lap and began to purr.

"This will all change when Jaxon and Fraser are lairds." She resumed with her sewing. "You shall see. Our families will be united again."

"Will they? I think not. Their land is almost as weak as ours." Gavin slid his fingers through the cat's soft fur. "Jaxon being the eldest will inherit, and Fraser will have to live off the scraps offered by his brother. I see a fight brewing."

"They get along now," his mother replied, jamming the needle through the cloth.

Gavin laughed. "Aye. But now is not later. They will fight, and the stronger will win, and the other will have to forge his own way in the world. Just like *Da* and Hew had to whittle out their own brother."

His mother glared at him without stopping her task. "That is not how it was. Colban fell off his horse and broke his neck."

Gavin puffed and pushed the soft feline from his lap. "A seasoned *reiver* would fall off his horse when a rabbit came hopping by? Nay. Think on it. Why did Father give land to Hew? They formed a pack against their own brother. You know I speak the truth."

"I know nothing of the kind. The hills can be fierce. An excellent rider could meet his demise by one wayward stone." His mother stubbed her finger with the needle, dropping her sewing onto her lap. "I know in my heart your father would never kill his brother over a piece of dirt."

Clenching his teeth to prevent further words, Gavin stood. "I *dinnae* care to rehash the past. I'm going to ride the marches."

"Alone? I dare say, last I noticed, Jaxon had his arms wrapped around Mistress Audrey. I am not sure a good whipping would scare him off. And Fraser has not been about in days. Of course, you could take Clyde."

A loud snore cut the air from where Clyde slept against the wall. His mother could needle him better than she did her mending. Now challenged, she wished to continue the fight. He had no desire to discuss Jaxon and Mistress Audrey's disgusting display of affection with his mother. And as for Fraser…he had been the one man who had not fallen under the woman's spell. So just where was he spending his days? Unable to solve this puzzle, Gavin shrugged and answered, "I shall take Bairn."

His mother laughed. "If you can drag the beast away from Mistress Audrey's side."

Gavin shoved his fingers into his riding gloves and stomped toward the hall entry, unwilling to take the bait. "The *dug* prefers the marches much more than a lovely lass who should be mending with you." His gaze rotated to the sleeping moss-trooper. "Clyde! Let us go."

The bench tipped over as the old man scrambled to his feet, blinking bleary-eyed in Gavin's direction.

His mother's laughter followed him all the way out into the bright courtyard. He shielded his eyes to see Mistress Audrey leaning against a cart with Jaxon by her side. Bairn, like the traitor he was, sat on the lady's feet. Least he was keeping Jaxon honest.

The dog's ears perked when Gavin let out a high whistle. "Let's go, *dug*."

The lass whispered to the animal, who reluctantly gave up his seat to come to his master's side.

Gavin released his tight jaw. "Are you coming, Jaxon? There is work to be done. Or are you going to entertain the maid all day?"

Jaxon never let his gaze drift from Mistress Audrey. "I will be along a little later."

A little later. Bah. When the winter winds blew. Deep down Gavin understood. Who wouldn't want to look at a lass whose beauty rivaled the rolling hills of the marches? For certain after Truce Day, the lass would have to leave or Hew Armstrong would kick Jaxon's Scottish arse out of his home for good.

Duncan brought forth two horses. "The others are waiting for us outside the gate."

He spoke of the other moss-troopers who would join them. They were nothing more than cottars who fulfilled a duty to their laird. No doubt they were hoping for a quick ride so they could go back to their farm work.

Gavin nodded and swiftly mounted his beast. Audrey and Jaxon giggled like a pair of foolish children. With a swift kick, Gavin's horse trotted to the gate. May the both of them choke on their smiles and laughter.

Once out of the keep, Gavin rode vigorously, scanning the hills, glen, and woods for wayward livestock or dead carcasses. The bright rays of sunlight warmed his cheeks and sent a small trickle of sweat down his back. Bairn howled by his side, bounding to the left and then to the right to keep pace. The other moss-troopers followed in silence as if knowing their laird was in no mood for idle chatter.

Nothing in the marches seemed amiss. No English lurked in the thickets, and no strange Scots rode across the meadows. His mind so preoccupied with Mistress Audrey, Gavin did not realize how close they were to Maxwell land and the same small inn where he had been with Jaxon and Fraser.

Gavin pulled his horse to a stop. "Let's stop for a drink," he said, hoping the other moss-troopers would readily agree.

"Eh? On Maxwell land. Are ye mad?" Clyde said once he caught up to the pack. "Methinks I'll wait here. With the lad."

The excitement in Duncan's eyes began to dull. The young servant had never been on Maxwell land let alone in a neighboring tavern in his life.

The others held back also. At this time of the year, they probably wanted to keep their heads clear so they could complete their work once they returned home.

"Why *dinnae* the rest of ye return to Warring. Clyde and Duncan can wait for me. I'll not be long."

Before Clyde could give protest, the others had ridden off, a wake of dust following behind them.

"What ye want in there?" Clyde grumbled. "Ye'll get yer head knocked in."

Duncan maneuvered his horse closer to Gavin's. "I *dinnae* mind going with ye."

Gavin shook his head. The less anyone knew about his plan the better. "Stay here. I'll be back shortly." Bairn barked. "Aye, ye can come with me."

The dog answered by licking his chops.

"We both could use a cool drink."

Gavin rode up to the inn and then tied his mount outside. He entered the tavern with Bairn in tow. The innkeeper's daughter gave him a lusty grin. "Would ye like a brew, Laird Armstrong?"

"Aye, and a bit of water for me *dug*." Gavin made his way to an empty table while Bairn drank heartily from a bowl of water.

"That fleabag should be outside," Rory Maxwell chastised from the same table he had been sitting at a few days' past.

"Bairn is cleaner than you, I wager." Gavin stretched out his legs and gave a coin to the lass who brought a small beer.

"I was speakin' about ye, Armstrong, not yer *dug*." Maxwell showed his dark stained teeth. "Though I have to wonder, why *dinnae* ye drink on yer own lands?"

Gavin took a long pull from his mug. "I like the company here better."

His remark drew a crusty laugh from Maxwell's throat. "Ye better not be talkin' about me cousin Lorna." He motioned to the innkeeper's daughter.

"Nay, though she be tempting. I am here to converse with you."

Maxwell stared at his brew. "We have nothin' to say, ye and me."

Gavin hefted a small bag of coins onto Maxwell's table. "A word, nothing more."

Maxwell rubbed his grubby cheek and gave a nod.

Swiftly, Gavin pulled out a chair across from Maxwell.

"Ye come to toss the dice? I'd be happy to take yer

land away again," he guffawed. "Ye can always marry another rich English lass to buy it back."

Gavin's blood heated. He'd love to kick Maxwell's arse all the way to the Highlands. Instead, Gavin gripped the wooden handle of his mug and hoped it wouldn't snap. He took a long drink to wash away his anger, then carefully placed the mug on the table. "I want to speak to Hetta."

Maxwell sat back, suspicion filled his gaze. "She *dinnae* want to talk to ye."

"Please." Gavin leaned over the table. "I *willnae* hurt her. I only want to speak to her." He picked up the bag of coins. "One talk is all I'm asking for. An easy task for a handsome sum. Consider it payment for her keep."

Another grainy guffaw filled the air. "The spit of coins ye have *willnae* tempt me. Be gone. And *dinnae* come here again." Maxwell gave him his shoulder.

Gavin grabbed Maxwell's arm. "Wait. I will help you in your cause."

"What cause do ye speak of?" Maxwell pulled his arm away.

"The one a man of the True Faith would be involved in. Those who *dinnae* wish to see the Reformer John Knox and his kind come into power."

Maxwell shifted. His eyes became thin slits. "Ye be willin' to betray yer own *ma's* beliefs? Some say she is more loyal to the English queen than to our own."

Gavin dropped his gaze to the table, his chest tightened. "I care little about religion and politics; it has torn this land apart. I care even less for Queen Elizabeth."

"Careful, the English would say those be words of treason," Maxwell whispered. "Yer *ma* would be so disappointed in ye."

A large knot developed in Gavin's throat. He tried to clear the obstacle away, but the tightness would not budge. Finally, he just nodded.

Maxwell's stale breath swirled around Gavin's face. "I never trust a man of mixed blood. Ye never know where they stand on things." Maxwell puckered his aged lips and let his gaze roam across Gavin's face as if searching for the answer. "Aye then. I'll hold ye to yer word, and if ye betray me, I'll cut out yer lyin' tongue and feed it to yer *dug*."

The lump let go. "I never go back on my word, and if I do, ye can place a dagger in my chest."

Maxwell sat back and finished his ale before wiping his mouth with the back of his hand. "Ye can count on that, Warrin'. I'll have to talk to the rest of me friends. They may not want ye involved in our affairs."

"When can I speak to Hetta?" Gavin snapped, dropping one hand to his lap, squeezing it into a fist.

Maxwell shrugged, tossing the coin bag in his palm to feel its weight. "When I think the time is right." He rose and tucked the bag into his jack. "Lorna, give Laird Armstrong another brew. He'll be needin' it."

Without another word Maxwell left, leaving Gavin to stare at the tavern's wooden door. For all he knew, winter might arrive before he met Maxwell again. Gavin gulped down his drink before Lorna refilled his mug. He needed an answer from the murdering Maxwell soon or his sons and Warring Tower would truly be lost.

Chapter 10

Thomas placed the brick back into the wall. "Are you sure this is a safe place?" he said to Audrey. "What if Gran or *Da* find the ring here?"

His quick thinking warmed Audrey's heart. She wondered what the boy would say if he knew it was his grandmother who had suggested the hiding place. "Nay, they will not. Your father never comes into the chapel, and your gran never looks behind this altar. Besides, God will be watching; He will keep your mother's ring safe."

The boy lifted his eyes toward the wooden cross on the altar, then nodded. "I think I shall come to prayers tomorrow morn."

His grandmother would be so pleased, though she would know the real reason for his sudden devotion to the Lord. At least the servants and villagers would be excellent examples of Christian piety. Audrey rose to her feet. "I think that would be wonderful."

"If I come every day, then I can remind God to take care of the ring." Thomas ran his fingers on the altar stone. "Do you think I can ask God to watch my things by the river?"

She brushed the dust from the front of her gown, trying

desperately not to chuckle. "I think that is a splendid idea."

Thomas gave a firm nod.

"Come. The sun has begun to set, and your grandmother will be wondering where you are."

The boy took Audrey's hand but kept looking back at the hiding place while they made their way to the door. "I know God will keep it safe. I just know He will."

Audrey squeezed Thomas's hand when they entered the hall. Already some of the servants were preparing for the evening meal. Lady Francis sat in her usual spot by the hearth, stroking her cat. All waited for the boar to make his presence known.

When Thomas saw Mistress Jonet by one of the tables, he raced for the scullery. Audrey at first considered giving chase, but she knew he would be back the moment his father entered the hall.

She strolled up to Lady Francis and took a seat next to her. "I have to say your hiding place was brilliant. Thomas already is considering coming to morning chapel to keep an eye on his prize."

"Had I known such a simple thing would bring him to prayers, then I would have shown him the spot years ago." Lady Francis scratched the purring cat under his chin.

"'Tis a grand secret for him to hide something from you and Laird Armstrong." Audrey yawned. The day had been long, and the fire eased her weary bones.

"Just what Warring Tower needs, more secrets," Lady Francis said, watching the fire dance in the hearth.

The cryptic words pricked Audrey's interest. There might be something there that would interest the queen. She meant to query further when a dusty Laird Armstrong strode into the hall followed by Bairn. The dog's jowls juggled back and forth; a long strand of drool hung from his mouth. Even caked in dirt, Laird Armstrong cut a fine figure. The annoying thought rattled Audrey. What care she if he was handsome or not?

"Hard ride today, Gavin?" Lady Francis asked, her fingers tenderly playing with the cat's ears.

He plopped into a chair opposite his mother while Bairn came to sit next to Audrey. "Aye, but I have good news. From what I can see, our land is free of any unwanted predators, four- and two-legged." He rubbed the bridge of his nose. "'Twould be nice to have a quiet summer." He stared off as if he knew what he asked for was nothing more than a fairy's tale.

"Well then, if all is calm, maybe you can join Mistress Audrey and me in prayers tomorrow?"

Gavin crossed one leg over his thigh and let his head fall back against the chair. "You know I *dinna*e believe anymore."

"Do not say such, your soul is in danger." Lady Francis pushed the cat from her lap, who quickly hopped up onto Gavin's. Bairn gave out a low growl.

Laird Armstrong's long fingers began to gently glide through the cat's fur. Audrey's breath caught when her mind wondered what those fingertips would feel like next to her cheek.

"I *dinnae* care about something that *doesnae* exists." He scrubbed a hand over his face.

His blond lashes accentuated the dark circles under his eyes. Audrey wanted to soothe his worry away with one simple touch. A war must wage in his soul.

"You know such words upset me. What happened in the past is not God's fault. Quit blaming Him for your own sins." Lady Francis slammed her hands on the armrests and bolted from her seat. She glared at her son. Her lips twitched with unspoken words. Knowing they would fall on deaf ears, she stormed toward the stone stairs. "Have Blair send up my meal. I shall be in my chamber."

Feeling awkward and a little embarrassed by her own wayward thinking, Audrey sat still though her heart raced like a galloping border pony. Gavin casually watched until his mother vanished from sight. Whatever went on inside his head he kept well hidden under a hooded expression. There was much to learn here. "Well, Mistress Audrey, it looks as if it will be just you and me this eve. Though I am certain Thomas's rumbling stomach will bring him to the hall."

"He is already in the scullery, probably filling his belly as we speak." Audrey patted Bairn on the head, trying to calm her senses. She threw in a yawn for good measure, though any fatigue had vanished the moment he walked into the hall.

"The fresh Scottish air making you tired? It has that effect on many." His gaze almost sensual, his fingers twisted and turned through the fur.

A warm glow seemed to fill her belly. "I think it is from chasing around with Thom…"

The heat in his eyes receded as a deep frown marred his face. His hand paused on the cat's back. "Once again you were with Thomas. Little more than a day has passed and you are back traipsing around with my son. But that is not all you do, is it? You play the innocent maid with Jaxon and others as well."

Why did he choose to be cross with her when all she

wanted to do was soothe the weariness from his brow? Desperately she tried to put up a wall against him. "Why are you speaking to me in such a manner? I cause no harm. You are a—"

"You are everywhere except where you are supposed to be." He jabbed a finger in her direction. "By my mother's side."

Once again, his Scottish brogue faded away as his anger rose. Audrey was fast learning she was the key to his agitation. "May I remind you that I was just sitting next to your mother?" She sucked in her breath; she had overstepped the boundary again. He had a way of bringing out the worst in her.

He jerked back, and his blue eyes became as wide as a vast lake. Then as if a dam had stopped the waters, his gaze constricted. "*Dinnae* be flippant with me, mistress," he said in a low growl. "You know my meaning, but if you keep on this way—"

"Laird Armstrong, please forgive me." Audrey clasped her hands and brought them to her chest. "Thomas follows me everywhere, and with your mother's blessings. As for Jaxon, we only throw daggers. Nothing more."

A brooding look settled on the boar's face.

"To hone my talent for Truce Day," she added in an as penitent voice as she could muster.

He stood. The cat cried out in protest, scurrying for safety under a table. "And that is why you are still here. Remember the feats were designed for men, not for lasses. That the other families allowed you to participate is proof they expect you to fail. Whatever the outcome, you will leave soon." He wheeled toward the stairs.

She rose and stopped his departure with a touch to his

chest. Her heart skipped and flipped over on itself. "Please," she whispered. "Must we always fight?"

His solid chest rose and fell with each breath he took, warming her fingers. He stepped even closer, his sultry, sweet breath curling down her neck. Her mouth went dry.

A brief flash of yearning entered his sultry gaze, pulling her closer to the fire, but then the longing burned out, buried under a cold veil. He stepped back. "Mistress, it is better to be enemies for that is the only way I can keep you safe until you leave." He bowed slightly before walking out of the hall.

Audrey reached back and grabbed the arm of her chair to stop her shaking. The man had a way of undoing her, and his words left her mind in a muddle. What did he mean, keep her safe? No one threatened her. Did he mean the marches weren't safe? Or did he know the real reason why she was here? Or the desires that plagued her soul?

More and more Audrey wanted to peel away his frozen mask and see what scars held his heart in ice. A bold plan began to form, ceasing her fears. If she could reach him a little, then she would learn much.

Dressed and ready, Audrey listened to the early morn footfalls of Laird Armstrong. She hoped and prayed he would ride the marches this morn. The sun had barely risen when she heard him slam his chamber door and race down the stairs with the pants of Bairn right behind him. She pulled her shawl around her shoulders, following at a fair distance.

A flutter of gratitude flared inside her when she saw

him head for the stables. She picked up her pace and found him readying his horse. "My Laird, I-I wish to ride with you."

His hand stalled on the animal's back; his eyebrows kicked upward. "You? Wish to ride the marches, with me? Are you daft? It is no place for a lass."

An annoying burr dug deep in her confidence. She lifted her chin and threw back her shoulders. "I know how to ride, and I have noticed that as of late you are riding without your cousins. I fear I am partly to blame."

He snorted. "With Jaxon for sure. As for Frasier, he *hasnae* been himself for a while."

Audrey cleared her throat. "Then I should like to go with you. I need the fresh air, and I am sure the other moss-troopers will not care."

A devious smirk twisted the corners of his mouth. "Riding the marches is not a trot on a country trail. They are dangerous. There could be *reivers* about. They have been known to take lovely wenches for ransom. And if that be your fate, then you are lost to us. For I *willnae* waste good coin on getting you back."

Bairn let out a low whine and sat on Audrey's feet. *Lovely wenches! Was he trying to be complimentary or cruel?*

"You are trying to scare me." She folded her arms across her chest and tipped her head. "It will not work."

"You're a brave one, are you? I wonder what you would do if Rory Maxwell kidnapped you."

She blinked. "Who?"

Gavin Armstrong frowned and shook his head. "A thorn in my...someone to watch out for." He motioned his head to the grey palfrey. "Since all looked peaceful yesterday, only Duncan and Clyde are riding with me this morn. I am sure they will not mind if you come along. Take Bessy. She is as docile as a milking *coo.*"

Elation and pride shot through Audrey. She had managed to persuade him with little resistance.

Laird Armstrong called for a stable boy to ready her horse. "With luck, the English will be roaming my lands. Then I can give you back to them." He winked before guiding his horse out to the courtyard. She quickly took her seat on the palfrey's back.

Duncan tipped his head with pleasure when he realized she would be joining them. Clyde spat on the dirt and mumbled his disapproval. All three men wore silver helmets and their jack of plates. Duncan and Clyde held a lang spear, while Gavin was armed with his sword and dagger. None of the men offered her any such weapons, which meant they truly did not expect trouble or they truly did not care about her welfare. Without a word, they took off into the early morning light with Laird Armstrong in the lead, Duncan at her side, and Clyde at her back.

Audrey lifted her gaze briefly to the heavens. *Lord, help me to safely get through this ride.* Satisfied, she gave her horse a good kick in the flanks and rode ahead with confidence.

Fresh cold mist hit her cheeks as she tried to keep pace. Gavin's broad back held her gaze, his muscles rippling with the horse's gallop. They were almost one and the same—two beasts striving to fulfill some unknown ambition. Each time she tried to reach his side he would push his horse harder, farther away, as if he feared someone might see, might know what tormented his soul.

Clyde laughed. "Ye *willnae* be catchin' him. There be no one in the west marches that can ride like Gavin Armstrong of Warring. Best ye stay back here with me."

Pushing the palfrey a little harder, Audrey pulled away. She needed to earn Laird Armstrong's trust and respect. She very well couldn't do that by acting like a weak English female. She had managed to get to his side when he pulled up his horse and came to a stop. Unable to halt her horse, Audrey rode past. "What now?" she asked, before circling back.

He lifted his chin to the hill before them. "There. On the horizon."

Audrey followed his vision. Three mounted men stared back at them. "Who are they?"

"That be Rory Maxwell, his son Ewart, and his cousin Ualan. We are close to their lands." Laird Armstrong maneuvered his horse in front of hers. Duncan and Clyde flanked her sides. The trio of brawn held their position.

"Are we givin' a greetin' or are we headin' back?" Clyde asked, pointing his spear at the men before them.

"You and Duncan will take Mistress Hayes to the top of yonder hill. I wish to speak to them alone."

"Nay, it be too risky. Ye need one of us with ye. Let the lad take her." Clyde lifted his sagging shoulders and locked the spear firmly under his armpit.

Gavin shook his head but did not argue with the relic. He turned his attention to Duncan. "Do not stop until you have her at the top of the hill."

The whole thing seemed absurd. Surely, they didn't intend to fight? "My laird, perhaps all we need to do is talk with them."

His eyes never left the threesome. "Not unless you want

to become their permanent guest. Do you not remember what I said about the Maxwells earlier?"

A spike of fear pierced her insides. Even from this distance, the small band did ooze malice. She resisted the urge to make the sign of the cross upon her chest. She timidly nodded.

"Listen carefully and do as I say," he said quietly, backing up his horse, dropping his hand to his sword. "Follow Duncan and head for the opposite hill and do not stop nor look back until you have reached its peak. Wait for us there." With a side glance, he whispered, "Ready?"

Her breath was imprisoned in her throat.

"Go," he shouted.

She and Duncan kicked their horses' flanks, and the beasts took off. A loud curdling cry cut the air and sent spirals of horror down her back. Her heavy breath matched that of the palfrey's as they galloped toward the hill. At the top, they stopped and swiveled back. She saw Laird Armstrong, sword raised high in his hand, charging the trio alone while Clyde stood like a stone warrior.

Audrey choked back the bile rising in her throat. "Why did he not charge with Laird Armstrong?"

"Because Clyde *isnae* any good in a fight. Those years for him are long past. All he can do is look fierce and pray Laird Armstrong knows what he is doin'."

The man was mad. They would cut him to pieces. She wanted to help, but she had no weapon. She had left her dagger in her room. Something she never planned to do again. "Please go help him," she pleaded.

"He wants me to stay here with ye. I know better than to gainsay him." Duncan held his reins in his hands, holding firm to the spot.

Such foolishness! She would have to head back to Warring Tower and alert the other moss-troopers. But which direction should she go? Helplessness rolled through her body. Intent on her earlier musings, she had not observed her surroundings. She knew not which way to go.

Laird Armstrong charged on with Bairn howling next to him. Rory Maxwell and the rest did not budge. Nor did they unsheathe their weapons. Less than a furlong he stopped, then trotted his horse back and forth in front of the trio. Shouts were exchanged, but Audrey could not distinguish their words. Finally, Laird Armstrong sheathed his sword. All four began to laugh as Bairn circled them, sniffing the ground. The jocularity continued as their attention floated up the hill to her.

The hair rose on the back of her neck. Her heart thudded wildly in her chest and echoed in her ears. Was all the bravado a show? Did he mean to bargain with them? Barter her for a few coins?

Duncan's wide eyes mirrored her conclusion. "Methinks this may not end well, mistress. Perhaps ye should head back to the keep. I'll go and help Laird Armstrong." Without giving her a second glance, he headed down the hill.

She glanced to her right and then to her left, which way should she go? *Anywhere but here.* Swiftly, she flicked the reins and took off over the hill.

The pounding of horse's hooves on the dry ground captured her hearing and stole her senses. She rode on and on, not giving thought to where she was or where she was going. Her breath came short, hard, and fast. Red, green, and yellow spots danced before her eyes. Trapped in her haze of horror, she did not notice the beast next to her or the hand that grabbed her horse's reins until it was too late.

She cried out, flaying her arms in every direction until her fist connected with a solid surface.

"Woof." The intrusive hand let go of the reins.

Tumbling forward, she grabbed the palfrey's neck, stalling the animal's steps. Audrey looked to her left to find Laird Armstrong holding his nose, a trickle of blood seeping through his fingers.

"You scared me! You should have made your presence known." She surveyed her surroundings to see Duncan and Clyde fast approaching, but none of the other men. Her breathing eased. A stab of guilt replaced her fear. "Are you all right?"

He shook his head. "You smacked me in the *nib.*"

Clyde and Duncan snickered but remained wordless.

Audrey straightened in the saddle and maneuvered her horse close to him. "Let me see."

"Nay," he cried when she reached out. Carefully, he removed his hands from his nose and swiped the blood away. "I'm fine." He sniffed. "Why did you run? I told you to stay at the top of the hill."

Her flesh heated. "I saw you laughing with...and Duncan and I thought you might—"

"You should know better than to listen to a green lad." He sighed and dabbed at his nose again. "In truth, if they wanted you, they would have taken you. They could have cut us all down."

"Then why did you charge in the first place?" Her horse danced away from his.

"To soothe a dangerous situation. And it worked. They believe only a crazy fool would charge with an old man to watch my back."

"Hey now," Clyde said in protest.

Gavin's horse danced around the two moss-troopers. "Return to the keep. We will head back shortly."

Duncan nodded, but Clyde would not budge. "Ye *cannae* be out here alone. Maxwell could return. Besides, we must think of Mistress Audrey...what might people think?"

Dabbing his nose again, Gavin gave her a cold appraisal. "Up ahead, there is a fine place near the river to rest the animals. You two can wait there. Mistress Hayes and I will be along shortly." He then trotted off, dismissing all of them.

Audrey followed quietly along, knowing he believed her to be a silly female. Queen Elizabeth would be disappointed in her actions. What man would tell a fragile female his secrets? She should raise the white flag right now and return to England.

He dismounted under a large oak tree. Audrey did likewise, though a good twenty paces away from him.

"Why are you mad?" he asked.

"I am not mad. I just..." She tucked a curl behind her ear and headed back to the tree where she sat down, clutching her knees.

"You are embarrassed because you listened to Duncan and fled?" He came to sit next to her. "*Dinnae* be. Had they killed me, they would have come after you. 'Twas a wise decision given what might have happened, though Duncan should have stayed with you. Later I will have to have a long talk with the lad."

101

"They still would have caught us." Defeat crept into her already flimsy resolve.

He put his back against the tree and stretched out his legs. His shoulder brushed against hers, sending a numbing tingle down her arm to her toes. "You have my father's dagger."

She grimaced. "I left it in my room."

He dabbed at his swollen nose. "That was very foolish. Keep it with you at all times from now on."

His sound advice made her heart slump. "Aye, I will."

"Perchance Jaxon would have come for you," he said playfully.

Audrey's skin began to heat. "I hardly think he is that smitten with me."

"It would have nothing to do with you. If they would have killed me for no good reason, then they would have the whole Armstrong family to deal with." His brow quirked up. "Unless you told me a tale earlier and there is something besides dagger throwing between you and Jaxon."

Her neck itched and was probably molten red. What a twit she was. Her knowledge of these people was so lacking. 'Twas almost as if Queen Elizabeth wanted her to fail. "There is nothing between us." Her protest came out a little louder than she'd wanted.

He chuckled, letting his gaze roam freely about her body. She should bristle at his forwardness, but instead, a sliver of delight tore through her, enjoying his appraisal. He cleared his throat and raised his gaze to scan the glen. "Where is that *dug*?" He let out a sharp whistle. In the distance, a series of barks and howls could be heard. Laird Armstrong stood and whistled again. "Bairn, Bairn," he called.

The hound bounded out of the brush and headed toward them. Covered in burrs, he jumped up and put his great paws on his master's chest.

"Ack, look at you, silly beast. Always got your nose in the wrong place." Laird Armstrong sat down again, and a panting Bairn managed to wedge himself between them.

Audrey laughed and began to pull burrs from the hound's back. "I must ask. Why would a mighty laird name his dog Bairn? He really is not a babe."

A deep frown chased away Laird Armstrong's joviality. Cavernous lines creased his forehead. "I am not so mighty. Quite the opposite, and as for the beast's name, it was given by another."

The heat in Audrey's body, which had begun to recede, kicked upward once again. Edlyn must have named the animal. 'Twas the only answer for his change of mood. "I am sorry," she mumbled.

"Sorry? For what? For the *dug's* name? It is what it is." He stood. "We must be getting back. I have other things I must do this day. I *cannae* waste all day spending time with a fair lass."

Audrey curled her tongue to hold in a gasp. Her heart tumbled in her chest. *Wasting time indeed.* But deep down she knew her heart skipped not because of his terse words, but because he called her fair.

Little was said by any as they journeyed to Warring Tower, nor did Gavin bid her well when he proceeded to his chamber. Audrey stood in the courtyard with Bairn by her side. To get a pet, the hound bumped his nose against her hand. Gently, she began stroking his head.

"Mistress Audrey." Thomas raced through the gate.

"I saw you riding with *Da*." The boy knelt down and gave Bairn a big hug. "Did you have fun?"

Audrey hesitated. She had no desire to lie to the boy. "It was pleasant." Other than the fear of being kidnapped.

"I wish I could go riding with *Da*. Can you talk to him? I would love to come along next time he goes out."

A chilly wave swept through Audrey. She had no desire to ask Laird Armstrong anything. "Your father rides very hard when he travels the marches. Keeping up might be a challenge."

Thomas stood and pushed out his chin. "I know how to ride. I used to ride with *Da* all the time until Marcas was born." The boy jammed a toe into the dirt, burying his face in Bairn's coat. "Then he stopped."

Compassion tumbled over in her chest. She doubted the boy rode far with Gavin. Thomas would say and do anything to get his father's attention. Audrey knelt next to the boy. "Your father is just very busy. He loves you as much as he loves Marcas."

"*Da doesnae* like Marcas either. *Da* just changed when Marcas was born."

What man doesn't love his children? Was he that heartless? Or did all of this have to do with Edlyn's death? The wind kicked up and swirled around her neck. She pulled up her shawl. "Your father has a keep to run."

Bairn licked the boy's face, breaking the sadness. Thomas gave the hound another hug. "But he let you ride with him."

Alas, they were back where they had started. How could she change the lad's thinking? A niggle of an idea began to bloom and blossom. "If you can tell me how Bairn got his name, then I shall speak to your father about riding." She expected the boy to frown and shake his head at the impossible task.

Instead, Thomas brightened and hopped up. "That is easy. I named him when *Da* brought him here as a pup. I named him Bairn." The hound barked, and Thomas rubbed the dog's broad head. "I get to go riding. Can I go tomorrow? I have to tell Gran!" The boy jumped into the air and clapped his hands before racing off to the tower with Bairn barking behind him.

Audrey's gaze drifted up to the boar's chamber window. By tomorrow morn she had to change Gavin's mind or Thomas's heart would be broken, and that was not going to happen.

CHAPTER 11

With the slash of the quill, Gavin crossed off another entry in his log. The past year's fighting had left Warring's finances dismal once again. The cottars who lived and worked on Armstrong lands faced a rough winter. A peaceful summer along with the purse from winning the Truce Day feats would help greatly. Unfortunately, neither was a certainty. The thought of *reiving* other families and the English through the winter once again left a cold empty pit inside him. Taking from those who were struggling just as badly was more than dishonorable, it was nothing short of murder.

He had seen enough death and starvation. And he was done with it. A timid knock on the door drew his attention. What now? Another squabble in the fields? Could his tenants not get along? Hunger had a way of tearing everyone apart.

"Enter," he bellowed, jamming the quill back into the inkwell. The door creaked open, and there stood Mistress Audrey. His interest piqued and chased away his glumness. "Mistress?"

She crept into his chamber like a timid mouse in search of a morsel of cheese. He frowned—this bode no good.

"I promise not to take up too much of your time." She wrung her hands, a habit that meant she was after something. "Just a moment."

Gavin rubbed the bridge of his nose, bracing himself for her request. "Speak, mistress. What do you want?"

Color flashed up her neck, and she fisted her hands. She puckered her lips and shifted her feet. Finally, the jumbling of her body slowed. She threw her shoulders back and looked him straight in the eye. "I promised Thomas that you would take him riding tomorrow." A gust of heavy breath followed her pronouncement.

A wave of anger ebbed and flowed through every muscle in his body. By all that was unholy, why would she do such? He pushed back his chair and ground his feet into the floor, fighting for composure. "You have no right to give away my time to my son or anyone else."

She opened her fist and smoothed her hands over her skirt. "I-I know, but Thomas and I made a bargain, and I lost."

He arched a brow, becoming interested in her words. "What type of bargain?"

The redness in her neck rushed up to her cheeks. He wondered if they were hot to the touch. Her gaze glazed over, and he feared her tears would break forth. Then her eyes cleared. "I told him if he knew how Bairn got his name, you would ride with him."

Gavin rose, toppling his chair. With three steps, they stood less than a hand apart. Her warm sweet breath caressed his cheeks, but that did not break his resolve. "Seems you were caught in your own trap. But that does not mean I have to try and set you free. I *willnae* ride with the lad on the morrow. 'Tis too dangerous out there, even if I called every moss-trooper to ride with us."

Mistress Audrey crossed her arms over her chest, and she had the audacity to glare at him. He fought the desire to kiss that look away. "You are the boy's father. He wants to spend time with you." To his amazement, she advanced on him, causing him to back up. "Why are you so uncaring? If you do not show some affection, the boy will grow up hating you. Is that what you want?"

A rayless cloud settled in his soul; she didn't know the half of it. "You promised me you would stay out of the rearing of my son." From within, he fought against the darkness. Against the rage that caused destructive damage. "You broke that vow. Truce Day or not, I think you should leave and return to England."

Unbridled terror filled her eyes, which reached out to grip his heart. What demon placed such horror in her? All color drained from her face. Her arms dropped to her sides. Gavin feared she would swoon again. He placed his hand on her hip. She flinched. Then slowly she thawed and touched his chest with soft fingers. His heart hammered. The softness of her curves crushed all of his anger, and he wondered if he would be the one who would swoon. He wanted to pull her closer and get lost in her deep midnight eyes. Run his hands through her silky black curls. Tease her lush red lips.

Gavin closed his eyes, fighting against the need to clasp her hand. He took another step back, shielding her from his desire. His breath slowed as her poise returned. Whatever frightened her had been forgotten. Her breathing was even, and she seemed unfazed.

But not him. Her star-studded eyes captured him once again, and he was undone.

Quickly he dropped his gaze, fearing it mirrored his want and knowing what that would cost. When he gained his composure, he looked up. "Forgive me, mistress. I thought you were ill and might swoon again."

"I am extremely fine." She lifted her breasts. "Your words no longer affect me. I am getting used to your bluster."

He would miss her spunk. Her eyes. Her lips. Perhaps he should reconsider sending her away.

"I shall leave on the morrow. But please spend time with Thomas. Think of the joy one morning of riding would bring to him and you."

She knew nothing about Thomas nor what had transpired long ago at Warring Tower. Nevertheless, she unwittingly had outmaneuvered him. She was the one chance for the Armstrongs to win the Truce Day feats and maybe change the past. The absurd notion almost teased laughter from his throat. Would she be willing to make another bargain?

"All right, mistress. I will take Thomas riding on the morrow as long as you join us."

First, her face filled with caution, then light as bright as a glowing tallow lifted her lips into a dazzling smile.

"But," he said, raising a finger, "after that, you *willnae* speak to the lad or spend any time with him. You will keep to your duties as being a companion to my mother, and when the Truce Day is over, you will leave and never return to Warring Tower again. If you *dinnae* accept my terms, I will send you away within the hour."

The stunning smile withered, and her cheeks drooped. What perplexed him even more was how his chest ached at her reaction.

He steeled his back, pushing away the troublesome thought. "Well?"

Her gloomy gaze glaciated his heart, and again he had the desire to hold and protect her against his own words.

Finally, that fine chin of hers rose. "I accept your terms." Mistress Audrey walked toward the door and stopped. "I assume you will tell Thomas of his good fortune since I am not allowed to speak to him."

Gavin gave a curt nod.

Her delicate hand smoothed out the spot on her waistline. The spot where his hand had been. She dropped into a submissive curtsy before quitting the room.

Though Mistress Audrey had acquiesced, Gavin felt like he had lost the battle.

Insufferable. There were no other words for him. That she ever believed he had a smidgen of a heart had been her folly. Audrey stormed through the hall and out into the courtyard with her dagger in hand. She stopped a good thirty paces from the butt before flipping the blade at the mark. Perfect strike.

Nay, there were many a word for him—vile, despicable, detestable, horrid, repugnant, and evil. Audrey winced at the last word. Not evil, but certainly he was obnoxious. She stomped over to the butt and snatched her dagger, returning to the line to violently release the blade again.

Zing! Again, on the mark.

For a second time, she made her way toward the target, slapping her feet against the dry ground. Though she rarely questioned God, she could not fathom what He was thinking to allow that man to have children. Straw flew out in all directions when she yanked out the knife a second time.

Liar! 'Tis that you enjoyed his touch that has your ire up.

How true. When he told her to leave, all that plagued her was Queen Elizabeth's wrath. She had to write to the queen. But what? Surely there was something that would interest her. Audrey tapped the blade in her hand. Lady Francis seemed sympathetic to the English. Would the queen care about that? Or perhaps the strife between the Maxwells would pique her interest. None of this would matter to a queen. Audrey bit her lip. None of it mattered to her except his touch...

Gavin's warm, powerful hand melted away her fears. She rubbed the spot where his grip had been. How close she had been to throwing her arms around his neck and kissing his vile words away. When had she become so wanton? And why was she attracted to such a detestable man?

Because deep down you know he is not. He may be damaged, but he is not unredeemable. He should be unredeemable, then everything would be fine. She could hate him with great satisfaction.

Working up a hearty anger again, she marched to the line and lifted the dagger over her shoulder.

"Hold there, Audrey. Do ye mean to destroy the butt?" Jaxon's smooth voice did not ease her fury.

She flicked the blade, hitting the mark again. "Your cousin is an intolerable lout." *Wounded.* "A dreadful man." *Suffering.* "A-a boar!" *Who has a heart that needs to be rescued.*

Jaxon strode to the butt and extracted the dagger from the cloth. Wisely, he tucked the blade into his jack before returning to her side. "So, Gavin has crawled under yer skin once again."

The idea of the man crawling anywhere near her sent her lips tingling. She tried to work up her old defense. "I know he misses his wife, but does he have to be such a cruel father? Truly, Thomas had nothing to do with his mother's death."

"Mmm..." Jaxon rubbed his chin. "Ye are right about the lad and his *ma's* death. But what Edlyn and Gavin had I *widnae* call love."

Could this be true, or was this just Jaxon's male perspective? "Surely you are mistaken. Maybe it just appeared that way—men being indifferent in front of other men."

Jaxon shook his head. "Nay. The pair hardly talked. Edlyn was the type of *wumman* who was afraid of a mild breeze. The only one who seemed to get her mouth to move at all was me brother, Fraser. Once in a while I would see them whisperin' and even laughin'. But Gavin and her, nay, never. He never seemed to notice her."

This had to be wrong. And yet...it seemed so right. The sadness in his eyes. The slump of his shoulders. The blustering mask he wore hid that vulnerability. Lady Francis had said he was a doting father until Marcas came along. Did he doubt the babe's parentage? Impossible. Marcas looked exactly like Gavin.

"But surely there must have been some affection? They did have children."

"I think he was more interested in the size of her purse." Hesitation entered Jaxon's voice. "Though there had to be somethin' else since they were secretly wed long before he brought Edlyn home."

A secret wedding? Questions flooded Audrey's mind. "Did not his father approve of the match?"

"Nay, Ian was long dead before Edlyn came to Warrin' Tower to live. Any way ye see it, the marriage *didnae* make any sense. Gavin was into drink, dice, and lasses." A fiery longing filled Jaxon's eyes. He placed his hand boldly on Audrey's shoulder. "How about we take a little ride. Use some of that heat in ye in a different manner?"

"One ride this morn is enough." Nor did she care to get that friendly with Jaxon. Her gaze shifted up the tower to Laird Armstrong's chamber window.

Jaxon cocked his head upward, wrinkling his forehead. "With Gavin? He rides fast with *wummin*."

She stepped back. "I do not like what you are implying."

"Perhaps not, but if Gavin let ye ride the marches with him, then he must have had somethin' in mind."

Audrey opened her mouth, ready to give the man a severe tongue-lashing, when a cart rolled through the gate.

Peter had returned, and he would be wanting a missive for Queen Elizabeth. A trying day had just become worse.

CHAPTER 12

Watching from his chamber window, Gavin fisted his hands. Jaxon never missed an opportunity to woo a maid. Mistress Audrey should be warned, but then again, she could take her blade to him if he tried to seduce her. She was a she-devil come to wreak havoc on Warring Tower and to any who crossed its gate.

Gavin surveyed his desk and rubbed the back of his neck. Enough with the figures today. Time to save the undeserving female from his cousin and find his wayward son. But upon entering the courtyard, Audrey was nowhere in sight. Jaxon sat flipping her dagger over and over in his hand.

"Where is Mistress Audrey?" Gavin asked.

"She went to speak with the merchant that come in that." Jaxon pointed to Peter's cart.

Peter showed up almost every week with English goods to trade, and sometimes, when they had nothing to trade, goods that were gotten in an unscrupulous manner. A scoundrel to be sure, but a Scottish one who helped fill many bellies when the weather cooled. What did Audrey want with him? A curl of wary settled in Gavin's gut.

"Where did they go?" He scanned the courtyard; his query wasn't anywhere. He came to save Mistress Audrey from one leech, and now he might have to save her from another. Though Peter was an old man and fonder of drink than women. Nay, something else drew them together.

Jaxon shrugged. "They went in the tower. She said the man had somethin' she needed."

That seemed impossible since Peter's cart was still covered with a heavy leather skin, and they weren't in the hall, or he would have seen them. So, where were they? In the kitchen? What were they up to? Gavin shielded his eyes against the bright sun. He would have to watch the merchant more closely.

"She said she would return shortly." Jaxon hitched up his breeks. "The lass is keen on my skills. Would ye care to wait with me?" The challenge in his voice could not be missed, but Gavin did not want to fight over Mistress Audrey like two murdering cocks. Best to leave now or he might just punch his cousin in the nose.

Gavin shook his head and adjusted his riding gloves. His fingers nearly tore the leather. "I have to find my son."

"I am thinking of taking Mistress Audrey out for a ride. Alone," Jaxon said, unwilling to give up the contest.

Gavin squeezed Jaxon's shoulder, pulling him to the tower stable. "Methinks it would be better for you to come with me. Unless you be wanting to lose some important parts of your body."

Jaxon wrinkled his nose. "But I have her dagger. And who knows what that merchant intends to do."

"Aye, but I *widnae* doubt that she harbors an ax under her skirts and can well take care of herself."

Early the next morn, Thomas stood in the courtyard with his humble steed. The mare was docile, old, and perfect for a young lad to ride. "I'm ready, *Da.*" He beamed from ear to ear. The loving eagerness in Thomas's eyes sent a wave of guilt rolling over Gavin's shoulders.

"Good," he said sternly, looking to Duncan and Clyde. They would take a short ride and return quickly, which would please Thomas and... "Where is Mistress Audrey?"

The lad's face wilted. "I *dinnae* know. She *willnae* speak to me."

At least the lass had heeded his order. Still he had to wonder, where was she now? Once again, her whereabouts had become a mystery. After dragging Thomas from his favorite fishing spot yesterday, he had found her sitting quietly by the hearth. Her odd behavior continued all last eve. Often Peter drew her attention while he ate and drank with the other servants. He was the one who brought her here and would be the one to take her away, but that did not explain her uneasy demeanor. Something reeked, and it wasn't Peter's ripe tunic.

As if his words had summoned the lass, Mistress Audrey stumbled into the courtyard. The bags under her eyes resembled bales of hay. A spiral of worry whirled up Gavin's spine. "Mistress, how fair you this morn?"

"I did not sleep well last eve. The wind kept me awake all night."

The night was quiet and pleasant. What wind did she speak of? Even this morn it had been calm and void of windy bluster. Something else disturbed her slumber.

A heavy sigh left her lips as she mounted the grey

palfrey. "I am ready," she said, looking straight ahead.

They rode out of the tower to Thomas's squeals of delight and Mistress Audrey's melancholy. Over the meadows they journeyed. All the while she remained silent. Thankfully, her gloominess had not been noticed by Thomas. He chattered away with Duncan and Clyde while riding between them.

Even in the company of the moody mistress, the early morn offered a preview of the fine day to come. Yellow-orange rays rose in the east, and the air was full of songbirds, bleating sheep, and mooing cows. The crisp air gave way to warm winds. Soon summer would settle in, and Gavin prayed it would be full of peace instead of constant fighting.

They zigzagged over the river and took the rolling hills in stride. The tension in his shoulders began to ease. Thomas started humming a merry tune, and Gavin, Clyde, and Duncan quickly joined in.

The glum mistress dropped some of her gloom. A smile teased her lips. "What song do you hum?"

"Something my father made up to woo my mother," Gavin said lightly.

"Sing it, *Da*," Thomas begged.

So merry the day, Gavin obliged the lad.

Me girl is a lass so fair that none would give a care
If she danced in bare feet and whistled a tweet
If she smiled so sweet while eating a treat
Me girl is a bonnie lass.

"That's terrible." Mistress Audrey laughed.

He shrugged. "She married my father anyway." Gavin winked, and Audrey's skin began to take on a familiar pink glow. A color he was beginning to appreciate.

Clyde noticed and wheezed a chuckle while Duncan's cheeks resembled Audrey's red hue.

"*Da,* look!" The lad pointed to a small hill near the Maxwell land. There stood a figure that swept away his joyful mood. *Hetta.* And she was alone, her long grey hair hanging to her round shoulders.

Gavin pulled the horse to a stop. "Hold, Thomas. We *cannae* go to her. For if she stands there, the rest of the Maxwells are not far off."

"But, *Da.* I only want to wish her well. She was my nurse," Thomas whined.

"Nay. Go back to Warring Tower, now. Clyde. Duncan. Take the lad back now!"

"But we *havenae* finished our ride." Thomas shot Gavin a venomous look.

Gavin yanked the reins from Thomas's hands and turned the animal around. With a swift slap on the rump, the horse took off. Thomas jostled from side to side before taking control. The lad wailed but rode on with the two moss-troopers racing behind him.

Let him be angry, soon he will understand all.

"Was that necessary?" Mistress Audrey pierced Gavin with a cold stare. "He just wanted to greet his old nurse."

Gavin cocked a warning brow. "Mistress, best you hold your tongue on things you *dinnae* understand."

"I am sure the old woman is very dangerous." Her flippant tone set him on edge.

He looked to the hill, but Hetta was gone. *Blast.* He wanted to speak with her—alone. Gavin scrutinized the high and mighty mistress. Last thing he needed was her bonnie nose in his dangerous affairs. Without a word, he headed back to Warring Tower knowing the lass would follow.

Once inside, the stable boy took his mount. He scanned the area for Thomas, but the lad was nowhere in sight. Probably hiding under his gran's skirts. The kink between Gavin's shoulder blades returned. He'd been a fool. If he had gone out this morn without the lad and Mistress Audrey, he would have had his opportunity. Now he would have to wait and meet Hetta under the watchful eye of Rory Maxwell.

"A word with you, my lord." The intrusive voice of Mistress Audrey paused his steps on the spiral stairs.

He spun about. "What now?"

"Why?" she snapped. "Why are you so cruel to your son?" Her pink cheeks now shone bright red, her breath short and fast.

His gaze raced around the courtyard. A few servants had paused in their tasks. "Not here, not now, mistress," Gavin said low through clenched teeth.

She folded her arms over her chest and fixed her stance like a tough termagant. "Then where and when?"

Enough. He was done fighting with her. He was done with her accusations and snobbish ways. He was done with her telling him what to do. "Follow me, mistress."

With long strides, he strode through the gate to the grassy meadows beyond. A good furlong away from the tower he stopped, waiting for her to catch up.

She stopped and wiped her sweaty brow with the back of her hand while trying to catch her breath. "Well, sir. We are alone. You can start with your yelling and shouting. I am sure no one will hear the boar from here."

The woman tested his resolve like no other. "Mistress, it seems you are incapable of keeping your thoughts to yourself. I have warned you many a time that things in the borders are not like things in London. Here you can trust no man or *wumman*."

"And London is different? You are sadly mistaken. There is much more intrigue and danger within that city than you can imagine."

His pulse increased at her loose words. "What intrigue do you speak of?"

She blanched and took a step back. Her high color draining away. "I-I spoke in generalities. Nothing more. Criminals abound on the city streets."

Obviously, but that was not what she meant by intrigue. He took a patient breath. "If you wish to stay, you must learn to censor your words."

The lass cast her eyes to the side. Plainly, she had heard the same reprimand from others. "I am trying," she said meekly. "But I just do not understand why you are so harsh with your son. He admires you so much. What harm is there in showing a little love and understanding to the boy?"

They were back to the same conversation they had had many a time. His ire rose, and his temper flared. "Stop meddling with the lad."

"Stop shouting at me. The boy is your seed. What father does not love his son?"

"He's not my son," Gavin bellowed.

Her hand shot to her throat as her eyes became as wide as a cart's wheel.

Anger drove him on. "Take a good look at him. Does he look like my son?"

"Nay, but I thought his mother…"

"He looks nothing like her either."

"But that does not mean—"

"In this case it does. The lad is not mine. Now leave it alone." He gave her his back and stomped to the keep. He had said too much. Truce Day couldn't come fast enough because he knew she wouldn't let the subject go, and that might put them all in danger.

Later that eve, as he sat in his chamber perusing Warring's accounts, he heard a creaking of a cart in the courtyard. Standing, he went to the window. There he saw Mistress Audrey and Peter exchanging words. She handed him a piece of parchment. As the cart rumbled out of the courtyard, she made the sign of the cross over her chest before she fled back into the tower.

A slow burn began to fill his belly. So, the lady was a Catholic. Why would Pimberly send a papist to Warring Tower and to whom did she write? Quickly Gavin reached for his sword and dagger. He knew Peter's habits well. Before heading for the English countryside, he would stop and quench his thirst at a local tavern. Gavin would be waiting.

CHAPTER 13

U nable to sleep, Audrey dressed and headed down the spiral stairs. She had hastily written the queen's missive and now regretted every word. Trying to gain some control in these lawless lands, would Queen Elizabeth use Thomas's paternity against Gavin? What would happen if he disowned the boy? Poor Thomas. He could be left a nameless, penniless pauper. And she had added to this tragedy.

Audrey placed a fist against her forehead. Why did she not stick to generalities as she had first planned? So set was she on proving her worthiness as a spy, she might have jeopardized the boy's future.

She slipped into the chapel, fell to her knees, and clutched her hands. *Dear Heavenly Father, forgive me of putting my own desires above those of others. Please let not my words harm Thomas. Keep him safe. Soften Laird Armstrong's heart toward Thomas. I ask all this in your son's name. Amen.*

"Oh my, what are you doing in here so early?"

Audrey froze and swiped a hand across her eyes. Clearly Lady Francis could not sleep either. Gaining control, Audrey rose. "I was just spending some time in prayer."

"You have missed a few days, have you not?" The reprimand in the older woman's voice was light, though her eyes kept darting to Thomas's hiding place. *Did she think I took the ring?*

Audrey gave a mental shake and focused on Lady Francis. "I am sorry. I was trying to grow the bond between Thomas and his father through riding."

"As I have heard from Thomas. But it did not go well, did it?"

Despair squeezed Audrey's chest. "Nay. Thomas wanted to greet his former nurse, Hetta, and your son became quite cross. The gap between them is even wider now, and I promised Laird Armstrong I would not speak to Thomas anymore."

The pleasantness slipped from Lady Francis's features. "Hetta," she whispered, stepping back and putting a hand to her heart.

"Do you need to sit, my lady?" Audrey reached out and took Lady Francis's elbow.

"Nay, aye..." Lady Francis pulled away. "But not here. Come, let us go to my solar."

Audrey guided Lady Francis up the stairs and pushed open the door to her room. The opulence caused Audrey to pause. A large four-poster bed with yellowing linen curtains stood against a wall. Animal skins were neatly placed in front of a large bronze brazier. Two old green fabric chairs sat next to a round table. On top of the table stood two silver goblets and a matching pitcher. An elegant, aged tapestry of three women dancing hung on another wall, and a large chest with brass handles fit snug in a corner.

Lady Francis stepped over the threshold and motioned

to Audrey. "Come. Though the fire has gone out, the room is very comfortable."

The chamber was almost as lavish as any Audrey had seen at Queen Mary's court. The opposite of Edlyn's room or even the boys' chamber. The solar was twice the size and clearly meant to be the laird's—yet it wasn't.

"Ah. I see your mind turning. This old woman lives like a queen." Lady Francis sat in one of the soft chairs and again motioned to the other. "Do sit down."

Audrey quickly complied, but she did not affirm the older woman's words.

Lady Francis reached for a pitcher and poured two goblets of water. "All of what you see here came from my home in England before I married. I offered all to Gavin to pay Warring's debts, but he refused." She paused, letting her sad gaze rest on each object. "If he had, perhaps all would be different now."

Audrey opened her mouth to speak, but Lady Francis seemed far away in the past and did not want to be disturbed.

"After my husband died, I wanted to move into the chamber above us, but Gavin would have none of it. So, I stayed—here." Lady Francis grabbed a goblet and took a long drink before wiping her mouth. "Even when things went bad."

"Bad?" Audrey leaned in, hoping to calm the lady's distress.

"Aye." Lady Francis's eyes filled with tears. "Gavin never got along with his father. The lad was an irritant to my husband. No matter how I tried to smooth things between them, they only got worse."

Audrey had already heard too much over the last few

days. What would be offered now? More sweet tidbits to pass on to the queen. She wanted to cover her ears. On the other hand, she wanted to hear more. Guilt gnawed at her insides. "My lady, you do not—"

"Of course, I do." Lady Francis croaked before taking another drink. "Gavin spent much of his time with Fraser and Jaxon. Mostly Fraser. They would run wild on the marches. Drinking, gambling, and carousing. My husband was at his wits' end."

What father wouldn't be? Audrey had seen many a young man ruin the family name by such antics. "But he did grow out of it."

Lady Francis sadly laughed. "Not right away. Gavin was still a wild rogue when my husband died. In truth, his behavior became worse. He was loud, brash, mean, and drunk most of the time. He tore through the tower like a wild boar."

That is how he got his name. "Surely guilt ate at him for not reconciling with his father before he died."

"Possibly. But all that changed once he wed Edlyn."

Then despite the questionable paternity of Thomas, Gavin Armstrong must have loved Edlyn regardless of what Jaxon had said. "A good woman can have a marvelous effect on some men."

Lady Francis raised her greying brows. "Really? I have never seen such, and especially not with Edlyn. Truth be told, it was quite the opposite."

"But—"

"Let me finish. Many months after my husband died, Gavin went on a rampage. In a drunken stupor, he tore the tower apart. Even knocked out a couple of Clyde's teeth. And he has few to spare. Seeing the man bloody on the floor, Gavin fled and was gone for almost a year. There were reports of how he was gambling, and drinking, and other things…"

Heat flooded Audrey's body. Even when he held himself in check, Gavin Armstrong oozed with manly desires. What would he be like out of control? A slight shiver skidded down her spine. "You do not have to tell me more. These are private matters."

Plus, Lady Francis could give some incriminating evidence that would link Laird Armstrong with those trying to cause a great rift between Dowager Mary de Guise's Catholics and those of the Reformed Church or worse against the English and Queen Elizabeth. Regret crushed Audrey's chest. She did not want to cause any more harm to a family who had obviously suffered so much.

Tears washed down the older woman's cheeks. "Nay, they need to be brought to light." Lady Francis picked at a nonexistent spot on her gown. "I tried to run Warring Tower by myself, but I never stopped praying that God would return my prodigal son to me."

Audrey picked up a cloth, handing it to Lady Francis. "And he has."

Lady Francis dabbed at the corners of her eyes. "But at what cost? When Gavin did return, he brought a wife and a babe. It all became clear to me then."

Audrey fought to purge the fog from her brain for nothing made sense to her. Nor did she care to know. Especially if her words would deem Gavin a traitor to his own people.

Lady Francis carried on. "It was not just my husband's death that plagued Gavin. He had a child out of wedlock."

The cloth fell to the floor. "Well, at least he did the right thing and married Edlyn. All was well for a while."

Audrey took a sip of her water to hold her speech. Laird Armstrong had said the child wasn't his. This tale was growing more perplexing by the moment. But why would Gavin reveal such a secret to her but keep his mother in the dark? Or had he lied and his mother held the truth?

"They resided as a fairly happy couple in the chamber above while Thomas slept where he does now, and his nurse Hetta slept in the chamber you now occupy."

"But I thought that was Edlyn's room?" Audrey blurted out. Her head began to pound from all the contradictions.

Clouds entered Lady Francis's eyes again. "That did not happen until after Marcas was born. Edlyn claimed she wanted to be closer to her children. I offered her my chamber, but she would not have it. She slept with Hetta, though I have no idea how they managed."

The narrow bed Audrey rested upon was never meant to hold two people. Something was still missing from this puzzling tale.

"Then when Edlyn died... I cannot tell you the words that were said between Gavin and Hetta." Fresh tears pooled in Lady Francis's eyes. "Soon after, Hetta fled and sought protection from Rory Maxwell."

Talons of foreboding grabbed at Audrey's heart. "Why would she need protection?"

"Because Hetta accused my son of murdering Edlyn."

CHAPTER 14

Gavin ordered another butt to be placed outside the tower wall where he could practice his archery skills in peace. He pulled the hemp string tight and fixed his bow, measuring the weight carefully in his hand. His father had been a superior archer; his arrow always struck the mark perfectly. Since it was Ian Armstrong's weapon of choice, Gavin chose another. He was an expert on horseback. A true *reiver*. He should have practiced his archery skills more.

No combat would be found in the Truce feats since the people of the borderlands were bone-weary from all the violence they experienced during their everyday lives. They wanted only joviality. No reminders of war, poverty, or starvation. It started with a few wrestling matches and then grew into much, much more.

Besides the Armstrongs and the Maxwells, two English families would participate in the feats. The Halls and the Dunneses were *reiving* families that just happened to settle on the English side of the border. Depending on the year, they could be an unbeatable force. However, this year would be the Armstrongs' year.

The horse race gave Gavin no concern. He could win

that while snoring. Rory Maxwell would be the victor in the archery contest; he had not lost in six years. Maxwell's cousin Ualan laid claim to the blade toss. If the English hadn't gone soft from last year, they would win the lang spear and the wrestling contest. Usually, the footrace settled the feats. Whoever had the fastest lad would win the day. If the games split evenly between any families, then an ax throw would determine the victor.

The Armstrongs had not won the games since Ian Armstrong died, but this year things would be different. They had the fastest runner in Duncan. If they won the horse race and the footrace, then they would only need to win one more feat. Most believed Audrey would outwit Ualan with her accurate dagger. But she was a woman, and experience had taught Gavin that women weren't very practicable. He wouldn't lose again and face the humiliation of allowing Maxwell the win or the English. Warring Tower may not be the grandest, but the Armstrong lineage begot many warriors. This year was theirs.

The muscles in Gavin's arm groaned as he pulled back the string, aiming for the brown cloth. Letting go of his breath, he loosed the arrow. All sound fell away as the arrow drifted on a mild breeze to land well below the mark.

Blast! Bairn whined and rolled onto his side away from the butt. Gavin eyed the dog. "Agreed, a poor showing to say the least." He wiped the sweat from his brow with a cloth, discarding the linen on a wooden bench that sat nearby.

Stomping his feet on the firm ground, Gavin approached the butt and yanked out the arrow. 'Twas all for naught.

Six arrows had missed the mark. The Maxwells or the English would win the feats again. In his mind he heard Rory's laughter. Perhaps he should forget about archery and focus on something else.

The feats were only one of his problems. The other was much bigger and had a saucy mouth—Mistress Audrey Hayes.

Gavin rubbed his bruised knuckles. The missive he had taken from Peter, after a little persuasion, spoke of the daily activities at Warring Tower and Thomas's questionable heritage. One drivel was obvious, while the other was troubling. Why did he tell her such an important secret? He should throw the bonnie traitor in chains right now, but that would not produce the needed answers. Who did she work for? He doubted she would just tell him outright, and he wasn't one to torture a maid, or a man for that matter.

He nocked his arrow and set his sight on the target once again, picturing the prim, secretive lass. The arrow flew straight and landed right in the middle of the drab cloth. Perfect. If he kept up his ire against the lady, he could beat Rory Maxwell and the English with the bow.

Peter claimed he only delivered the missives to a man in Lanercost and knew nothing more. To save his neck, he made an agreement. Each missive would be delivered to Gavin, and a different note would be substituted and sent to Mistress Pittman on Little Lane. Audrey acted like a courtly lady, not some poor mistress raised on a farm. Mistress Pittman had to be someone of importance. Someone who might have the ear of Queen Elizabeth. However, why would the queen be interested in him or Thomas? He needed answers. The thought of Thomas being harmed hit him like a backhanded blow.

Gavin pulled another arrow from his quiver and studied the butt. The cloth took on a look of Audrey's face. With perfect perfection, the arrow landed slightly above the other.

Out of the corner of his eye, he saw the traitorous woman sneaking away from the tower. "Mistress," he called out, but Audrey did not stop. Bairn sat and started to bark, wagging his tail. "Go fetch the lass," Gavin ordered.

The large hound took off and chased Audrey, knocking her to the ground. Bairn howled and slobbered her with affectionate licks.

"Get off me, you big oaf," she cried, but Bairn only answered her pleas by placing one large paw on her chest.

With long strides, Gavin came to her side and stifled a laugh at the wet mess of a woman before him. "Mistress, I told you to stop."

She wiped her hands over her face, trying to peek between her dark lashes. "Get this beast off of me. Do you want him to kill me with his slobber?"

Gavin laughed. "If I wanted to kill you, I would have used my bow."

She froze, and fright entered her eyes, chilling his bones. He had not seen such a look since Edlyn...

Shagging the dog away, Gavin held out his hand. Her fingers were cold to the touch and shaking. Swiftly he wrapped an arm around her shoulders, lifting her to her feet. A soft fragrance of heather wafted from her locks. She looked like a frightened child. Truly, did she believe he would harm her?

"Mistress," he said gently, giving her shoulders a protective squeeze. "I *willnae* harm ye."

She wormed away from his grasp, brushing an arm across her face to remove the rest of the dog's drool. "I... you should not scare a person so."

Grass stuck out of her braid in every direction. A smudge of dirt clung to one cheek. What a bonnie lass. If she were not a spy, he would kiss her until she did not know her own name. Perchance he would kiss her anyway.

He pulled a long stalk from her hair and handed it to her. "Forgive me, but you should not be wandering the meadows alone."

She dropped the twig and brushed dirt off her gown. "I was not going to be alo..." Her hand stalled on her frock. "What did you say?"

Another lie had almost slipped from her lips. "Nay, mistress. As you were saying, you *werenae* going to be..."

She curled her hands in her skirt and licked her lips, giving them the most delectable sheen.

Gavin placed his hands on his hips. "Who were you going to meet? Jaxon?"

A hand flew to her throat. "Absolutely not."

"Then who, Audrey?" His gaze captured her glossy lips. "Do I need to retrieve my bow?"

Her eyes widened. "Sir, I-I...you should not..." She blew a piece of wayward hair from her face. "I was going to see Thomas."

As he suspected. Why was the lad such an interest to her? "What am I going to do with you?" he said in a low voice.

Once again, she fiddled with her skirt. "My lord, I do not know what to say. I have heard some things, and I fear for the boy's safety."

What turn of events was this? Did she speak of whom she wrote the letter to, or did she fear someone else would harm Thomas? He frowned. Surely she did not think he would harm the lad. "Tell me what you have heard?"

Color rose in her cheeks, and she glanced past him to the tower gate. "I am a mite parched. Could we return to the hall?"

Her evasion tried his patience. "What about Thomas? How is he in danger?"

She touched her brow, and her eyes darted left then right. A forced laugh left her throat. "I may have been mistaken." She glanced at the hound sitting to her left, panting and drooling profusely. "I had a terrible fright. Let us go get that drink." He blocked her steps when she tried to get around him.

"Audrey," he said softly, leaning closer to her. "Are you afraid of me?"

A tight squeak followed by a whine left her throat before she nodded.

Looking heavenward, Gavin let out a long, patient sigh. His words would probably wind up in her next missive, but he could not abide a maid who would tremble at the sight of him or contemplate sticking a blade in his ribs.

He waved toward the wooden bench near the butt. "I have a flagon of water over yonder, and we shall be close enough to the tower in case you need to call out for help, which I assure you *willnae* be necessary."

Before offering her his arm, she took off with Bairn howling at her heels. She plunked down on the bench without even looking at the flagon. With measured steps, Gavin strode to stand in front of her. He picked up the flagon and offered her a drink. Without a word, she took the flask, drank, and then handed it back to him.

Carefully, he knelt in front of her and picked up the linen he had discarded earlier. He poured water over the cloth and gently wiped her face. "Audrey, you need to be honest with me. 'Tis the only way we will reach some agreement."

She reached up and took the linen from his hand, dabbing at her neck. "That is the third time you have used my given name."

"Aye."

"Why?"

The lass was too smart to be wooed by intimacy. He sat back on his heels. "Perhaps if we were more friendly, we might understand each other better."

She dropped the cloth to her lap. "Mmm. If you call me Audrey, then what shall I call you?"

"Whatever you want." He grinned, hoping to gain her trust and then find out the true reason why she was here. *And perhaps they could become much, much more.* His gut kicked at the intimate idea.

But her thoughts were elsewhere. "Can I call you Armstrong?"

"Aye."

"Or Warring?"

"That is fine too."

"What about Gavin?"

He paused. Only his mother and his cousins called him by that name. Not even Edlyn had been so bold. But for some reason he felt obliged to give Audrey his consent. "If you wish."

She dropped her lashes over her eyes. "I shall call you Warring."

A wave of disappointment surged through him. What was this? The maid befuddled him.

"Are you good with the bow?" she asked, picking up one of the discarded arrows.

Gavin shook his head. "Nay, though I wish I were. It would give us a better chance at the feats. In these parts, Rory Maxwell is the master of the bow."

"The man we saw on the meadow the other day?" She twirled the arrow over and over in her hand.

Thinking of her talent with the dagger, he wondered. "Do you hold any skill in archery?"

The arrow fell from her fingers. "Nay. I have never even held such a thing."

He rose to his feet and picked up his bow. Bairn let out a long whine and then stopped when Gavin handed the bow to Audrey. "Then I think it is time for you to learn."

A glowing smile spread across her face and tickled the edges of Gavin's heart. She strode to the line, and he followed, marveling at the gentle sway of her hips.

He handed her an arrow and stepped behind her. "Raise the bow and I will show you how to fix your arrow."

She hesitated, but then settled her warm body against his. He placed one hand over hers on the bow and the other on hers that held the string and arrow. A piece of her soft dark hair blew against his cheek. Briefly, he closed his eyes and inhaled the heather scent. Too bad she was a sneaky spy. Correction, a clumsy spy.

Her long lashes fluttered, and he felt the rapid beat of her heart against his ribcage. "Keep your eyes on the cloth," he whispered in her delicate ear. Slowly he helped her pull the string back. "When you are ready, release the arrow."

The arrow rolled up and down and landed in the bottom of the target. She cried out in delight. "I did it."

Bairn circled her, letting out a series of barks and ending with a long howl. The lass reached down and scratched the animal's head. Her face lit up, and then suddenly, she hugged him. Gavin went cold as his heart fell out of his chest like a poorly thrown dagger.

Releasing him, she grabbed another arrow and lifted the bow. "Again. Let us try again."

His arms hung like dead vines. He dared not aid her for he feared he would steal that kiss he thought about earlier. Getting tangled up with an English spy did not fit his plan.

"Well, are you going to help me or not?" She held the bow high in her hand, a look of determination on her face as she eyed the butt.

He rubbed his sweaty palms on his breeks and again stood behind her. Her heather scent tempted his nose. He ground his teeth against the onslaught. Her fingers twitched against his, and he almost let out a moan.

The arrow flew again, this time landing on the top of the target. She danced away, and Bairn barked, enjoying the gaiety. "Again," she shouted.

Nay, he had no more endurance. It had been a while since he had been with a woman. "I have work to attend to."

"Please," she bemoaned.

So, he obliged her. Over and over he put himself through the torture. Arrows flew above the mark, below the mark, in the bench where there was no mark. One even landed near a yonder cow. Finally, he brought an end to the torment.

"Audrey, enough, I have other tasks to see to today."

A playful frown rested on her lips. "Ah, so be it. I had such fun, Warring."

And he had never endured such pain, and for what? He had learned nothing. He took his bow from her fingers. "You did well for your first time."

"You are too kind." The joy fled from her face, and small lines etched her forehead.

Now what was wrong?

She began to twist her hands in her gown again. She pursed those lush lips. She cleared her throat. "I have something to say. I have not always been honest with you."

Finally. The truth?

"Tell me something I *dinnae* know."

CHAPTER 15

The words hung heavy in Audrey's mouth. She should just be honest and tell him about the communication with the queen. But what would he do then? Making her leave probably was the best scenario. Then she wouldn't have to betray his trust. More than likely he would throw her in chains until he came up with some other vile punishment. A shiver skidded down her spine. She could very well wind up like Edlyn.

The thaw she had seen in his clear blue eyes frosted over. "Well, mistress, what is it?"

He was back to calling her mistress, not her given name. The winter chill blew again. Her given name flowed so naturally from his lips and seeped into every sore spot of her body. Just what would he call her once she told him the truth? The wisdom to be honest shriveled. She desired to hear him speak her name again.

Another idea crept into her mind. She stepped closer but didn't meet his gaze. "I have heard some very troublesome rumors and…"

He took his familiar stance, crossing his arms over his chest, his jaw tight. Bairn stood sentinel next to him. "They were about me."

"Um…" She rolled her hands into her gown.

"Out with it," he snapped.

Her words were held fast in her throat, and her heart pounded in her ears. Her breath came short and rapid. Her words broke their bonds. "Some say you did not love your wife and that—"

"I killed her." His voice dropped heavy, and his face resembled a cold stone slab.

"Aye," she said weakly. "But I am sure that is not true." The tone of her voice spoke just the opposite. She glanced up at him.

He did not budge, nor did he even blink, nor did he disagree with her conclusion. A strong warm breath expelled from his lungs and rushed over her face. The dog licked his chops. "I should tell you nothing. I know what I say will go elsewhere."

Prickles of fear swept down her back. *He knows why I am here.* He gently unwrapped her fingers from her gown and held her hand. His tenderness confounded her. Why was he not shouting and stamping about?

"Please sit." Like a dutiful servant, he guided her to the bench and sat next to her. Bairn plopped in front of the pair, his smelly breath filling the air around them.

She did not know what to make of Gavin's swinging moods. Was this a ruse to win her confidence, or was he insincere? Truthfully, she was not made to live a life of intrigue.

"I was not the respectful son. I ignored my father's advice, scoffed at his stories, laughed at his backward attitudes. We never saw eye to eye. I cannot tell you why, but he always seemed to look at me like I belonged somewhere else." Gavin leaned over and put his elbows on his knees. "I was exceedingly rowdy. Fraser and I tore up the countryside like none other. But then my father died."

Why was he telling her all of this? Had he not just said he knew his words would go elsewhere? She wanted him to stop talking, and she wanted him to speak on. God have mercy on them both for she knew not what to do.

Pain and devastation rippled across his face, and Audrey's heart tore open. She tenderly placed her hand on his shoulder. "You should not blame yourself. I am sure he knew you loved him."

"Nay, that was the problem. I *dinnae* think I cared for him at all."

His confession startled her. She was closer to her father than her mother, but all the same, she loved them both.

"I began to drink more, gamble more, all because I felt nothing. I watched my mother weep, and still I remained cold and uncaring." His voice cracked. "I was a despicable, disgusting human being."

The desire to embrace him grew deep within her, but she dared not. She stroked her hand gently over his back. "You were plagued by guilt."

He glanced up before looking down at his feet, giving Bairn a scratch on the ear. "I suppose."

"Then worry no more on this, God forgives all."

"Ah, there it is again. God." Gavin moved the sole of his boot back and forth across the earth. "I *dinnae* seek God's forgiveness. Save your tales of salvation for others."

"I just meant—"

His hand paused on the dog's head. "There is more, which might change your consideration of forgiveness.

Soon after his death, I left and things became worse. The drinking, the gambling, the...anything you can conjure up, I am sure I have done it."

'Twas exactly as his mother had said. Audrey wanted him to pause, but he did not.

"Once, I was so drunk I could barely stand. Rory Maxwell coaxed me into a game of chance." Gavin sat back and shook his head. "I lost everything, more than everything. I lost Warring Tower."

She gasped. His mother had said none of this. "But—"

"I'm not finished," he said more forcefully. "You asked to hear my defense of murder, and now you will hear all of it."

His shoulders tightened under her touch. Her hand slid from his back.

"Not only did I lose my favorite Galloway pony and my personal possessions, but I lost my family home and lands. I begged Rory. I even offered to fight under the Maxwell name if he would release my debt, but he just laughed and laughed." Gavin stared out into the fields. "He threw a coin at my feet and told me to leave Scotland. From now on he would take care of my mother and all those at Warring."

"But you are master of Warring Tower. I don't understand."

A past weariness hunched his shoulders. "Another long tale."

He opened his mouth as if to speak more, then suddenly stopped. Over the hill came three riders. Bairn and Gavin rose, standing straight. "Listen. I want you to go to your chamber and wait there until they have left."

"Nay, I won't leave—"

"Hush. Take Bairn with you," he ordered. "I will probably go with them. If I do, find Thomas and keep him in your sight until I have returned."

Audrey stood. "You told me never—"

"Go now," he shouted as the threesome fast approached.

His murderous scowl stifled any protest. Her heart banged in her chest as she fled to the tower. Bairn and she had barely cleared the gate when she heard Gavin call out.

"Rory Maxwell and your sow of a son. What brings you here?"

Audrey made the sign of the cross over her chest and prayed the scoundrel would not strike Gavin dead.

The sly cunning fox. Maxwell's bold visit just put Gavin's loyalties in question. Everyone knew the Maxwells followed the Catholic faith and wanted to crush those of the Reformed Kirk. What would the English Crown make of this? Why did he even care? Obviously, Rory Maxwell wanted to make sure Gavin would hold his end of the bargain and help the Catholics keep control of Scotland. But what would the Reformers think? Reformers like John Knox wanted to see no queen sit on the Scottish throne, be she raised by the French or living down in London.

All Gavin wanted was peace. And here he was stirring the pot of rebellion. For Thomas's sake, he hoped it would all be worth it.

The three Maxwells brought their horses to a halt. Rory leaned forward. "Time for ye to come with us, Warrin'."

Gavin held his stance. "Good day to you too, Maxwell. Just where are we planning on going?"

"I believed ye wanted this meetin'," Maxwell roared in a voice that would reach all in the tower.

What a smart fellow. Making it look as if this was Gavin's wish would ensure his neck would stretch along with the Maxwells if they ever got caught in their schemes. All in all, it was a small price to pay to meet with Hetta. Now that the time was upon him, Gavin hesitated. Was he doing the right thing? What he was about to do would change Thomas's life forever. A twinge twisted his heart. Could he live without Thomas? The lad's beautiful face clouded his vision. Would the child ever forgive him?

Gavin pushed the troubling thought away. He would deal with the consequences later. "All right. Let me get my horse."

"Not so fast. Ewart and me cousin Ualan have been ridin' all morn on the marches and would prefer to wait here until we return."

The crafty swine. If anything went wrong this day, his mother and sons would suffer, but to back out now would be futile. Gavin held his anger in check and motioned to the gate. "By all means. It would be a pleasure." He swiftly followed the horses into the courtyard.

To his surprise, his mother was already standing near the tower with Bairn at her side. Gavin scanned the courtyard. Thankfully, Mistress Audrey was nowhere in sight.

His mother cleared her throat. The dog growled. Gavin wanted to assure her things would be fine, but her gaze was firm on Maxwell as his was on her.

"I thought I smelled a foul odor. What brings you here again, Rory Maxwell?" she said, her voice echoing off the courtyard walls.

What had gotten into her, provoking the man like that? The horrific scar on Maxwell's face whitened. How he had come by the scar no one seemed to know. For as long as Gavin could remember, the man possessed the mark.

Maxwell pushed his horse toward Gavin's mother and nodded. According to Clyde, Rory had spent many an hour here when he had control of Warring Tower. Gavin's stomach rolled. A rancid taste grew in his mouth. *Only a monster would leave her with such a devil.*

Gavin's hands curled into fists. *And now he was leaving her with the devil's son.* "Mother, Laird Maxwell and I have some affairs to attend to. His son Ewart and his cousin Ualan would like to stay until I return." He tried to put enough censure in his tone to quell her tongue.

"But of course, we must always do what the Maxwells want," she said sarcastically. Bairn let out another fierce growl, showing his teeth.

Maxwell rubbed the scar on his face. "*Willnae* be long," he said almost apologetically. "And they will behave." He shot a threatening glance to his son and cousin, who immediately cowered under his glare.

Gavin's mother rolled her eyes and gave them her back, returning to the tower.

"Get yer horse, Warrin'. I have other things that need attendin' this day."

The horse was brought forth, and Gavin quickly mounted. Again, a niggle of doubt bothered him. Was he doing the right thing?

Rory grabbed his reins and circled his son and cousin

as they dismounted. "I mean it," Maxwell voice rumbled.
"No playin' with the *wummin* and keep yer wits about ye.
Dinnae give Lady Francis a mite of trouble."

Gavin surveyed the courtyard once more for Audrey
and Thomas. Hopefully, they were safely tucked away. He
watched Ewart and Ualan enter the lower level of the
tower. Even with Maxwell's warning, the pair should not
be trusted. By the way his mother glared at Rory, she
would be just fine with the pair. His mother was stronger
than he imagined to take on a grizzly old laird. Or maybe
Bairn had frightened Maxwell, but that seemed unlikely.
What *reiver* would be afraid of a dog?

"Ye commin'?" Maxwell called. "I *dinnae* have all
day." He rode out of the gate without a look back.

They rode to a small village surrounded by lush green
fields located on the western side of Maxwell's land. All
the way there, dread filled Gavin's soul. Once he set this
plan in motion, there was no turning back. *Oh, Thomas,
can I let you go? But the survival of Warring depends on
this. Hopefully someday you will understand.*

Slowly they meandered through the village where
dwellers were poorly dressed in worn tunics and rough
breeks. Dirty faces with dull eyes stared as Laird Maxwell
trotted the muddy paths. In every pathetic face he saw
Thomas. Gavin resisted the urge to turn his horse around
and return home. *You wanted this, now see it through.*

The foul smell of unwashed bodies and animal dung
slammed into Gavin's senses and hindered his resolve.
What if Thomas's future was nothing more than this? The
lad deserved a better destiny. They stopped outside a
rickety cottage on the edge of the village. Smoke swirled
out through several holes in the roof.

"In there." Maxwell pointed, keeping his seat on his horse. "Be quick about it."

Gavin adjusted his blade and searched his surroundings before he dismounted. He tied his horse to a nearby tree. Ducking his head, he entered the cottage. The smell of roasted fowl filled his nostrils and tripped his memory. Hetta would help Cook prepare the same dish at Warring Tower. He could still hear her barking out orders. *Don't roast the bird too long.*

His eyes adjusted to the dimly lit room. There in a dark corner sat Hetta with her familiar scowl on her wrinkled face. Her gnarled fingers held a shawl tight to her sagging breasts. Two dark eyes stared out of sunken sockets.

"Hetta," Gavin whispered.

Her jaw clicked when she opened her mouth. "What ye want, whelp?"

As respectful as ever. He made his way to a wobbly chair near the shabby table and sat across from her. "I have come to talk about the lad."

The old woman curled her lips inward but said nothing.

Gavin put his elbows on the table and folded his hands. "He *cannae* stay at Warring Tower any longer." His words sounded foreign to his own ears.

A heavy cough left Hetta's lips and poisoned the air between them. She wiped her mouth with the back of her sleeve and wheezed. "Why, is he interferin' with yer other son or botherin' yer new guest?"

Gavin pulled back, remembering the ride on the marches with Audrey. "Mistress Hayes is not my guest. She is my mother's companion. Nothing more."

"I wager she is more than that. Best ye watch yer back, whelp."

Was Hetta searching for the truth, or did she know Audrey was a spy? The woman had a sense about these things. Her eyes and ears were always open. "I would think you would be pleased if someone stuck a knife between my shoulder blades."

The old woman cackled, which quickly turned into a laborious wheeze. "There was a time, but now I'm thinkin' it's best if yer cold heart suffers a little more."

"I *didnae* kill Edlyn."

"Ye didn't push her from the tower, but yer words sent her to her death."

Edlyn and he did fight viciously that awful night. *I dinnae care what you do. Take your son. Leave.*

Gavin shook his head to wipe away the memory. "I never—"

"Aye, ye never thought about anybody but yerself. And now ye want me to believe yer thinkin' of the boy?" Hetta sneezed into her sleeve. "Go back to yer cold tower, whelp."

He slammed his fist on the table. "I *dinnae* have much time. Maxwell will be coming through that door at any moment. Please. Just listen."

Hetta pursed her cracked lips and nodded.

"You know Warring Tower can have only one heir. I *willnae* have my sons fighting over the land. One might die like my father's brother. I *willnae* have it."

"Then leave the land and tower to yer precious new son if yer afraid Thomas might kill the boy when they get older."

Gavin shook his head. "Nay. I *willnae* have others question Thomas's heritage."

The older woman's eyes tapered. "Ye are an odd man,

Gavin Armstrong. Ye want the boy gone, but ye care about his future."

Flexing his fingers for patience, Gavin drew in a long breath. "That is why I am here. If I help you leave this place, can you get Thomas to his father?"

A rumble built up in Hetta's throat before uncontrollable laughter spewed out. Gavin's ire rose as she kept on with her glee.

"I *dinnae* jest," he growled.

"Aye, I am sure." Hetta wiped her eyes and let out one more hearty hoot. "Ye are such a fool. Did ye really think Edlyn's father had enough coin to purchase Warring Tower from Maxwell? Think back, who else was present at yer weddin'?"

Gavin pressed his mind, digging up five years past. Broke and drunk, he begged in the streets of Lanercost. Many a day Edlyn's father, Lord Hadley, passed by, ignoring Gavin. Until one day, Hadley stopped and invited Gavin to his home. There he met Edlyn and another man of the clergy, John Feckenham. Lord Hadley offered Gavin salvation. If he married Edlyn and claimed her illegitimate son as his own legal child, not telling a soul the truth about the boy's parentage, then Lord Hadley would purchase Warring Tower from Rory Maxwell, giving it back to Gavin as a wedding present. Never did he think Maxwell would sell, but he did. A week later Gavin found himself a married man and owner of Warring Tower again.

"I see nothing amiss. Edlyn was in trouble, no respectable Englishman would have her. Feckenham married us."

"Feckenham married ye. Do ye know who he is?" Hetta waved a boney finger in front of Gavin.

"A clergyman. What of it?"

Hetta tapped the table with her withered fingers, her eyes glowed in the hazy cottage light. "Not just a clergy. A priest."

"So what?" Gavin rubbed his hands together to keep from throttling the old crone.

"My sweet Edlyn was of the Reformed Faith. A righteous girl." Hetta hung her head and sighed.

"Apparently not that righteous, she did have a child out of wedlock. Feckenham married us because Hadley *didnae* want his daughter married by their local clergy. He knew there would be talk."

For the third time, Hetta barked out a gut-wrenching guffaw. "So that is what Hadley told ye." She lifted her chin and stuck out her jaw. "Ye were given a bushel of muck. Edlyn was as pure as the driven snow when she married ye. She never knew a man."

"Nay, that is impossible." Clouds parted revealing the past to his wedding night. He remembered being overly drunk, though he had sworn he had very little to drink. The whole room shifted and swirled—Edlyn's soft body warm against him, her cries, gripping his arms tight. Fear in her eyes. He shook away the dreadful memory. "There *wasnae* any blood."

Hetta's worn lips snaked upward. "Ye woke up on the floor. Do ye remember that? By Hadley's command I drugged ye. Ye took a virgin to bed and didn't even know it. Edlyn and I rolled ye off the bed, and I changed the linen."

The night wobbled before Gavin's eyes. Edlyn's cries filled his ears as he carelessly used her. He clutched his head between his hands. "I had been drunk so often. I just believed…" Gavin stared up into Hetta's bottomless eyes. "Why? Why would a man want to make his daughter out to be a whore?"

"A poor one, that's who."

"But Hadley paid a high price to purchase Warring Tower."

Hetta leaned over the table, her sour breath seeping into Gavin's soul. "He didn't buy it, Feckenham did."

Gavin's temper rose. Why did she play with him? "Where would a priest get enough—"

"The coin wasn't his either. It came from royal coffers. Back then, Feckenham was Queen Mary Tudor's chaplain. He came with the boy and paid off Hadley's debts and yers." She nodded, reading the doubt in Gavin's eyes.

The muscles in his back and shoulders tightened, bracing for the truth that was to come.

"Take a good look at the boy. Red hair, pale skin, Tudor looks."

"But Queen Mary wanted children," Gavin said lamely.

"The child isn't hers. Who sits on the throne now?"

Gavin drew back and almost fell off his chair. There had been rumors that Queen Elizabeth had been intimate with Thomas Seymour while living with Catherine Parr, the last wife of Henry VIII. A chill of betrayal slid down Gavin's back. Could his Thomas be the son of Thomas Seymour? Nay, it *wasnae* possible. Thomas Seymour died years before young Thomas's birth.

But there probably were others. In fact, it was known that the Princess Elizabeth had many suitors. Gavin gripped the table. "A bastard *cannae* inherit the throne."

"But what if the child was born of a legal union?"

What would Queen Mary do if she found out Elizabeth had married and had a child? A child that the English people might embrace over a barren queen, especially a male child. She'd kill it or give it away.

Hetta roared with laughter. "Aye, whelp. Ye might just be raisin' the future king of England."

Chapter 16

Audry peeked out of the scullery at the pair sitting in the hall. One man was of middling years and another younger, possibly thirty summers old. Both were dressed in leather jack of plates and brown breeks. And both had long unkempt coppery beards.

"That be Ewart Maxwell and his cousin Ualan," Blair said, pouring a couple of mugs of small beer. "Ewart is as dull as the cows grazing in our fields, but Ualan is as sharp as Cook's ax. He be the one ye best watch out for. Laird Armstrong left Clyde to protect us, and he be takin' his nap in the corner." Blair shook her head.

A twist of worry curled down Audrey's spine. "Laird Armstrong asked me to find Thomas. How am I to do so with these two lurking in the hall?"

Blair hefted a mug in each hand. "Worry not. I will take them some beer and make a fuss over them. That be the time to sneak out." She motioned with her head. "Cover yer hair with me cap."

Audrey swiftly complied, jamming her thick braid into the well-worn cap.

"There. We are ready. Once I have made it to the table, ye scurry away. And *dinnae* come back until these brutes have left. Laird Armstrong's *dug* is upstairs with Lady Francis. She should be safe."

How Audrey hoped this would work. One false move and she could be entertaining the two men as well. Not to mention how cross Laird Armstrong would be if she did not make sure Thomas stayed out of harm's way.

Blair waltzed into the hall sashaying her hips. "Are ye thirsty, gents?" she called as she approached the table.

Their wide eyes on Blair, Audrey stayed in the shadows and quickly made her way outside the keep. She escaped to Thomas's favorite place and gave up a thankful prayer when she saw the boy fishing.

"I thought I would find you here," she said cheerily, taking a seat next to him.

He glanced at her saying nothing, his eyes filled with distrust before he turned his attention back to his pole.

"Oh, Thomas. Please do not be this way. Your father ordered me to stay away from you."

"Then why are you talkin' to me now?" His brows drew down, and his lips grew tight.

"Because now he asked me to come and find you."

Thomas lifted a doubtful gaze. *"Dinnae* make any sense. Why would *Da* say not to talk to me, then change his mind?"

For a young child, Thomas was quite astute. She did not want to scare him with the truth, knowing he would dash back to the hall and pull out his wooden sword challenging Ewart Maxwell. Or worse, Ualan.

Audrey reached over and tousled the boy's curly locks. "I think his heart softened when he saw how sad you were."

Thomas's frown deepened as he pulled his head away. "Me *da doesnae* care."

Right, he would not. Poor Thomas, suffering, looking for love. Audrey searched her brain, trying to come up with a feasible tale. One to heal the hurt without revealing the reason for her presence. When none came forth, she went with the truth regardless of the consequences. "There are Maxwells at the tower, and your father is worried about your safety. He wants me to stay with you until they leave."

Thomas glanced in the direction of the tower, probably digesting her words. His frown softened, and he concentrated on his pole "Then I guess we should stay here, fishin'."

"Sounds like a wonderful plan." Audrey placed her hands on the ground and lifted her face to the sun. Honesty was always the right course.

"But I sure would like to see them up close. Me *da* says you should never trust a Maxwell."

Her brief relief skipped away. "Thomas, that would be foolish. Your father does not want you to be hurt."

"My brother is there."

"He is hidden in your room with Mistress Jonet. We should stay here until they leave."

Thomas wrinkled his nose. "I could help *Da.*"

And there it was. The boy constantly trying to prove his worth to his father. This child loved Gavin unconditionally. That type of love should be given by a father, not a son.

"Your father is not there. He went somewhere with Laird Maxwell, and I am not sure when he will be back."

Thomas jumped to his feet. "Then we must go back. Gran is there! She should not be alone with those men."

Why had she not weaved some fanciful tale instead of speaking the truth? Audrey stood. There was no way she was letting Thomas near those men. "I think your grandmother will be fine. Bairn is with her. Besides, she did not seem afraid of them at all."

"Gran is strong, but she might need our help." He slipped around Audrey and started walking toward the tower with his fishing pole in hand.

Audrey let out a heavy sigh and ran after him. She reached out and grabbed his shoulder. "Let us not go charging in there. Methinks it would be wiser to stay here and wait for your father to return."

"Those Maxwells can be trouble. I'll not let Gran and me brother with them." Thomas wiggled loose from her grasp and shot off like a slender hare shaking off a dog.

"Ugh." Audrey gave chase. The boy was so much like his father.

Sneaking into their own home like a pair of robbers was going to take a sack full of cunning. Audrey tapped her skirt, searching for her dagger. She let out a heavy sigh. She'd left the weapon in her room again. Gavin's reprimand boomed in her head. He warned her not to go anywhere without the blade.

"Thomas, we should turn back. I left my dagger in my chamber."

He did not pause at her omission. "*Dinnae* worry. We can get weapons in the stable. Surely there is something there that will crush a Maxwell's head."

She should have kept her discovery to herself. Thomas dashed to the stable. Hopefully, she could find a way to keep the boy there until Ewart and Ualan left.

The stable master started to shoo Thomas away, then stopped when he saw Audrey. "Good day to ye, mistress," the older man said, pulling his cap from his head. "What can I do for ye?"

"We are just looking for a few things. Thomas wishes to build another tower." The stable master blanched, no doubt remembering the mess Thomas had caused the last time he was on such a mission. When he appeared with a pair of rusty spurs and a mud-caked horseshoe, the poor man all but passed out.

"What ye be needin' those for buildin' a tower?" The stable master hobbled over to get a bucket of pitch. "Here, take this and be gone."

But Thomas would not relinquish his prizes, putting them behind his back. "I need these for something else."

The man started to shake. "Yer *da willnae* like this. Takin' things from his stables."

Audrey stepped in front of Thomas and bent down until their eyes were level. "We do not need those things." She tapped her head. "We have our wits. And my wits are telling me we should stay here for a while."

A look of defiance crossed the boy's face as he stuck out his chin and leaned in. "We *cannae* stay here. What if they are hurting Gran? What if they hurt Bairn or Marcas? I forgot me knife just like you did," he whispered.

He spoke of the rusty blade hidden under his special rock. "We should go back and get it." Anything would be better than confronting the two visitors.

Thomas shook his head. "We may not be able to sneak back into the tower." He glanced at the stable master. "Can I at least have the horseshoe?"

The older man itched his nose. "I suppose. 'Tis worn and not good for anything."

Beaming once again, Thomas handed over the spurs and tightened his grasp on the shoe. With fast feet, he made a dash to the tower and up the spiral stairs. Then he paused, pressing his body against the stone wall next to the hall entry. Audrey trailed along, trying to figure out a way to prevent this folly.

Thomas peeked into the hall. "We shall try to sneak along the inner wall without being noticed, until we can reach the scullery. I am sure Cook has a large knife," he whispered.

Audrey reached out and pulled the boy back. Her mind racing. She had to figure out a way to keep Thomas safe. "Nay, we will be spotted. I will draw their attention while you sneak into the scullery. Stay there until you hear me say, 'leave now.'"

The boy nodded, and Audrey inwardly breathed a sigh of relief. She had no intentions of ever uttering those words. "Are you ready?" The boy nodded.

Taking a deep breath, Audrey walked in with her head held high. Ewart Maxwell's eyes flared, and Ualan's lips moved upward in a lecherous grin.

"Well now. What do we have here?" Ualan pushed Blair off his lap. "The dagger lady has come to test our mettle?"

Both men guffawed. A quick scan of the hall confirmed that Lady Francis was nowhere in sight. Smart woman. Clyde sat snoring on a bench against the wall. Perhaps if she was loud enough he might wake up and come to her aid.

"Come here, mistress," Ewart called, motioning with his hand. "Come show us yer precious blade." The men laughed again.

Audrey swallowed and stepped further into the lion's den. How she wished she did have her weapon, for she would slit these villains in two. Whatever these fools had planned could not be any worse than the intrigue at court. Many a time she had to fight off lustful courtiers. She pulled out a chair a fair distance from the pair.

Blair picked up another mug and placed it in front of Audrey, pouring the amber liquid. "A drink, mistress? Are things fine out in the meadows?"

Audrey touched her ear, knowing the maid spoke of Thomas. "Aye. Our guests look hungry. Please bring some oatcakes and cheese. I am sure there is some in the scullery," she all but shouted this command, but Clyde slept on. Gad, the man was deaf as well as old.

Dawning flashed in Blair's eyes, and she swiftly retreated. Believing the boy to be safe, Audrey contemplated the wolves in front of her. "So then, after we have eaten, shall we go to the courtyard and have a throw with the blades?"

The pair howled with laughter again. "Mistress, we would really like to see yer skills with the dagger, but we are wonderin' if ye have other talents as well?"

Their lewd comments made her skin crawl. Would they speak to her in such a way if she were the lady of these lands? Where had such a grand reflection come from? Even when she lived at court, she never presumed she would ever rise above her station. She was a poor merchant's daughter. All her life she relied on the good-will of others for her keeping. These oafs did not have a care for her welfare.

"Good sirs, you tease. Surely you would not in earnest make such a suggestion of a guest of Laird Armstrong's?"

Audrey played with the handle of the mug, trying to hide her fear.

Blair came with oatcakes and a bit of cheese, and momentarily the men were preoccupied with the food set before them. "Mistress, could I have a word with ye? There seems to be a problem in the scullery."

"But of course." Audrey quickly rose at the chance to escape the pair.

Ewart flashed out of his seat and grabbed her arm, holding his dagger to her throat. "Not so fast, mistress. I'll not be havin' ye scurry away."

Blair cried out as Ualan jumped up and wrapped an arm around her waist. "And ye too, sweet. *Dinnae* run off."

"Remove your hands, sir." Audrey twisted and turned, trying to gain her freedom, but Ewart's grip tightened until he had the audacity to plant a wet kiss on her cheek. "You're disgusting," she hissed.

Ewart threw back his head and roared. "Ah, mistress, such flattery."

When he bent down for another kiss, Audrey stomped on his foot and then gave a swift kick to his shin. He released her, hopping about on one foot.

At the same time, Blair raised her knee and caught Ualan in a most unfortunate place. The man crumpled to his knees.

"Leave now," Audrey shouted as Ewart reached out and grabbed the hem of her gown.

A squeal of a scream echoed in the hall. Like a banshee, Thomas tore across the hall with the iron horseshoe high above his head. With great force, he slammed the shoe on Ewart's head, laying him flat on the floor. Blair took an enthusiastic swing at Ualan's nose when he tried to stand. He too landed in a heap next to his cousin.

"Hey? Lord's mercy." Clyde jumped to his feet, fumbling for his dagger.

"What is happening here?" thundered a familiar voice.

Audrey spun about and gulped. There stood Gavin Armstrong with flames of fury igniting his face. Next to him stood a stone-faced Rory Maxwell.

The battle had just begun.

CHAPTER 17

The pandemonium in his hall was only a small irritation compared to the brewing contempt that stirred up his wrath. Not only was Audrey Hayes a spy, she was here to systematically destroy everything he had worked to restore. The demure, innocent maid was a fine disguise for a conniving, evil witch. Playing the coy maid when, in fact, she might have known all along about Thomas's parentage. She probably even welcomed Ewart's slimy touch. He'd deal with her soon, but one problem at a time. He needed to first get Rory Maxwell and the rest of his brutish family out of Warring Tower.

"He kept gropin' me, Laird Armstrong," Blair whined as Ualan made another attempt to rise to his feet.

As if Ualan was the first to lay a hand on the wench. Gavin fought the urge not to shake his head. Without question, she and Audrey had a hand in whetting the lustful appetites that provoked the Maxwells.

Thomas beamed from ear to ear, holding out an old horseshoe. "I rescued Mistress Audrey."

That Thomas was in the middle of all of this fired up Gavin's innards. He glared at Clyde. "And where were you?"

Clyde rubbed his jaw and dropped his gaze to the floor without answer.

"Please, this is not Clyde's fault." Audrey stood in the middle of the carnage and had the audacity to blush. "If you must blame someone, blame me."

Aye, he would love to, but everyone present seemed to have played a part in this tale.

"Ach, the devil take them." Rory Maxwell marched over to his son and pulled him up by the back of his neck. He then cast a furious glance at his cousin. "I told ye not to give Lady Francis any trouble, and here ye are, tryin' to bump her *wummin*."

At that very moment, Gavin's mother with her head held high like a regal queen entered the hall with Bairn in tow. "What goes on here?"

The dog charged forward and leaped on Ualan, knocking him to the ground. Immediately Bairn clamped down on his arm.

"Let go," Gavin shouted, his temper flaring at the whole fiasco before him. Though he was sorely tempted to let the dog have his way with the cretin, the Maxwells were already subdued. The dog released Ualan and came to Gavin's side.

"I should kill that *dug*." Ualan rubbed his sore arm before coming to his feet.

"Leave off, Ualan, or I'll gut ye where ye stand." Maxwell flushed a deep shade of purple, then concentrated his anger on Ewart, who finally seemed to be regaining his senses. Maxwell slapped Ewart on the back of his head. "Ye have to forgive my son and my kin. They are a bunch of fools. We be leavin'. I'm sorry for all the ruckus they have caused, Lady Francis."

162

A grim tightness held her lips as she appraised Maxwell.

After a push in the shoulder by his father, Ewart stumbled forward. Ualan came to his aid and helped the younger man out of the hall. Rory pulled his cap from his head and bowed low to Gavin's mother. "Beg yer forgiveness, my lady."

Gavin's mother stared at the man as if he were nothing more than a pile of dung.

When she said nothing, a cold mask fell across Maxwell's features, and he stormed to the entry pausing only briefly at Gavin's side. "I'll be contactin' ye shortly to collect me payment." Maxwell jammed his cap back on his head and left.

Payment. Of course, he would not forget the debt Gavin owed—helping the Scottish Catholics reduce the Reformers' power, securing Mary Stuart's rights to the Scottish throne and possibly more—the English Crown. What a fine mess. Gavin lifted his gaze and directed his fury at a most worthy opponent. One who did not keep young Thomas safe.

"Escort Mistress Audrey to her chamber," he ordered Clyde. "And make sure she stays there until she is summoned." Clyde came to her side, his head hung low. "One more thing, your dagger, mistress."

"'Tis in my chamber," she snapped.

Gavin wanted to scold her for leaving herself and Thomas unprotected, but instead he answered, "How unfortunate." He looked to Clyde. "Retrieve the blade and bring it to me."

The glare in the lass's eyes could have frosted a frog, but it had no effect on him. Wisely, she did not open her mouth but gave him her back as she headed for the stairs. Clyde gave his opinion by shaking his head. Once they were out of sight, Gavin focused on Thomas. Agony clawed through his body. *How long before they came to take his son? A son only hours ago he was willing to give up. But now...*

The lad proudly held out the horseshoe. "I got him good, *Da*. I defended a maid's honor just like you taught me."

Tears burned at the back of Gavin's eyes. He knelt down and pulled his son into his arms, kissing his auburn locks. "You are a brave lad, but in the future, I want you to be careful. Had I not returned, those men may have harmed you and the ladies. Promise me you *willnae* take such a chance again?"

Thomas pulled back, his face grave. "*Da*, are you all right? Why are you cryin'?"

Gavin winced and wiped his cheek. A mule should kick him. For months, he had been pushing the lad away. No wonder Thomas questioned his father's sanity.

"I am fine. Just heed my words. In the future, I *dinnae* want you to go out into the meadows alone."

A familiar pout punched out Thomas's lip. "I am not a *bairn*. I know how to take care of meself."

He didn't want to scare the lad. His life was more important than anyone else's in the tower. Why hadn't Edlyn told him? Didn't she know the truth? Perhaps not. But someone did, and she resided under his own roof.

Gavin gripped Thomas's shoulders. "Listen to me. For the time being, I want you to stay within the tower walls. There is trouble brewing."

"Worse than usual?" The lad's eyes shone with excitement.

The constant border fighting had become an ordinary part of living here. Thomas had been taught to be strong and not fear anything. How could years of such training be undone? Or perchance they were just the skills a king would need.

An idea sprung forth. "I am most proud of how you defended Blair and Mistress Audrey this day, but I fear Gran might be in trouble too. Stay close to her. We have to make sure no harm comes to our *wummin*."

Thomas puffed out his chest. "Aye, *Da,* I will keep a close eye on our family." He lifted the horseshoe. "And if someone tries to hurt Gran, they will answer to me."

Another wave of pride rushed through Gavin's chest. His son would be a mighty warrior someday, and if possible, an honorable king.

Audrey paced back and forth across her tiny chamber. Whatever trust she had gained with Gavin over the past few days had been lost by not heeding his words. Sin or not, she should have lied to Thomas and kept him safe by the river, making her plead to God for forgiveness later. There was no doubt that Gavin would hold her responsible for this raucous folly. Instead of pacing the room, she should be packing her few belongings. Peter should be returning any day. Best to leave immediately, feign a failure in her mission, and beg Queen Elizabeth to be merciful.

But right now, Audrey had a more immediate problem. How was she going to ease the boar's temper? For certain he would lay blame for the whole Ewart Maxwell incident at her feet. The dark hues of purple and orange filtered through the small chamber window signaling the fast approach of the end of the day, and yet Gavin had not appeared. Did he plan to come at all? Or did he wish to punish her by keeping her cloistered in this room forever?

Loud voices rose in the nursery. Audrey put an ear to the door.

"What? We're movin' to where?" Mistress Jonet's voice drifted down the hall. "Why do we have to leave now? 'Twill be dark soon."

Gavin was moving the children out of their chamber. Why? Something must have happened to make him act so rash. Surely, he did not fear her? She would never harm the boys. Anger bubbled up as she headed toward the door. On this matter she would set him straight. They were as precious to her as if they were her own children. Audrey pulled the latch, but it would not budge. She wiggled it again. Locked. Why would Gavin do such a thing?

With both fists, she pounded on the door, crying and then finally begging for release, but no one answered her plea. She slid down, leaning her back against the entry. Carefully she folded her hands in her lap.

Dear Lord, I know I have not always been a faithful servant, but I beg you, watch over Thomas and Marcas during this uncertain time. If it be thy will, free me from these confines and show me what I am supposed to do. I am so confused. I ask all this in your son's name. Amen.

A sense of calm rushed over Audrey's spirit. Her eyelids grew heavy. Pleasant dreams filled her mind…
She walked in a grand meadow. Blossoms of heather and wild pansies brushed against her bare feet. Laugher of young children filled the air while a dog's howl drifted on

the wind. Her fingers brushed against the rough wood floor...

With a start, she awoke, her hand splayed on the worn floor. Dust particles danced on the bright morning rays slowly drifting in from the window. She rolled her shoulders to ease the stiffness in her neck. Somehow, she had slept the whole night on the floor. Rising, she made her way to the window. The courtyard was unusually quiet. Feet pattered on the floor above her, followed by Bairn's usual bark. Gavin had moved the children upstairs. Whatever for?

The slip of the latch drew Audrey's attention. Blair rushed in with a bowl of pottage and oatcakes, placing them on the table. "Here we go, mistress. A little somethin' to fill yer belly."

In the doorway stood a burly man with crossed arms.

"Where is Clyde? Am I to be locked up like a prisoner? Where is Laird Armstrong? I wish to speak to him," Audrey demanded.

The brute did not change his expression, but Blair wiped her hands on her apron, giving her an apologetic look. "I am not sure what to tell ye, mistress. Laird Armstrong was in a foul mood all night. Ye are supposed to stay here for a while. I am sorry."

"While his lordship rides the marches and goes about his usual day." Audrey glared at the pair. The lout standing in the door prevented an escape. Blair dropped her chin. "If it makes ye feel any better, he slept outside the little one's new cham—"

The man cleared his throat, and Blair scurried to the door. She glanced back. "I am so sorry, mistress." The door slammed shut, and the latch fell into place.

Audrey stood alone. The lord of the manor had spoken. How dare he judge her without giving her a voice. Her only crime was trying to keep his son safe. *Which she had failed at miserably.* She slammed her hands on the table. *Could she not do anything right?*

Steam curled upward from the warm bowl of pottage, and Audrey's stomach rumbled. She had not eaten since yesterday afternoon. Pulling out a chair, she sat down at the table and ate the pottage, then drank the last of the remaining water in the pitcher. With her belly full, she lay back down on the bed and went over all her shortcomings and, more importantly, all the ways she was going to kill Gavin Armstrong once she got out of this chamber.

Her list exhausted on both fronts, she closed her eyes. The next time she opened them midday shadows filled the corners. She slapped her hands on the sides of the bed before standing. Her throat parched; she tipped the clay pitcher. Not a drop. Did the boar mean to have her die of thirst?

Audrey strode to the door and banged her fists against the solid surface. "Lout, tell your master I need water. Tell him I wish to speak to him."

Not a sound could be heard.

She slammed, kicked, and scratched at the door. "Do you hear me? I need water. I need to talk to your master, now!"

Her tantrum was finally rewarded when she heard the latch open again. But the face that greeted her constricted her dry throat.

Wearing a deep frown and a black leather jack of plates and breeks, Gavin held out a pitcher. "Mistress, your water." He shuffled a step back. "And I believe you have something to tell me."

All the words she had rehearsed earlier floated away. She wobbled her head like a silly goose. How was she going to make him believe what she spoke was truth and from her heart?

He kicked the door closed, then placed the pitcher on the table. "Sit, mistress. Have a drink and then we shall talk." His eyes narrowed like sharp daggers.

Moving to the table, Audrey stood and, barring her good graces, drank straight from the pitcher, wiping her mouth with the back of her hand. "What right do you have to keep me locked up?"

His hands curled into fists, and his chest expanded. She gripped the pitcher to her breast for defense.

"Sit," he said in a cold lethal voice.

When she did not comply, he stepped closer, towering over her, his stare riveted to her face. He dug into his jack and pulled out a missive, throwing it on the table.

A wave of defeat swept from the top of Audrey's head to the tips of her toes at the sight of the familiar note. She eased away and perched on the edge of her chair. He would want her dead now. "Where did you get that?"

"I know all that goes on at Warring Tower. Did you think your deception would go unnoticed?" The warm spring wind outside brought the promise that summer was close, but his chilly gaze and icy stance spoke of a harsh winter instead. The ruse was up, and she had lost.

"Please let me explain."

"I want the truth. All of it," he snapped. "The lives of my children are at stake. Are you capable of giving me the truth?"

Every muscle in her body tensed. "I did not want to do this."

He slammed his hand on the table, causing her to jump. "Stop with your useless prattle. Who sent you here to spy on us?"

Audrey licked her lips trying to form the words that would convict her. "I am trying to tell you, but you must stop shouting."

He brushed a hand through his long blond hair and pinned her again with his glacial blue glaze. "Mistress, I never shout. Now, the truth."

"You do not understand. If I tell you, my family will suffer."

Gavin pointed to the missive. "You would rather my family suffer?"

"Nay!" Tears sprung in her eyes. "I have no desire to hurt anyone. The queen just did not give me a choice."

His lips slit into a mock grin. "The queen? Out with it. All of it."

As if the noose had already been put around her neck, Audrey took a stiff swallow. "Queen Elizabeth sent me. She feared you were conspiring with the papists and the dowager queen. With those who want to put Mary of Scots on the English throne."

Some of the frost fell from his features. "Go on," he said coolly.

As her heart rate kicked up, Audrey began to see colors, but she fought away the fear. She had to be strong for her family's sake. For Thomas's sake.

"I am waiting. No fake swoon will save you from the punishment you deserve."

The colored spots grew. "Please, a little more water."

Gavin poured half a cup and pushed it toward her. The cold water sluiced down her throat, returning a bit of calm.

"She also wanted me to keep an eye on Thomas."

The icy reserve melted from his eyes as if a blazing fire burned his soul. He leaned over, placing his hands on the back of her chair. A scent of the marches and leather filled her nostrils. "Why? Why would Queen Elizabeth send a spy to check up on my son? Why do you keep lying to me when all here have been nothing but kind to you?" His voice barely above a whisper, his eyes filled with a sadness that gripped her heart.

She had faced poverty as a child, intrigue at court, and humiliation from her stepfather, but never had she encountered such venom laced with such agony. Fingers of fear scraped across her chest and shredded her stomach. She pushed him away and tried to stand. "I-I do not know. I was just supposed to report your comings and goings and what the boy did. I did not want to do it. She forced me. She promised to harm my family if I did not help her."

The colorful spots swirled and danced in Audrey's vision. She stumbled, trying to get to the door. "You cannot keep me here. I promise I will not report back." She hurried forward. Her slipper caught on a jagged stone. She reached out but could not brace herself against the threshold. She tumbled down, and with a smack, everything turned black.

CHAPTER 18

Gavin rushed over and lifted Audrey by the shoulders, looking for any injury to her head. Relief rushed through him when he found none. But what of injuries he could not see? "Audrey, Audrey." He patted her cheeks. She did not respond. In fact, her face was ashen and her red lips faded. A vision of a lifeless Edlyn filled his memory and stole his breath. His stomach began to burn. Quickly he scooped Audrey up in his arms and carried her to the bed.

"Audrey, Audrey," he cried again. Yet she remained still. What had he done? "May I be burned in oil." Once again, his words and actions might cause another woman's demise. He stepped back and ran a hand through his hair. "Mother, Mother," he yelled.

The attached chamber door swung open. "What is it, my son?" Lady Francis asked, clutching a cape to her body.

"'Tis Audrey. She fell and hit her head." He motioned to the bed, then slapped his hands against his thighs. "Can you help her? I fear...the worst."

His mother pushed past him and rushed to the bed, examining Audrey for injuries. Finding none, she placed a hand on Audrey's forehead. "Audrey, Audrey. Thomas is waiting for you," she said, trying to rouse the maid. "Oh dear. She must have hit her head extremely hard. Let us pray she comes around quickly."

She lay on the bed so still as if the shadow of the grave hung about ready to take her away. Gavin knelt down next to the bed; his chest gripped in horror. "Mother, please, is there nothing else we can do?"

"Go get my medicinal basket and be quick about it," his mother ordered, keeping her gaze on Audrey.

Gavin hurried into his mother's chamber, grabbed her basket, and returned to find her piling the coverlet under Audrey's feet. The lass groaned. The pain in his chest gave way. "Is she coming around?"

His mother yanked the basket from his arms. "Aye, in spite of your brutishness." She pulled out a bottle, popped the cork, and held it under Audrey's nose. "I believe she may have fainted before she hit her head. Either way, she will have a healthy bruise on her forehead."

Immediately her eyes fluttered open, and Gavin let out a slow breath. Either the Queen of England was a fool or the shrewdest person to ever live to send such an inadequate, fragile spy. "My thanks, Mother, you may leave now."

"I think not." His mother sat on the side of the bed. "I'll not have this poor girl suffer your boorish behavior. Only God knows what you will do next to her."

The accusation was given as a reminder. She need not worry. Edlyn's death haunted him daily.

Audrey's eyes glazed over. "I-I'm so...so sorry." Her lashes floated over her eyes.

Though his questions remained unanswered, what happened to Audrey was his fault. He had been so furious after talking to Hetta. Why could he not hold on to his temper? Better to leave the lass in the care of his mother. Perhaps tomorrow they could talk in a more amiable fashion.

"Then I leave her in your hands." Gavin bowed slightly to his mother and gazed into Audrey's eyes before he strode from the room. He headed up to the battlements to clear his mind. He passed his old chamber, hearing the soft voices of his children playing within. If Thomas was truly Queen Elizabeth's son, then why had there not been other spies? Perhaps there were and he just never noticed. And if there were more capable spies, then why send Audrey at all? His feet stalled. Certainly, another spy lurked in their mist. Who? Peter?

Nay, the man's visits were short. Then who? Who among them was sending word to the English court? Gavin pushed open the door to the battlements and took a long breath of fresh spring air. He searched the meadows and hills. All seemed so peaceful, but how long would that last?

He slammed his fist into the stone wall. This was all his fault. Had he not lost his family lands to Maxwell in the first place, none of this would have happened. Untrue. Thomas still existed, and Lord Hadley and John Feckenham would have found another husband for Edlyn. Another man raising Thomas seemed unthinkable and bore a hole through Gavin's middle.

He moaned and let out a pathetic laugh. Poor, poor Edlyn, she had been a pawn in this mess as well. So meek, she did whatever her father told her to do. Perhaps he threatened to send her away with Feckenham, send her to a Catholic convent. What fear that would put in the heart of a woman raised in the Reformed Faith. No wonder

Edlyn went along with her father's wishes. Gavin shook his head. And he added to her troubles.

Raising his fists, Gavin struck the stone wall again and again until his knuckles bled. He flexed his fingers, watching the blood trickle down his hand. A small price to pay for such a great crime.

The sound of galloping horses caught his hearing. He squinted at the approaching figures. Maxwell and his son. What could they possibly want now? Gavin raced down the steps and entered the courtyard just as the pair approached the gate. He waved to the guard to let them enter.

Once in the courtyard, Maxwell leaned forward without dismounting. "Get yer horse, Warrin'. We have a few friends to meet."

Gavin gritted his teeth. So soon the debt was being called in. There was nothing for it. Honor demanded he keep his word. He had been a fool to make such a pact with such a devil. Gavin didn't give a fig what happened to him, but Thomas was an innocent. If these monsters ever found out who he was...what a disaster.

He strode back to get his horse.

"Hold there," Maxwell said. "Ye might be needin' yer sword and a good dagger."

True. For a disaster truly brewed.

They rode until Maxwell's keep loomed high before them. Tall stone walls heavily guarded let all know this was not a fortress that would easily fall. Maxwell's wealth would ensure his family would grow and be secure for many generations to come. Unless his Catholic beliefs became his undoing. Inside the gate, a group of saddled Galloway ponies drank from a trough. Some were familiar mounts, while others were not. Gavin dismounted and handed his beast over to a groomsman before entering the hall. There assembled were well-known papists from very influential families.

Ualan Maxwell nodded and kicked out a chair. "Have a seat, Warrin'."

Gavin sat down and glanced at the gaunt and gluttonous faces around a large round table. Some were well-groomed, while others were not. Some had merry eyes, while others were sunken and sullen. Some clean-shaven, while others had heavy beards. But all carried hatred in their hearts for the Reformers who wished to change the way Scotland was ruled.

"We come here today to discuss how we can destroy the Lords of the Congregation and give aid to our own Queen Mary." Maxwell's head swiveled around the room, pinning all with a sharp look.

The men erupted with agreement. Perspiration beaded on Gavin's neck. He had no stomach for setting Scots against Scots for religious reasons or anything else. The Lords of the Congregation, powerful Scottish, new faith Reformers were against the marriage of Mary of Scots to the French dauphin. Fueled by the preaching of John Knox, a priest turned Reformer, the Lords of the Congregation rallied around James Stewart, the illegitimate son of King James V. At best, there would be rioting around Perth and Edinburgh. At worst, there might be a war, Scottish Reformers on one side and Scottish papists on the other side. Either way, Scotland would lose.

Why didn't the Scots unite for Scotland? The families and clans all wanted power but hid under the disguise of faith. What would these men say if told being a Catholic or of the Reformed Faith made no difference since there wasn't a God?

Ualan leaned closer; his breath smelled like horse manure lying out in the warm summer sun. "Where's yer enthusiasm, Warrin'? *Dinnae* want to see our queen ruling what is rightfully hers without the interference of the Reformers?"

Gavin took a pull from the mug of ale placed before him, giving his nose a more inviting scent. Of course, Maxwell could afford ale, while those at Warring Tower drank watered-down small beer. "I have learned many things come with a price, and I am wondering what your price will be."

A rumble of laughter launched around the table. "Worse than you think." Ualan slapped Gavin on the back.

"Quiet, all of ye," Rory Maxwell scolded. "There is a serious matter before us, and Warrin' has offered his services."

The sly and eager grins that dripped on the men's nasty lips made Gavin's chest constrict. He wiped a sweaty hand over his jaw and eased back in the chair. "What do you want me to do?"

Wickedness contorted Ualan's face. "Ye and I will be takin' a wee trip to Perth and be havin' a meetin' with James Stewart and possibly that heretic John Knox. If I remember, Stewart's a friend of yers."

A trip to Perth? Not if he could help it. Gavin eased back in his chair and gave a casual smile. "Aye, we know one another, but I would not say we are great friends. Where you be hearing that yarn? As far as Knox, my father knew him before he was exiled. I have never met the theist."

"But ye do know Stewart." Ualan pulled out his dagger, twirling it on the table.

Gavin shrugged. "Aye, but not well." Stewart was known to favor the Reformers with ambitions of his own, but he also had close ties with Mary of Scots's mother, Mary de Guise. The man played on both sides. He played a dangerous game.

"He thinks ye support the Reformed Kirk like him." Ualan roared, jamming his blade in the table.

"What he thinks or believes is not my affair. I have no stomach for trickery or fighting against any Scot. How will Scotland ever stand strong if we keep squabbling among ourselves? The English and the French would love to swallow us up. Mark my words, if we *dinnae* stand together, one of those countries will rule us, and they will not care which faith we practice."

Ualan flew from his seat, putting his dagger to Gavin's throat. "We are fightin' for God and for Scotland."

"Hold, Ualan. No matter how temptin', we need Warrin'," Rory Maxwell shouted.

Taking a deep breath, Gavin calmly pushed the blade away. "I love Scotland too. That is why I am here."

Ualan grumbled and sat back in his seat, putting his dagger back in its sheath.

Rory cleared his throat and pointed at all in the room. "Remember why we are here. There be plenty of time to argue over other things later." His grizzly gaze settled on Gavin. "All we are wantin' is for you to go and have a nice meal with Stewart. There ye will be contacted by a man who will hand you a missive. Bring that back to me."

This mission mirrored someone else's. A lass with dark hair and eyes that shone like a starry night. His mind's eye saw her bent over her table writing a secret missive to the queen before she passed it off to her courier. In this case, he would play the courier for Maxwell's informant. The taste of all this intrigue curdled in Gavin's mouth.

"That's it?" He placed his elbows on the table and feigned indifference. "I thought you were going to ask me to kill the man."

Again, the room erupted with laughter. Ualan raised his arms and laced his hands behind the back of his greasy head. "Ye are one of us now. No turnin' back."

"Bring me a quill and some parchment. Warrin' needs to write to his friend James Stewart," Rory Maxwell ordered. "And just to make sure he follows our orders, Ewart will be keepin' an eye on Warrin' Tower, makin' sure the Armstrong children will be safe and that lovely lass ye have stayin' with ye."

Gavin clenched his teeth and held his calm, though he wanted to smash his mug into Maxwell's head. Someday the man would regret threatening Gavin's family and Audrey. And then, as if a rock had flown through the air and hit him square in the head, Gavin understood Audrey's dilemma. A new appreciation for her filled his soul. Both of them were being forced against their will to do a task neither of them wanted to do. When this was done, and if he survived, perhaps they could move forward on a different footing.

Gavin feigned a chuckle and raised his mug to his lips,

though he did not drink. He'd go to Perth and get the missive, but then he was done. Now more than ever he had to be careful. His soul filled with the fear of a thousand ghosts…a freshly dug child's grave. What would this bunch of murderers do if they knew Thomas might be Queen Elizabeth's child?

CHAPTER 19

A udry was thankful that Lady Francis sat on the edge of her bed when she awoke, but she knew the boar would be back. What would he do now? Send her back to England or stretch her neck for being a spy. Either way, her future looked bleak. Alas, there was naught she could do but throw herself on his mercy.

Lady Francis held out a bowl of watery soup. "Here, drink this. It will calm your belly and soothe what agitates you."

How a bowl of broth could ease her woes Audrey did not know. She dutifully sipped at the soup. The warm liquid did settle her stomach, though it could not change her predicament.

"Now then, how are you feeling? Does your head hurt? You did take a mighty fall." Lady Francis leaned over and placed the backside of her hand against Audrey's cheek.

"I am fine, my lady. I just stumbled." Audrey felt her skin warm and so did Lady Francis.

"Tell me, what did my son say that upset you so? Why would he put a guard outside your door?"

A queasiness disrupted Audrey's stomach. She settled the bowl in her lap. "I am ashamed to tell you."

"Surely it cannot be that bad?" Lady Francis took the bowl and placed it on the table.

"But it is. I beg you, talk to your son and have him send me back to England immediately." Audrey slipped deeper under the coverlet, not wanting to disappoint the elegant woman.

"But I thought you wanted to stay?"

"I have changed my mind," Audrey mumbled.

Lady Francis stood near the bed, her arms crossed, her eyes narrowed to resemble arrow slits. "When I came to Scotland all those years ago, many believed I was a traitor to my own people, others thought I was a spy. No one trusted me. During those first years I was so lonely I almost left my husband."

Audrey closed her eyes briefly and gave up a brief prayer, glad the conversation had changed. "But you did not. Why? Did you begin to love Ian Armstrong?"

"In a way I did." A deep sadness entered Lady Francis's voice. "And in a way I did not."

The perplexing words piqued Audrey's curiosity. She inched higher in the bed. "What do you mean?"

Lady Francis seemed to drift to a time that no longer existed. "Toward the middle of my third year here I became pregnant."

"So you stayed because of the babe, not because you loved your husband? You said your marriage was arranged."

"I do not even know where to begin." Lady Francis clutched her hand to her chest and faced Audrey. "I was sixteen summers when we met." She stepped further into the past. A softness entered her features. "I was young but of an age to be married. I was infatuated with a handsome young man in our local village outside of London, and my father feared the man would take liberties with me. Without a word, he packed me up and sent me north to visit my aunt in Lanercost."

"I am sorry." Audrey picked at the edge of the coverlet. She too had been separated from her family at the same age.

"One sunny morning I went to pick wildflowers in the meadows. So engrossed was I in the array of oxeye daises, scarlet poppies, and yellow buttercups, when I looked up, I did not recognize my surroundings. I was so frightened, and then out of nowhere stood Ian Armstrong. Tall, older, his wild brown hair shaped his face like a pirate on the sea." Lady Francis shook her head. "He kidnapped me and held me for ransom."

"Nay! You said your marriage was arranged." Audrey scooted to the edge of the bed, not wanting to miss a morsel of this tale.

Lady Francis chuckled and took a seat by the table. "Not at first. My father came with a few men and the coin to pay the ransom. But over the month of my captivity, Ian fell in love with me and wanted to strike a different bargain with my father."

Audrey placed her feet on the floor. "How awful."

"It was not that bad. Ian never laid a hand on me and was remarkably cordial. To a young girl he could be most attractive. My father was furious in the beginning. Ian was a Scotsman and a papist."

Fear trickled down Audrey's spine. She too held the same belief. "What happened then?"

"Ian verbally gave up his papist faith. He also pledged protection and a large sum to be paid to my father over a period of years." Lady Francis glanced around the chamber. "'Tis why Warring Tower is so poor today." A heavy sigh floated from her lips. "I should have left when..." She then shrugged and gazed upon her bare fingers.

One could only assume that somewhere along the way their love bloomed or at least they had reached an agreeable settlement. Audrey wanted to ask more, but Lady Francis rose and made her way to the door. "Rest now. We shall talk about your problems with my son later."

Disappointed the story had ended, Audrey slipped back into bed. She pursed her lips thinking of asking more, but then she changed her mind. As of now, she had a reprieve, but she was not deceived, by nightfall, all within the tower would know the truth that she was a spy.

Around dusk, a clomp of horse's hooves drew Audrey's attention to the window. Gavin threw the reins to a young stable boy before entering. His loud voice snapped and boomed throughout the tower. Oh, he was in a foul mood. Her door crashed open revealing his ominous presence. His blond hair resembled a mass of ropes wildly coiled around his face. Dark smudges of dirt streaked across his cleft chin. In one hand he carried a flagon of wine and in the other two wooden cups.

"How are you feeling, Mistress? Better I hope?" His gaze shifted to her forehead where she had hit her head. A deep frown settled on his lips.

"Much better, my laird." She touched the sore spot. "It looks far worse than it feels."

Gavin slowly nodded and then strode across the room. He dropped the flagon and cups on the table. "Do you feel fit to have a drink with me?" He motioned to the chair.

Her heart racing, Audrey prudently sat without giving a comment. No sense in poking the boar.

He poured the wine and quickly took a drink, draining his cup. After pouring more, he leaned his muscular frame against the wall. "Take a drink. It will clear your senses and prevent you from swooning. I *dinnae* want you to fall and hurt yourself again."

His words seemed unwise, but saying so would be foolhardy. Audrey took a sip, then placed the cup back on the table. Her stomach burned and balked against the warm drink. She put a hand to her belly, hoping she did not retch.

Taking another swig of his wine, Gavin just stared at her. "What am I going to do with you?" His voice was low and somewhat sensual, and it seemed to settle her rolling stomach.

Her heart fluttered. "Send the guard away from my door and then let me be." She licked her dry lips.

"Unfortunately, I *cannae* do that. I *cannae* have a spy stepping freely through my home." His gaze traveled over her form.

Audrey's pulse quickened. "I have already told you all. Queen Elizabeth threatened to harm my family. Please, I am just a simple maid of simple means."

"So you say. But if that were true, how would Queen Elizabeth even know who you are?" He paused, letting his question sink deep into her. "I have no desire to fight or argue with you. I only seek the truth. How long have you been a spy for the queen, and what does she want?"

Audrey rubbed her perspiring hands on her gown, and a shiver skidded down her back. His gaze penetrated her all the way to her soul. She tried to keep her thoughts on his questions and not on his rugged lips. "My father was a successful merchant who lost most of his business because he would not turn from the True Faith."

"I know you are a papist, and I am beginning to understand why you would work for a Protestant queen. Sometimes we are forced to do things against our wishes," he said softly.

His sudden calm almost pulled her from her chair. Was his change honest, or did he use it as a ploy to get answers...or something else? She took a hard swallow to wash away her rising desire. "Years ago, when I was young, my brother Asher did everything to keep our family out of debt. After King Edward died, Asher learned some information that helped save Mary Tudor's life."

"We all know how this tale goes," he continued casually. "John Dudley, Lord Northumberland, tried to put his daughter-in-law, Lady Jane Grey, on the throne, all in hopes of keeping control of England. Yet this ruse did not work, and Jane Grey was but a queen for nine days. So I fail to see what any of this has to do with you." He pushed off the wall and filled his cup again, coming ever closer to her.

A gasp begged for release from her throat. Again, she swallowed. "Asher was the one who alerted Queen Mary that her life was in danger. That Dudley wanted to kidnap her and probably kill her. With Dudley's plan thwarted, Asher then became one of her favorite agents."

"And later on you joined him in his sneaky affairs." Gavin leaned forward, closing the gap between them.

"Nay, not at all," Audrey whispered, looking away from his towering presence. "That is not how it happened. My father started gambling again, and we wound up in

debtors' prison. Asher gained our freedom, and Queen
Mary placed me in her court. I remained there until her
death. I then happily went back to my family."

Gavin reached out and removed a lock of hair from her
shoulder. His tantalizing fingers teased her neck. "You
mean to your brother the spy?"

Audrey's breath caught in her throat. His familiar scent
of meadow grass and leather overwhelmed her. She closed
her eyes briefly to clear her senses. "Nay, Asher left the
country with his new wife. I have not seen him for many
years."

His fingers dropped to her bare collarbone. "Are you
trying to tell me that suddenly Queen Elizabeth contacted
you because your brother used to be a spy for her sister?"

"Aye," she gasped, lifting her face to his. Wishing
he would... "I know you do not believe me." Her hands
itched to grab his fingers and bring them to her lips. She
fought to finish her defense. "I think she sent me because
I was of the True Faith, and if you were sympathetic to the
religion—"

"I might confide in you. Trust you." His fingers brushed
her cheek. "You are very comely. That can loosen a man's
tongue." His gaze rested heavy on hers.

A rush like lightning coursed through her body. She
fought the onslaught with a look of indifference.

"This is all about Thomas. What are her plans for him?"

His words started to make her head ache as her body
pulsed with the desire to wrap her arms around his neck.
"What do you mean?" she asked breathlessly. "The queen
said little about Thomas. Any comments she made of him
were afterthoughts." Audrey wanted to put a gentle kiss
on his rough cheek.

He gently bent forward and took her hands, bringing her out of the chair.

His warm touch sent heat from her head to her toes. His gaze held hers for a brief moment before he cleared his throat and stepped away. His shoulders straightened like a soldier ready for battle.

Craving for his touch again, she stepped forward. "If the queen knew you had a son named Thomas and your possible connections to Scottish Catholics, then I would say she already has a spy in your midst."

"True." He backed away.

Her heart dropped as she watched the fire drain from his eyes. She turned and took her seat again. "I have told you all I know."

"I need your help. I need you to write a quick letter to the mysterious Mistress Pittman." His words were spoken like a commander giving out an order.

Audrey's insides began to burn again, this time with anger. Deceiving Queen Elizabeth was a reckless move and could get them and her family killed. "I do not think that is wise."

He ignored her pleas and extracted a piece of blank parchment from his shirt. "Tell Mistress Pittman that she was right about me. I am working with Mary de Guise. The French will be heading to our shores, and they will join a large Scottish army here."

Audrey gulped. Her heart bumped off her ribs. "Are you mad? She will come with her army. She'll kill us all."

His granite gaze held her fast. "Perhaps or perhaps not." He placed the sheet on the table and held out the quill. "But she will send someone."

Audrey's stomach roiled; she grabbed the quill and

quickly wrote the words. When finished, she lifted her gaze. "Please think before you send this."

He took the parchment and rolled it up. "I am always thinking. I am leaving for a few days, but have no fear, I shall leave you and Thomas in capable hands."

"Capable hands?" She watched his strong back ripple as he headed for the door. "Like Clyde?"

At the threshold, he paused. "Nay. All my moss-troopers will be on alert. You shall be safe."

"I want you to know I am not your enemy. I care what happens to you and your family."

His back stiffened momentarily before he looked down at the missive in his hand. "I know," he whispered, his voice deep and sultry. He took a deep breath, and his hot gaze ripped through her. "All the more reason to keep you safe. Fraser is in the hall and will be your companion while I am gone."

"Fraser! Why him? He does not care for me. It would be better to have Jaxon, at least he is pleasant." She reached out. "Gavin, please."

He turned toward her, and she wondered if he might take her in his arms...but he didn't. Instead, his words came out like a slap. "Nay, you would have him dancing your deeds before I even crossed Liddel Water. You may come and go as you please as long as Fraser is at your side. I have said so, and this is done."

She folded her arms across her chest, fighting not to throttle him *or kiss him*. "This is absurd. I won't have it."

A tender but serious smile grew on his lips. "You will, or would you prefer spending a few days in the cells?"

The cells! Did he mean the dark, dank ones down below? As if reading her thoughts, he nodded.

"You wouldn't."

"Aye. I would. No one would gainsay me. After all, where else would you put a spy?"

And she was actually starting to care for him. *Callous cretin.*

He bowed and headed for the door. "Good day to you, mistress."

The merriment in his voice drove her to madness. But what truly drove her insane was the desire to kiss his smug face.

CHAPTER 20

The next morn, Audrey stomped down the tower stairs with Fraser a few steps behind her. At least she was no longer restricted to her chamber, but when she entered the hall, the vision that greeted her was less satisfying than the ogre who guarded her back. "Ewart! What is he doing here?"

"He and a few of his men, who are in the courtyard, are to be guests until Gavin returns," Fraser answered. He then handed her a familiar dagger. "Gavin wanted me to give this to ye while he was gone."

The gift stunned Audrey. Gavin Armstrong was more than a puzzlement. He locked her up, and then when released, he gave her a weapon. Nothing made sense around here anymore. Audrey tapped the blade against her fingers. "I could use this to get rid of you."

Fraser snorted and folded his arms over his chest. "Aye, ye can try if ye like."

She hid the blade in her skirt. "Nay, there are others here who would be more deserving of seeing my skill." Her attention settled on Ewart. "Why would Laird Armstrong allow such a beast entry to his home once again?"

Fraser remained silent, though the deep scowl on his face reflected his agreement.

With a quick scan around the hall, Audrey breathed a sigh of relief. Blair hung close to the scullery, while Duncan poured Ewart a healthy mug of beer. But neither Thomas nor Lady Francis were present. Where were they?

Fraser touched her arm. "Gavin's children are with their nurse, and a guard is at their door."

"Ah, mistress," Ewart called, waving his mug in the air, "come join me. I do so enjoy yer spiritedness."

Audrey was tempted to turn around and hike back up the steps she had just descended, but being stuck in her chamber another day was insufferable. Besides, she did have Fraser to defend her dignity if things worked out poorly. She strolled to the table and took a seat a good fifteen hands away from Ewart. "I have no desire to indulge in strong drink this early in the day." Waving, she called for Duncan. "Bring me an oatcake and some goat's milk."

The lad took off on his swift feet and returned before Ewart finished off the contents of his mug. "Fill it again," he growled at Duncan.

Things would not bode well if Ewart kept up his drinking. He might very well be the only man who had ever gotten drunk drinking small beer. Fraser sighed and leaned against a nearby wall.

A loud belch burst through the air followed by a grotesque laugh. Ewart's stale breath drifted toward Audrey. She worked hard to keep from gagging.

"So, Warrin' has left his *dug* of a cousin to watch over ye. That *willnae* change the outcome. Soon my *da* will own all this, and he has promised to give Warrin' Tower to me."

Fraser pushed off the wall and lifted his fist. "Shut yer mouth. No Maxwell will ever own Armstrong land. Not without a fight."

Ewart took another slurp from his mug and then scratched his skinny protruding belly. "Believe what you want." He sat back in his seat and leered at Audrey. "When that happens, this lovely mistress will be my wife. Drinkin' always gives me the best ideas."

Audrey's insides crawled. Death would be a preferable option than to be wed to this fool. Without a word, she focused on her oatcake.

"I *cannae* wait." Ewart smacked his lips and inched closer to her. "What happens in Perth will decide the outcome."

The drink must already be addling the fool's brain. Still, one had to wonder what he meant.

"Yer daft." Fraser came closer to the table and put his one foot on a bench. "I think ye can wait for Gavin's return out in the courtyard. Yer not welcomed in here."

"My father and Ualan *willnae* be back for a few days, and I refuse to sleep in a stable or in the filthy courtyard."

"Well, we *dinnae* want yer stinkin' hide in here." Fraser flew behind Ewart and grabbed him by the back of the neck and raised him to his feet. "Now get yer arse out of here."

"Hold," Lady Francis shouted, walking into the hall. "Let him be. He is a guest in our home and should be treated as such."

Fraser dumped Ewart on the floor. "Fine, then, but *dinnae* be cryin' when the buffoon spills his guts all over yer clean rushes. He's been drinkin' all morn."

Lady Francis rushed across the hall and helped Ewart

to his seat. "I promised my son I would entertain Master Ewart while he is with us." She motioned to Duncan. "Bring us some cheese and more cakes."

"And beer," Ewart shouted.

Mumbling under his breath, Fraser lumbered back to the wall.

"Now then," Lady Francis said, raising a cautionary glance to Audrey and Fraser. "Perchance you can enlighten me, just why would my son be going to Perth with your father and Ualan?"

Audrey admonished herself. Why had she not come up with such a tactic? Kindness and smooth smiles always disarmed an enemy more than a strong fist.

Ewart adjusted his tunic and glared at Fraser. "Ye'll find out soon enough when my *da* returns."

"But we are all friends here." Lady Francis filled Ewart's mug and motioned to Audrey to take a seat next to him.

Audrey's insides curled, but better to know what your adversary planned than not. Besides, she did have the dagger. She gritted her teeth and moved toward him. Immediately he flopped his hand on her thigh. Fraser took a step forward, then paused when Lady Francis glared at him.

"Will be even friendlier in a little while." Ewart winked, adding a pinch that burned like a flash of fire.

Before she could react, Fraser stormed across the floor and launched his fist into Ewart's jaw.

"What have you done?" Lady Francis jumped to feet and came to Ewart's aid. "Are you all right?"

Bleary-eyed, Ewart's head wobbled. "My *da* will be comin' for ye next, Fraser Armstrong. Just as soon as he is finished with Warrin'."

"Always chirpin' about yer *da*. Ye act like a sniveling lad. When ye goin' to act like a man?" Frasier flexed his fist.

"What nonsense." Lady Francis dabbed at the mark forming on Ewart's cheek. "My son and your father are on good terms." She then cast a healthy glare at Fraser. "No one is going to finish anyone off."

"*Dinnae* listen to him, my lady. The man is short in the noggin." Fraser brushed his bruised knuckles under his chin.

"Warrin' is a dead man," Ewart seethed. "He thinks he is in Perth to retrieve a message, but in truth, he is never comin' back. He is goin' to see James Stewart and John Knox. The pair has been meetin' in secret. Warrin's been sent to kill them. He just *doesnae* know it yet. Ualan will make sure the deed is done and then..." Ewart sliced a finger under his neck.

"Oh Lord." Blood drained from Lady Francis's face. She wobbled and pushed Ewart away. "What is this? You ambush my son?"

Audrey's breath caught and hung like a wet cloth in her throat. Gavin may be a boar and a brute, but he did not deserve to die. A memory of their archery lesson and his warm kiss floated through her mind. Truly, Warring Tower without him would be a dismal and dark place. She inwardly shook her head to dispel such a troubling thought.

Ewart struggled to his feet. "Ye will see. He will be swingin' in a tree soon for the murder of those two filthy Reformers."

Lady Francis gasped, placing a hand on her throat.

"Warrin' is walking into a trap," Fraser said.

"He has to be warned." Audrey lifted her pleading eyes to Fraser.

Taking a deep breath, Fraser gave her a stony look. "Gavin asked me to watch ye, nothin' more. I care *nae* what happens to a bunch of wayward Reformers. In case ye have forgotten, I am of the True Faith. Gavin can take care of himself."

At one time Gavin and Fraser were close, but something or someone had driven a wedge between the cousins. Surely a spark of that bond still existed? Audrey squared her shoulders. "You know he would come to your aid if you were in danger."

The tight skin around Fraser's eyes softened, and briefly a memory of friendship seemed to linger in his eyes. "He's a half day's ride ahead of us, and there are at least five of Maxwell's men outside."

Audrey grabbed his arm. "There has to be a way."

Ewart struggled to get up. Lady Francis quickly called for him to be bound and moved to the cells below. After the hall cleared, she whispered to Fraser and Audrey, "I think I have the answer. Follow me." She led them to the chapel, and once inside, she ordered Fraser to give the altar a heavy push, revealing a set of downward stairs. "This will lead you outside the tower walls, but you will not get far on foot."

"Aye, if I have to search out another mount, I will lose even more time." Fraser slammed his fist on the altar. "I am sorry, my lady. Perchance Gavin will uncover the plot."

"And if he doesn't? My son is as good as dead." Horror rippled through Lady Francis's eyes.

Dead. Nay, not while she drew breath. Audrey's hand

slid to her dagger. She boldly stepped forward. "Perhaps not. I shall see if I can persuade one of Ewart's men to take me out for a ride on the marches."

Lady Francis deeply inhaled her breath. "'Tis too dangerous. You could be harmed."

"Getting away might be treacherous. A pretty lass always sets men to brawlin'." Fraser shook his head. "Gavin would skin me where I stand if I let anythin' happen to ye."

"Worry not about that. Remember, I have a dagger. Just meet me outside the gate."

Doubt briefly flickered across Fraser's face. "Even if we manage to carry out this plan, I fear Maxwell will send others to kill Gavin's lads."

"I will send swift Duncan to your father," Lady Francis added. "Surely, he will come to our aid. Hew Armstrong may not care for me and my son, but he hates Maxwell more."

Fraser slowly nodded. "Then, my lady, get me a rope and a cloth, for we have a plan to carry out."

In no time, Lady Francis returned with the items Fraser wanted. He threw the rope over his shoulder and stuffed the cloth into his jack before descending the stairs under the altar.

"I wish there was another way." Lady Francis touched Audrey's arm.

A mixture of grief, guilt, and gratitude emanated from that simple touch. The years had left a heavy mark on the woman. Audrey clasped Lady Francis's hand. "We both know this is the only way to save your son. If we don't warn him, he will be murdered by Maxwell's scheme."

"Then go with God. I shall pray until you return."

Audrey squeezed the older woman's hand. "Be careful, you will still have to deal with Ewart's men once they realize what has happened."

Lady Francis's lips pressed thin. The determined gleam in her eye gave Audrey courage. "We will disarm them before their puny noggins can sort out the details. Just find my son and bring him safely home."

After giving Lady Francis a hug, Audrey swiftly left the chapel, descended the spiral steps, and saw Ewart's men standing at the base of the tower. With a swish of her hips, she approached them. "My, what a lovely day." She puffed out her chest and shielded her eyes from the sun. "I would so love to take a ride."

Three men voiced their agreement while staring at her as if she was a savory treat. One frowned, and the fifth, who clearly was in charge, shook his head. "Not possible, mistress. Only Master Ewart can take ye out."

Audrey sighed. "Nay, he is already in his cups, snoring away. I fear he will not awake until later, and I do so want to ride, to dip my toes in the river." She twirled a lock of her hair around a finger and slid her slipper temptingly across the ground.

The leader rubbed his stubble beard while the others cheered, offering to be her chaperone. "I *dinnae* think it would be a good idea. What if Master Ewart wakes?"

Flipping her long braid over her shoulder, Audrey strolled toward the leader. "He'll not wake for some time. Surely a little ride could not hurt," she whispered in his ear.

The man's eyeballs bulged when she licked her lips. "What's a short ride." He pulled at the top of his breeks and ordered another to take charge.

They were out of the gate before another soul protested. With a swift kick, Audrey's horse galloped away. The eager man followed and did not notice Fraser standing behind a copse of trees with his sword drawn.

Carefully, Audrey brought her palfrey to a stop before jumping to the ground. "Come, follow me." She giggled and twisted her hips, before running right to the trees where Fraser hid.

Whack! The man didn't know what hit him.

"Is he dead?" Audrey asked, not wanting to cause another man's death, even if he was a leech.

Fraser hauled the man up against a tree, tied him up, and stuffed a cloth in his mouth. "I'm hopin' so. But I will not take the chance." He motioned to the two horses. "We have no time to waste."

Audrey closed her eyes and sent up a quick prayer. *Dear Lord, this scoundrel is in your hands. You decide his fate. And please, let us not be too late to save your servant, Gavin.*

The hollowness reappeared in her chest as Gavin's words reverberated through her memory. *"Save your prayers. I do not believe in God."*

Chapter 21

Heavy rain pelted Gavin's back as they rode into Perth. The ride had been rough and long. All he wanted was a plate of food, a mug of ale, and a soft bed. However, considering the late hour and the dark buildings, he'd be lucky to find a hard stone to place his head.

At least Ualan, Maxwell, and his men were dressed like servants and not like a bunch of marauding *reivers* come to ransack the town. That didn't mean they wouldn't meet the hangman's noose.

Lightning cracked above their heads. "We should seek shelter and continue on in the morning," Gavin suggested.

Maxwell scratched his beard. "Ye might be right. No sense raisin' suspicions by arrivin' in the middle of the night. We passed an inn not far back. Let us try to rouse the innkeeper."

After retracing their route, Maxwell dismounted and pounded on the inn's door. The innkeeper was not amused at being woken from his warm bed in the middle of the night, but he quickly changed his demeanor when Maxwell laid a healthy sum of coins before him. The men drank ale and ate cold mutton while Gavin and Maxwell were led to a room at the end of the hall.

"'Tis all I have." The innkeeper rubbed his large belly as the voices of Ualan and the others filled the inn. "If they break anythin', it will cost ye extra."

Maxwell waved off the landlord and shut the chamber door in his face. He eyed the narrow bed in the corner. "I'll be takin' the bed. Ye can have the floor. In the mornin', ye will go along with Ualan and a few others. I will stay here since Stewart knows me. We *dinnae* need him to become suspicious." Maxwell rolled onto the bed without giving Gavin a second glance.

If this missive was so important, why would Maxwell put a bumbling fool like Ualan in charge? All the way here, he drank excessively and did not seem to care who followed them. The man would have no compunction to kill any who crossed his path. 'Twas like they were purposely trying to draw attention to themselves. Something was amiss.

Gavin placed his bundle under his head and stared at the ceiling, listening to Maxwell's heavy breathing. Obtaining one mysterious message was a small price to pay to fulfill his bargain. At least they *dinnae* ask him to spill a Reformer's blood.

A swift kick in the leg awoke Gavin with a start. Rays of early morning light streamed into the small window. Every bone in his body ached. He rolled to his side before Maxwell kicked him again.

"Get up and make yerself presentable. Yer goin' to be meetin' James Stewart today," Maxwell snarled.

Gavin sat up and reached for his bundle, which

possessed a clean leather jack and breeks. At least this day the roles would be reversed. He would be the laird while Ualan would be his servant. "How long will it be before your man with the missive contacts me?"

"*Dinnae* be worried about that. He will find ye and make sure ye do exactly what he tells ye."

The back of Gavin's neck itched. "What do you mean, do whatever he says? I'm picking up the message and nothing more."

Maxwell shrugged, opened the door, and called for Ualan. "Be quick about it. The exchange needs to be done before John Knox makes any more fancy speeches." The talk of the preacher surprised Gavin. Was he the man who would give him the missive? Nay, probably not. What would a Reformer have to do with a bunch of staunch papists?

Gavin yanked on his boots and followed Maxwell out the door.

"Besides Ualan, only two others will go with ye. We *dinnae* need to draw attention."

This? Just what did this missive contain? There had to be more to this plan than what he was told.

With few words, they mounted their horses and headed farther into town. They made their way to a row of rough stone houses off a narrow road. A heavy stench of urine wafted from the buildings' corners. They stopped in the shadows not far from Stewart's house. Ualan's gaze fixed on a thick wooden door with a crumbling stoop littered with broken branches and bird droppings. One would think this was the home of a poor merchant instead of the temporary residence of James Stewart. A guard dressed in a heavy cloak stood at door.

Ualan pointed at the structure. "That be the place." His gaze shifted to the other riders. "Stay here. Armstrong and I will go on alone. Once the guard is dead, one of ye can follow. The other stay here in case there is trouble." Ualan took out a wheel-lock pistol and exposed the dagger in his belt. He glared at Gavin. "*Dinnae* try anything. Now then, let's get this deed over with."

"Deed?" Gavin stuttered. "You mean kill Stewart?" Ualan's venomous eyes answered Gavin's question.

"Aye, and ye are along to take the blame." Ualan spat on the ground. "Small price to pay to keep yer children breathin'."

The message was well taken. Gavin would be used as the scapegoat in order to get rid of a powerful man that influenced many in Scotland. "The court would be in an uproar if Stewart, the half-brother of Queen Mary, was murdered."

"Stewart is a traitor to our queen and to our faith. But he be only one of the targets. Knox is in there with him. Now get goin' before the guard becomes suspicious." Ualan aimed the pistol at Gavin and used his thighs to urge the horses forward, keeping his hands free. They rode on in parallel formation.

It all made sense now. Knox being a powerful orator was swaying many to the Reformed Faith. His death could break the backs of his followers. Or the man could become a martyr to a cause. Either way, there could be a war between Scots if both Knox and Stewart perished.

This was lunacy. This was a disaster. This was Maxwell's brilliant plan. He didn't care about his faith or who ruled Scotland. Not with so many lives in peril. Maxwell saw this as a way to destroy Gavin and probably gain control of Warring Tower once again, expanding his power in the borderlands. Why did Maxwell's hatred run so deep? Gavin needed a plan, and quickly, to save these men and his family from butchery.

His mind raced as he tried to figure out a way to disarm Ualan and alert those within. A loud shout from behind momentarily distracted Ualan's attention. Gavin leaned over and reached for the gun. The horses lurched, sending both of them to the ground. The guard at Stewart's door called out a warning, pulling his sword from its sheath. Sweat broke on Gavin's brow, and his arms shook as he rolled in the mud trying to disarm Ualan. Gavin lost his grip, and Ualan jumped to his feet, pointing the weapon at Gavin's head. This was it, he had tried his best, but he had failed his family once again. If there was a hell, he was on his way to it.

Ualan laughed and took aim. "It be my pleasure to stop yer heart."

A slap of footsteps and a loud cry bounced off the buildings. A boot like a flash of lightning came out of nowhere and kicked the gun from Ualan's hand. He cried out, watching the weapon fly through the air. Quickly, Gavin stood up and grabbed the dagger from Ualan's belt, plunging it into the man's chest.

And then time slowed. Ualan's eyes widened as his body pitched forward. With a gurgle, he fell face-first into the mud.

Behind Ualan, rumpled and out of breath, stood Audrey. The loveliest lass in the world.

"Is he dead?" she asked, paling. "I feared we would be too late."

Gavin nudged Ualan's body with his foot. "Aye, I

believe so." He wanted to wrap her in his arms forever. "Are you hurt? I told Fraser to keep you safe."

Stewart's guard was upon them, poking a sword into Gavin's back. "Hold there."

Fraser came limping down the *wynd*, blood oozing from his shoulder. Reading the concern in Gavin's eyes, Fraser waved off. "'Tis only a small stab wound." He glanced down at Ualan's body. "I see ye are still a better fighter than a Maxwell."

"Not at all. I still breathe because Mistress Audrey has a fair kick." He gave her a smile filled with delight. Tearing his gaze from her, Gavin looked to his cousin, wincing as the guard still held the blade to his back. "Are ye all right?"

"Aye, but one of them got away."

The gravity of the situation chilled Gavin's soul. If alerted, Maxwell would head straight for Warring Tower. Before Gavin could make his case to the guard, the door burst open and out stepped two more armed guards followed by James Stewart and an older bearded gentleman who could only be John Knox.

"What goes here?" Stewart demanded, holding a sword in his hand.

The guard stammered about trying to explain the fight that killed Ualan.

"If you please, I can clear this up," Gavin said, inching closer toward Stewart. Immediately all weapons turned on him.

Recognition came slowly to Stewart. "Laird Armstrong? Is that you? What happened, man?"

"This papist was sent to kill you and Knox." Gavin flinched. He should have chosen his words more carefully for Audrey and Fraser were Catholics too, and yet they had come to his aid.

"I knew this place *wasnae* safe," Knox said, stepping to Stewart's side.

"Hush, John," Stewart cautioned, his gaze traveling up and down the *wynd*. "This is not the place to have this discussion."

Gavin carefully clasped his hands. "This man's kin, Laird Rory Maxwell, holds my family hostage, and unless I followed his orders, he will kill my sons and my mother. Had I known about such a plot to kill you earlier, I would have found a way to send a warning, but I only discovered the truth moments ago. I beg you to let me go. My family's lives are at stake."

Fraser stumbled forward. "Ewart was tied up like a goose when we left, and yer mother was goin' to send Duncan to my *da* for help. I think they are safe at the moment."

Only if Hew Armstrong chose to help. He might just as well ignore Duncan's pleas. The look of uncertainty in Fraser's eyes spoke of his doubts as well. "If your father is in a forgiving mood. Maxwell will rip every brick from Warring's foundation to get to my family. Maybe 'tis best you stay here and heal up. Mistress Audrey and you can follow later."

Stewart frowned listening to the exchange. He seemed to be mulling the situation over in his mind. If he did not believe Gavin, then his family was doomed.

"We *cannae* afford a border squabble at this time. We have much at stake. *Dinnae* get involved in this," Knox pleaded.

Again Stewart scanned his surroundings and then

nodded. "I have no proof if your words are false or true. But I have always known you to be a fair man. Take one of my guards and I hope you can find this Maxwell."

"My thanks." Even though Gavin was eager to depart, the weariness in Audrey's face did not escape him. "I have one other request. Could you give aid to my friends? Without Mistress Hayes's and my cousin Fraser Armstrong's help, I am sure we all would be dead."

"I'm fine," Fraser growled, wincing as he tried to throw his shoulders back.

"Nay, you are not," Gavin snapped before he turned back to Stewart.

For the second time, Stewart hesitated while Knox shook his head. Audrey folded her hands and bowed her head. Her lips began to silently move. Did she pray?

The uncertainty in Stewart's countenance seeped away. "All right. They may stay until they are well and able to travel." Stepping aside, Stewart gave them entry.

Knox shrugged and recited a prayer as he went back into the house.

Before Gavin could make it to his horse, Audrey rushed over and gave him a hug. "Godspeed," she whispered.

He tightened the embrace, cherishing the moment, absorbing the warmth and spring garden fragrance that was his lovely Audrey. "All will be fine. Come along when Fraser is healed." He pulled away and looked into her moist eyes. How he wished to kiss her tears away, but not now, not in front of Stewart and Fraser. "Thank ye for saving me. You are as good with a kick as you are with a dagger."

Her thick lashes fluttered as she blushed and stifled a smile.

Fraser coughed as beads of sweat formed on his brow. "I am fine now. No need for us to stay."

"Nay, and I have no time to argue." Gavin picked up Ualan's dagger, then pinned Fraser with a rigid glare. "This time watch over her, or I swear I will have your head."

Fraser's shoulders slumped, and his head tipped to his chest. Audrey rushed over to him. "He has lost a lot of blood. Worry not. We will be fine. Go."

How he admired her determined spirit, but now was not the time to think of all her good qualities. His family must be saved.

When Gavin rushed to his horse, he heard Stewart say, "So then, mistress, are you betrothed to Laird Armstrong?" He did not hear her response as he left the *wynd*, but the question that once would have curled his gut now invigorated his spirit as he went to search out his nemesis and right his home.

Chapter 22

They were too late. By the time Gavin and Stewart's man made it to the inn, Maxwell was gone. Gavin franticly looked to the open road before turning back to the guard. "He must have heard what happened. Maxwell will make for Warring Tower. He plans to kill my sons and probably my mother as well."

The guard shook his head. "I *cannae* go farther. I must stay and protect my laird."

Indeed. In Scotland, Stewart's life would outweigh two young lads of insignificant value. Gavin wondered if their thinking would change if they knew Thomas was Queen Elizabeth's child.

"I understand." Gavin turned his mount around. "Please thank your laird for his generosity to my friends, and I will compensate him for his troubles later." He kicked the sides of his horse in earnest.

Gavin tore out of town, doubts stabbing at his soul. Never in his life had he ever felt so alone and so useless. The hollowness in his chest overwhelmed him. He tightened his grip on the horse's reins, trying to find some resolve, but there was nowhere to draw strength. Bleakness surrounded him.

In his despair, a flicker of hope begged to be heard. What was it? A picture of scripture niggled his mind. *"Trust in the Lord..."* As much as he tried to remember, the message seeped away. Peering into the bleak night, he galloped on, full of worry, desperation, and fear.

A day and a half later, he arrived home. From a distance, all seemed well. One of Gavin's servants stood near the gate. That did not mean no trouble lurked within. Cautiously he approached with his hand on Ualan's blade. Once crossing the threshold, he found his mother and Hew Armstrong standing in the courtyard. But where were his children?

He scanned the yard; there was no sign of Maxwell. If all was well, then why did foreboding engulf his soul? What was it? Something was missing, something wasn't right. His mother looked weary but also...troubled. Horror crept into his soul. Where were the lads?

"Where are my sons?" Gavin leapt from his mount and pulled the beast toward Hew.

Squaring his shoulders, Hew stepped in front of Gavin's mother. "Where's my son and that English lass?" Hew bellowed to give Gavin rival.

"Fraser should be along within a few days with Mistress Audrey. He suffered a mild wound." Handing over his horse to the stable master, Gavin entered the lower level of the tower.

"A mild wound?" Hew raised his fist to eye level and chased after Gavin. "If somethin' happens to me lad, I'll—"

"Hew, stop." Gavin's mother stayed at Hew's side. "I am sure he will be fine."

Barrels were being rolled to the kitchen as a few

chickens squawked in makeshift crates. A servant sat counting the few sacks of grain they had left from last winter. Everyone was going about their usual duties. All seemed normal, yet Gavin could not hold his unease a moment longer. "Where are my sons?" he shouted. "Has Maxwell been here?"

All activity stopped. Even the chickens ceased their protest. His servants looked upon him as if he had been dropped on his head at birth.

"Yer sons are safe. Maxwell did show his ugly face here, but we sent him on his way with his scrawny whimpering son. I swear if I had such a lad for my heir, I would run him through before he held his first blade." Hew always had such an eloquent way of saying things.

A tightness left Gavin's chest, but he still could not shake his fear. He did not see his sons anywhere. "You have my thanks for protecting my family. Where are the lads?" His words came out as a strangled howl.

"They are fine." His mother wrapped her arm around his, giving him a faint but reassuring smile. "At this very moment, Thomas is playing swords with Jaxon in the hall." She paused. "He has been very...noisy being kept inside."

His mother was being kind. No doubt, Thomas was being a holy terror. Gavin raced up the steps to the hall. His prediction had been correct. Thomas stood on the long table, jabbing his wooden sword at Jaxon, who screamed for mercy. Bairn ran around the table howling like a fiend. Gavin gave out a sigh of relief.

Thomas dropped the sword and jumped down, his face red with embarrassment. He folded his hands behind his back like a repentant child.

The desire to hug and kiss the lad was great, but Gavin held back. "Where are your nurse and brother?"

"Upstairs sleepin'. That's what old ladies and babes do." Thomas raised his chin like a royal.

Royal or not, he was an Armstrong. Gavin scooped the lad up in his arms and hugged him tight.

"*Da* I *cannae* breathe," Thomas whined.

Gavin's worries drained away. He wanted nothing more than to spend the day laughing and playing with his son.

Jaxon wiped his brow and took a seat at the table. "The lad will make a fine swordsman someday. He fights like a man with purpose. He's not the timid sort."

Nor is his mother. The thought of Queen Elizabeth sobered Gavin. Foiling Maxwell's plan to kill Stewart and Knox had been like playing with wooden swords. His encounter with the English queen over Thomas's future would be far more lethal.

"I am thirsty," Thomas complained.

"Blair," Gavin called, "take the lad to the scullery and get him a cool drink. Then bring Jaxon a mug of beer."

Thomas ran off to the scullery before Blair could grab his hand. In a few more years, he would be as swift as Duncan. A dull ache settled in Gavin's chest. Would the lad still be here, or would the queen find a safer haven for her son? Once again, the idea of Thomas leaving Warring Tower turned his gut raw. Clenching his teeth, he turned away from the idea. Another problem sprung forth. Even though Audrey saved his life, what was he supposed to about the brash female?

Blair brought back two mugs. Accepting his drink, Gavin sat down next to his cousin. "I *cannae* believe your father came to our aid."

Jaxon took a long drink, then smacked his lips. "When he heard Maxwell was involved, he *couldnae* get to his horse fast enough. A drop of Armstrong blood outweighs old feuds. Besides, he'd rather have yer sorry hide livin' next to our lands than that skinny pup of Maxwell's."

Just then Hew Armstrong sauntered into the hall with Gavin's mother, laughing and whispering like a pair of old friends—more than friends. The man who claimed to hate the English seemed awfully content having a lady of such birth on his arm.

"Someday we might be brothers." Jaxon winked.

Gavin's stomach soured. The sooner Hew Armstrong left, the better. "Nay, I think not."

His mother came over and put her hand on Gavin's shoulders. "If it is all the same to you, I think I will go upstairs and take a little rest. It has been a trying few days. We will talk later, my son."

The dark circles under her eyes and the lines around her mouth seemed more pronounced. Guilt slammed into Gavin's chest. He had caused all of this. Had he not wished to see Hetta, none of this would have happened. Now, Ualan was dead and Maxwell would want revenge. All here knew it.

Gavin gave his mother's hand a tight squeeze. "Rest easy."

"'Tis good to have you home." She leaned over and kissed his temple before heading for the stairs.

Hew took the seat across from him and grabbed Gavin's mug, finishing off the contents. With a sigh and a belch, he leveled Gavin with an intense glare. "Well, lad. We have a fine mess here. I need to know all."

'Twas the least Gavin could do. Most of the details

poured from his lips, though he did not divulge his meeting with Hetta and the parentage of Thomas.

"Killin' Ualan *willnae* be taken lightly. Maxwell will want ye dead." Hew waved the empty mug in the air, looking for more drink. "What do ye plan to do about it?"

Gavin flexed his fingers and then rested them on his thighs. "I will give him what he wants."

His uncle slammed a fist on the table. "Are ye mad? Yer goin' to give up yer sons' inheritance? Let me call the rest of the family together. We'll ride tonight."

"That's not the answer. John Knox is stirring up the Reformers in Perth. Mary de Guise is allowing the French free rein within our borders, hoping to crush them. The English will not sit quietly by and watch the French gain control of Scotland. A war is brewing. These lands will be washed with blood soon enough."

Hew drummed his fingers on the table. "I like the foreigners less than I like ye. But ye *cannae* just give up."

"That is why I need your help. Truce Day is in a fortnight. I will wager Warring Tower against any purse Maxwell is willing to put up. That will change his desire of revenging Ualan's death to his favorite loves—land, gold, and power."

Hew leaned across the table and lifted his fist until it was level with Gavin's eyes. "I thought ye had given up yer foolish ways, but I see I was wrong. We *havenae* won the Truce feats in years. Even with your knife-throwing wench, our chances are very slim."

A flash of Audrey tossing the blade at the target warmed his heart. "I know. But that is where we will turn the tables on him. You are going to become his ally."

"Hey? I just kicked his arse out of here. He'll not be trustin' me now."

"He would if you believed I was a weak, stinking, double-tongue Reformer." Gavin held his breath as he watched the workings of Hew's mind play out on his face. If the crusty old man didn't help him, then all would truly be lost.

Hew scratched his beard. "Some of that be true, but what's yer plan?"

A small stream of elation lifted Gavin's heavy soul. He may have a chance at saving Warring Tower and his sons' future after all.

Audrey prayed and fretted all the way back to the tower. Fraser's injury was little more than a flesh wound. He was ready to leave the following day. Stewart insisted they stay until he was certain they meant no ill to him or John Knox.

In the end, it was Knox that persuaded Stewart to let them leave, not wanting the attention. "The borderlands are the least of our concerns at the moment."

Audrey didn't know what he meant, but she was happy their pleasant captivity would end. Three days later, they left Perth. Another day passed when they finally rode through Warring Tower's gate.

When they entered the hall, they were greeted by Lady Francis sitting cozily next to Hew Armstrong, laughing and whispering like a maid with a young knight.

"What is this?" Fraser asked, letting out a steady stream of air. "Me *da* looks as if he is laird here."

He scanned the hall. "Where is Warrin'?"

Audrey eyed the grizzly laird with the unkempt beard and wide girth. So, this was Gavin's uncle, but where was the laird of the keep? Jaxon sat by the table deep in conversation with Blair. Duncan was serving drink, and Clyde sat in his favorite corner, sleeping. Fear squeezed her heart. Hopefully, Gavin did not ride the marches alone. Surely, he took some moss-troopers with him. But if he didn't...why would he be so foolhardy? Maxwell would kill him on sight.

"Ah, Mistress Audrey, come here," Lady Francis called.

With swift steps, she made her way to the matron's side while Fraser drifted toward Jaxon. "My lady, I am so pleased to find you well."

"Come." Lady Francis glanced over to Fraser. "How are things?"

"Fraser is fine. He says soon it will be just another scar." Audrey watched Jaxon gently tap Fraser's injured arm.

Hew eagerly sat up, looking toward his sons. Though he did not call Fraser over, Hew's attention was hawk-eyed on his son's injury. When satisfied at what he saw, he feigned indifference. "Ack, I'm sure he will have many more scratches before he draws his last breath. How was the journey?"

"We looked over our shoulder the whole way. We could not wait to be home." *Home.* When had her thoughts changed? Gavin's fleeting face skipped through her mind. *What nonsense!* This was not her home.

"I am glad to hear so," Lady Francis said. "I am not sure if you have ever been introduced to Jaxon and Fraser's father. This is Laird Hew Armstrong."

216

Audrey dropped into a curtsy. "A pleasure, my laird."

The older man's gaze zigzagged over her form. "Now I see why Jaxon is always wanderin' this way." He raised a hand and called for another chair. "Sit and tell me, what brings ye to Scotland?"

Lady Francis stiffened at his words, but Audrey had no intention of betraying their confidences. Deftly, she took her seat. "I am a companion to Lady Francis."

"She came to give me comfort after Edlyn's death," the older woman added in a rush.

Hew stroked his beard, there would be no fooling this man. "There was no loss there, the wench barely spoke. One bland look would send Edlyn tremblin'."

"That is not true. She conversed with Fraser and, of course, Gavin," Lady Francis corrected. "How would you know? You rarely stepped foot in this keep."

"I hear things." Hew shifted in his chair. "'Twas told yer son ignored her, and Fraser…" Hew assessed his son on the opposite side of the room. "He is kind to all the lasses."

Audrey begged to give a different opinion. To her, Fraser was cool and apathetic. But instead of voicing her views, a more urgent need pressed on her chest. "Where is Laird Armstrong?"

Hew chuckled. "So ye be worried about him."

She glanced away. "'Tis I just do not see him about."

"He will be back soon." Hew hooded his hazel eyes. "He's gone to speak to Maxwell."

Audrey jumped out of her seat. "Maxwell! Why, he will kill Gavin!"

The older laird's eyebrows pushed upward. "Methinks ye are overly concerned."

Lady Francis sat up straight. "I share that concern."

"Ack, I told ye. Maxwell *willnae* touch a hair on Warrin's bonnie head once he says his piece."

"If he is able to speak first." Lady Francis scowled at Hew.

Just as Audrey sought to argue, a loud howl followed by a boisterous bark filled the hall. Bairn came lumbering over to Audrey's side, his tongue hanging long from his mouth. She whirled to the entrance.

"Ah, you have returned," Gavin called from the entry. With meaningful steps, he strode toward them. "Pray tell, did you encounter any troubles?"

Fraser strolled up with a tankard in hand. "Nay. We tried to keep yer name out of it."

A brief look of friendship passed between them. "I thank thee."

"*Dinnae* be thankin' me." Fraser tilted his head. "Thank Mistress Audrey. She convinced Stewart and Knox to weave a different tale. One where ye never set foot in Perth."

Gavin bowed slightly. "I am in your debt."

He stepped closer to her side. His heady smell of leather and meadow grass caused her knees to quake. She gave a short nod.

"You should sit." The lines around his mouth softened.

Her heart kicked up tenfold when he offered his hand. Casually she placed her fingers in his palm, trying to play the action down while the other hawks watched on.

"What of it, Warrin'? Did Maxwell take the bait?" Hew asked.

Gavin's gaze lingered on Audrey, causing her insides to puddle. The sensation did not cease when he addressed his uncle.

"Like a pig to his slop."

Hew slapped his knee. "I knew he would. The clod *cannae* see past his own greed."

"I doubt that had anything to do with it. He would have killed me where I stood had you not spoken to him first." A conspiratorial look flashed between the two men.

Her curiosity on alert, Audrey calmed her pounding heart. His fingers held hers firm, giving them a tight squeeze. Was Gavin placing himself in danger? Why couldn't the man hole up in the tower? She pierced him with her gaze.

Gavin cleared his throat. "Perhaps Mistress Audrey would like to rest after her long journey."

"Nay, I am truly fine. Though a rest might suit me," she said, trying to please him. Suddenly another query entered her mind. "Where is Thomas? Is he all right?"

Hew grunted. "The lad is fine. Probably hiding out in the chapel again. I swear he is destined for the clergy."

"Mmm," Lady Francis studied Audrey. "He has been coming to chapel almost every morn. Surely God has touched his heart."

Audrey chuckled while Gavin watched her intently. The man was forever measuring every action or word she spoke. Why could he not just accept that she genuinely cared for the boy? "Only time will tell if he has a calling."

Gavin shook his head. "I do not see the church in his future." A coolness swept his countenance. "Mistress Audrey, you look pale. I insist you rest. Let me escort you to your chamber."

Alas, did he mean to place her in prison again? The ungrateful wretch. She pushed his hand away. "I can go on my own accord." She walked with measured steps to the stairs.

Bairn followed along with his master at his side. "I will see you safely there. The stairs can be slippery. I would not like to see you take a wrong step."

Wrong step. The man was a mass of muscular contradictions—grateful for her help in Perth, yet suspicious of her motives. Would he never trust her?

Dark circles mooned his eyes, and his shoulders seemed to have shrunk since she last saw him. Gavin Armstrong lived in a world of secrets and distrust. What ate at his soul happened long ago. The only thing she prayed for was the reformation of his heart. For if that did not happen soon, she feared he would be lost forever.

He placed his hand at her back, guiding her along. He bent his head closer to her ear. "Audrey, I need you."

CHAPTER 23

Thomas raced from the chapel and stopped Audrey and Gavin's ascent. "Mistress Audrey, yer back. Where are ye goin' now? Jaxon is too tired, and Duncan is too busy to play swords with me." Though he addressed her, he timidly glanced at his father.

Gavin ran a hand over the boy's head. "Perhaps later." An answer Thomas probably heard often.

Audrey knelt down and looked into Thomas's sad copper eyes. "Your father is very tired. He has had a long trying day and so have I. On the morrow we both will play swords with you."

The boy's shoulders drooped. Without looking his father's way, Thomas trudged off toward Lady Francis, dragging his wooden sword behind him.

Audrey stood. She hated disappointing the child.

Gavin didn't even look in Thomas's direction. "After you, mistress."

Not a single sound did she utter until they were standing in her room. Then she whirled on him like a cat with her claws out. "What is wrong with you? Could you not make the effort to entertain your son for a little while? Are you that unfeeling? Many care for you, and you

221

trample on them like they are nothing more than dirt under your feet."

"Care for me? Pray tell, who are all these people?" He trudged into the chamber, closing the door behind him.

Her arms flailed about as she continued, "Thomas, your mother, and…many more."

He sat down in the only chair in the room and stretched out his legs as if this was his chamber. "Who are the more?" he asked calmly. A spark of heat glowed in his eyes and sent her heart a tumbling.

Why did he want to know? Did he set a trap so he could keep her locked up for the rest of her life? Fire brewed in her belly as he watched her under heavy blond lashes. His smooth cheeks carried a hint of color, a lock of flaxen hair floated down across his forehead. The desire to brush the hair back drove up her mad.

Her gaze dropped to the floor. "What care you who they are?"

"I *dinnae* wish to be ungrateful to anyone."

Her eyes met his, and she whispered, "Except me and Thomas." She bit down on her lower lip before anymore words betrayed her.

He smiled like he had feasted on a hearty mutton stew. "Ah, Audrey, trust me, I would never take you for granted nor the lad. You made it possible for me to come home to my family. I will never forget your…favor, bravery… I've never known a woman like you."

Her heart flopped at his familiarity and the warmth in his tone. What game did he play now? "Then what do you want from me? I am no longer a threat to you. I mean you no harm. I mean your family no harm. I have grown exceedingly close to your mother and your son Thomas."

"He's not my son," Gavin said, without blinking an eye.

Hurt exploded in her chest. She came and knelt at his side. "Does that matter? Surely at one time you loved his mother. Could you not love him as you had once loved her?"

Gavin threw back his head and laughed. "How can I love a woman I never met?"

The man had truly lost his wits. The urge to make the sign of the cross over her chest was great. What torment brought him to this that he could not see the truth? She should have prayed harder for him. Cautiously, she reached out and placed her fingers on his hand. "Your wife, Edlyn, was Thomas's mother."

"That is not Thomas's mother." Gavin pulled his hand away and leaned forward, placing his elbows on his knees.

Confusion swept through Audrey as she glanced to Edlyn's picture. The boy did not look like either parent, but that did not mean Edlyn wasn't Thomas's mother. "If not, then who is?"

Gavin lifted his head. "You truly *dinnae* know?"

She placed a hand over her heart. "If you wish me to swear, I shall. But I beg you to believe me. What I told you is the truth."

For a while, he said naught, examining her features. New lines she had not noticed before creased his forehead. Finally, he nodded. "That became apparent when you rode into Perth and saved my life."

A deep well of joy sprung forth, and she almost hugged him. "I would never want to see any harm come to you or your family."

"I know." A misery covered him like a heavy cloak.

"Giving trust is not easy for me."

If he trusted her, then maybe someday… "From this moment on, let us speak nothing but the truth to each other. Now tell, if not Edlyn, who do you believe to be Thomas's mother?"

"Who ordered you to come here?"

Audrey's brain tripped. Her eyes flipping to Edlyn's picture and then to the memory of Queen Elizabeth's face. "That is why you forced me to write that letter? You believe the queen is…" Audrey fell back on her heels. "Nay, that cannot be. She is a virgin."

"There are rumors—"

"There are always rumors. I cannot believe you would be taken in by such gossip."

"Not gossip. I went to Perth to fulfill a debt to Maxwell. I offered my services to him, if he would allow me to talk to Hetta."

"The boys' old nurse?"

"Aye, I wanted to send Thomas away, back to his original father." He raised his hand, no doubt shielding himself from the horror he probably saw in her eyes. "That sounds terrible. Looking back, I know I could have never done it. The lad means everything to… I *dinnae* want to choose who would inherit Warring Tower. I *dinnae* want to see my children fighting over this scrap of land. One could end up like my father's brother Colban. I know my father and Hew killed him. That is why they divided up this land."

"You think Thomas would kill Marcas?"

"Or the other way around. I *cannae* lose either of them." He looked away as if hiding something in his soul. "Hetta told me how Thomas came to Lanercost."

Audrey sat on the floor in front of him as Gavin spoke of his past. The bargain struck at his marriage, Edlyn's virginity, and Thomas's possible mother. She did not doubt that Gavin spoke the truth, but she wondered about his reasoning. "But you do not know for sure?"

With a huff, Gavin rose to his feet. "If it were not true, then why would Queen Elizabeth send you here? By your own admission, you said she wanted you to keep an eye on the lad."

"I know, but I cannot believe she would not have claimed the boy the moment she ascended the throne." Audrey fought not to rub her aching temples.

"I agree, which makes me think there are many parts missing from this tale. Who is the lad's father? Where is he now? Was the queen married or not?"

The same questions plagued her, but why would Gavin goad the queen? She could very well come to Scotland. Understanding dawned like a bright morning sun. "You wish to challenge the queen for Thomas." Audrey rose to her knees and reached out, placing a hand on his cheek. "You play a deadly game."

His warm skin tingled against hers. An earnest twinkle rose in his brilliant blue eyes. "I know." He rested his forehead against hers. His warm breath soothed like a sweet balm. "I am sorry that you are in the middle of this," he murmured.

All sound slipped away. Her mind focused on nothing else but the nearness of his lips. He drew away ever so slightly. Their gazes met and all she saw was a lonely man and a father. Her lips parted. He leaned in and gently brushed his against hers. She sighed and lifted her chin, welcoming his long, lingering kiss. He tried to pull away, but she would not let him. Her senses craved more. She pulled him close and captured his lips again. He moaned, wrapping his arms around her. From that moment on, Audrey knew that her heart belonged to this perplexing man. To him alone.

A quick rap and the door swung open. "Excuse me, but…"

The rapture broken, both rose. Fraser stood in the doorway. A fierce frown on his fiery face.

"Fraser. What is it?" Gavin briskly asked.

The large Scot did not answer but stomped away. Neither Audrey nor Gavin spoke a word, but both knew a friendship had been broken that day. Unfortunately, they didn't know why.

A sennight had passed since Fraser stormed out of Warring Tower after finding Gavin and her in an intimate embrace. In truth, the kiss meant nothing, for not once since that time did Gavin deem to touch her. Instead, he immediately apologized profusely for his actions. But his repentance did not bring his cousin back to the tower. Fraser's anger mystified her. Gavin believed that his cousin carried some affection for her, but such an idea felt false. Nay, there had to be another reason why Fraser left in such a huff.

Sweat dripped down Audrey's back as she shielded her eyes from the sun's intense rays. The sweet mild days of spring had given way to summer's heat. The butt outside the tower walls loomed before her like an impenetrable barrier. Though Gavin had not included her in all the plans he arranged with Hew Armstrong, she knew that its success rested on her winning the blade toss.

Pulling her dagger from its sheath, Audrey took her stance, reaching out her hand to measure her aim while the red cloth pinned to the butt fluttered in the wind. She flipped her wrist, and the knife flew to the mark. It landed slightly to the left of the cloth. That would not do. If she could not hit the target every time, then they were all doomed.

At least according to Lady Francis, they were. She claimed if the Armstrongs did not win the Truce Day coin, Gavin would not be able to pay Warring's debts. Knowing that alone made Audrey want to do her best. She was riddled with enough guilt as it was for not being honest with Gavin from the beginning. Adding to Warring Tower's demise by writing secret missives to the queen was not acceptable.

What worried Audrey all the more was that her last message to the queen was the one Gavin told her to write. Surely Queen Elizabeth would send someone to find out what exactly was going on at Warring Tower. What would happen to Gavin and his children then? What would happen to her family? The queen was not the most kind and tolerant person.

Audrey pulled the blade from the butt and walked back to the line. She used the back of her arm to wipe the sweat from her brow before taking aim once again. Inhaling deeply, she let the blade sail through the air. A spark of elation jumped within her when the knife landed square in the middle of the target.

"Well done, Audrey. Our chances of winning the games grow greater every day."

A flaming blush ascended on her already heated skin hearing Gavin's voice. How she wished she could control the embarrassing condition, but alas, it was impossible. "My thanks, but I wish my aim was better. I just pray when Truce Day does come, I will not lose the little skill that I do have."

Dressed in just a white shirt and a pair of tan breeks, Gavin strolled to her side. "You will not falter. Look at what you have accomplished in your life."

His words surprised her. For she could not think of one thing she had ever done correctly. "Though I am grateful for your faith in me, I possess no great skill in anything."

His lips twitched, and the memory of their kiss filled her mind. "I can think of several. Except being an astute spy."

Ignoring his tease, she worked on taming her unruly thoughts, trying to concentrate on the target instead of his beautiful solid chest. She took a deep breath and let the dagger fly. Another perfect strike.

"See. Many talents." He strode to the butt to retrieve the knife. "I must speak with you privately on another matter."

For a sennight, they had not been alone. In all likelihood by his design. Surely, he did not wish to whisper sweet words into her ears, nay, something else was amiss. Yet, she could not help but hope he longed for her as she did for him.

She nodded and followed him to a copse of trees. Once in the shade, away from prying eyes, he stopped. "What's wrong?" Audrey asked.

"I have been watching you over this past week."

Her pulse kicked up. She closed her eyes, and once

again she was in his warm, strong embrace. When she opened her eyes, she found him leaning against a tree, staring out into the fields. "I have watched you with my mother and Thomas. You are very kind and patient with both of them."

Audrey's heart sagged. No words of love would be forth coming. She tried to hold on to the tears that begged to flow. "They grow dearer to my heart every day."

"I know." He rested his hand on his sword, which had become a daily part of his dress since returning from Perth. "I notice you practice diligently with the blade."

His pleasantries were like a simple dance before the floods would whisk away the merriment. "I know what is at stake."

"You *dinnae* know all of it." He paused, watching a small bee buzz through the air. "At first I wanted to keep you in the dark, fearing you would betray my confidences."

A ball of indignation ripened in her stomach. What must she do to win this man's trust?

"But not once have you tried to seek out Maxwell or write a missive to Queen Elizabeth. You speak no ill of any in the tower but cheer those who are forlorn. My mother is attached to you, and Thomas adores you. So, I must trust you."

Again, another thing that had been established before. Or was it just she who had given her trust and love so completely? What then must she do to make him see where her loyalties lie? She shortened the distance between them until he was but a breath away. "I would never hurt Thomas or anyone here. This family is as precious as my own."

229

A jab of pain pierced her heart. Her family would suffer if she did not make Queen Elizabeth understand. She would not let a betrayal go unpunished. Audrey remembered the squeaking rats clawing at the meager food she and her family received when they were in debtors' prison. The years had taken a toll on her father. He did not live long after they were released. If her mother was forced back into prison, she would not last long. No matter what happened here, Audrey knew she would have to return to England and beg for mercy. She could not let them suffer.

"That is why I want you to know all in case our plan falters." Gavin bent down and picked up a few sticks and began running them over the smooth ground.

She focused on his words, trying to put the worries of her family to the back of her mind.

"Do you know why Maxwell never came seeking my head after Ualan died?"

"I assumed it was because there was no proof of a real crime in Perth. Certainly, he doesn't want his failed plot to come to light."

Gavin lifted his chin to the heavens and laughed. "Oh, you know so little about Scotsmen. These are the Debatable Lands. No law reigns here. If Maxwell wanted to rally his kinsmen this eve, no one would think twice about it. Nay, I sent Hew first with an offer Maxwell could not refuse, and then I added more to the pot to sweeten his appetite."

His last word offered little comfort. The glint in his eye bespoke of a plan of trickery. And a plan developed on such a shifty foundation would not stand. Audrey squeezed her hands together. "What are the details of this plan?"

"Warring Tower is in poor straits. If our land does not produce good crops this year, we will starve come winter. Maxwell knows this, so I bargained with him. If the Armstrongs win the feats, not only do we get the coin prize, but Maxwell will have to supply us with grain all winter long. If we lose and he wins, then the prize is Warring Tower and my lands."

"'Tis a foolish bet. Why would you do such? Why would you once again give Warring Tower to him?" Audrey's mind buzzed with the implications of such a pact. She began to pace, destroying the drawings he had dug in the dirt. "By your own admission, the Armstrongs have not won these feats in years." Her spirits lightened slightly. "There is also the possibility that you both might lose. What then? What makes you think he would not just kill you and take your lands anyway?"

"Because he found another way to do it without spilling a drop of Maxwell blood."

Audrey stalled her steps. "What do you mean?"

"Because Hew offered to double-cross me." Gavin's words were said so nonchalantly that Audrey had a great desire to throttle him.

"How?" she asked, tightening her hands into fists.

"Hew will lose the archery event, or so Maxwell believes, in exchange for a large sum of money. Coin he will use to buy land from the English. He will give this land to his youngest, Fraser, and Jaxon will inherit the Scottish land. This will strengthen the family as a whole on both sides of the border. A plausible idea."

In truth, it was. The hair started rising on her neck. What prevented Hew from going through with such a plan?

"Hew told Maxwell your skill with the blade is fair and beatable. Making it sound as if we no longer hold the advantage." Gavin almost leapt into the air as he rubbed his hands together. "But we know you are the best with the blade and Duncan has the swiftest feet. We will not lose those two feats. I have figured it all out."

A large lump formed in Audrey's throat and descended to her stomach. The man put too much faith in her. 'Twould have been better had he kept his plan to himself.

"I will win the horse race," he continued.

"If all happens as you say, then we shall win the feats, but something still could go wrong. Like me losing." Her belly sizzled. She wanted to bash him in the chest for putting such a heavy burden on all of them.

"You will not. But if something does go wrong, then Hew will win the games for us in the archery match. Only the English can beat him."

"What if he loses?"

"Ah! If a tie happens. Then Fraser will win the ax throw." Gavin circled Audrey's waist with his hands, lifting her high and twirling her about in the air.

"Put me down, you oaf. Your plan is nothing but maybes and mights."

He placed her on her feet; disappointment wrinkled his forehead.

She brushed invisible creases out of her gown, trying to control her riotous senses, hoping he might just kiss her again. "'Tis still a risky plan."

"If I thought there was another way to keep the peace in the land, do you not think I would follow that course?" He kicked the soft dirt with his boot. "Nay, there is no other way, and we will not lose." He hid his worry behind a false smile. "Think on it. There are three possibilities. We win, the English win, or Maxwell wins. Maxwell would never start a war over losing the feats on Truce Day. 'Twould be a cowardly thing to do."

"What makes you think he will not take your head in any case? All know Truce Day can be quite rowdy. He could claim someone else did the deed. Look at what he tried to do in Perth?" A vision of Gavin lying on the ground dead sucked her breath away. Audrey fought to fill her lungs; this was no time to be weak.

Gently, he placed his palm against her cheek, becoming deadly serious. "If that happens, I want you to take my mother and my sons to Queen Elizabeth. Beg for mercy. For them and your family."

Audrey placed her hand over his, relishing his tender touch. He had not forgotten about the plight of her family. A lone tear slipped from her eye. Nothing could happen to either family—or to him. No matter the outcome next week, she had to be strong. "I will make sure no one comes to any harm."

With his thumb, Gavin swiped her tears away and then placed a tender kiss on her lips, before pulling back. "All will be well. We have you praying for us."

"I thought you do not believe in our Lord?" She struggled to lift a smile to her lips, even as she wished for another kiss.

"True. But on the chance I am wrong, then I have the most pious Audrey Hayes making intercessions for me and our families."

Her voice was lost among the tears that clogged her throat. He grabbed her hand and kissed it, sending her heart into a tumble.

"Come. Let us leave this melancholy behind." Hand in hand they started walking back to the tower. "'Tis a bonnie day to go riding."

And they did. They rode the marches until the sun glided away, until purple and pink hues filled the skies. But no matter how splendid the day was, both knew a torrent stood on the horizon, which would change the lives of all in Warring Tower forever.

Chapter 24

Another week swiftly passed, and the gaiety of Truce Day buzzed through the tower. In the past there would have always been several days a year and mostly held at the border. A while back it was decided that the summer Truce Day would be held by one of the families. Last year's events was held on the English side of the border at the Hall family keep. This year it would be held on the Scottish side of the borders at one of the Armstrong holdings.

Hew, being the eldest kin, decided the place. "Best at yer keep," he said a fortnight ago. "Seeing and possibly owning yer lands might excite Maxwell to make a grave mistake."

Gavin wished he had his uncle's confidence. He stood on the battlements and watched the visitors from each family assemble in the fields below. Having Truce Day on familiar ground would give them the advantage, but it would not be a sign of instant victory. His mother, Audrey, and even Thomas had spent many an hour in the chapel. Perchance their prayers had been answered for not a cloud dotted the sky and the winds were mild. The land was dry and in perfect condition. A perfect day for the feats.

From the east, Maxwell approached with his family while the Dunneses and the Halls were already erecting their pavilions in front of the gate. Quickly, Gavin descended the stairs, eager to welcome his guests. But alas, a most alarming scene met him in the hall. There lay Duncan on a bench, his long legs stretched out before him.

"His stomach, has been retchin' all mornin'," Blair announced, patting Duncan's face with a cool cloth. "I fear there is no race in his future."

Of all the times for this to happen. The cold emptiness that Gavin had felt on the road from Perth resurfaced once again. Why should he be surprised? As he suspected, no God stood on Warring Tower's side. Gavin rolled his eyes heavenward before fixing them on the ill lad. "We shall have to forfeit the feat. Where is Lady Francis and Mistress Audrey?"

"They still be in the chapel, prayin' for God's help." Blair motioned her head toward the chapel. "Look, here they come."

His mother, Audrey, and Thomas, upon seeing Duncan lying prostrate, rushed to his side. The astonished looks on their faces produced an awkward laugh in Gavin's throat. Did they truly believe time on their knees, pressed against a cold floor, would wake up a nonexistent God?

"How did this happen?" Lady Francis asked.

Blair shrugged. "Not sure. He was fine last eve. Hoppin' around like a rabbit. Racin' up and down the steps and through the courtyard. He even raced with Master Fraser and Jaxon."

"Is that all they did?" Gavin leaned over Duncan's body and took a sniff.

Blair shrugged again.

"Did you drink beer last night?" Gavin asked Duncan.

The lad shook his weary head before he spewed his guts into the bucket next to him. All stepped back, not wanting to catch what ailed him.

Audrey grabbed a clean cloth and wiped Duncan's face. "I have never seen the boy drink anything but goat's milk and water."

"There is nothing for it. We are out of the foot race for there is no one else in the Armstrong family that has swift enough feet to beat the Maxwells, Dunneses, and Halls, but we still have a chance to win."

Thomas tugged on his father's doublet. "Let me try. I have been practicin' with Duncan, and I can run fast."

Gavin burst with pride, before a dull empty ache settled in his chest. He placed a hand on the lad's soft curly head and knelt down. "You are incredibly fast, but you are too young. In a few years you will be able to run the race. Then you will beat all, I am sure of it."

Thomas's lower lip quivered. "I can run as fast as a man. I have beaten Clyde."

Clyde could barely walk a straight line. His greatest feats were lifting a mug of beer to his lips and sleeping the afternoon away. But such a point was lost on Thomas. "Aye, but you must be at least six and ten to run the race."

Letting out a hearty huff, Thomas stomped away, his head hanging low.

Gavin stood. Someday Thomas would be a fine man, but today he would have to be watched closely. "Blair, stay close to Thomas or I fear he will be into mischief."

Wrinkling her nose and squinting her eyes, Blair motioned her head to Mistress Jonet. "Can he not be with his nurse?"

"Nay, she will have her hands full with Marcas. The task must fall to you."

The sullen maid nodded her head, but her gaze shifted around the hall to all the visiting young men. 'Twas a lot to ask of a youthful servant who had been looking forward to a day of merriment. There was nothing for it, no one else knew the lad's habits better than Blair.

Gavin dug into his pocket and pressed a silver coin into her hand. "For your trouble this day."

"I really could use a new frock." Blair tucked the coin into her bodice, then brushed her hands over her drab brown dress.

He lifted a brow in surprise. Blair was a shrewd lass. "And a new fancy frock as well."

With a flutter of her eyelashes, Blair picked up her skirt and hurried off after Thomas, which left Gavin with the problem lying on the bench.

"Take Duncan to his quarters," Gavin ordered two servants.

"I shall attend him and meet you at the games later." Lady Francis picked up a wet cloth. "Have no fear. All will be fine. I am sure 'tis not serious." She squeezed Gavin's arm. "My prayers are with you this day. If it is God's will, the Armstrongs will win the day."

He almost said skill would win the day, not God, but he did not wish to upset her. Most women needed such beliefs to keep them calm and happy.

"Well then, I guess it is up to us to make sure these games are won." Audrey's mesmerizing obsidian eyes drew him in.

The fair Audrey who usually wore simple and demure clothing was nothing of the sort this day. Dressed in a dark skirt and a black leather doublet, her dark hair plaited, she resembled a woman warrior. For certain, she would win the blade throw by skill or intimidation. Or perhaps by distracting the other contestants with her alluring smile.

He placed her hand on his arm. "Mistress, allow me to escort you to Truce Day." Together they took the stairs and stepped toward the door, then into the beaming light. Whatever came this formidable day, at least he had the loveliest lass at his side.

They weaved their way through the pavilions and the boisterous crowds. Many already reeked of beer or ale. Merry voices and happy faces floated everywhere. Pipes and tambourines heightened the festivities. Maids danced while others stood near the fields vying for the optimal place to watch the feats.

Audrey marveled at all. Never had she witnessed such a spectacle. How easy it would be to get caught up in the gaiety instead of focusing on the blade toss.

Each family rallied beneath their standard. The Halls, Dunneses, Maxwells, and Armstrongs all proudly hailing the strength of their family. A crier listed off the names of all the feats—*reiver* horse race, wrestling, lang spear throw, archery, blade toss, and footrace. Dice would be rolled; the winner would name the first feat.

God answered Audrey's prayers, and the Armstrongs were allowed to choose first, followed by the Dunneses, Maxwells, and then the Halls. An early lead might build the Armstrongs' confidence.

"The horse race," Hew Armstrong yelled. Immediately Gavin took to his mount.

Shouts of agreement and encouragement sprung from every present Armstrong. The other families cheered on their own riders as they made their way to the starting line. Those who were able ran to various parts of the trail to rally their rider. At the line, the four contenders struggled to keep control of their horses among all the revelry. A servant called for silence and then raised a flag high. With a powerful yell, he dropped the flag and the riders were off, their mounts kicking up dirt as they flew down the path.

Thomas came out of nowhere with Bairn on his heels. The boy grabbed Audrey's hand, tugging her down the path. "Come on, let us follow as long as we can."

Audrey laughed and then let go of his fingers. "You go along. I wish to save my strength for the blade toss." The lad raced ahead without a look back, weaving in and out of the crowd. If Thomas kept up such a pace, within a few years he would be the best in the footrace.

Stopping at Audrey's side, Blair placed her hands on her knees, taking deep labored breaths. "I took me eyes off the lad for a moment, and *poof,* he raced away like a rabbit with a hound on his tail."

"That is exactly what it was, Bairn racing after him. Your task is not easy." Audrey stretched her neck but could not spot the boy anywhere. "Let us make way for the finish line. I am certain he will be there by the time the riders cross."

Blair nodded and followed Audrey to the line. There stood Hew Armstrong.

"'Twill be a while before they come," Audrey said, shielding her eyes from the sun.

"Aye," Hew confirmed. "They have to loop across the waters and then over the hills that mark off Armstrong land to the east, then back around to the west."

Her insides tumbled up and down as if they stood on the deck of a ship instead of dry land. "Do you think Gavin will win?"

"Of course," Blair chimed. "There be none finer on a horse than Laird Warrin'."

Her smitten look pricked Audrey's ire. This was no time to be jealous of another maid's desires. She needed to keep her mind clear and stay focused on her own feat.

Perspiration dotted Audrey's forehead as they waited and waited. She closed her eyes and tried to block out all the joviality around her, searching for a deep calm. A jumpy spirit would not do, especially when it came time for her to perform her own skill.

Finally, an approaching rumble shook the ground. Two horses, neck and neck, came thundering toward the finish line. The crowd began to roar. Hew's words boomed encouragement. Audrey's voice caught in her throat; her ears rang as Gavin's horse began to pull away.

Thomas appeared out of nowhere, perched on the side of the lane. He jumped high in the air when his father crossed the line first. Gavin had done it. The Armstrongs had won the first game.

The race had barely ended when the Dunneses shouted, "Lang spear."

As expected, all ran to where the spears would be thrown. The best of three throws would determine the winner. Going first, Allan Dunnes's spear flew like an arrow being loosed from a bow. Hall's and Jaxon's spears landed far behind, but at least both had bested the

Maxwells. Jaxon managed to win the second round, knocking the Maxwells and Halls out of the competition. But alas, Jaxon could not find the strength to beat Allan. The Dunneses had won the lang spear throw.

Before congratulations were shared, Rory Maxwell roared, "Archery."

Here, Rory Maxwell stood against Hew Armstrong, Will Hall, and Edward Dunnes. All the men were of the same age, and all were known to be excellent bowmen. A few practice rounds were given to measure the length of the butts.

Gavin strolled up to Audrey's side. "Hew should win this," he said, assessing all the archers.

Audrey did not hold Gavin's confidence. The feats were more than just skill. If Hew lost, the burden for her would become even greater. Hew let loose an arrow, which landed close to the mark. Audrey stole a look at Gavin's strong profile, but his expression told nothing. "He is the best, right?"

"Aye. But I have bested him at the butts more often than not and so has Rory and Will. Edward Hall has an aim with the bow like yours."

She ignored his jab and tried to remain serious. "Then why are you not standing out there?"

Gavin folded his arms across his chest as Hew let go of another arrow. This one fared slightly better, but not well enough to beat Rory Maxwell's arrow. "At the time I *didnae* think we would need the event. I knew I would win the horse race and Duncan would win the footrace, and you—"

"I could lose." Audrey's spirits dipped when Hew's last arrow bounced off the butt.

"I am certain you will seal the win for us." Gavin did not look at her nor blink an eye as if her winning the blade toss was a forgone conclusion.

Despair and helplessness pricked at her soul like a vulture plucks meat from an aged corpse. "You should not place so much faith in me. I could fail."

Gavin tipped his head toward hers, a grin on his lips. "'Tis not faith I have in you. I know your skill and that of those you compete against. You will win."

Joy should be erupting from her soul. He believed in her. No matter if she did win the toss, they needed one more event to save Warring Tower. Her high spirits plunged. With Duncan's illness, the footrace was lost. "And if Hew loses?"

"Pray for a tie," he mumbled.

"What? I thought you do not believe in God and prayer?"

His gaze met hers, the corners of his mouth curved upward. "But you do," he said before he strode closer to the butt. "And that is good enough for me."

How true, she did, and she would pray all the more that all would turn out in their favor.

The command was given for the archers to stand on the line. They flexed their bows and eyed the red cloth that served as the mark. Since Maxwell had called for the event, he went first. The others rolled the dice to see who would be next. The crowd roared and gasped as the favor fell to Hew. He would be second, then Will Hall, and Edward Dunnes would go last.

The contest was simple. There would be three rounds. The arrow farthest from the mark would be eliminated each round. Maxwell readied his stance and eyed the target. A mild breeze ruffled his greying hair. With little effort, he loosed his arrow, which landed slightly above the cloth. The crowd murmured at the fine placement.

Next, Hew stepped forward. His focus solely on the butt. The breath Audrey held in her throat burned. Her eyes fixed on the scene before her. The bowstring pinged, and the arrow landed slightly below the mark. Slowly her breath seeped out. Will Hall had the skill to best them both.

With a nod, Will stepped up. He raised his bow, then dropped it at his side. Audrey's heart tumbled to her toes when Will strolled over to the target to examine the other two arrows. Was such a practice allowed? No one stopped his steps or seemed surprised. The warmth of the sun made her leather doublet feel heavy. The sun had hit its zenith. This day was only half over, and already sweat snaked down her back. Her nerves tight as the competition continued. How was she to remain calm when her time came?

Seeming satisfied, Will Hall returned to the line. He aimed; his arrow buzzed to the target, landing far off the cloth, but still on the butt. Last came Edward Dunnes. He barely took aim before his arrow sailed through the air and almost hit a woman in the crowd. Clearly Dunnes was eliminated.

Again the archers prepared for the next round. Maxwell went first once again and placed the arrow in the same place as before. Hew did the same. One had to wonder if they had planned such a feat. If so, then indeed they were both fine bowmen. Lastly, Will Hall took to the line and just like last time took his time evaluating the butt. He released his arrow, and this time it landed a hair above Maxwell's. The oatcake she ate this morn twirled in her stomach. The Halls were out.

Will Hall waved, then left the field. A servant handed Hew and Maxwell each a cup of water. Both wiped their brows before standing at the line. The crowd shouted and encouraged their favorite.

A familiar arm looped through Audrey's. "'Tis highly exciting, is it not?" Perfectly put together in a spring green gown, Lady Francis looked as if she did not have a present worry. Hopefully that meant that Duncan was feeling better.

"How can you remain so calm? Warring Tower's future is decided this day."

The older woman stared straight ahead as if she were looking for something buried in the past. "Whatever happens, I will be content. I have shared my peace with God. It is all in His hands now."

Content. All in Warring Tower by the end of the day could be at the mercy of Rory Maxwell. His long scar seemed to pucker and whiten as concentration rested on his face. A dark glint of intolerance burrowed in his brown eyes. Like a mighty oak with crooked branches, his hatred made him strong. Rory Maxwell did not exhibit an ounce of mercy. How then could Lady Francis find contentment if such a man became her laird?

"You will see, all will work out. You must have a little faith," she whispered in Audrey's ear.

And there it was—faith. How many professed to have a faith in God yet worried about daily woes? Did not God say, "Have no fear, for I am with you." If God's words were true, then Lady Francis was right. There was nothing to worry over.

245

The sound of an arrow whirled through the air, and Maxwell hit the mark right in the middle. Audrey's heart plummeted in spite of her faith.

"'Tis fine. You shall see, Hew will split his arrow." Lady Francis squeezed Audrey's upper arm.

Hew lifted his bow, inhaled deeply, and loosed his arrow, which sailed high on the mild wind. The arrow landed far off the mark. So far that Audrey had to wonder if Hew deliberately threw the contest.

Cries of glee rang out from the Maxwell family. Rory lifted his bow high above his head and roared. Then he did the most chilling thing. His icy gaze swept over Lady Francis. Though Audrey's knees grew weak, Lady Francis's stance never wavered, nor did she look away from his frozen stare. Something was wrong, but what only these two knew.

A lad came running up and handed Lady Francis a missive. Her face shone white as she quickly read the note. "I must go. A small situation has arisen."

"Should I go with you? All will rest a bit before the next event."

Looking away, Lady Francis crushed the note in her hand. "Nay, this is nothing for you to worry about. Best you get ready for your own feat."

Lady Francis rushed away as if the ground were covered in hot ash. Audrey meant to follow, but Thomas and Blair came up wearing long faces.

"*Dinnae* look so good for the Armstrongs," Blair grumbled. "A blind man could have landed a better arrow."

"*Da* should let me run the footrace." Thomas's head hung long and low like a goose at the chopping block.

Audrey knelt down, hoping to bolster his spirits. "This will all change after the noonday meal. You shall see. The Armstrongs will have the day."

Taking Thomas's hand, Audrey walked back to the tower. All the while praying for a miracle that would grant the Armstrongs victory.

Chapter 25

Audrey nibbled offered oatcakes and couldn't even take a sip of her small beer. No matter how she tried to calm her senses, her coming event left her insides in a shamble. She laughed when Jaxon told a joke, even though his words sounded like a garbled mess. Gavin lay on his side cooing and playing with little Marcas. Every so often she would catch him looking her way, smiling. Blair flirted with any man that passed, while Thomas ran back and forth, showing off his swiftness of feet. Not one of them seemed to have a worry about the impending contest.

Except her.

The call was given for the feats to resume. Audrey said a quick prayer. *Let the dagger toss be next, O Lord. For I am not sure I can keep my wits much longer.*

Once again Hew Armstrong, Rory Maxwell, Will Hall, and Allan Dunnes shook the dice. Audrey's heart sank when the Halls won the first event call. "Wrestling," shouted Will.

Few wagers were cast on this event as Will Hall's son, Henry, was sure to win. Though not muscular, he had speed and quick moves. He'd slip through his opponents' grasps until they tired. Then like a fast wind, he would have his sorry challenger down on the ground, giving up the match. As predicted, he vanquished his foes effortlessly.

Audrey wrung her hands as Hew, Allan, and Rory rolled the dice again. Audrey's heart dropped when the Maxwells won.

"Footrace," yelled Rory. All rushed to find a good place to watch the race. Only the Maxwells, Halls, and Dunneses had runners since the Armstrongs could not find a suitable replacement for Duncan. The shout was given to start; the racers left the line.

Time dragged. Audrey paced back and forth far from the crowd, trying desperately to focus on her own event. Closing her eyes, she visualized her dagger floating through the air, then landing squarely on the cloth. Taking it one step further, she added the motions to accompany her thoughts.

"*Dinnae* try to overthink it."

Her eyes flew open to find Gavin standing in front of her. Her throat grew dry like the oatcake she had just eaten. "I-I'm just so anxious. I fear I will not succeed. And then…" She lowered her gaze to the ground, hiding her disappointment.

"Look at me, Audrey."

With effort, she pulled her gaze upward to meet his. Not a mite of doubt, dread, or defeat graced his gaze.

He gently touched her shoulder, tilting his head to the side. "Did not Paul say in Philippians, 'Be careful for nothing; but in everything by prayer and supplication with thanksgiving let your requests be made to God'?"

His words dumbfounded her. "But you claim not to

believe in God and here you are quoting scripture?"

"Even the devil knows scripture. I *dinnae* have to believe to know the words." He grinned. "But in truth, 'twas years of my mother's training that has burned such passages in my memory forever. All that matters is that you believe them."

She had trained for days. God knew her wishes and her desire to win. She was trying to fight this battle by herself instead of handing it over to God. He was so much more powerful and wiser than her. Win or lose, whatever happened would be God's will.

"Come." Gavin squeezed her shoulder. "Best to change your thinking. Let us watch the rest of the race together."

And they did, and slowly Audrey began to get caught up in the enthusiasm around her. The Maxwell lad and the Hall lad were less than a hand pace apart when they hastened across the finish line. Cheers exploded from the crowd. The Maxwells had been victorious.

Audrey's heart became numb. The feats would continue. The Halls had won the wrestling match. The Dunneses were victorious in the lang spear throw. The Maxwells had won the footrace and the archery event. The Armstrongs had won the horse race. The tie rested on her shoulders.

"Shall we proceed?" The confidence in Gavin's tone and the belief on his face spurred Audrey to the butt. Once there, he brushed a wisp of her hair from her cheek. "Worry not. This day is yours."

She wanted to throw her arms around his neck and stay in his embrace—he believed in her.

"Come now, your opponents await," his words whispered close to her ear.

Taking a deep breath, with her head held high, she strode to meet Keir Hall, Robert Dunnes, and Ewart Maxwell. Since Ualan had died, Rory had been forced to find another suitable blade thrower. The best replacement was Ewart. Or more than likely, Rory had to find an event for his son or lose face among the other families. Audrey was fairly certain Ewart could be beat. So could Robert Dunnes. Known to be fair with the blade, he was also known to like his drink, and he had consumed much at the noonday meal. It would be hard for him to keep a straight aim.

But then there was Keir Hall. Strong and masterful at dagger throwing. And more importantly, determined not to let a *wumman* win. Audrey threw her shoulders back. He would be the challenge.

"To the line," Hew Armstrong called.

Her insides jumped when he cast a cold glare her way. She dared not think what would happen if she did not win.

Then another gaze pulled her. Gavin nodded and called out, "All will be fine."

His assurance in her was humbling. He stood to lose everything, nevertheless he chose not to burden her. Oh, how she had grown to love him. He may play the cruel boar, but deep down he had great faith. He just needed the Holy Spirit to help him find it again. Before he could read her thoughts, she stepped to the line.

"All shall have three practice throws," Hew explained. "Then we begin."

Sweat streaked down her back as she watched Keir flip his dagger with his muscular arms. Each time the blade landed on the mark. Robert's aim was likewise accurate, but he took a drink of ale between each throw, causing each strike to be farther from the mark than the last. Alas there was Ewart. Constantly fiddling with his knife and glancing to his father, who stood nearby. His dagger landed wide to the left and then to the right. He looked as if he might cry.

A smile washed over Audrey's face, but then pity took hold of her soul. Did not God say, "Do unto others as you would have them do unto you." Perhaps a few wise words could make his showing with the blade a little less disastrous. She leaned over. "Clear your mind. Keep your eye on the mark. Watch the blade go from your fingers to the cloth."

Though he did not reply, his stance and demeanor spoke volumes of gratitude. The dagger left his fingers and landed firm on the mark. A shout of shock left his lips, and his mood lightened. Hew Armstrong frowned all the more.

Her own practice tosses were marginal at best. Two landing close to the mark and one directly on the center of the cloth. If she could do that twice more, then the feat would be hers.

The call was given to start. Audrey would go first. Closing her eyes, she mentally went through the motions. She said a swift prayer. *Lord, make my aim straight.*

Opening her eyes, she took a deep breath, the air smelled of leather, sweat, and unwashed bodies. The crowd seemed to move ever closer, suffocating her determination and courage. The heat of every gaze burrowed into her soul. The words she used to instruct Ewart pressed tightly into her brain. *Keep your eye on the mark. Watch the blade go from your fingers to the cloth.*

She released the dagger. It zinged to the butt, close to

the mark but not exactly on the cloth. Not a bad strike, but not perfect either. The crowd murmured as Robert Dunnes stepped forward. He barely made it to the line when he released his knife. The blade landed slightly right of the cloth. Then Keir Hall stepped up and slowly took aim. A perfect strike. The roar of voices hammered in her ears.

Several moments had passed before Ewart crept up to the line, his face etched with doubt. If he remembered her advice, he might beat her. Ewart pointed his dagger at the butt and then pulled his arm back again. Audrey's breath caught in her throat when his arm stretched out again, but he did not release the blade. The crowd began to mumble, a few goading him on. Ewart looked to his father, who impatiently crossed his arms over his chest. Once again, Ewart pointed the knife at the target, his Adam's apple bobbing with every breath. His focus fixed, the dagger left his fingertips and tumbled toward the butt, landing directly on the cloth.

"I did it." Ewart hopped and danced about before seeking his father's approval. Rory puffed out his chest with pride.

Air seeped slowly from Audrey's mouth. Did she create a foe that she could not vanquish? Robert, losing the first throw, shook Ewart's hand and walked from the field.

Now they were three. Keir being the winner went first. Once again he took his time, but just as he was ready to let go of the blade, Ewart sneezed. Though he was quick to apologize, many grumbled that it was a dirty trick. Keir's blade landed far to the left of the cloth.

Ewart ignored their complaints and marched up to the line, this time with much more confidence. To everyone's astonishment, the blade landed on the cloth again. Audrey focused on the target. The red cloth blurred in front of her. She closed her eyes to regain her focus. Slowly she opened them and the blade left her fingers, landing on top of the cloth. She had beaten Keir, but not Ewart.

Keir was not as gracious when he left the field vowing he would beat Ewart next year. Ewart ignored the threat and strutted to the line as if he had already won. Once again his blade landed effortlessly on the cloth. Shouts erupted. Thinking the feat was over, many began to congratulate the Maxwells. Some even strolled away deeming the match was over. After all, in what world would a *wumman* ever beat a man, even one as wanting as Ewart Maxwell? Already many were calling the Armstrongs fools for letting a woman partake in the feats.

But this contest wasn't over. Standing firm near the line was Gavin. A small smile sitting on his stalwart face. Even though she came as a spy, he believed in her. His fate rested in her hands.

Nay. His fate rested in God's hands. *Dear Lord, I know Gavin claims not to believe in you, but he was raised to know you. Your word says, 'Train up a child in the way they should go: and when he is old, he will not depart from it.' Lord, Gavin is your child, show him your hand in this contest so that he believes again.*

Instant calm swept through her. With a nod, she strode to the line. She pulled her dagger from its sheath once again and felt the weight of the blade in her hand. A beam of late afternoon sunlight reflected off the shiny metal, sending a wide range of colors across the ground. She wrapped her hand around the hilt of the blade and eyed the target before her. Though echoes of merrymaking reverberated from the tower and the fields, Audrey held fast her focus. With a quick flip of the wrist, she let the dagger go. *Thy will be done.*

A perfect strike. Audrey's blade stood in the middle of the cloth. A tie.

The shouts of the tie rolled through the field, and the crowd began to return. There would be another round. Audrey bobbed her head to Ewart, who turned red.

Gavin came forward and offered her a cool drink. "You have him. He's rattled. Just throw the blade straight."

Audrey took a long drink, then wiped the back of her hand across her mouth. "I shall win this."

Gavin nodded, his body brimming with assurance—in her. She couldn't let him down. With God's help, she wouldn't let him down.

Causing the tie, she would be the first to throw. Shifting her shoulders back, Audrey marched to the line. She pictured herself releasing the blade, over and over striking the cloth. She would not falter. Lifting her hand, she let loose the dagger and watched it sail to the target. Her blade hit the mark, dead center.

Roars reverberated through the Armstrong family. Someone began playing a pipe. Ewart's mouth hung open, though he quickly recovered. A few of his family members gave him an encouraging slap on the back. Rory Maxwell glared at her. All noise stopped and silence reigned when Ewart stepped to the line.

Audrey forced the rapid beat of her heart to calm. There could very well be another tie. If so, she needed to remain engrossed in her task. She needed to put her faith in God. Whatever happened was His will.

Ewart leaned forward. He took his time, weighing and

measuring every move. When the blade finally did leave his fingers, it glided slowly on the breeze. End over end, the shiny knife wheeled to the target.

Thump. The dagger landed a hair to the left of mark.

Audrey was the champion.

Sound rushed back into her ears as Gavin came and whirled her around in the air. Gently, he placed her on her feet. "You did it. I knew you would," he said, giving her a hug.

Her body began to melt into his, but then he pulled away, looking at those around them. Clearly, he did not want to compromise his or his family's future in any way.

"Forgive me for I do not wish to embarrass the lady," he said without an ounce of contrition in his voice.

She laughed. "Truly, there is little that could offend me this joyous day."

But all were not happy. Turning red like a deep wound, Rory Maxwell stomped up to Ewart. "Ye lost to a *wumman.* What kind of a man are ye?" He waved his hand in disgust before storming away.

Ewart's head drooped as the teasing intensified. Without congratulating her, he shuffled from the field.

"Though I do not care for the man, I cannot help but feel sorry for him. For the rest of his days he will be known as the man who got beat by a lass." Gavin winked.

Audrey slapped his shoulder. "I wager I could beat you too."

"No doubt." He placed a discreet kiss on her temple. "I think the day will be ours, for Fraser can throw an ax almost as well as you can throw a blade." Gavin placed another soft kiss on her lips before they strode to where the Armstrong family stood.

Unfortunately, Fraser did not share Gavin's exuberance. For he sat away from the crowd, hunched on a large rock in a slump defeat, sharpening his already whetted ax.

CHAPTER 26

"He seems a mite odd this day." Hew Armstrong watched his younger son sitting on a boulder, examining his ax.

Gavin did not gainsay his uncle's words. In truth, Fraser had not been the same for months, nor would he talk about it. The cause of his malady was buried deep inside him. "A lot weighs on his shoulders."

Hew chuckled. "The lad has been up against worse than this. 'Tis not his hide that is threatened this day. Nor the loss of his future. That be yers alone."

The words were well taken. If Fraser lost, he would return to his father's household just as he did every day of his life. Of course, what would happen once Hew died and Jaxon inherited the land? Would Jaxon want his younger brother around? Perhaps they would make the same bargain Gavin's father and Hew had made all those years ago and split the land. The brothers were close, but greed had a way of changing a man's heart.

Gavin rubbed his chin. And what of him? He stood to lose everything. His land, his home, his family. All that he held dear rested on Fraser's ability to hurl an ax.

"I shall speak to him." Gavin gave Audrey a reassuring nod and then strode to his cousin's side.

"What ye be wantin'?" Fraser barely glanced up, his gaze fixed on his gleaming ax.

"Your *da* is a little concerned. How are you feeling?"

Fraser paused his polishing. "*Dinnae* worry. I know what is at stake here," he said gruffly before returning to his task. "And I will do what's right."

What's right. This wasn't a contest of honor; it was a game of skill. Perchance Fraser wanted to make this right by winning the event.

Gavin knelt so that his gaze was level with Fraser's. "I just want you to know that whatever happens, you will always be my friend."

Again, Fraser's fingers stalled. His brow knitted, and his hands started to shake. Suddenly, he nodded, his focus locked on the ax.

Whatever tormented him would not be shared this day, but for certain someday Fraser would open up, and once again, they would be close. Gavin stood. "I look forward to having a mug of beer with you afterward."

With no acknowledgment coming from Fraser, Gavin went to Mistress Audrey's side.

"How is he?" she asked.

Gavin stroked his chin. "He's not worrying over his skill. Something else gnaws at him and has for quite some time."

"He does not like us together. And he has grown even colder since he found us..."

She spoke of the kiss and embrace Fraser had witnessed. Gavin believed the opposite was true, that

Fraser was captivated by Audrey. 'Twould explain much of his bizarre behavior as of late, though not all of it.

"I believe you search for something that is not there." Gavin motioned his head back to the butt. "Come, the call has been given. The feat will start shortly."

With strong determined strides, Fraser trod to where his competitors stood. There were only two families competing since only the Armstrongs and Maxwells won the same number of feats. By the throw of the dice the Maxwells would start, followed by the Armstrongs. Each man was strong, and each man seemed comfortable with the ax. The Maxwell man seemed determined to win, but not Fraser. His gaze darted among the crowd as if he were searching for someone.

Knowing Fraser for most of his life, Gavin had no problem interpreting the moods which rode across his cousin's face. First, he pushed his lip and chin out like he would not falter. Then his eyes clouded and his eyebrows slanted, his face filling with doubt. But most chilling was when he set his jaw, his grip white on the ax handle. If Gavin didn't know better, he would believe murder festered in Fraser's heart.

All the while Hew guffawed with Rory Maxwell as if the event meant nothing. Didn't Hew see Fraser's distress? A prick of unease wrestled for a place in Gavin's soul. Could other deals have been dealt?

He guided Audrey away from the family. "Whatever happens, I want you to make for the tower immediately."

Confusion rested in her eyes. "What do you mean? You fear something is amiss?"

"I am not sure, but something is terribly wrong here. Fraser is a puzzlement. And my uncle is too at ease."

"Is that not how all men act before a fight?" Audrey worried her lip, examining the pair.

Quite right. Bluster was a tool used to fool an enemy. But Hew and Rory seemed too familiar. Too friendly. The men parted and stood near their own families. Hew's face shone like granite as he watched Fraser.

One of Maxwell's men came up next to him and whispered into his ear. A subtle smirk settled on his lips before the man sprinted away.

Gavin could not make sense of what was happening, but his gut told him something was wrong, very wrong.

"All will be decided now," Audrey said breathlessly.

True. The future of Warring Tower rested on Fraser's ability to wield his ax. Gavin rubbed the back of his neck, then an idea occurred. "Would you say a prayer?"

Her eyes widened. "But you do not believe."

A quiver caught his lips. "Nay. But you do."

She stared at him for a moment and then nodded. Closing her eyes, she lifted her face to the daylight. "Dear Lord," she said quietly, "we know you are in control of everything. We come to you this day to stretch out your strong hand on our servant, Fraser. Give him the knowledge and ability to follow your will wherever that leads. We ask all this in your son's name who saved us all. Amen."

A peacefulness washed briefly through Gavin but was quickly replaced by a niggle of doubt. "You did not ask to have Fraser win?"

She concentrated on the butt; a shadow cloaked the side of her face. "Nay, I did not. God knows what is best for all of us, and if that is having Fraser win, then he will. And if he loses the match, then God has another plan."

If he had a crumb of her faith, then perhaps he would be the laird Warring Tower deserved. Perhaps Edlyn would still be alive. Perhaps he would truly love Thomas as a father should.

But he did not have the faith. He did not believe. No one heard his words. No one recognized his voice. No one answered his prayers. Possibly someone heard Audrey's.

Instead of taking the first throw, which was his right, Fraser offered the choice to the Maxwells. Immediately Rory ordered his man to take the throw. The lad nodded, setting his position. Aiming straight, the ax left his fingers and struck a sliver to the left of the cloth.

A heavy breath left Gavin's lungs. To win, Fraser would have to land his ax directly on the mark. If he were focused, this would not be a problem. Trouble was afoot. Instead of taking to the line, Fraser paced, then rubbed the back of his neck, all the while staring out into the yonder field as if he were looking for a ghost.

"What ails him?" Audrey asked.

"I wish I knew." Gavin searched the crowd. Fraser wasn't the only one who fidgeted. Hew looked as if he stood next to a grave of a dear friend. Rory Maxwell carried an expression of ease. As if he knew the outcome...

Fraser finally found the line. He reached out his muscular arm. The furrows in his brow melted away. With a warrior's yell, he hurled the ax. Shouts of joy filled the air. Fraser's ax struck the middle of the cloth.

Above the cheers a powerful roar of anguish sailed on the wind. "What have ye done?" Hew thundered. "Ye have given away yer birthright. May the devil take ye." Hew stomped away, leaving most of the Armstrong family flummoxed.

Audrey placed a delicate hand on Gavin's arm. "What's happening? I do not understand. Shouldn't he be cheering his son's win?"

Gavin quickly scanned the crowd; Maxwell was nowhere to be found. "I think Fraser was supposed to lose the feat."

"But why? That is foolish. He stands to gain as much as Warring Tower does."

"Maybe not." Gavin took her hand in his. "Come. Let us find Fraser."

They did not have to go far for he was surrounded by a congratulatory crowd. However, he did not look like the victor. He stood as still as his plunged ax while others slapped his back and offered him a celebratory beer.

Gavin and Audrey pushed to his side. The crowd dispersed in search of livelier company. Fraser peered at them through contrite eyes. "Ye get to keep yer tower." He took a drink and then spat the beer on the ground.

"You were told to lose the feat?" Gavin asked, already knowing the answer.

Fraser wiped his mouth. "Aye."

"But why?" Audrey gasped. "Why would your father wish you to lose? It makes no sense."

The present truth stared at Gavin from the past. "Hew made a bargain with Maxwell for a large sum of coin."

"Enough for him to buy more land from the English. Ye gave him the idea when ye cooked up yer plan." Fraser hung his head.

"Hew hates the English. Why would he buy their land?" Audrey stood wide-eyed and naïve.

Gavin sighed. She had not listened to a word he had said about lands, borders, and families. He would have to enlighten her once again. "Jaxon will inherit Hew's lands upon his death. His land is only slightly larger than mine. Not enough to sustain two brothers who wish to have families of their own someday. The land Hew wants is for Fraser. A gift he would give as soon as Truce Day ended."

Audrey placed a hand on her heart. "Oh, Fraser, you sacrificed yourself to do what is right."

Gavin wanted to wash away the sadness in her eyes. Somehow through all the intrigue and distrust she had witnessed in her life, she still believed men were basically good and would sacrifice their own needs to save others. He eyed his dejected cousin. "What changed your mind to throw away your future?"

Fraser raised his ghostly gaze to the tower, to Edlyn's chamber window. "She would have wanted me to."

It took Gavin a few moments to decipher Fraser's words. Then the truth came rushing forward. "You speak of Edlyn."

"Aye." His head fell back down to his chest.

Guilt slammed into Gavin's chest. He had always suspected there was someone else that held Edlyn's heart. Her quiet countenance and daydreaming eyes gave away her thinking. To be honest, he really didn't care whom she loved until she became pregnant. Then the thought of her bearing another man's child drove him wild. How dare she find another when he'd forgiven her past indiscretion by giving her first child his name. His wounded pride would not let him see the truth.

The awful past burned in Gavin's belly. He was the true monster. He threw her out of their chamber, forcing her to sleep with Hetta. To make matters worse, after

Marcas was born and Gavin was satisfied the child was his, he did the most unthinkable thing—he taunted her.

The memory of the night of her death tore open the old wound. They had been arguing on the battlements. The eve had been cold and rainy, a perfect omen for what was to happen. His words were ruthless and meant to cut. To hurt her as he believed she had shamed him.

"I dinnae care what you do. Take your first whelp and leave. I will happily pay your lover to take you off my hands. If he will still have you. But my child, Marcas, stays with me."

She begged and swore that she had never been with another man. Gavin knew her words were true. He had her body, but someone else consumed her heart and soul. Being selfish, he suddenly wanted all of her.

A wash of anguish gushed over Gavin, and his throat clugged. "Edlyn loved you."

Pain oozed across Fraser's face when he lifted up his head once again. "She was never unfaithful to ye, though God knows I tried to make her leave ye." His jaw grew tight, and the veins in his neck bulged. "Ye never appreciated her. Ye treated her like she was a piece of mud caked on the bottom of yer boot."

Gavin wanted to rip out his own hard heart; Fraser spoke the truth. Only a cruel cretin would have treated his wife in such a way. Though he hadn't physically pushed Edlyn from the walls above, her death rested heavy in his hands. "You are right. I should have let her go. I killed her."

Audrey gasped, and Gavin turned away from the hurt in her eyes. He had slain any chance of having a future with her. The word murderer fit him completely.

Fraser dug his hands into his hair. "Nay, ye *didnae* kill her. I saw all of it. I was there."

He saw? A coil of self-loathing tightened in Gavin's stomach. No wonder Fraser had become so distant, he had witnessed every harsh word hurled, every action of indifference. That Fraser didn't use his sword to run Gavin through was nothing short of a miracle.

"We used to meet near the large meadow where our lands touched English soil. We would just sit and talk about birds, sunsets, or anything that would suit Edlyn's fancy." Tears began to trickle down Fraser's cheeks. "Sometimes we would go fishin'." A small smile tugged at his lips. "She baited a hook poorly." Then a coldness swept over him. He glared at Gavin. "But never was she unfaithful to ye. She *widnae* even let me steal a kiss."

Gavin laid a hand on his friend's shoulder, hoping the man would slug him in the face. "I am sorry." Tears stung Gavin's eyes. "I unjustly hurt her and not a day goes by that I *dinnae* regret what I did."

"Ye *didnae* see it, but I did. Ye left her there. Alone," Fraser choked out his memory.

He had. Gavin had gone back into his chamber, slamming the door behind him. He left Edlyn at the top of the tower, the rain mixing with her own tears. *How could he have been so evil?* He swiped the moisture from his eyes.

"I saw her crawl up. Standin' there, the storm peltin' her beautiful face. I tried to get to her, but I slipped in the mud." Fraser raised a fist and banged it against his head. "She saw me lyin' there, and then she said"—his voice choked with fresh tears—"she said, 'My love, I'm comin'.'" He shook his head. "Then she jumped and landed right in front of me. There was nothin' I could do."

"Forgive me, Fraser. You *dinnae* need to—"

"The scream everyone thought was Edlyn's was really mine. Instead of stayin' by her, I got scared and ran like a coward. I went and hid near the stable."

Gavin remembered the hoarse cry that tore away his soul and tore away his faith in God. He had rushed back to where he had left Edlyn and peered over the edge, seeing her lying there, her neck twisted and bent.

"When Lady Francis come out and she saw ye standin' up there, she made up that foolish tale of Edlyn jumpin' from Hetta's chamber. I saw the anguish in yer *ma's* eyes, she believed ye killed Edlyn, and I did nothin' to change her thinkin'."

Nor had Gavin. He knew what his mother believed, and he did not try to enlighten her. In truth, he relished in her sorrow and disappointment. It was another way of punishing himself for his cruelty to his wife. He had taken Edlyn from her love, so why not sacrifice his mother's love for him? It only seemed fair.

Gavin scanned the field. Where was his mother? He had not seen her since early morn. No doubt, she was busy with feast preparations.

"I am sorry, Gavin. I should have told all what happened," Fraser whispered.

This time, Gavin embraced him and would not let go. "You have nothing to apologize for. Though I *didnae* push her off the wall, I am guilty of Edlyn's death. Will you ever forgive me?"

Fraser raised his remorseful eyes and held Gavin's wretched gaze. "We both are at fault. Me for pesterin' her to leave with me and ye for not lovin' her. We both brought sadness to her heart. And bein' a gentle soul, the pain was too great. Now in death, I *cannae* cause her pain. I *couldnae* have a hand in ye losin' ycr lands. It belongs to her sons."

Gavin nodded. "Edlyn will always live on in her sons. You have my word I will protect them with my life."

"I have one more confession." Fraser scraped his hand across his wrinkled brow. "Me *da* gave me somethin' to put in Duncan's food last eve so he *widnae* be able to run in the footrace. I am sorry. It just took me awhile to see things straight."

Gavin had suspected as much, though he believed Maxwell was responsible for the nefarious deed. "Worry not. I am sure he will recover."

"My laird, my laird. A word with ye," Blair called from behind.

Gavin rose to his feet and swung around. "What is it?"

Blair twisted and churned her raw hands in distress. "I *cannae* find Thomas. He took off when the footrace started. He wanted to run along with the runners a bit. But after the race was over, I *couldnae* find him anywhere. I searched by the butts, the hall, the courtyards, and in all the tents. I searched all the chamber rooms, the stables, the kitchen, and even the garderobe. He's nowhere, my laird. Thomas is gone."

CHAPTER 27

The strong empty hollowness Gavin had felt so often lately swept through his body and soul. He scanned the fields around him. The festivities had already begun. Men and women alike sang and danced while waving mugs of small beer and ale in the air. Soon some of the laughter and merriment would turn sour and fights would break out among the revelry. This was not the place for a young lad to be left alone. Surely Thomas was hiding somewhere.

"I told you to watch him," Gavin snapped at Blair.

The woman blanched and ducked her head as if she had been slapped.

Audrey's soft hand touched his shoulder. "Yelling at her will not help us find Thomas."

He wanted to hold and squeeze her hand forever, hoping to squash the fear building inside of him. She was right. Blaming Bair solved nothing. "I'm sorry. Thomas is a strong-willed lad. Even with me, he will go where he chooses."

Blair wiped away her tears. "I searched everywhere. 'Tis like he vanished, like a ghost."

Thomas had become artful in sneaking about, taking a

bauble here and there. Being silent like a delicate breeze so as not to be seen or heard. Gavin wanted to yank his hair out. He had no one to blame but himself. How often had he stormed about the keep shouting at Thomas for making a ruckus? That the lad had chosen not to be seen now wasn't a big surprise.

"I shall help ye look for the lad." Fraser rose to his feet. "Blair and I will search the tower again."

Gavin nodded, humbled by the help of a friend he did not deserve. "Find my mother, perhaps the lad is with her. I will call the servants to search the grounds and pavilions. He *cannae* have gone far."

Audrey's hand slipped from his shoulder. "I think I know where he is."

The brightness in her eyes gave Gavin hope. "Where? I shall go with you."

Quickly he instructed his servants and was further warmed by those of other families that wished to help. Calls for Thomas rang out from the multitudes, echoing across the landscape as Audrey and Gavin slipped into the countryside.

She took his hand and led him through the tall grass. "Thomas has a secret hiding spot where he keeps all the treasures he has taken or found. It is his place of refuge."

In such a short time, Audrey had gained the lad's trust and knew his habits. To Gavin, the lad remained mostly a stranger. Only a pathetic parent would know so little about his own child.

"He might be there. He was awfully upset you would not let him run in the race," she said hopefully.

They stopped along the water's edge near a field of boulders. There was no sign of Thomas. Every spot that

Audrey claimed held a treasure had been undisturbed for some time. 'Twas apparent the lad had not been there.

Bewilderment filled her face. "Where could he be?"

Where had Thomas gone? The rest of the afternoon and into the evening everyone continued the search. Exhaustion gave way, and many lay down and took their rest, but not Gavin. He rode the marches all night long and did not stop until the black night faded into the golden rays of morning.

Shoulders slumped, he jerked back and forth on his mount. Defeat plagued his soul, and his hope of finding Thomas plummeted. For years he had been pushing the lad away. And for what purpose? The truth Gavin had been trying to erase whispered in his ears—*because you didn't want to love the lad.* But he had failed, for his love for Thomas was deep. The love lived in his mind, heart, and soul. And there lay the problem. Gavin could not find his son to tell him.

Far from the tower, Gavin slipped off his horse and fell to his knees. He folded his hands and wept. Then he did something he had not done since before Edlyn's death, he raised his tear-soaked eyes to the heavens.

"Dear Lord, though I denied your presence, I know you are there. I know I have put my own will above yours. I am heartily sorry for doing so. I am sorry for the way I have treated others. Forgive me, Lord. I know I *havenae* always been a good father. I have often thought to discard one son in favor of another son, but I beg you, please help me find Thomas. Let me know that he is well. I know with you all things are possible. I place his and my future in your hands. Amen."

A rush of peace momentarily pushed away his despair

and filled the emptiness in his chest. Now all was left up to God. On foot, Gavin led his tired horse back to the tower. He had barely crossed the entry when Audrey and Fraser came running toward him.

"We were worried something happened to you." In her hand she clutched a missive. "This came for you while you were out searching."

Her hand shook as she held out the parchment. Gavin didn't have to read the words to know what was in them. "Who has him?"

"Maxwell and he wants you to honor the terms of your last agreement or he will deliver Thomas to Mary de Guise."

So Hetta had told Maxwell about Thomas's parentage. There was naught for him to do but comply and pray that his son would be returned once he gave up Warring Tower.

Fraser scratched his head. "I think Maxwell has a crack in his head, for why would he take Thomas to Mary de Guise? What would the dowager queen want with the lad?"

Gavin cast a glance at Audrey before crumpling the missive in his hand. Sooner or later the truth would come out. If Queen Elizabeth was truly married and Thomas was the legitimate heir to the English throne, then Queen Elizabeth would do anything to ensure his safety. Even form an army to take control of Scotland.

"It matters not his reasoning. I am turning over the tower to get Thomas back." Gavin started walking toward the stable.

Fraser reached out and grabbed Gavin's arm. "There is one more thing," he whispered. "Yer mother is missin'."

"No one has seen her since yesterday morn,'" Audrey continued.

Now he remembered. She had not been seen since the archery feat. At the time Gavin thought someone else had fallen ill and sought his mother's healing skills. Or that she was preparing for the later festivities. Had she been kidnapped too? The ransom note didn't mention her.

A slither of apprehension weaved through Gavin's gut. Could Hew have her? After all, he had made a bargain with Maxwell. But if they had Thomas, why would they need his mother?

Gavin played the events of the past few weeks over and over in his head. His mother had been exceptionally friendly with Hew when he was here. And had not Rory specifically ordered Ualan and Ewart not to harm his mother when he went to the papist meeting? An unbearable idea slithered through his brain like a serpent in search of its prey. Could his mother be in league with his uncle and Maxwell?

His chest squeezed with loss. Would no one stand by his side? *And why should they?* Had he not nettled and chastised his mother for her English ways and her coddling of Thomas? Had he not stomped around Warring Tower shouting at anyone who would not do his bidding? Had he not pushed away all those who ever cared about him?

He had done all those things. He had been a big, brash boar. Then it might be possible that his mother would join the enemy.

"We will find them both," Audrey said softly, clearly seeing the defeat in his manner. Why she stayed with him, he did not know.

"Aye," encouraged Fraser. "We will figure a way to foil Maxwell's plot."

Overwhelmed by the support from those he had hurt the most, Gavin shook his head. "Nay. Maxwell has won. He can have my lands. All I want is my son back. And as for my mother... I am certain we will hear from her in due time."

Again, Gavin started toward the stables. But he did not get far when Blair came running from the tower. "Laird Armstrong, a word please."

Now what? Could they not see that time was of the essence? He inhaled a patient breath, giving her his attention. "What do you want?"

"I think ye should come to the scullery, there's somethin' ye need to see."

"Can it not wait? I need to get Thomas back."

Blair flipped her long braid over her shoulder. "I agree. And what lays in the scullery might aid ye."

Her cryptic words intrigued him and invigorated Audrey's and Fraser's interests as well. "Then by all means lead on, Mistress Blair."

What they discovered in the scullery did indeed change Gavin's course. There lay Ewart among the pots and rubbish, sleeping like a babe.

"What have we here?" Fraser said, tossing a bucket of water over Ewart's face.

The man sputtered and raised a hand. "Leave off. I ain't ready to wake."

Gavin kicked Ewart in the shin. "Get up. We have some questions that need answers."

Ewart finally shook his head and sat up, staring bleary-eyed and blankly, swaying to and fro. "What about?"

"Where did your father take Thomas?" Gavin barked.

Putting a hand to his forehead, Ewart placed his other hand on the floor to hold his position. "What ye mean? What care I about yer whelp? I come straight to the hall after I lost the blade toss."

Either Ewart hid the truth with a foggy head or he was being honest. "Are you saying you knew naught of your father's plan?" Gavin asked.

"I know that he and Hew Armstrong were cookin' up a brew of trouble for ye. But what that trouble be, I know not."

"Well, I know what to do," Fraser said, hauling Ewart to his feet. In a flash, Fraser pulled out his dagger and cut off a piece of Ewart's hair and a bit of fabric from his shirt. "Get some parchment Mistress Audrey, Gavin needs to send Maxwell a message."

Once the messenger had been sent, Gavin closed the gate and reinforced the entrance. He wasn't fool enough to believe Maxwell would willingly make the trade. There was naught they could do but wait and pray that God would be merciful.

They waited another full day, but no word came from Maxwell. Would he come for his son, or would he let him rot in Warring Tower's cells? The pavilions that scattered the field the day before were gone. A dark mood had descended on the keep as all waited to see what would happen.

Besides all of this, his mother was still missing. Some feared she was dead while others claimed she left with an English lord. Neither scenario could be proven, but if his mother did leave of her own accord, she left all her belongings behind, which would be unusual since she was so attached to them. No, Gavin was certain her leaving had not been planned. Wherever she was, he hoped she was safe.

The next morning's coolness gave way to midday's heat when a shout from a moss-trooper sent Gavin, Audrey, and Fraser to the battlements. As if rising out of the hills came Maxwell and a massive army on horseback.

None of this surprised Gavin. Even if it cost Ewart his life, Maxwell would fight. What cut Gavin to the heart was the sight of Thomas sitting in front of Maxwell like a shield.

The man truly crawled out of Satan's pit. Maxwell cared nothing for his own kin or the life of a young child. A demon drove him. Nonetheless, Gavin planned to sacrifice his life to the beast to save his son.

"We're goin' to be havin' a grand fight." Fraser beamed and raised his ax. "Whatever happens, I want ye to know I never meant to fall in love with Edlyn."

Gavin grabbed the back of his friend's neck, giving it a gentle squeeze. "We *cannae* control where our heart goes." His gaze glided briefly to Audrey. "Promise me you will look after her. Get her back to her family."

Fraser wrinkled his brow. "If that's what ye wish, but surely ye can..." His words drifted away as understanding dawned in his eyes.

The interaction had not been lost on Audrey. "What are you planning to do?"

"I aim to stop the bloodshed. 'Tis not only the land that Maxwell wants. He wants my head for killing Ualan." Gavin took her hands and kissed them.

She fell into his arms. "Do not do this. Surely there is another way?"

He stepped back and placed his hand against her cheek. "Go home, Audrey. Go home and marry a man who will love and protect you. Who can give you a brood of children." He kissed her gently, tasting her bittersweet tears. His lips lingered, capturing her goodness, her kindness, her devotion, and one more thing...

"I love you," she cried.

Ah, there it was, and he loved her. But that was not the last memory he wanted her to have of him. He wanted her life to be merry and complete. Free from him.

He touched her forehead with his. "More the pity for you," he whispered. She flinched, and his words tortured his own heart more deeply than she would ever know. He then pulled away and grabbed his sword, calling for the gate to be opened.

Chapter 28

God protect him! Audrey tried to run after Gavin when a hand snaked out and circled her wrist.

"Ye *dinnae* want to do that. He's doin' what is best for all." Though Fraser's words were true, she didn't want to hear them.

"They'll kill him before he has a chance to speak." Even if Gavin did not love her, she couldn't just watch him die.

"Possibly, but Maxwell is a proud man, and I am guessin' he will accept Gavin's challenge."

Gavin strode from the tower gate and raised a hand. "Maxwell. Let us settle this like men of honor. Fight me. If you win, you can have my lands and my life."

Audrey shuddered, fearing any moment an arrow would pierce Gavin's heart. She fought against Fraser's hold. "Let me go to him, please."

"Ye *cannae*. If ye go runnin' out there, all will be lost for sure. He needs to know ye are safe."

She wanted to smack Fraser, but no matter what punishment she would inflict on him, she knew he would not release her.

Maxwell guided his mount forward while Thomas

squirmed in front of him. "I could have all those things by this eve and yer skin. What need do I have to accept yer challenge?"

"Think, what will your prize be? A burnt-out tower and trampled crops. Plus, the responsibility of more mouths to feed and little means to do it. Your fight is with me. Let Thomas go or your son will die as well." Gavin stepped closer.

"Where is Ewart?" Maxwell demanded, backing up his horse. "I want to see that the lad is all right."

"He is in the cells, ye flamin' coward," Fraser shouted from above. "And there he's goin' to stay."

Even from where she stood, Audrey knew Maxwell bubbled with rage. "What are you doing?" she whispered. "The man is wild enough."

"Ah, just tryin' to move things along a bit." Fraser grinned before he spat on the ground.

"Get Ewart," Gavin called out.

Fraser handed Audrey over to another moss-trooper and took off, thumping down the stairs like a mad cow. Before her mind cleared, Fraser dragged a chained, beaten Ewart to the gate. "Here he is, ye horse's dung. Here's yer snivelin' son."

Ewart sobbed, slobbered, and sniffed. Like a dog, strings of drool hung from the corners of his bruised mouth. Rory puffed out his scarlet cheeks. "Stop yer cryin'. Yer a Maxwell!"

The sight of Ewart had pushed Maxwell into agreement. He called for one of his men to take Thomas. Once done, Maxwell got off his horse and drew his sword.

Audrey's breath froze in her chest, and her heart began to sink to the far recesses of her stomach. Rory Maxwell had murder in his eyes, and he would not stop until Gavin lay bloody and dead.

Breaking free from the moss-trooper's hold, Audrey sunk down behind the battlement wall, unable to see what would soon transpire. *What could she do?* The clanging of swords thundered in her ears. *What could she do?* Maxwell's roars swallowed up her mind leaving it black and blank. *What could she do?*

Pray. The single word cut through the ringing of sharp metal against metal. Pierced through the groans and moans coming from outside the tower walls. *She could pray.* Bowing her head and clasping her hands against her chest she began.

Dear Lord, I know Gavin has not always been a man of peace or a follower of your ways, but now he plans to give his life to save others. To save Thomas and those of Warring Tower. I know you do not condone bloodshed. Please find a peaceful way to end this conflict. Thy will be done. I ask all this in your son's name. Amen.

"Well, would you look at that," one of the moss-troopers said, pointing above the wall.

The grunts and clanging of a sword fight stopped, and the rumbling of the earth drew Audrey to her feet. There on a rolling hill south of Warring Tower sat at least twenty-five or more horses. They carried no markings of a family or colors of a country.

Maxwell and Gavin paused their fighting and gazed at the riders on the hill. 'Twas then that two horses broke the rank and galloped toward them. One a man with grey hair, wearing a brown leather doublet and black breeches. The other a woman who was familiar to all—Lady Francis. What turn of events was this? The closer the pair got,

Audrey recognized the man as well. Sir Walter Pimberly, Lady Francis's cousin and an agent for Queen Elizabeth. The pair rode between Maxwell and Gavin before stopping.

Terror should be coursing through Audrey's veins, but it didn't. Her heart exploded with joy. God had stopped the fight, at least for now. She sent up a quick prayer of thanksgiving as she raced down the tower steps and out of the keep to come to stand at Gavin's side. Whatever her fate, God had seen fit to save Gavin and Thomas. Nothing else mattered.

Regrettably, Gavin did not seem as pleased when he saw his mother. In fact, he greeted her with open hostility. "Where have you been?" he shouted, his knuckles white on his sword. "We were all afraid something terrible happened to you."

Lady Francis steadied her mount as her thin veil flapped in the early eve breeze. "I had something to take care of."

"'Tis wonderful to see you again, Laird Warring. I remember you as a lad," Lord Pimberly injected.

His polite manners were met with Gavin's scowl. "I know why you are here, Pimberly. Tell the qu—"

Sir Pimberly coughed, sending out a warning look.

Gavin gritted his teeth. "Mistress Pittman she can't have my son."

"God's bones," Maxwell shouted. "Do you mean the English qu—"

Again, Pimberly let out a horrific hack.

"Go back from where you came and tell the witch she will never be welcomed in Scotland." Maxwell raised his sword as if he were ready to run Sir Pimberly through.

"Hold, Rory," Lady Francis warned sweetly. "Unless you plan on making another foolhardy mistake as you did years ago."

Maxwell stalled and slowly lowered his weapon, a look of respectful penance on his face.

"We need to speak in a civil manner or all will be lost for both of our families." Lady Francis swiveled her attention to the men on the hill. "First, you must let go of Thomas. Then, you must send your men away."

Maxwell frowned. "Why should I do—"

"Stop being so stubborn. Let my grandson go and send the others away. Then come into the tower. All will be explained there." Lady Francis brooked no argument. "It is that or a large army will attack. Are you prepared to meet them?"

"I *dinnae* believe ye." Maxwell held his stance fast.

"All right, come, see for yourself." Pimberly sniffed. "I assure you, Lady Francis does not jest."

Maxwell's tongue slid across his teeth. "Methinks this is a trap to lure me away from my men."

"My word, you are thick," Lady Francis scolded. "We are trying to *save* your life."

Rubbing his jaw with his free hand, Maxwell's gaze traveled over Lady Francis. "I have a better idea." Maxwell went to his horse and motioned the guard to give him Thomas.

Gavin stepped forward. "Return my son."

"In due time if what Lady Francis and this Englishman says is true. Right now yer son and *ma* are goin' with me to see how many stand against us. The Englishman will stay here. If somethin' happens to me, my men will gut him where he stands." Rory's men laughed.

Lady Francis nudged her horse closer to Maxwell's. "Very well, but do not try anything, for if you plan to harm me or my grandson, I can assure you, you will incur the wrath of the most powerful."

"Quit the dramatics, Francis. I give my word. Let us get this over with. I have yer son to kill this day."

The three of them rode over the hill while Sir Pimberly and the rest of his men kept watch over the others.

"We could retire to the hall," Audrey offered, hoping that Sir Pimberly would jump at her suggestion.

Gavin slowly shook his head. "Nay, we wait here. I have no desire on letting any of Maxwell's men into Warring Tower."

Pimberly dismounted. "This could take some time. Though I have to say our timing is quite remarkable. With your Truce Day festivities going on, our entourage literally marched right up to the edge of your lands undetected."

All present seemed to view Sir Pimberly's words with skepticism. Quite possibly the English families knew something was afoot. 'Twould be another reason they left with haste yesterday morn. Audrey sat down, and Maxwell's men dismounted. No one was going anywhere.

The afternoon sun faded in the sky, and the winds turned cool. The sky became dark, and the smell of rain filled the air. Still, the trio had not returned. Maxwell's men were starting to grumble that some ill had befallen their laird. Those on the hill still held their position, though they, too, had left their horses preferring to stand.

Just when Gavin called for torches, two familiar horses appeared and immediately all became alert. Maxwell stopped his horse in front of Gavin, handing Thomas over.

"Half of the English army lay there. We best get ready. Methinks there might be a fight," Maxwell said.

Gavin ignored the man and hugged his son. Audrey's heart leapt at the tender scene.

"There, there, Thomas. You are safe now," Gavin's soft voice floated on the wind.

Thomas's narrow shoulders shook as he wept against his father's chest. "Yer not mad at me?"

Gavin softened his hold and swept back the curls that had fallen into the boy's eyes. "Nay. How can I? I love you."

Audrey's heart sang as she gave thanksgiving to God.

"I only wanted to run the race. They came out of nowhere," Thomas said, sniffing back his tears.

"I know." Gavin kissed the top of his son's head. "Now go quickly to your chamber and wait there with your nurse."

Thomas didn't have to be told twice. He ran right past Audrey and through the gate as if fire nipped at his heels. She wanted to follow, but her legs felt like ice. A gentle hand on her shoulder began the thaw.

"Audrey," Gavin whispered, "I think it is best we go inside too." Solemnly, he took her hand and led her into the keep. She inhaled his warm leathery scent, hoping it would soothe her troubling soul, for after this day, she wasn't certain she would ever see Gavin again.

In less time than it takes for sand to go through an hourglass, all of importance were situated in the hall. The rest of the servants returned to their homes, and the guards were kept at bay outside in the courtyard or the fields around the tower.

Inside the hall an uncomfortable silence reigned. Gavin, Audrey, and Fraser stood on one side of the room while Maxwell and Ewart stood on the other. Sir Pimberly and Gavin's mother stood in the middle like a wall between two warring countries.

"So," Gavin said sternly, facing his mother, "you are the queen's other agent."

A stab of guilt pierced Audrey's chest. Though Gavin had forgiven her, he had not forgotten, and never would, that she too had been a spy.

Lady Francis flapped her arms at her sides and sighed. "Gavin, 'tis not what you think."

His whole body tightened like a taut rope. He said not a word, nor would he look in her direction.

Maxwell shook his head. "I know Ian was not much of a husband, but I never would have believed ye would have betrayed yer own kin." He waved to Sir Pimberly. "What I saw and this skinny runt here proves ye prefer the English. What has become of ye, Francis?"

Gavin pulled out his sword and pointed the tip of the blade at Maxwell. "How dare you be so familiar to my mother."

With a fierce yell, Maxwell slid his sword from its sheath and charged forward. Sir Pimberly grabbed Lady Francis's arm and pulled her out of the way. Swinging their swords left and then right, Gavin and Maxwell continued the battle they had started on the fields.

Icy tendrils twisted through Audrey's insides. What was wrong with them? Queen Elizabeth's army sat outside their door, and all these two could think about was their hatred for one another.

They kept on striking blow for blow. Audrey clutched her chest as she watched Gavin's footing slip under the mesmerizing power of hurt and betrayal. He fought with his heart while Maxwell fought with his head.

Lady Francis fell to her knees, tears pouring forth. "Please. Please you...do not...understand..."

Audrey tried to rush forward, but Fraser circled her waist with his arm. "They are in a blood lust. They will not stop until one of them falls."

As she feared. In such a state, Gavin would tire first and Maxwell would give the final blow. "Let me go." She wrestled against Fraser's chest. "He'll kill Gavin."

Dear Lord, please place your vast hand between them. Only you have the power to prevent this madness.

But God seemed so far away. What if He didn't want this to stop? What if He wanted Gavin to die?

Her lungs squeezed for air. Her breath became short. The room floated away. Nay. She would not faint. She would fight. Pushing out her chest to fill her lungs, she stomped on Fraser's foot. He let out a howl, releasing his hold.

Just as she tried to rush forward, a young boy raced in front of her and stood between the fighting duo, a barking dog at his heels.

From the doorway, a cool mist seeped in, twirling up the stairs. Like a specter stepping into the human world, a woman draped in a black veil and ebony gown stepped out of the shadows. Flanked by her dark ghastly demons.

"Stop this at once," she cried.

Her guards rushed forward, their swords drawn. In the middle stood Thomas. "It's gone. Someone stole it. God *didnae* protect my ring," he wailed.

Gavin's and Maxwell's swords locked together above the boy's head. The fever fled from their eyes. Audrey's knees buckled. *Thank you, God.*

CHAPTER 29

Just when Gavin could not carry on, Thomas's auburn head lay right below Maxwell's sword. Bairn barked and nipped at the man's heels. Gavin blocked the blade's descent with the strength of a titan. His arms shook, and his back muscles burned, but he would not give way, not until he saw the fury leave Maxwell's eyes.

"Get away from me *dug.*" Maxwell kicked Bairn and then realized who he tried to protect. "By the Holy Mother," the elder laird cried at Thomas. "I could have killed ye." Maxwell dropped his sword.

The woman in black all but floated into the room and came to a stop next to the fighting men. Mist-damp droplets spotted her long veil. Her guards' sharp-pointed swords were aimed at his and Maxwell's chest.

"Take all their weapons." Upon her command, her men picked up the swords and took their daggers from their belts. They then took away Fraser's and Ewart's arms as well until none but the veiled woman's guard held a blade. When satisfied, she continued, "Now then. What nonsense is this?"

Audrey paled while Gavin had a pretty good idea who stood before them. Maxwell scrubbed his straggly beard.

"Beggin' yer pardon, but just who the blazes are ye to be tellin' us what to do?"

Pimberly stepped forward on weak knees. "Allow me to introduce, Laird Maxwell, Laird Armstrong, and Mistress Hayes. This is Mistress Pittman." He paused and stared at Ewart. "And I believe this is Laird Maxwell's heir."

A moment of excitement sizzled through Gavin. Never had he expected the queen to make an appearance in Scotland. 'Twas a risk. And well she knew it. Thus the disguise. He assumed her entourage still sat on the English side of the border, but he wondered how long it would remain there.

Gavin bowed sightly while all the others remained stiff as sticks. "My lady, perhaps you would like to sit by the fire?"

Her veil swished as she swiveled her head to the warm hearth. "Aye. What a splendid idea. I am not accustomed to traveling at night."

Quite so. Once Mistress Pittman took her seat, she raised her veil. She sent a look of censure to those who recognized her.

Maxwell's eyes narrowed. "Ye have an air of a—"

"Perhaps it would be best if Laird Maxwell and his son would retire?" Pimberly interjected.

Queen Elizabeth shook her head. "Think on it, Walter. He is no fool. 'Twill not take him long to figure out what goes here. Nay, he stays where I can keep an eye on him."

Thomas thumped to Gavin's side and placed his fists on his hips. "Me ring is missin', and I wager he took it." He pointed at Ewart.

"Me," Ewart croaked, shaking like a newborn lamb. "I *dinnae* even know what the lad speaks of."

"I saw you. I saw you sneakin' around the chapel before the feats started." Thomas raised a fist. "Give it back."

The queen's perusal went from Thomas to Ewart and then back to Thomas. Maxwell and Bairn both growled and glared at Ewart.

Seeing his father's reaction, Ewart rallied and stood up straight and proud like a Maxwell should. "I was lookin' for Mistress Blair, not for yer stupid ring."

"I want me ring!" Then Thomas rushed at Ewart, but Gavin quickly grabbed him by the back of his tunic before a punch landed in Ewart's stomach.

"What goes on here?" Queen Elizabeth asked while glaring at Ewart.

Gavin had the same question. What ring had the lad possessed? Searching the room, he found who held the answer—his mother and Audrey.

Before he could seek answers, Audrey came forward and gently knelt next to Thomas, facing the queen. "All this is my fault. I discovered what I believed to be a safe hiding place for Thomas's mother's ring, but apparently I was in error."

Mother's ring. Did she speak of Edlyn's ring? The one he had absentmindedly thrown away? Or had he? Gavin glared at Thomas. All knew the lad was a thief, taking objects from the keep and the tenants as well. Apparently, he had absconded with Edlyn's ring.

"I just want it back." Thomas's shoulders became rigid. His fists tight as his side. "Make him give it back to me, *Da*. Or I will."

Gavin's heart lurched. Soon the lad would be a fierce warrior. If possible, he'd give his son so much more than that insignificant ring.

"Hush, son. We will find the ring," he soothed.

"Would someone tell me what this is all about? Does anyone know the whereabouts of this piece of jewelry so that we can get unto things of more importance?" Queen Elizabeth asked, penetrating every face in the room with her stiff glare. "Well?"

Bairn bound up to the queen and plopped his head in her lap and whined.

The queen threw her hands in the air. "Good heavens."

"He wants you to stroke his head," Thomas said, coming to her chair. "Like this." Thomas started petting Bairn.

The queen delicately rested her finger on the animal's head, ignoring the drool dripping down her gown. "So this is your dog?"

"His name is Bairn. I bet if he could talk, he would tell me where me ring is." Thomas pursed his lips and let out a sad sigh.

Elizabeth wrinkled her nose and swept the room with a look of indignation. "No one here knows where this boy's ring is?" she asked incredulously.

Gavin's mother crept forward. Her eyes averted. "I know," she said barely above a whisper.

Astonishment flickered in Audrey's eyes as she rose. "I don't understand. You were the one to show me the hiding place. Why would you remove the ring?"

"I feared someone else would discover where it was hidden during the feats, and I couldn't bear it being lost again." Gavin's mother looked pleadingly at Thomas. "It is safe. I will fetch the ring from my chamber."

"Please do," Queen Elizabeth ordered. "For I, too, would like to examine this prize possession."

291

"It's mine," Thomas spat out, clearly fearing he might lose it again.

The queen lifted a slim eyebrow. "Indeed, sir. But surely I can have a quick peek?"

The scowl on Thomas's face did not speak of charity. Gavin stepped forward and bent down to whisper into his son's ear. "It would not hurt to show a little kindness."

Thomas poured a pout on his lips. "Will you make sure she gives it back?"

"Aye. I promise." Gavin put a hand across his heart.

Thomas folded his arms over his chest, took a firm stance, and resolutely held the queen's gaze. "All right, ye can look at it, but only for a little while."

Her cheeks quirked up. She looked to one of her guards. "Accompany Lady Francis to her chamber."

So silent was the hall, if one tried, you could hear the dust settle on the benches. The queen continued to stroke Bairn's head, assessing every fiber of Thomas's appearance and mannerisms. Her face softened; she must be pleased with the lad. Though she claimed Thomas by blood, Gavin had every intention of fighting for the lad as a father should. But both knew the fight would not take place in his son's presence.

Gavin had not taken in more than a handful of breaths when his mother came down the stairs carrying the ring.

Thomas rushed toward his gran, snatching the jewel from her fingers. "That's it. That's me ring."

The blue stone caught the sparkle of the afternoon sunlight streaming through the windows. Fractures of color danced off the walls and seemed to make Thomas's copper eyes glow. Suddenly the radiance disappeared when he clutched the ring tightly in his fist.

"Come, boy. I wish to see your ring." Queen Elizabeth leaned forward, but Thomas was having none of it. He pulled his hands to his chest.

Gavin cleared his throat. "A promise made must be kept."

"I *didnae* make no promise." Thomas curled his lips in, knowing that wasn't really true. "I just said she could peek at it."

"Well then. Show her," Gavin said sternly.

The queen pushed the dog's head off her lap. Thomas shuffled closer like a turtle crossing a path. Finally, he stood less than a hand from the queen's skirts. "Only a peek," Thomas warned.

Not one readable reaction crossed the queen's face. "Boy, I hold to my promises." She stretched out her hand.

Thomas glanced down at the ring he closely guarded and then up at the queen, assessing her as if she was a villain, then he turned to Audrey. "What do ye think? Is she trustworthy?"

Taking a sharp breath, a bubble of air lodged in Gavin's throat. He should have taken more interest in his son's education and how to address his betters.

But the queen let out a minute chuckle and dropped her hand to her side. When recovered, she tipped her head toward Audrey. "Well, Mistress Hayes, is my word right and true?"

"Of course, Your..."

The queen lifted a brow.

"Mistress Pittman," Audrey corrected. "Thomas, 'tis not polite to judge a lady's character."

"Why ever not? Everyone questions mine." Thomas set his jaw.

A howl of laughter escaped the queen's lips, and Bairn

joined in barking. She pushed out of her chair and knelt down until her eyes were even with Thomas's. "What a delightful child you are. I will let you in on a secret. Everyone questions mine too, they just do not have the courage to say it to my face."

"Me *da* says ye should always be forthright."

Now the lad remembers his lessons. Gavin resisted the urge to clear his throat again.

Queen Elizabeth pinned him with a glare. "Ah."

Thomas nodded.

"Then I look forward to having a forthright conversation with him very soon." Her temperament eased as she focused on Thomas. "Now then. May I have a look?"

Thomas twisted his lips into a pout and dropped the ring into Queen Elizabeth's hand. She rose and held the jewelry to the light. "The blue stone is exquisite. Sapphire. And these markings. The head of a horse on one side and bluebells on the other. Most interesting."

"Hey now," Maxwell piped up, stepping forward. "That be the ring I…"

"Yes?" Queen Elizabeth asked with a look that challenged his interruption.

Maxwell stalled and stared at Gavin's mother. Tears began to form in her eyes as some unknown knowledge passed between the pair.

Gavin's mother dabbed at her eyes. "Please. I can explain, but not in front of the boy…and some of the rest."

Foreboding seeped through the hall like a fine mist creeps across the lowlands. Gavin swore a sinister scheme slid between the couple. Had she lied when she said the ring was given to her by his father? At that very moment, he realized he did not know his mother at all.

But the queen did. She handed the ring back to Thomas. "Thank you for giving me a look. Perchance later you will let me look upon it a little more?"

Thomas snatched the ring and shrugged.

"Right." Fraser stepped forward. "I'm expectin' ye will want me gone too." He held out his hand to Thomas. "Come along, lad. Methinks there be some sweet tarts in the kitchens." Bairn perked up too and followed the pair.

"I will go with them," Audrey offered.

"Nay," the queen said as Gavin's mother cut off Audrey's retreat. "If I am right…then this concerns you also."

If she were right? What secret between Maxwell and his mother would be of importance to Audrey?

Her eyes burned with curiosity. But she was not alone, for he too wondered about the mystery of the ring.

Ewart slapped and rubbed his hands together. "This is goin' be quite interestin'."

Both Gavin's mother and Maxwell blanched.

"Nay, lad. This is not for your ears either. Go wait in the courtyard with the others," Maxwell ordered.

"But *she* gets to stay." Ewart pointed a long narrow finger at Audrey. "And she *isnae* part of anyone's family."

Audrey blushed, clearly agreeing with Ewart. However, Maxwell would not back down, and Ewart was ushered to the doorway by one of the queen's guard.

The queen glared at Pimberly until he understood her wishes. "I think I shall accompany our guest to the courtyard as well." He bowed and quit the room.

When they stood alone in the hall, the queen lifted her chin. "Well. Out with it. What is the great secret about this ring?"

Gavin's mother clutched her hands and scanned the large room. "My lady. This is a private matter. Nothing I am sure that would interest you."

"Are you dismissing me?" Queen Elizabeth rose to her full height. "Methinks what you have to say might be part of the reason I had to drag half my..." She paused. "Entertain me nonetheless."

Gavin's mother looked to the stairs and at the guards. "Surely there is a more intimate place? For I fear the walls have ears."

The queen let out a huff. "I will cut off any of those ears and lop off their tongues too if they deem to hear and tell."

Her words did not seem to quell his mother's worry as the color drained from her face and her body began to shake.

Gavin stepped forward to take hold of his mother's arm. "Do you need to sit down?"

She shook her head, dropping her chin to her chest.

"Oh, all right." Queen Elizabeth took a heavy breath at the other woman's hysterics. "Where, Lady Francis, do you propose we go?"

Gavin's mother raised her chin. "If you please, the chapel, Your... Mistress Pittman."

Queen Elizabeth rolled eyes. "Where is this chapel?"

It did not take long to assemble their small group. A chair was brought in for the queen while the others stood in a half circle around her. Even though the stone chapel was cool, Gavin's back dripped with sweat, and he was not alone. Dots of prescription rested on Maxwell's forehead, while moisture graced his mother's upper lip. Audrey took a piece of linen and wiped her damp neck. The only one who seemed fresh and bright like spring meadow flowers was Queen Elizabeth. Once seated, she adjusted her gown before resting her hands on the arms of the chair.

Maxwell raised a finger, dawning resting on his face. "I know who ye are."

Gavin almost laughed. So like a Maxwell, slow to figure things out.

"Then you best keep your thoughts to yourself." The queen glared at the old Scotsman with reproach.

His gaze darted around the room. "'Tis true then. The wee lad be yer bastard?"

"I have no idea what you are talking about. I am just here to visit friends, and well you should remember that as my guards are entertaining *your* son in the courtyard." She turned her attention to the others. "Now then. Shall we proceed? What is the story behind this ring?"

Maxwell itched the crooked scar on his face. Wisely he did not seek to push the issue of Thomas's parentage. "'Tis a tale Francis and I promised never to speak of again."

Francis! Gavin's jaw slacked. Just how well did his mother know this man? When this was all over, and if Maxwell still drew breath, Gavin vowed...his anger stalled. Years ago, when he was a lad, Fraser and he had gotten into a fist fight. So furious, he had been ready to bash Fraser's face in. A traveling priest had come upon them and broke up the fight, correcting them with scriptural words. Before losing his faith, Gavin had recited those words often whenever his anger flared or he was ready to punch another. When he turned his back on God, he had forgotten those words. Now with his faith renewed, they rang loudly in his ears.

For all they that take the sword shall perish with the sword.

He had almost forgotten the phrase. Thankfully, the Lord had reminded him. Gavin closed his eyes, digging deep for calm.

His mother put a hand on Maxwell's arm and gave it a squeeze, then she stepped closer to the queen. "I was very young when I was married, and 'twas no secret, the marriage was not forged in love."

"Few are," Queen Elizabeth dryly interjected.

"Quite so. Nonetheless, I was ready to fulfill my duties and produce an heir for Ian Armstrong." Her voice filled with sorrow. Gavin answered her sadness by crossing his arms over his chest. "But the years rolled on, and no child came. I believed I was barren. In his disappointment, Ian took his affections elsewhere. I was certain he would have our marriage annulled as soon as he found a more suitable wife."

With every word she uttered, Gavin swore another new line creased his mother's face. How he wanted to stroke every single mark away, for he was certain his antics had created many of them.

To his surprise, Maxwell came forward and continued the story. "Ian and I were good friends in our youth, even though we came from different families. I *cannae* tell ye how jealous I was when he married one of the most beautiful *wummin* I had ever seen. But I wished them well."

"Yes, yes, this is all well and good, but what does this have to do with the ring?" the queen asked.

For as long as Gavin could remember, his father had always hated Rory Maxwell. A string of curses would roll out of Ian Armstrong's mouth whenever the Maxwell name was mentioned. What then broke up this friendship?

"We are gettin' to that," Maxwell snapped.

Queen Elizabeth bristled at his tone. "Then by all means, sir. Quicken your tale."

Maxwell rubbed a hand across his mouth. "Ian never appreciated his beautiful wife. A week after he was wed, I saw him dallying with any maid who would look his way. It angered me, but I held my tongue. He was my friend after all. But then I got to know Francis better."

The sheepish look Maxwell swiveled to Gavin's mother filled in most of the mystery. They were like Fraser and Edlyn. Gavin took a long swallow. And he was like his father.

"Rory was so kind and treated me like I was the most precious stone," Gavin's mother said.

"When Ian said he was going to get an annulment"— Maxwell paused "because he believed Francis was barren, I began to woo her. First, it was just to console..." He stared at his boots and folded his hands behind him. "I am not proud of what I did."

Gavin's mother placed a gentle hand on Maxwell's back. "What we did. I welcomed your attentions."

The truth did not set well with Gavin. He felt his rage well up inside him again. God's love seemed so far away. He made to leave when his mother reached out.

"You must hear all of this. The ring was given to me by Rory. The horse represents him as he was a fine horseman in those days."

"And the bluebell is a symbol of your mother as she was always a delicate flower to me," Maxwell said quietly.

Gavin's whole body quaked, and the devil crept back

into his soul. "You told me it was my father who gave you that ring," he yelled. "Can you not be honest about anything?" Tears rolled down his mother's face, but his heart remained hard.

"Gavin, please. This does not help." Audrey reached out, but he lifted his shoulder, bumping her hand away.

"I think it explains much." The queen tapped her chin. "But there is more. Isn't there?"

Her cryptic words baffled and heightened Gavin's fury. What more could there possibly be? Clearly his father had been a cuckold. "I have heard enough." He pivoted to leave, and this time no one would stop him.

"Hold." Queen Elizabeth rose to her feet. "I have not dismissed you."

Gavin wanted to remind her he was not one of her subjects, but wisely he said nothing. Instead, he leaned against the wall next to the door, folded his arms over his chest, and crossed his feet.

The queen's lips slimmed, but she did not demand he stand in front of her. She sat down and nodded to Gavin's mother. "Go on."

"We met often. Days stretched into weeks and weeks into months." The wistfulness in his mother's eyes had clearly taken her back to a more pleasurable time. When she was young and wanton.

"But Ian Armstrong never did find another wife," the queen said, drawing Gavin's mother back to the present.

She shook her head. "Nay, and then—"

"She told Ian," Maxwell interrupted. "He went into a rage and came lookin' for me." Rory reached up and traced the weathered scar on his face. "That's how I got this. Ian swore he'd take me manhood if I ever saw

Francis again." Despite the rugged scar, Maxwell's face softened. "No matter, I was determined to rescue Francis. But she would not answer any of me missives, nor would she even look in my direction when I would see her in yonder villages." He sighed. "Then I heard she was with child. Ian's child." He reached up and touched the old scar again. "That's when this became hard to bear."

"I see," Queen Elizabeth said, stroking her long neck.

Audrey reached out and rubbed Gavin's mother's shoulder. Why would she give sympathy to a woman who played all false? A spy for the queen. All made sense now. How she wanted Thomas to be schooled in English ways. Why she was so intent on having Audrey come to Warring Tower. His mother knew about Thomas's heritage. Not only had she cuckolded his father, she had lied to her son.

Tell me God? How can I show mercy and love to someone who has lied to me all her life?

Hot bile rose in his throat when his mother rotated and held out her hand to him. "Come here, Gavin. There is still more to this tale."

"I shall hear it from here. Or leave and not hear it at all. You are a deceitful woman, Mother."

Audrey and Maxwell protested. Both taking steps toward Gavin. One with a hand held in caution, the other with his hand folded into a fist.

"Cease this," shouted the queen. "Laird Armstrong, you will come and stand near me. I fear that you might run, and then I will never hear the end of this story. And that would trouble me greatly."

Gavin held his position, eyeing the door. He wondered how far he would get before the queen would call her guard. With a heavy sigh, he pushed off the wall and came to stand before the queen. After all, what could he possibly learn that would change his already low opinion about his mother and Maxwell?

Satisfied, Queen Elizabeth settled back in her seat. "Now then, Lady Francis, please continue."

His mother fidgeted. Her cheeks flushed, and her hands trembled. Her sad eyes seemed to droop all the more. Her gaze traveled between Gavin and Maxwell. "There is a reason I told Ian about the affair." Her lips quivered, and she shook her head as if the words got stuck in her throat.

"Ah," said the queen. "Let me guess. The child was not your husband's."

Gavin's mother gave a timid nod.

"What?" Rory Maxwell roared and grabbed her by the shoulders. "Is that true, Francis?"

Audrey paled and covered her mouth.

Gavin wished he still had the wall to brace his stance for his legs wobbled and his head spun. Surely his mother jested. What cruel trick was this?

Though the queen was keen for more, Gavin's mother spoke only to him. "'Tis all true. You have the same cleft in your chins. Your wide shoulders. You even have the same gait."

Gavin and Maxwell assessed each other, but Gavin rejected the premise.

His mother carried on. "When I told Ian I carried another man's child, he flew into a rage. I begged him to let me go. This was the chance to get the annulment he sought. But he was so livid he stormed out of the tower. I was certain he would kill Rory. I prayed. How I prayed that Ian would relent and not harm him. When Ian returned, he was so calm. I feared Rory was dead, and I expected to follow him. Instead, he offered another bargain."

"Why *didnae* ye come and tell me the truth?" Maxwell moaned. "I'd have moved hell itself to free ye."

"You are the best swordsman in these parts now, but not back then. No man survived a fight when Ian held a blade against him. But that is not why I never spoke the truth." Gavin's mother fisted her hands over her heart. "Ian was no fool. He knew now without a doubt that he was the one unable to sire a child. With no heir, Warring Tower would have gone to his brother, Hew. An unbearable thought. So, he offered to recognize my child as his own."

"The lad was mine," Maxwell roared.

Those words being said out loud punched a hole in Gavin's chest. Nay, this revolting beast wasn't his father? His mother lied before, she could easily be lying now. If she truly cared about Maxwell, she would have left Warring Tower. Something wasn't right.

His mother boldly came to stand in front of Gavin. "If I did not agree, he swore to kill my child. And that was one thing I could not abide by."

Gavin searched his mother's gaze. His heart lurched. Her eyes were open and hid nothing. This was the truth. All she did, she did for him.

CHAPTER 30

Gavin stormed from the chapel, and Audrey wanted to run after him, but a gaggle of guards brought him back. "I'll not stay and listen to any more of this," he shouted to the queen.

Wisely, she did not demand he stay. Instead, she ordered him to his chamber with a guard placed outside his door.

"This is my home, not yours," Gavin spat, struggling against his captors.

The queen rose to her feet. "Perhaps so. But we have other things which need to be discussed, and until you can conduct yourself in a civilized manner, you will remain in your chamber. I'll not have you run off and lick your wounds in some tavern. Not while I am here!" Her hand slashed the air. "Take him away."

His shouts and screams could be heard throughout the keep. Audrey wanted to soothe away his anguish, but she could not. Nor would her attention be appreciated in his present mood. Twice Gavin broke free, and twice he had to be subdued. Finally, the queen ordered him to be taken to the cells below the tower.

'Twas wrong. How could the queen be so cruel and

lock Gavin up in his own home? Something had to be done. Audrey inched forward. "Your Majest—"

"Say not a word. The man is not thinking right and needs to cool his heels," the queen clipped.

Then all was silent. The queen let out a heavy huff and sat back in her chair with a thump. "Now then, where were we?"

Audrey stole a glance around the room at those who were still present. Any affection Rory Maxwell had ever harbored for Lady Francis seemed to evaporate before her eyes. The veins in his neck stuck out like purple snakes as he ground his teeth.

"Ye should have told me," he spat at Lady Francis before stomping to the door.

"And where are you going?" the queen asked, raising her voice an octave.

He turned back. "Home. I have no wish to stay here anymore."

"I have not dismissed you." Queen Elizabeth lifted her chin.

"Ye are not my queen. And even if ye were, I would leave. The truth be, I *dinnae* care who our rulers are because none of them care about the borderland people. I only sent Warrin' to Perth to get rid of him so I could have his lands again." He looked toward Lady Francis. "I missed...having control of these lands. Years ago, the lust of gold caught my eye and I sold them back to Gavin Armstrong." Maxwell looked away. "But I no longer have the desire to own this keep and those within." He then cocked his head and glared at the queen. "And I *dinnae* care if James Stewart or that heretic John Knox lives or dies. I *dinnae* care what faith rules here, True Faith or

Reformed Faith. For the only demon that reigns in these lands is the devil. So go back home and let the demon angel have his ground or he may just come for yers."

Queen Elizabeth flinched and rose to her feet. "This may be a godforsaken country, but as long as I stand on its soil, you will not leave this keep until I am satisfied your words are true." She raised a finger and pointed it at him. "Do you understand?"

Rory gave a sarcastic smile and bowed. "Aye, Mistress Pittman." His scar puckered on his face. "I'd be happy to tell ye the names of those who wish to harm ye, if it gets me out of this stinkin' tower. There's a whole bushel of zealots in these parts. Until then, I'll be with me men in the courtyard."

Queen Elizabeth nodded. Without looking at another soul, Rory Maxwell left, the chapel door slamming behind him. A ripple of revulsion raced through Audrey. The man would sell his soul to save his own neck. Perhaps he already had. Poor Gavin to have such a cold sire. Then again, she must remember it was time and circumstance that hardened the man. All she could do was pray he would have a change of heart.

"What an impertinent man. What did you ever see in him?" The queen did not wait for Lady Francis to answer. "Well, I think that is enough for one day. Do you not agree?" Queen Elizabeth asked to no one in particular. "I am sure there is a nice quiet chamber for me to rest in this eve."

"You may have my chamber. I shall sleep with the children," Lady Francis said with a shaky breath. She resembled and sounded like an apparition, void and bland of any real substance. "I shall go and ready the room for your comforts." With quiet feet she left the chapel, leaving Audrey alone with the queen.

"These Scots truly do not think of their own necks. For never has a room emptied so quickly in my presence. And without my permission." The queen sighed.

"You must remember they have been addressing Mistress Pittman and not a queen."

"Aye, you are quite right. And Mistress Pittman would like to see her chamber."

Audrey led the queen to Lady Francis's room and was glad the chamber had many luxuries. Though worn and not as fine as her palaces, Queen Elizabeth would have some of the amenities she was used to, and she would be far safer than setting up a pavilion in the fields.

Few words were exchanged before the queen requested the services of one of her own ladies. "I have traveled light to stay undetected, but not without some comforts."

Once the queen was settled in, Audrey went back to the hall. "Come, mistress, have a drink with me," Sir Pimberly called from a table placed in a shadowy niche.

She stepped closer and saw he sat with a full pitcher of ale and two mugs before him. He picked up the pitcher of ale and filled each mug. He then sat back and pushed the cup toward Audrey. "First, Laird Armstrong is led away under guard, and then Laird Maxwell storms out of here. Care to enlighten me on what transpired in the chapel?"

Audrey took the offered drink, letting the cool ale moisten her throat. She had never been fond of the brew, but right now it did seem splendid. "Perhaps you would like to ask Mistress Pittman, for I am not at liberty to say."

His lips curved downward. "Then I may never learn what happened."

"In all honesty, you are the most fortunate for not knowing."

At that very moment, one of the queen's guards descended the stairs and entered the hall. "Sir Pimberly, the queen wishes to speak to you."

With great care, he gently placed his mug back on the table. "Ah, it looks like I shall have no rest tonight either. For I am certain the queen has a task for me to complete before morn." He rose quietly and gave Audrey a neat bow before he slipped away on silent feet. The man was born to his sneaky ways, and whatever the queen wished to discover, there was no doubt he would uncover it.

"I suppose I should go to bed," Audrey said to herself, but when she got to the stairs, she descended them instead of ascending them. There was one person she wished to see yet this night.

The lower level of the tower always stank of aging brew and mold. The damp space sent goosebumps to her arms and a shiver to her spine. Few torches lit the area, so she had to step carefully to the cells where Gavin was kept. She yelped once when a rat squeaked and scurried out from behind one of the large wooden barrels. Her heart seemed to bang off her ribcage as she kept moving her feet forward.

Finally, she saw two large wooden doors. One open with no occupants and another closed flanked by two guards. Their faces etched with years of battle and service to those who ruled England. Sweet words would not give her entry. Honesty and perhaps an act of omission would gain her admittance.

"Hold there," one of the guards said as she approached. "Come no closer."

"Good sirs, I only wish to speak to Laird Armstrong, nothing else. I know the queen would not mind."

The guards looked to one another but did not move or offer a word.

She timidly stepped closer and reached out her arms. "I have no weapon upon me." She twirled about. "You may search me if you like."

One of the guards coughed, and the other looked pained. Their sinful thoughts formed on their faces. Surely, they would not take advantage of her with the queen sleeping above?

"What do you want with the likes of him?" one guard finally asked.

"Just to speak. I know Mistress Pittman did not deny him visitors." Indeed, the queen had just given her guard orders to take him to the cell for safekeeping. Audrey cautiously crept forward. "Please, just for a moment. He cannot escape, and I think I can get valuable information from him that the queen would be most appreciative to hear. I would tell her of your aid to me."

The guards exchanged a look, and then one of them stepped to the door, slipping open the lock. "Not long," he said gruffly.

With light feet, she rushed into the dark cell before the guard changed his mind. The door slammed into place, and a small window cut within slid open, leaving a dim ray of light to snake across the floor. The foul odor of waste assailed her nostrils. She reached for a cloth in her bodice and covered her nose. She tiptoed farther into the dark cell. "Gavin," she whispered. "Where are you?"

It took a while for her eyes to adjust to the darkness, and then she found him sitting against a moist wall, his legs stretched out before him like a bruised and beaten caged animal. Tearstained dirt etched his face. "Ye *shouldnae* be here," he croaked.

The desire to embrace him in her arms and kiss all his hurt away overwhelmed her. In a half a day's time, everything he knew to be true had been shattered. His true father was an enemy, his mother a spy, and she...wasn't much better. If she opened her heart and spoke of her love, would he accept her or reject her?

She licked her lips and tried to find the words. "Perhaps not, but many are concerned about you." *What a safe answer.* She was nothing but a coward.

"Many?" His voice came out like a grainy cough. "Like who? My mother? I think not. My father?" He spat out, shaking his head. "My whole life has been a lie."

The self-pity did not suit him. Nor was it good to wallow in something that was impossible to change. Right now he did not believe in love, nor would her admission chase away the dark demons that scraped at his soul. So she would fight them head-on.

"Tell me," she said, straightening her shoulders. "Would your life have been any different if you had known the truth? Would it have been better to be raised by Maxwell?"

He left out a snort. "Heavens no. The man is an ignorant bore. Crude and ill-mannered. What my mother ever saw in him..."

"She saw love. At one time, I think he was a very handsome and a kind man. But time and tragedies have a way of whittling away the good. Your mother did what she did to protect you. Because she loved you. She saved you from disgrace."

"She saved herself from disgrace," he sneered. "And then she further humiliated the Armstrongs by becoming a spy for the queen. How she must have hated my... Ian Armstrong." Gavin slammed the dirt floor between his feet.

"You do not know for certain that she was willingly giving information to the queen. I believe she was just conversing with her cousin. I know firsthand that Pimberly has a knack for twisting words to gain an answer he is seeking. More than likely your mother was trying to protect you, like I tried to protect my family." She paused, wondering how he would accept her next words. "Like you are trying to protect Thomas."

Even in the darkness she knew his eyes shone with contempt. He lifted his shoulder and turned away. "Leave me."

"Nay, not yet. There is one thing I do know about your mother: she loves you, and she would do anything to keep you from harm."

He turned back and rose to his feet, his breeks full of filthy straw. His hands rounded into fists. "You know nothing," he growled.

"Think my words are false? You are not the only one whose life has been a lie. Let us talk about a man who hides the truth from a young boy all in the hopes to protect him from his mother."

Gavin dropped his head to his chest. "That is different."

"Is it?"

"I may have planned to give Thomas away until I found out who his mother really was, then..."

"Not so. No matter if Thomas was the queen's child or not. You never would have given him up. I wager when the time came you would have changed your mind because you love the boy."

He shook his head and wiped his nose, trying to hide his tears.

"'Tis true. Do not be so tough on your mother. She chose the life she has because of you. Just as you are willing to take on a queen for Thomas."

'Twas then Gavin lifted his moist eyes to hers. "Aye. But what does that matter to you? When the fight is over, you will leave with your queen."

An ache grew to a cavern of despair, as if a fine blade had sliced her heart. She should tell him she wanted to stay, but just like everyone else in Warring Tower, she held on to her secret. Without another word, she fled to her chamber.

Bleary-eyed and weary, Audrey rose from her bed. The only person who seemed to get a good night's sleep had been the queen as her snores and snorts could be heard through the walls. Lady Francis hummed and sang to the children all night long while Audrey sat by the window and watched as the full moon traveled across the sky.

She trudged to the hall and sat down on a long bench next to a bleary-eyed Sir Pimberly, who slurped up a large bowl of pottage. Her stomach tumbled with each smack of his lips. "Did you sleep well, Mistress?" he asked.

For a man who had been out all night on the queen's business, he seemed quite cheery and chipper. Audrey passed on the pottage when Blair offered her a bowl. "I have had better nights."

"Mmm. Cheer up, soon you will be back in London. Though I must say I do enjoy my time away from the place. Though it does seem to make Mistress Pittman exceedingly grumpy." He then carried on devouring his pottage.

Nothing could be cheery from this day forth. The thought of going to London withered her spirits, and today would bring more interrogations. Or worse, if the queen longs for London, she might just grab Thomas and leave. *How horrifying!* Pulling a six-year-old boy from the only family he has ever known would be unthinkable.

She rose. "Have you seen Thomas this morning?"

"The boy is at prayers with Lady Francis."

"And you did not see fit to join them? Are you not a strong man of God?" He arched his brows, and Audrey bit her lip. She shouldn't have questioned his faith when she had not gone to chapel either this morn.

"I am at Mistress Pittman's call. Since she did not attend, neither would I."

His merry mood fled, and how Audrey wished she could call it back. 'Twas wrong to punish someone else for her own foul mood. "Do forgive me for questioning your choices. I do bid you a good day."

Sir Pimberly's slurps echoed behind her as she made her way to the chapel. Slipping inside, she stood against the wall. She joined in on the final prayers and then lingered while the servants shuffled out of the room. Lady Francis and Thomas stood near the altar whispering to one another.

A wide grin split Thomas's face when Audrey

approached the pair. "Mistress Audrey, come look. Gran has found a new hiding place for my ring."

Audrey almost laughed, who else would want the boy's ring, except for his nurse, Mistress Jonet. Nonetheless, Thomas proudly showed a loose cornerstone at the base of the altar.

"Gran says no one would ever look in the same room where the ring had been before." Thomas dropped the jewel into a little wooden box and placed it in the secret spot.

Quite so, Lady Francis would take to task anyone who would dare try to remove it. The woman seemed to have aged at least ten years since yester eve.

"How are you feeling?" Audrey asked the older woman.

"Oh," Lady Francis sighed, "as well as anyone could be after losing the love of her son."

The flatness of her voice froze like ice in Audrey's veins, but she did not know how to mend the break between mother and son.

Lady Francis placed a hand on the boy's shoulder. "Thomas is going to show me his other secret treasures. He was telling me all about them last night."

"Gran is going to help me find new hiding places for all of them." A special alliance had formed between the pair last eve. At least something good came out of a day of disasters. Though no one knew how long that confidence would last now that the queen was here.

"Well, we are off. If the que—Mistress Pittman has need of us, you know where we shall be." Lady Francis ruffled Thomas's hair.

He pulled his grandmother through the door. Gales of

their laughter echoed down the hall. Audrey took a deep breath and faced the simple altar. The rough wooden cross gave little comfort to her disheartened soul.

She fell to her knees and folded her hands, her gaze fixed on the rugged cross. *Dear Lord, you created this world, and I know you have the power to make the wind blow and the meadows to bloom. All is within your power. I come to you this day to ask that you bind this family together in love. Heal old hurts and allow Thomas to stay in this caring home. Your wisdom is greater than all. In your son's name, thy will be done.*

"Mistress Audrey," Blair called from the entry. "Mistress Pittman is awake and wishes to see ye."

Audrey rose to her feet and with renewed strength strode out of the chapel.

CHAPTER 31

The next morning Gavin was led like a criminal to his mother's chamber. Waiting inside and dressed in her black disguise sat Queen Elizabeth flanked by Audrey. The deep shadows under her eyes spoke of little sleep. Something Gavin and she had in common this morn.

The queen, on the other hand, looked bright and cheery; however, she raised a cloth to her nose as he entered the room. "Good heavens, you smell like a donkey who has rolled in his own dung."

He fought the urge to give the queen a wicked smile. "My apologies, I do believe the waste you smell is from other past residents of the cell and not a donkey's."

"Methinks you should clean out those cells. When we are finished, make sure you bathe," the queen ordered.

He tipped his head. "On both accounts, we are in agreement."

"Now then. What is this nonsense about a great French army come to help Mary de Guise and you leading a Scottish army into England?" Her fingers rapidly tapped the arms of her chair. His answer had best be forthright or she would take his head and any others she pleased.

"I am sorry, Mistress Pittman. I forced Mistress Hayes

to write such a missive to you. Everything in it was false."

"So I have learned." The queen's fingers stilled.

Audrey had given him up so easily. His gut grew tight. Though she said she cared for him, her true loyalties would always be to her queen. Gavin tried to hide his despondency by looking away.

"Come, come now, Laird Armstrong. Do not be so disheartened. Mistress Audrey has said nothing. My information came from a man named Peter Boyd. He claims you have been twisting the mistress's words for some time. Though I must say I only received a few communications from Mistress Hayes to begin with."

"What would any of that matter? You could have gotten what you wanted from my mother."

"Lady Francis was never a willing confident. She just on occasion conversed with her cousin. Pimberly has a talent for asking the right questions. Your mother was always willing to share about her family. But you must know that we cannot trust every word a mother writes about her son. 'Twas your own erratic actions that brought Mistress Audrey here." She paused. "And, of course, the boy."

So the queen admitted to her interest in Thomas. Audrey's eyes grew wide as if her ears could not believe what she had just heard.

"My son—"

"Stop." The queen held up her hand. "We shall talk about that later. First, we must discuss your lies and deceit to England and Scotland alike. I have come here under false pretenses." Her hand came down gently to her lap, and her gaze pierced him like a sleek blade. "What games do you play, Laird Armstrong?"

He wanted to argue that she started this game when she ordered Pimberly to make inquiries or when she sent Audrey to his door, but neither revelation would bring about a satisfactory ending. "With all respect, you are here because you fear these things may happen someday. The borderlands shift their loyalties often because they have suffered much. Aye, I have brought you here under false pretense, but then, you and your sister used trickery many years ago. And I will not give up what I claim is rightfully mine."

The queen slammed the arms of her chair and rose. "How dare you. I should take your head now and sack your keep as a warning not to trifle with England."

"Then you will start a war indeed," he spat.

Audrey quickly stepped forward and curtsied deep before the queen. "Please, Your Majesty, it is his love for his son that makes him say such vile things. He would move heaven and earth to keep the boy safe. Please forgive Laird Armstrong."

The fire in the queen's eyes receded, and she sat back down. Once again her fingers strummed the arms of her chair. "You are fortunate that Mistress Hayes thinks so highly of you. I must think on this matter some more." She waved a hand in dismissal. "Go and bathe. We shall talk again soon for I have no wish to stay on this repulsive soil much longer."

Gavin wisely bowed. But before he left, he shot Audrey a thankful glance for this morn she had truly saved his life and that of his kin.

During his bath, Gavin played the next conversation he would have with the queen. 'Twould be about Thomas. Somehow, he would have to convince her that the lad would be better off raised in Scotland than in a palace in London. Every argument he produced to sway the queen had more deficits than Warring Tower's ledgers, and he had to offer them up as a sound venture. He couldn't lose Thomas.

Once finished and dressed in clean clothing, he headed to the hall, but the queen was not present. Gavin let out a slow breath. Certainly, she did not leave already. Unless…his heart began to wildly gallop. "Where is my son? Where is Thomas?" he shouted to the servants.

Pimberly rose from a table situated in a dark corner. The man was becoming like Clyde, always favoring a special spot. "Laird Armstrong," he called. "Shall we go find Mistress Pittman? I believe they are walking along the river."

They? Who was they? Again he let his gaze shift around the hall. Where was Thomas? Knowing Pimberly held the answer, Gavin followed. All the way to the river Pimberly rambled on. They had not gone far when laughter greeted their ears.

"You got him, Mistress." Thomas's excitement rose above the noise of the rushing stream. "Give it a quick yank to secure the hook."

At water's edge stood the queen with a pole in hand trying to land a rather large trout. Audrey and Gavin's mother waved their hands, encouraging the queen to land the fish.

"Good heavens, he is a fighter," Queen Elizabeth chortled. The fish flopped and landed on a rock in the middle of the stream.

Immediately, Thomas waded into the water and secured the prize. He held it up proudly. "I wager it's about four hands long. And at least two stones in weight."

The lad exaggerated. If the fish were half that size, it would be a stretch. With great enthusiasm, Her Majesty, Gavin's mother, and Audrey appeared to agree with Thomas's assessment.

"*Da*," he called as Gavin approached. "Look at the fine fish Mistress Pittman caught." Thomas rushed out of the water, proudly holding the wiggling trout.

"Methinks Mistress Pittman should give up her other responsibilities and become Warring Tower's official fisherman." Gavin winked at Audrey who paled slightly at the comment.

Queen Elizabeth winced and raised her hands when Thomas tried to give her the fish. "Nay, I think all fishing should be left to Thomas."

The lad smiled, and the queen smiled back. For the first time, Gavin saw a resemblance between the pair. The moment of bonding seemed to end when Queen Elizabeth handed Pimberly the fishing pole. "How about you, Thomas, and Lady Francis take this fine catch and clean it for our supper later?"

Lady Francis lowered her chin, and Pimberly's jowls sagged as Thomas grabbed his hand. "Come on. I'll show you how to gut it. 'Tis easy." The lad then turned back to the queen. "I am sure you will be okay with me *da*. I *dinnae* think you need all them guards. Me *da* will protect you."

The queen chuckled and waved at Thomas. "I am certain I am in good hands." Though her guards remained in place.

Thomas skipped down the path holding the fish out to Pimberly, who looked positively grey. "Look at the color on him. What kind of a fish do you think he..."

The lad's voice drifted away, and Gavin's chest was ready to burst with an undeniable boast. The basking in parental pride dissipated when his gaze rested upon his mother's sad face.

Lady Francis gave a weak, longing smile to Gavin before she followed the pair. He should make peace with her as that would be what Christ would want him to do. But his heart still fought against the idea. Right now, he had a queen to persuade.

"I think I should leave also," Audrey added.

"Certainly not," the queen ordered. "What goes forth now will concern you too." The queen paused. "Shall we continue down this way?" She held out a hand to her guards. "Stay here. I shall not wander far."

The uneasy looks the guards held did not channel their agreement. Nonetheless, the men did not move.

The confidence Gavin had tried to muster all night seemed to dissolve on the gentle morning wind. Somehow, he had to find the courage to show the queen what a fine teacher and proxy parent he would be for Thomas.

Looking up, Gavin noticed that puffy clouds floated across the bright blue sky. A few golden finches weaved through the air as a spotted woodpecker hammered on a nearby tree. If this day were a judge of how his conversation with Queen Elizabeth would go, then all of his desires would be granted. But weather was never a predictor of human conduct and best he chose his words wisely.

He led the queen along the river path while Audrey followed behind them. The silvery ripples and gentle burbles of the stream he hoped would keep the queen in a cheery and charitable mood.

She stopped under the shade of a large oak, searching for a place to sit. Gavin spied a fallen log. He placed it beneath the tree for her comforts. "Your—Mistress Pittman, this would be a nice place to rest?"

She nodded and sat. Her large black gown spilled across the log and over the lush moist grass. "Though this is truly a lovely spot, we are not out here for our amusements. I have decided to overlook your treachery. And if all remains quiet here, I will leave within the day. However, if you truly do plan to form an army against me..."

Gavin fell to his knees. "Your Majesty, I would never do so. I only wish for peace to reign in this land."

"Good." The queen nodded. "That is settled. Which brings us to another matter. What are your plans for Thomas?"

His plans? Gavin expected the queen to tell him what would happen to Thomas. Never had he suspected she would want his opinion on the matter. "I-I—"

"Out with it. Last night, Pimberly had a long conversation with your old nurse and that boorish father of yours. Do you still plan to give the child away?"

It amazed Gavin how quick the queen acted on small bits of information. But then he must remember Thomas was the queen's son and his protection was of great importance.

"Do not stand there gaping like a cavernous cave. There is little that goes on in my kingdom that I do not know about."

He wanted to state that Scotland wasn't part of her kingdom, but a warning look from Audrey blocked any words on that matter. Instead, he stood and got to the heart of the matter. "Will you let me choose what is best for Thomas, or is this just a tactic to test my loyalties concerning the lad?"

The queen ran a slim finger down her neck. "How odd that you would twist a conversation about the boy into your allegiance."

"Is that not what this is about? Am I a loyal enough servant to you to raise your son?"

"My son!" Queen Elizabeth jumped to her feet. Her arms became rigid while her hands curled into tight fists. Flashes of red ripened her cheeks. "Who would utter such nonsense? Ah, did your thinking come from that fool, Maxwell? Scots are always so thickheaded and misguided."

Gavin assessed the two women. Audrey seemed just as bewildered by the queen's outburst. With the boldness of a lioness, Audrey stepped forward. "My queen, you asked me to keep an eye on Thomas, and when we found out that he came from England—"

"You believed he was mine!" the queen spat. "My sister Mary sent the boy north when she was queen, not I, but you do not think she could be the mother?" The heat left Queen Elizabeth's eyes. Even she knew that wasn't possible. Mary Tudor desperately wanted a child and would have claimed even a bastard as royal if she could have gotten away with it. Nay, this child was another's. But whose?

Gavin and Audrey remained silent. The gentle flowing water seemed to help the queen regain her composure. She fixed a stern eye on Audrey. "The child is not mine."

Audrey did not back down. "Then why are you so interested in Thomas? Why send me to make queries?"

"You recruited my mother to your schemes," Gavin added, suddenly not caring what the queen would do to him as long as Thomas was safe.

Queen Elizabeth began to pace back and forth. "This is more complicated than I thought. Pimberly tried to pull more information out of Lady Francis, but she was very protective of the boy. In truth, Lady Francis believes you are Thomas's father." She pierced Gavin with a stern look. "Once I read my sister's writings, I needed to know more. That is when Pimberly established a steady stream of communication with your mother. I didn't want Thomas to become a pawn used between Scotland, England, and France."

Gavin rubbed a hand across his jaw. "I *dinnae* understand. If you *arenae* Thomas's mother, then why are you concerned about his future, and how can he be used against you?"

Queen Elizabeth frowned. "We all know how Thomas came to be your son, but you do not know all of the story. Nor had I until I came upon my sister's papers. Sometimes I believe 'tis her guilty conscience that killed her and not the disease that ravaged her body."

A twinge of unease wiggled through Gavin's insides. Could the queen be an emissary from Thomas's real father? If so, then the man had to be influential. More powerful than the Queen of England. Someone not easily persuaded. His jaw clenched. How was he to fight an invisible foe? A man stronger than royalty.

The queen released her breath. "Though I was held at the tower, I was not the only would-be queen imprisoned."

Audrey stepped forward. "Do you speak of Lady Jane Grey? She was rightly beheaded for treason."

"On this we are in agreement. But one queen killing another tends to set a precedent. And in truth, the young Lady Jane was used by very ambitious men. My sister did not believe the girl ever wanted to become queen, even for nine days."

Gavin impatiently folded his arms across his chest. If Elizabeth were not a queen, he would direct her conversation back to Thomas's future instead of discussing the tragic death of a traitorous queen.

"According to my sister's writings, being of soft-heart, she refused to kill Lady Jane." Like a royal, the queen paused for effect. Obviously, she realized how preposterous her statement must sound, for all knew Lady Jane Grey did die that cold February day in 1554. "Instead, my sister found someone else to take Jane's place at the block."

"Say again?" Gavin dropped his hands to his side, not wanting to miss what she would say next. Either she was mad or found humor in telling such a ridiculous lie.

Audrey gasped and wobbled before the queen. "Do you jest?"

Queen Elizabeth put her hands on her hips. "I never jest." She lifted her chin, forbidding anyone to gainsay her. "She sent Lady Jane Grey to a convent in France, but the girl escaped to the German Nations." The hair on Gavin's neck began to rise when the queen paused. "And here, my dear Audrey, is where your brother comes in."

CHAPTER 32

The past started taking focus in Audrey's memory. Her brother would do almost anything to put food on the family's table. "You speak of Asher?"

"Of course, I speak of Asher," the queen confirmed. "Do you have another brother that was a spy for my sister?"

Why did the queen taunt her? She was just an innocent in all of this mess. 'Twas her brother not she who had spied against the Protestants when Queen Mary sat on the throne.

"After Jane's escape, my sister realized her folly in letting the girl live. She sent your brother to kill Lady Jane Grey."

The cold cruel words sent a clammy chill down Audrey's back. Surely, she was mistaken. Asher rounded up the Protestants, but he never...eerie screams of those being burned at the stake cried out from the past. The smell of burnt flesh singed her nose once again. Audrey put her hands against temples. "I cannot believe he would..."

The queen waved a hand. "Do not worry, he did not kill her, he married her."

"What?" Audrey stumbled back, and Gavin reached out to steady her.

He held her tight while casting an accusing glare at the queen. "Have care, Your Majesty."

"Have care? How dare you threaten me. I am England." Elizabeth regally took her seat on the log.

"With respect, you are not in England, and you are not Scotland," Gavin challenged.

Audrey squeezed his arm. They were in no position to correct her words with a gaggle of guards less than a shout away. Besides, what the queen said had to be false. Her brother would never marry a dethroned queen. Why, he was married to a German woman. A person Audrey had never met.

Audrey untangled herself from Gavin's arms and stood straight before the queen. "This cannot be true."

Queen Elizabeth slapped the front of her gown with her hands. "Of course, it is true. Why do you think he lives halfway around the world?"

"I remember the last time we spoke. He said his wedding was a secret...that I would never see him again."

The queen nodded. "And you haven't, have you?"

"No," Audrey feebly answered as all the pieces began to fall into place.

"Nor will you unless he becomes a widower or you decide to take a long trip far from Scotland and England." The queen sighed when Audrey blanched. "Have no fear. As long as Jane Grey is content to be a merchant's wife and does not seek the throne, I am willing to forget the matter completely as should all of you." The queen leveled them with a threatening glare.

"I am sure Mistress Audrey agrees that neither of us would want to cause harm to England." Gavin stepped to Audrey's side.

The queen seemed pleased with that answer. "Then we shall forget this conversation ever happened."

Audrey was in full agreement. If this secret ever became known, her brother's safety would be jeopardized. She was ready to put this whole affair behind her, but then Gavin opened his mouth.

"Your Majesty, one thing remains a mystery. I am wondering what does all this have to do with Thomas?"

The queen slapped her hands against her chest. "Goodness. Do you not see? Thomas is the son of the poor woman who took Jane's place at the block and got her head chopped off."

Gavin wanted to close his ears as the queen told the tale of how this poor woman chose to die in order to give her son a better life.

"At first I did not believe the tale myself. That is why I had Pimberly make inquiries. I had to know if my sister's words were true. It seems she had her chaplain, John Feckenham, drug the real Lady Jane and replace her with a common woman of similar looks. Thomas could very well be the key to unlock the past. There are still those in my realm that would like to remove me from my throne."

Audrey worried her lower lip. She feared for her brother. The past was never really forgotten until all who knew the truth were dead. If the queen ever came after Jane Grey, Asher would lose his life as well.

Slitting her eyes, the queen motioned to Gavin. "Now that you know the whole story, what think you of Thomas's future? Are you worthy enough to be his father and protect the secret, or should I find another who would raise him to be an honor to the sacrifice his mother made?"

The queen's condemnation was well deserved. For never was there a worse father than he. Nevertheless, he wanted the lad, even if he was lowborn. He had to make the queen see. Gone were the years of hatred. Gone were the years of bitterness. Gone were the years of blaming. He would protect his family from harm because he loved them all.

He went down on one knee before Queen Elizabeth and beat his chest. "I know I have no claim on the lad, but I promise, from this day forth, I will be a good father."

The queen lifted her brows. "According to your mother, you harbor little feeling for your children. I fear if I question Mistress Hayes, she would agree. Give me one good reason why I should leave the boy here when I can think of many excellent English families that would rear the child to be an asset to England."

His heart sagged. Her words were true. Gavin licked the dryness from his lips. "I *dinnae* disagree with your thinking. But there is one thing I can give the lad that others *cannae*."

The queen puckered her lips. "And what is that?"

"I love him. This I say with my whole heart. I will honor your decision, but wherever Thomas goes, he will always be my son in my heart." Gavin touched his chest. "May God's will be done."

"God's will." The queen chuckled. "I have heard you

carry no faith." Audrey took a step forward, but swiftly the queen raised her hand, blocking any protest.

The stream seemed to slow, and the wind died. The birds grew quiet. Either God was contemplating her words or Gavin had been rendered deaf.

Finally, the queen stood and ruffled her gown. "Well, I may be mistaken. Perchance you could fulfill your fatherly duties and protect the Crown's secret."

Gavin rose to his feet but humbly kept his head bowed. "I promise. I will rear Thomas in the Protestant faith."

"Mmm. Mistress Hayes might have another opinion on that. I would prefer that you would just raise him to be a good Christian. Of course, one that loves England."

"And Scotland, Your Majesty," Audrey interjected.

The queen sniffed. "I need your word, Armstrong, that the boy continues to be educated in the English ways."

A ray of optimism pierced Gavin's hopeless heart. "I promise. His education will not be slighted."

"And that you will bring him to London at least once a year."

On this, Gavin paused. The lad's presence at court would set tongues wagging, but if Queen Elizabeth did not care, then why should he. "Aye, Your Majesty, if it would please you, I shall."

"I am sure Mistress Hayes would enjoy seeing the boy again too."

The queen's words all but froze Gavin's insides. He had forgotten Audrey would be leaving now that Truce Day was over. For so long he had wanted her to leave, and now that the time had come, he couldn't bear it.

"I am sure you are ready to leave this place and see your family again?" The queen held out her hand to Audrey.

"I do miss my mother." Audrey looked away, hiding her heart. In fact, her voice became light as she and the queen discussed London's markets on their walk back to Warring Tower.

Gavin's mood grew darker, and he finally begged off and headed for the stables. There he found Fraser preparing his mount to leave.

"What say you to a ride on the marches?" Gavin called.

Fraser shook his head. "I have to go and drag Jaxon out of one of his favorite taverns close to Maxwell land. Mistress Pittman let Rory and his men leave after he swore not to be a threat to her. I think that was a foolish decision, but what care I what happens to an English queen."

So even Fraser had figured out Mistress Pittman's identity. It would not be long before her enemies knew she was here. The queen would return to her own soil soon, taking Audrey with her.

"I have heard Jaxon is causin' quite a ruckus. Seems yesterday's festivities moved there and have been goin' on for quite a while."

"Do you mind if I ride along?" Gavin asked. "I need to clear my own head."

"Suit yerself, but once I drag him out, I will return him to me father. Someone needs to inherit his lands." Fraser would be banished from his home for what he did on Truce Day, and yet, he cared what would happen to his brother. The man deserved a kingdom for his family loyalty. Perhaps someday God would grant him peace and prosperity.

"You will always have a home at Warring Tower. I want you to know that." Though he meant what he said,

Gavin wondered what Hew and Fraser would do if they knew about Gavin's parentage. Another secret that would need protection.

Fraser's sad eyes held gratitude, but also a deep longing of a missed future. "Nay. My time has come to move on. This world is a big place, and I am itching to discover it."

Gavin called for his horse, and the pair rode out into the meadow as the sun rose high in the sky. This season would not only be a new beginning for Fraser but also a new beginning for Warring Tower. He would rear his sons to be good stewards of the place and devoted disciples of God. Gavin frowned. He had always believed that Audrey would be around to help him in this task, but clearly, she had no desire to do so.

By the time they arrived at the tavern, Gavin's mood had spoiled. He worried that he might have to defend Warring Tower against Hew, and he dreaded the lonely years ahead without Audrey at his side.

Merrymakers were lying outside the inn, and singing boomed within. He smiled. This was exactly where he needed to be. The heavy, stale air assailed Gavin's nostrils the moment he crossed the threshold. Not a chair sat unoccupied as they shuffled through the cramped space. Near the hearth sat Jaxon with a buxom wench on his lap. He was waving a mug of small beer in his hand, singing crude songs off-key.

"Brother," he called to Fraser. "Tell me ye have brought us some ale, for the innkeeper has run out hours ago. He has naught but this watered-down beer."

"Nay, I come to take ye home. *Da* will be lookin' for ye and *willnae* be happy until his favored son has returned." Fraser put his fists on the table.

The woman on Jaxon's lap wisely departed, knowing when a fight brewed. "I wish ye would beg his forgiveness, for I have no desire to inherit such a crumblin' keep. I plan to take that fair maid and set out for a brighter future." Jaxon took a swig of his beer and pointed his mug toward the lass.

The table cleared, and wagers on the presumed fight filled the air. "Ye can tell him yerself. Come along now. 'Tis time to go home."

Jaxon rose and took a swing, missing Fraser's head completely but hitting one of Maxwell's men. Faster than it would take a mule to kick, the whole tavern erupted. Bubbling over with his own anger, Gavin heartily joined in.

Bones cracked as punches connected with jaws. Tables and chairs were tossed about the room as if they were a pile of feathers. Blood oozed, and teeth lay like pebbles on the floor. Gavin could not remember having a grander time. He gladly smashed each face and body that appeared before him. Even with blood dripping down from a nasty gash above his eye, his vigor did not slow.

His fists were raw, but Gavin kept swinging, throwing punches and taking them until his head spun. Ready to stop, a man with a long white scar stumbled into Gavin's arms. His greying brows and brown eyes were well known.

"Rory Maxwell. This will be a pleasure." Shoving him away, Gavin spat into his hands, then hurled his fist into Rory's left cheek.

The older man fell back but recovered quickly. Screaming, he ran full force into Gavin, slamming him into a dirt wall. Rory laughed and started walking away, thinking Gavin wouldn't recover. That had been his mistake. Gavin fought to stay on his feet. He took a full breath. "Maxwell," he shouted, coiling his hands into tight fists.

The two men sparred until neither of them had the strength to lift their arms and the inn was nothing but a ramshackle mess. "Leave off," shouted the innkeeper. "There be nothin' left for ye to ruin."

Bodies lay strewn about the floor or sitting dazed against the walls. Not a stick of furniture stood intact. The tavern was nothing more than a smelly, sweaty, shambled shack. Bloody shirts decorated the rafters. A chorus of moans and groans drifted through the air.

Fraser dragged Jaxon out the door and winked. "See ye later, cousin. I have to be gettin' me brother home."

Gavin nodded at his dear friend, hoping they would spend more time in the future riding the marches.

Maxwell gave out a belly laugh and spat out a tooth. "Now that's a good fight."

"Aye, and the Maxwells and the Armstrongs will pay for fixin' the place up again." The innkeeper took a rag and tried to wipe up some beer on a broken table.

Gavin stood and wiped the blood from his nose. Maxwell slapped him on the back. "Two beers and be quick about it. Before Armstrong and I die of thirst."

"May God make the both of ye choke on yer own spit." The innkeeper poured two small beers. "Take them outside."

Maxwell picked up his mug and downed it in two gulps. "Another." Gavin finished his off just as quickly. "Give him another too."

"Nay, not until I see some coin." The bartender held the pitcher of beer far from their reach.

Maxwell threw a couple of coins at the innkeeper. "Now give me the whole pitcher and leave us be."

Satisfied with the generous amount offered, the innkeeper handed over the pitcher, then went to salvaging his furniture. Gavin and Maxwell exited the tavern and slid down the side of the building until they were seated on the ground. Both took a long pull from their drinks before staring at each other.

"I *cannae* remember havin' such a grand fight." Maxwell polished off his mug and poured himself another.

"Nor I," Gavin agreed.

The humor in Maxwell's eyes left, and his face seemed to age years. "Had I known, I would have fought heaven and hell to get yer *ma* and ye out of there."

"I know." The pain oozed out of Gavin's memory. His father's coldness, his mother's tears, all made sense now.

"*Dinnae* be so bitter." Maxwell rubbed a hand over his face.

"I'm not bitter," Gavin snapped.

"Ye are. 'Tis as plain as yer bloody nose on yer pasty bloody face. Francis did what she did to stop a war and save many a life. Yers included. If anything, she is a saint, she is." Maxwell tossed back his mug, taking a healthy slurp before resting his head against the wooden building. "Ye look like her, but now I can see the Maxwell in ye too." He pointed to his chin. "Right here." He then slapped Gavin's shoulders. "And in yer brawn."

Gavin had not taken the time to think on any resemblance. The thought that this man was his sire did not rest well. "I want nothing from you."

"Nor am I offerin' anythin'. Ewart for all his faults will

335

inherit me lands. All I am askin' is to get to know ye a little better."

Another troubling matter pricked at Gavin's soul. "If Hew finds out the truth…"

"Aye, that could be a problem." Maxwell took another swig of beer and then gave Gavin a sideways glance. "He'll not hear it from me. And I doubt yer *ma* will say a word. She's carried the secret for a long time. Fear not, Warring Tower will be yers. And if Hew tries to take it, I'll stand by yer side. I owe that to ye and Francis."

"You might rekindle your friendship again?" *A disgusting idea!*

A sad laugh floated from Maxwell's lips. "I think not. What is done is done. I will say this, I am glad ye *didnae* die in Perth. Knowin' what I know now, I *couldnae* have lived with such a sin on me conscience."

Gavin squeezed Maxwell's shoulder. "I am glad to hear it. perhaps the Maxwells and the Armstrongs will be friends once again."

A crusty laugh followed by a hard hack pushed out of Maxwell's throat. "Aye, at least while I breathe air. God only knows what will happen once Ewert is laird." He paused and took another drink before continuing. "What about the lad? Will the queen be claimin' her son?"

"That's where we both were wrong. The lad is not her heir but some common maid's child." Gavin stretched out his legs in front of him to ease the pain in his knees. He couldn't speak the whole truth, but he could speak part of it.

"Huh? Then what be the fuss about the lad?" Doubt clouded Maxwell's eyes, and his guard began to rise.

Gavin waved off and poured the older man another

brew. "Seems Thomas's real mother gave invaluable service to the Tudor family. When she died, Mary Tudor wanted the boy to be well taken care of."

Maxwell's shoulders relaxed as he chuckled. "Looks like another Armstrong is raisin' another man's child."

Gavin shrugged. "So be it. He is a smart lad, and I am proud to call him my son. He will be my heir. Another secret that needs to be kept."

With a nod and a slow appraisal, Maxwell grinned. "Ye are a fine man, and I am proud to call ye son too. Even if that be kept a secret."

A warmth spread through Gavin and between the two men. They might never be close like a father and son should be, but they would never be enemies again. Both men held up their mugs and tapped them together. "May God be with thee," they said in unison before taking a long quenching drink.

CHAPTER 33

Audrey watched as Queen Elizabeth and Thomas played a game of chess. With his tongue hanging out the side of his mouth, he valiantly captured the queen's rook. All within the room hesitated to praise Thomas until the queen showered him with her approval.

Looking at the board sparsely sprinkled with the queen's black pieces, she shook her head. "I dare say, I believe you will win again."

'Twas obvious she was letting Thomas have the upper hand, so enthralled was she by the boy. Audrey held her hands to her heart. He had that effect on almost everyone he met. So forthright and bold. No wonder it was easy to believe he was Queen Elizabeth's son.

Yet, he wasn't. A common boy with extraordinary talents. And he had a father that loved him. Happiness should be exploding from Audrey's chest, but it wasn't. She would be leaving with the queen's entourage in the morning. How she would miss the lad...and his father.

Though things seemed normal at Warring Tower, a heavy sadness hung within. Audrey strolled to where Lady Francis sat mending one of Thomas's tunics. Her red-rimmed eyes spoke of a night of tears. Her heart must be in pieces. She had lost the love of her son yesterday and the respect of an old love. How any of this would turn out, only God knew.

And I pray He heals this family quickly. Audrey sighed and sat down next to the miserable woman. "Mistress Pittman truly enjoys Thomas's company."

"Agreed," Lady Francis answered with a small quiver in her voice.

Audrey reached out and squeezed the older woman's hand. "Gavin still loves you."

Tightening her lips, Lady Francis shook her head.

"You must give him time to accept all that has happened. I am certain when he has sorted everything out, he will understand the choices you made."

"I never wanted any scandal to touch his life, and in the end, it did anyway." Lady Francis pulled her hand away from Audrey's grasp and dabbed the corners of her eyes. "Ian was so desperate for an heir, and he was willing to claim Gavin as his own. I guess I made the wrong decision for the truth came out anyway."

"Do not let the past eat up your future. God will work this out for everyone's good. You shall see."

Slowly, the tears dried and were replaced with a tenderness. "You are a remarkable young lady. Someday you will make an excellent wife."

Audrey's throat grew thick. Oh, that Gavin would see such a quality in her. How much she wanted to stay here and become a wife and a mother to his children. But it did no good to dream. He would never love an English Catholic, and certainly not one that came to spy on him. "I am flattered by your words and only can pray that someday they will come true."

Lady Francis reached out and stroked Audrey's cheek. "I am sure of it. You deserve love for what you did for Thomas."

Thomas threw up his hands in victory. Audrey shook her head. "I did nothing for the boy. He still acts like a Scot, and he is as brash and bold as ever."

"You taught me to accept my grandson as he is, a beautiful, intelligent boy who loves life. Blood or not, he is an Armstrong through and through. I am proud to be his gran." Lady Francis's gloom washed away as she reached out and took Audrey's hands in hers. "Thank you, my dear. You will be sorely missed."

Now it was Audrey who fought to keep the tears from rolling down her cheeks. "I will miss you too."

Just then Gavin entered, a tattered, bloody, and disheveled mess, followed by Bairn.

"Gads man, what happened to you?" Queen Elizabeth asked.

"*Da.*" Thomas ran over and jumped into his father's arms. He then pinched his nose. "You smell awful."

Gavin tossed the boy in the air and once caught started tickling his belly. Bairn howled and jumped up on the pair. "I was rolling around with a herd of pigs."

"*Da*, leave off." Thomas laughed, trying to push away the amusing fingers. Bairn licked the boy's face.

Gavin knelt and greeted Thomas eye to eye. "What have you been up to this day?"

"I beat Mistress Pittman three times in chess." Thomas wiped his face with the back of his hand before proudly holding up three fingers.

"The boy is a fine opponent." Queen Elizabeth stood, folding her hands in front of her.

"Is that so? Methinks he is rather a charmer." Gavin winked, and Thomas scooted behind the queen's chair.

She reached around, trying to grab him to no avail. "How about we take one more turn at fishing?"

Thomas jumped out and nodded. "I also found a new snake hole. I bet we could find another hole if we look hard enough. Snakes always have two holes. One for the snake to come in and one for escape. If I stand at one and you at the other, I bet we could catch the snake."

"Good heavens." Queen Elizabeth slapped a hand against her throat.

The lad grabbed her other hand and led her to the entry. He glanced back and gave a wave. "See you later, *Da.* Come on, Bairn. We have to show Mistress Pittman how to snag a snake." The barking dog loped merrily behind the pair.

Another soft ache tripped through Audrey's chest. Father and son would be just fine. And in time, Thomas might not even remember her name, but she would never forget either of them. She would hold them close to her heart and pray for them daily.

Calling for a wet cloth, Gavin wiped his face and hands. He then strolled over to where she and Lady Francis sat. "I would like to have a word with my mother."

The dismissal was given with a smile, but Audrey took it as a punch to the gut. She should be happy for surely Gavin was going to make amends with Lady Francis. Nonetheless, she had a difficult time hiding her hurt. How selfish of her. The whole Armstrong family was forming a strong bond and all she worried about was her own weeping heart.

Audrey stood. "Of course. I am sure you have much to discuss, and I have to prepare my things for my journey south tomorrow."

Gavin's brow wrinkled, then smoothed quickly. He nodded without adding a word.

"Well then, God's peace to you both." Audrey gave a slight curtsy to Lady Francis and quickened her pace to the stairs. This eve she would take her meal in her room for she could not bear the sight of this beautiful family one moment longer.

Music from a lute, flute, and drum glided up to Audrey's humble chamber while she chewed on an oatcake and fish scraps. There was much more food down in the hall, but she had asked for simple fare for her last supper at Warring Tower. With each chew, the laughter and singing seemed to intensify and further darken her mood. Finally, she slammed a hand on the table and tossed the cake into the chamber pot.

"Everything sours in my mouth. Why try to eat at all." She rose and strolled to the window and watched a star skim across the cloudless night sky. "And this is the last time I shall look into the Scottish heavens."

How she had hoped and how she had prayed that Gavin would come and beg her to join the festivities this eve. But he did not. Nay, she was already forgotten. With a deep sigh she wandered over to her open chest and picked up her bunched-up cloak, refolding it into a new heap. "'Tis all for the best. I am sure my mother needs me."

Another lie. Her mother had been relieved when Audrey left, even joyous. One less mouth to feed. She tossed the cloak back into the chest. The queen had made it plain she did not want Audrey as an agent anymore. Possibly she might find employment elsewhere. *Doing what?* Just what was she capable of doing? She failed at court intrigue and was a terrible spy. She had talent with a dagger, but who would want a woman with such a skill?

She fell back onto her bed. "I am good at nothing."

"I *wouldnae* say that."

Immediately she sat up. Her skin began to heat. She glanced over her shoulder to find Gavin leaning in the doorway. "My laird, you should have made your presence known."

"The door was ajar, and I heard a voice."

He would think her a ninny talking to herself. She rose and primly placed her hands over her skirt. "I talk to myself sometimes."

"Oh." He sauntered into the room. "I thought things like that *didnae* happen until a person was many summers old."

She cleared her throat and pressed her sweaty palms together. He'd think her daft. "Is there something you want?"

He ran a hand over the open lid of the trunk. "You will be leaving early in the morn?"

"Aye," she said cautiously, wondering his purpose for being here. "Mistress Pittman wishes to get to English soil as quickly as possible."

"Before you leave… I wanted to give you my thanks."

Her heart sank. What was she expecting? His undying love? "I did naught."

Gavin stepped closer, his gaze resting warmly on hers.

"You brought truth where there were lies. You made a young lad open up, and you mended many a broken heart. I would say that is quite a bit."

She shrugged and backed up a step. "None of which had anything to do with me."

"Really? Had you not come, I would have given Thomas away. I would have never found out who my real father was or what sacrifices my mother had made. I would have remained bitter. Blaming others for my own doings. And most importantly, I never would have found my faith again."

He took two more steps closer; his leather and meadow scent swam through her ailing heart. She moved back until her heels hit the wall. "I remember doing none of those things. You should thank God."

"I do. For in His wisdom He sent you here." Gavin moved forward until the tips of his boots touched the toes of her slippers.

"This might be God's will," she whispered, her body paralyzed by his closeness.

"Possibly." He placed his hands against the wall on either side of her head.

A flush of heat shot up her neck as his blue eyes penetrated her soul. Her heart thudded. "My laird," she said weakly. "Methinks you should step back."

"You do? Huh." He pushed a wayward lock out of her face. "You *willnae* be leaving on the morrow." His sultry breath licked against her throat.

"No?" she squeaked.

Slowly he shook his head. "The queen is staying to witness a marriage."

"A marriage?" she croaked.

"She sanctioned it this eve, and I *dinnae* think we should gainsay her. She even is providing her own clergyman." He lifted a hand off the wall and slid a finger down her burning neck.

A rock-sized lump jammed her words in her throat. Colors rolled in front of her eyes.

"So only one thing remains." His soft lips placed a tender kiss on her neck. "Will the lady say yes?"

Slowly she unraveled his speech. *Would the lady say yes?* Did he mean...

"Audrey?" His brows knitted together before he pulled back.

Joy rushed through her body chasing the spots away. "Is the woman of the True Faith and the man of the Reformed Faith?"

He grinned and nodded. "Aye, but the queen thinks they can work out their differences. After all, they both believe that Jesus Christ saved them from their sins. I agree with the queen."

Audrey leaped forward and threw her arms around his neck, planting a reckless kiss on his lips. He pulled her close, deepening their love.

When they finally parted, he placed his forehead against hers. "Then shall I tell the queen the bride will be attending?"

"Only if the groom wants me to."

"He would love to have you there." He placed another long luxuriant kiss on her lips.

After catching her breath, she placed a hand on his chest. Her mind began to reorganize. She could not marry him, not without love. "Does the groom have feelings for the lady?"

His smile traveled up to his eyes. "He loves her deeply."

Her heart soared. Another heady kiss swept across her lips, taking away all doubts.

This time when he stepped back, his eyes held a question. "And the lady? What are her thoughts?"

"Loves him with every bit of Scottish air she breathes."

They sealed their bond with one more kiss. God had indeed blessed them all.

Epilogue

Thomas sat on the hall steps with a chicken thigh in his hand while all within sang and danced, wishing his *Da* and Mistress Audrey much happiness. He took a bite and chewed the tasty meat. He wasn't sure if he liked the idea of having a new *ma,* but he did enjoy the food and the celebration offered.

A drooling Bairn sat next to him, eyeing the few morsels that remained on the leg. Thomas plucked off a piece and held it in front of the dog's nose. "If I give this to you, do you promise to stop all that slobberin'?"

The dog licked his chops and eagerly sniffed the offered morsel. "Gently." Bairn timidly took the food. Thomas wiped his fingers on his tunic and frowned when a drip of drool once again hung from Bairn's jowls.

"He is rather a sloppy dog, is he not?" Mistress Audrey sat down on the step next to Thomas.

He shrugged. "Bairn's a hound. He's supposed to be sloppy."

"Ah, you are so right. We cannot expect a creature with such long jowls to act any other way." Mistress Audrey reached out and scratched Bairn's head.

Thomas shrugged again. Why didn't she go back inside? Or better yet, why didn't she leave Warring Tower altogether?

She inched closer to him. "Thomas, why are you so quiet?"

He shrugged again, turning his head away from her.

"Are you still mad at me? I thought we were good friends?"

Why didn't she just go away? Her face was so close to his, she smelled like heather, which he used to like because it reminded him of the meadow grass near his hiding places. But now…it made him sick.

"Are you upset that I married your father?"

Thomas's bottom lip pushed out. "Yer not my *ma*." He gave her his whole back.

"Thomas, look at me."

"*Dinnae* want to," he grumbled. "Go away."

"I know I will never take your mother's place, and I do not wish to, but your father and I love each other, and we want to be together. We hope to make a happy home for you and your brother." She was so close she was practically whispering in his ear.

Thomas tossed the chicken leg between them, then folded his arms across his chest. She wasn't going to make him like her anymore. Bairn whined, eyeing the leg, but Thomas shook his head. "Them bones *arenae* good for you."

"I am sorry, Thomas." Mistress Audrey just *widnae* go away. "I guess we should have talked to you first before we married. But it is done now, and it would be a sin for us to part."

Thomas lifted his chin and gave her a determined look. "Why not ask Mistress Pittman to talk to God? Everybody seems to do what she wants."

Mistress Audrey laughed. "So true, but even she has to do what God wants." Her face grew somber. "All I want is for us to have the same relationship as before. I want us to go riding, fishing, and find new treasures for you to hide. Please, give me a chance?"

She'd always been great fun when they did those things, but that wasn't the problem. Slowly he gazed at her. "My *da* and *ma* hardly ever talked, and when they did, they fought. You used to fight with my *da*. What if something happens…"

"Oh, Thomas." She slowly put her arm around his shoulder. "Nothing is going to happen to me, you, your brother, or your gran. I told you, your father and I love each other, and we both love you. We want this to become a happy place to live, full of comfort, joy, and love."

She whispered close to his ear. At least she wasn't slobbery like Bairn.

"You don't have to call me Mother. Audrey will do." She paused again and gave him a pleading look. "Will you not give it a try?"

A lightness began to grow in Thomas's chest. "All right. I guess we might be friends again. Maybe you could talk to *Da* about getting rid of Mistress Jonet, she isn't very good at being a nurse. I think she should go back to the kitchens. We could ask Mistress Pittman if she would like to be our new nanny."

Audrey doubled over and grabbed her sides as laughter seized her body. He didn't see what was so funny about the request. He stood and put his hands on his hips. "I think she likes us very much. She might stay if we ask her."

Mistress Audrey rose and lightly tapped the tip of his nose. "Why, I think you should ask her. Otherwise I have made arrangements for Hetta to return. Would you like that?"

Thomas jumped to his feet. "Very much. She can be Marcas's new nanny. But I would like Mistress Pittman to stay too." He patted his dog's head. "Come on, Bairn, we have to convince Mistress Pittman to be our new nanny."

And off he ran into his future.

Author Note

Researching for a historical novel is always a challenge. What one historian may believe to be historical fact another might not. In *A Life Redeemed*, I used the term Moss-troopers. Though historical records show the term did not appear in print until the mid-17th century, it was in fact, like many words, used verbally well before it was written. I have it on good authority, that many 16th century *reivers* were indeed called Moss-troopers. Thus is why I chose to use the term in my book.

The borderlands were very lawless during this historical period. Often goods and livestock was stolen from one border family to feed another. This was most common among English and Scottish border families. As the situation became worse, Wardens, Deputies, Keepers, Captains, Land Sergeants, and Troopers on both sides instituted Truce Days. On these days English and Scots would come together in order to 'keep the wild people of the Marches in order.' These days were originally made to bring about peace between the English and the Scots, but in time they became days of rowdy fun. Though they did not have such organized feats as I have in *A Life Redeemed*, they did have wrestling matches and other feats of strength. I recommend *The Border Reivers* by Keith Durham or *The Debatable Land: The Lost World Between Scotland and England* by Graham Robb if you would like to learn more.

Finally, any other historical inaccuracies are mine alone. They were used to give flavor and dimension to the story, and are not meant to give offense.

Dear Reader,

Thank you for taking the time to read my book, *A Life Redeemed*. I know your time is valuable and that you have a lot of book choices. From the bottom of my heart, I feel so blessed that you chose mine. I do hope you enjoyed your time with the Armstrong family. The story continues when Thomas comes of age in book three, *A Life Reclaimed*. This adventure will start out in London and then head to some very exciting places, and even a trip back to Scotland.

Don't forget to check out the books in **The Sword and The Cross Chronicles**. Or my contemporary romance, *Joshua's Prayer*. All my books are clean reads and carry a strong Christian message. You may find all these books on my website oliviaraebooks.com

And once again I make a humble plea. If you enjoyed any or all of my books, please leave a review where you purchased them. A review on Goodreads would be appreciated too. A kind review can go a long way. And we all know this world could do with a little more kindness. May God hold you forever in his loving hands.

Until next time…abundant blessings,
Olivia

A LIFE RECLAIMED

SECRETS OF THE QUEENS · BOOK 3

OLIVIA RAE

PROLOGUE

September, 1571
Warring Tower
Borderlands, Scotland

Anguishing cries tore down the cold dark hallway, rending Thomas's heart in two. Ma Audrey's wails meant one thing—his father was dead. His illness had been so sudden. One day he was riding the marches and bellowing out orders to his moss-troopers and the next he had fallen ill. No one knew what caused his affliction. He awoke one morning and fell flat on his drooping face.

From there his father's health deteriorate with every passing day. Even with all her wise apothecary skills, Gran could not alleviate his pain or determine what had caused the illness. Her face etched with fresh suffering; she wiped her nose with the back of her hand. "There is nothing more I can do. 'Twill not be long before he meets his maker."

Gran's chilling words clutched and clawed at Thomas's heart as he made his way to the tower' s small chapel nestled near the spiral staircase. He removed a weathered stone from the simple alter and dragged out a worn wooden box. Carefully he raised the lid and looked at the few precious possessions he had collected when he was a young lad—a bit of cloth, an old knife, a horseshoe, and a stick tower. He lifted the tower and held it up to the dim chapel light. His mind sailed back to when he had made the object. It had been the year after his mother had died, when Ma Audrey had come from London to live with them. Of course back then he called her Mistress Audrey. They were good friends and she had helped him build the sturdy tower. He smiled and gently placed the treasure back in the box.

"Being English herself," Gran had said back then, "Mistress Audrey was an angel sent from heaven for she softened his father's heart and restored his faith." Indeed, things did change after she arrived. She had become a mother to Thomas and his wee brother, Marcas. Mistress Audrey was the only mother his brother ever knew.

Thomas reached beneath his shirt and clasped the ring he wore around his neck. From far beyond, he could hear his real mother's voice, soft and delicate. She would hum and sing him to sleep and tell him stories of great knights and mighty sultans. His fingers brushed over the raised blue stone. He'd never forget his *ma,* Edlyn Armstrong. Never.

Aye, Ma Audrey had brought joy to their small family when she gave birth to Isla. His new sister strengthened their family bond. Yet, none of them could steal the special place in his heart he held for his true mother.

The memory of his birth mother did not ease the growing sorrow that roiled up from his stomach and captured his throat now. His father was dead. He shook the box. A few pebbles rolled exposing a red ribbon he had found in a stable stall long ago. Nothing inside the box revealed the meaning of his father's mysterious words.

"My son. I am sorry. I should have been honest. You have the right to know. Look in the box." His father's words plagued Thomas. There was naught here that would give a clue to their meaning.

The chapel door scrapped opened and Ma Audrey entered. "Oh, I did not know you were here." She dabbed at her red-rimmed eyes with a soft cloth. "Your father…" She Hiccupped a sob.

"Aye, I know." He should go and see his father's body, but he could not bring himself to view the gaunt skeleton his father had become. Thomas focused on his possessions, fearing his own misery would spill causing Ma Audrey more distress.

She knelt beside him and put her arm around his shoulders. "He loved you very much." Her tear-clogged voice threatened to open the water gates in his own eyes.

"I know," Thomas said softly, shaking the box. "He left me something, but I *cannae* seem to find it? Something he wanted me to know about."

Ma Audrey drew in a sharp breath and clutched Thomas's shoulder until it ached. "You won't find the answer here."

He swiveled his head and met her gaze. "What do you mean? He said to look in the box."

"Your father was going to tell you, when you were a little older. He meant to protect you. There is another secret box." She fell back and placed a hand against her forehead. "Please Thomas, we shall talk about this once your father is buried."

Secret box. He should have honored her wishes. 'Twas the right thing to do. This was a house of mourning and he should conduct himself in a worthy manner as the new Laird of Warring Tower should. But a betraying, impatient serpent twisted through his gut and wanted answers.

With his grief blinding him, Thomas stood, and wrapped his fingers into tight fists. "I am eight and ten. I am old enough. Where can this mysterious box be found?"

"Nay, Thomas. This is not the time." Ma Audrey held out her hand for his assistance.

Instead of helping her up, he backed away, reading the fear in her eyes. "Where?" The question came out like an icy stick, jabbing through his pain.

Her body sagged and her eyes pooled with fresh tears. "I love you and don't want you to be hurt. Not at a time like this."

The evasive words did not calm him, more the contrary. His spine pricked with foreboding. A tightness grew in his chest and nothing but the truth would cure what ailed him. "I want to know now. Where is the box?"

Ma Audrey shook her head as fresh tears spilled from her eyes. "Can you not wait?"

Her gaze pleaded, but he stood stone stiff. A raged cry tore from her throat and Thomas almost relented.

She shook her head in defeat. "Your grandmother has it."

For a moment her words took him aback. Why would *Da* trust Gran with such an important item and not his wife? Thomas tucked the question away and walked briskly to the door.

"Thomas. It will only add to your agony," Ma Audrey cried. "Please wait."

He did not break his stride as he took the spiral stairs two at a time. Without a knock, he stepped into his grandmother's chamber. She stood, staring into the hearth's dancing flames. Her long white hair swept over her sagging shoulders and framed her teared-etched cheeks.

With a frail hand she poked at the fire with a gnarled stick. "My son is dead. I loved him dearly."

Briefly Thomas's fury ebbed and he wanted to take her delicate body in his strong arms to comfort her. "Gran," his voice cracked. "So did I."

Her blue eyes circled by dark purple skin met his. "But you are not here to speak words of adoration for your father, are you? I heard what he said to you."

Thomas brushed a hand through his russet hair, trying to tamp down his impulsive desire. "I need to know what my *da* meant. I need to know now and I *cannae* wait until...where is the box?"

"Of course you cannot. You are so much alike, and yet that is not possible, is it?"

Thomas did not understand her cryptic words nor was he in the mood to figure them out. "Please, Gran. I'll not rest until I know."

"You'll not rest once you do." She shook her head and with a heavy sigh shuffled over to a large ornate chest.

Quickly Thomas rushed to her side and assisted her in opening the lid.

She bent forward tossing gowns, veils, and shifts onto the floor until she extracted a gold-gilded case. Thomas remembered the decorative box. His father had bought it on an English and Scottish Truce Day. At the time, Thomas believed it was a gift for Ma Audrey, obviously he was wrong.

"What does it hold, Gran?" he asked quietly like an awestruck child.

"A few years back after a raid on the English went terribly wrong and many moss-troopers lost their lives, your father feared his own life could be taken before telling you the truth."

"Why *didnae* he tell me then. Thomas reached out for the case, but Gran was quicker and pulled the box to her chest.

"You were not ready and methinks you still aren't. But you are laird now and the truth cannot be kept from you forever." She closed her eyes as an old torment tore across her face. "A secret kept too long can choke the life out of those it was meant to protect. Know this, I will always protect you."

Why could no one in this family ever speak plainly? Just because Warring Tower looked like it harbored ghosts did not mean that all within had to speak in shadowy language. Thomas firmly stuck out his hand. "Gran, that is for me."

"Aye, so it is." She gently placed the case in his hand and wrapped her fingers around his. "Everyone here loves you. No matter what you read, we are kin. Always."

Thomas jerked his hand away and eagerly flipped open the lid. Inside he found a folded piece of parchment protected with his father's waxed seal. With a snap the seal broke. His fingers trembled as he hurried to open the letter. His heart hitched and raced as he took in his father's scribbled handwriting.

"Perhaps you would like to sit down before you read," his gran suggested, offering a chair.

"Nay," he said gruffly, turning his attention back to the

letter. The words swam before his eyes as they began to take focus.

My dearest son, if you are reading this missive then it means I am no longer alive. I meant to have this conversation with you when you were a man."

Thomas paused, and his body heated with a mite of anger. At what age did his father deem that to be? He was a man now. Shaking off the troubling thought he continued to read.

I do not know how to put this delicately, so I will give you the truth and hope that you will understand my reasoning for not telling you when you were young. You were already born when I met your mother. At the time, I was heavily in debt. I had lost the ownership to Warring Tower. Your departed grandfather offered me a great sum of money to buy Warring Tower back if I married his daughter.

Gavin Armstrong was not his true father? Thomas worked his mind trying to remember how things were before his mother died. His parents fought often. They hardly spent any time together. Yet never had he thought Gavin of Warring wasn't his father. Dread seeped through Thomas as he forced himself to read on.

It was not until after her death that I learned she was not your mother either.

Thomas's breath stalled. His heart sank to his belly. Nay, that cannot be true. He went back and read the line over and over again. He could feel Gran's tight gaze on him, but he dared not look up, not until he read the entire letter.

It seems your grandfather was heavily in debt also. You were brought as a bairn to his household by a clergyman from the English Tudor court. All your grandfather's debts and mine were paid by Queen Mary Tudor. Your true mother died at the block in the place of Lady Jane Grey, who was queen of England for nine days. Your mother sacrificed herself to give you a better life.

Know this, what started out as an act of greed has turned into love and devotion. I look back on the day I married Edlyn as one of the best days in my life as I became your da that day. With all my heart, I love and consider you my true kin and heir. All I ask is that you take care of your brother in return.

My love is with you forever.

Da

Tears built up behind Thomas's eyes even as rage built up in his soul. Everyone had lied to him. His real mother died for some English queen. No one here was his kin. He had always believed the glens, rivers, hills, and the very air that made Scotland, lived in his bones. He had been wrong. Not a drop of his blood had ties to this land.

He crushed the letter in his hand and fixed his gaze on his gran. Nay, not his gran, just some old woman who could not be truthful.

"Thomas, this changes nothing. I love you. We all love you. You will always be my Grandson." He shifted away when she reached out to touch him.

"You are all liars!" His hand shook as he tossed the note into the hearth. The letter twisted and curled as hot embers licked and burned away his father's words. Nay, a foreigner's words.

Thomas stormed out of the room and strode to his chamber, kicking open the door. He'd go to London and seek out the truth. Perhaps find his real father. With clumsy fingers, he jammed a few articles of clothing into a sack and fixed his Jack of Plates over his shirt. The wind outside whistled as rain began to pummel the tower. Thomas grabbed his sword and dirk and secured them to his belt before heading for the staircase.

At the base of the stairs, he found the fortress of Ma Audrey and Gran, standing shoulder to shoulder. He paused, gritted his teeth and pushed through them as if they were stalks of wheat blowing in the wind.

"You are not thinking right," Ma Audrey cried, running after him, grabbing the back of his jack. "Has not this family suffered enough this day? Your father is dead."

Thomas stopped. Like a slow rotating wheel he turned and stared at the deceivers. "He is not my *da*. Both of you knew and not one of you thought fit to tell me." He fought to keep his fury high as his throat constricted. "Not one of you."

He whirled away and blinked his eyes trying to hold back his tears. He would not cry. He would not feel pity for those who held the truth from him. With quick steps, he raced out into the wet, sloppy courtyard. The wind caught his auburn hair, swirling it around his head like a red storm cloud. Behind he heard the sound of feet slapping in the mud. Their cries of remorse chased after him. Did they truly think they could stop him?

A jagged bolt of lightning split the sky, followed by a loud rumble of thunder. "Return to the tower," he ordered. "Ye will all catch your death out here." He glanced over his shoulder expecting to find Ma Audrey and Gran standing there. Instead he found his brother Marcas, dripping, soaking wet. His narrow shoulders shaking.

"Where ye goin', Thomas?"

Though the lad had seen twelve summer, he was reed-thin. If the wind kept coming, he could very well be tossed about like a pile of withered leaves. Easily, Thomas scooped Marcas up into his arms and carried him to the stables. Once inside Thomas gentle set the lad on his feet, brushing his wet blond locks out of his soft blue eyes.

"Ye should not be out in this." Thomas grabbed a cloth from one of the stalls and handed it to Marcas. "Here. Wipe your face. When the rain stops return to the tower, Gran and Ma Audrey will be looking for your comfort."

Marcas accepted the cloth, but held his gaze on Thomas. "But where are you goin, brother?"

Thomas let out a heavy sigh and washed a hand over his face. "I *cannae* stay here anymore."

"Why? *Da* is dead and you be laird now. You are the head of the family now." Such bold words from a lad who but a few months ago played with wooden swords and stole Cook's chickens, wishing to save their miserable necks.

"Listen to me. I am not laird, you are. 'Tis your birthright." Thomas looked away and readied his mount, "Gran and Ma Audrey can explain. Look after them and Isla too."

"I *dinnae* understand. You are the eldest. You are Warring Tower's laird." Marcas reached out and grabbed the horse's reigns. "*Da* was teachin' and trainin' you to be laird. You *cannae* be runnin' away."

The worry in Marcas's eyes, made Thomas pause. Being responsible for your family, moss-troopers, and tenants would frighten even the strongest of men let alone a spindly lad. Thomas placed his hand on Marcas's shoulder and gave it a squeeze. "I have no claim on this land, but you do. You will be a fine laird. If you be needing help, ask Rory Maxwell, he dotes on you like a *grandda.*"

"But you are my brother. I *dinnae* want you to go."

Tears rolled down Marcas's cheeks and ripped opened Thomas's heart. He pulled Marcas into a tight embrace. "Aye. Remember that. We will always be brothers." Thomas drank in the field and stream scent that was his younger sibling, tucking it into his memory.

Releasing his brother, Thomas took his horse to the courtyard, knowing one glance back at Marcas would bring him to his knees.

Once Thomas mounted his horse, another flash of lightening filled the grey sky. The beast reared up in fright and threatened to unseat him. Swiftly, he gained control and headed for the gate. Before crossing the threshold, he glanced back. Heavy drops of rain pelted Marcas's face, covering his tears. He raised up a weak hand in farewell.

"Brother, brother," Marcas shouted.

Thomas's gut wrenched, but he could not offer up one comforting word, not without breaking down himself. He yanked his mount around and took off down the rutted path as if all that was unholy waited for him out in the storm.

ABOUT THE AUTHOR

OLIVIA RAE is an award-winning author of historical and contemporary inspirational romance. She spent her school days dreaming of knights, princesses and far away kingdoms; it made those long, boring days in the classroom go by much faster. Nobody was more shocked than her when she decided to become a teacher. Besides getting her Master's degree, marrying her own prince, and raising a couple of kids, Olivia decided to breathe a little more life into her childhood stories by adding in what she's learned as an adult living in a small town on the edge of a big city. When not writing, she loves to travel, dragging her family to old castles and forts all across the world.

Olivia is the winner of the Angel Award, Book Buyer Best Award, Golden Quill Award, New England Readers' Choice Award, Southern Magic Contest, and the American Fiction Award. She is an Illumination Award Gold medalist and she has been a finalist in many other contests such as the National Readers' Choice Awards, and the National Romance Fiction Awards. She is currently hard at work on her next novel.

Contact Olivia at Oliviarae.books@gmail.com

For news and sneak peeks of upcoming novels visit:
www.oliviaraebooks.com